X-TREME POSSIBILITIES

A PARANOID RUMMAGE THROUGH *THE X-FILES*

Paul Cornell, Martin Day
and Keith Topping

By the same authors:

DOCTOR WHO – THE DISCONTINUITY GUIDE
THE NEW TREK PROGRAMME GUIDE

First published in Great Britain in 1997 by
Virgin Publishing Ltd
332 Ladbroke Grove
London W10 5AH

Reprinted 1997 (twice)

Copyright © Paul Cornell, Martin Day and Keith Topping 1997

The right of Paul Cornell, Martin Day and Keith Topping
to be identified as the Authors of this Work has been
asserted by them in accordance with the Copyright,
Designs and Patents act 1988.

ISBN 0 7535 0019 1

Typeset by Galleon Typesetting, Ipswich
Printed and bound in Great Britain by
Mackays of Chatham PLC

This book is sold subject to the condition that it shall
not, by way of trade or otherwise, be lent, resold, hired
out or otherwise circulated without the publisher's prior
written consent in any form of binding or cover other
than that in which it is published and without a similar
condition including this condition being imposed on the
subsequent purchaser.

Introduction

The X-Files has changed everything. Before it, American television, under the influence of series like *Star Trek: The Next Generation*, *Hill Street Blues* and *Twin Peaks*, was just starting to become more innovative, more interested in continuity and texts that could be usefully watched a number of times. *The X-Files* took this idea and ran with it, creating a vast (and difficult) intermittent running story that brought a large supporting cast with it. Having innovated in that direction, it innovated again in the way it used that story arc: the returning characters returned at strange points in the narrative; the central storyline wasn't restricted to episodes in which our heroes discovered something more about it, but informed other episodes as well. So far, and most surprisingly, all the dead characters have stayed dead. That's quite an achievement in a show about the supernatural.

It's true that *The X-Files* was a series whose time had come, one of those dead certs that only a TV critic would bet against. With the American psyche turning increasingly against its own government, against all authority, nobody, in the 1990s, can tell an American citizen what to believe. The skies are full of UFOs/black helicopters, containing aliens/UN troops who do experiments on/wilfully destroy herds of cattle. The American public has become thoroughly alienated, shocked that the betrayals of Watergate haven't stopped: Irangate, Whitewater, many other revelations that power is in the hands of people as mortal as those they govern. Their nation, the one that had always believed in freedom and democracy, is being ferociously shown the realities of power and capitalism. That these terrible things have happened cannot be the fault of the public themselves: it's the fault of those in power. Not those fallible presidents and their parties, who are just as much victims of the real world as the public are. The real people in power. Those whose presence amongst the government makes America such a scary place. The conspiracy. *The X-Files* is the product of a nation looking for such people to blame.

The second factor in the success of this series is that there is, now, a whole mythos to feed its stories. Thanks to Steven Spielberg (who invented them) and Whitley Strieber (who was abducted by them), the little grey aliens have become an omnipresent icon, that most miraculous of things, an archetype in a new form. Centuries ago, they'd have been fairies or demons. Now they're from Zeta Reticula. The innovation is that they bring with them a folk myth of total fear: we are helpless, totally vulnerable, and not safe anywhere. We have to conform to their agenda, we can't bargain with them, they have no human emotions to appeal to. It's a myth, in the end, of bureaucrats from outer space. Their skin colour is no accident. Even the eyes look like spectacles. The greys are also the dead of Belsen (an image that *The X-Files* takes literally), aborted foetuses, shaved experimental cats: all those things we've done, that we should be guilty about, externalised, mythologised, and back to do to us what we did to them.

The third factor in the series' success is the millennium. It's no surprise that Chris Carter's new show is entirely about the change from twentieth to twenty-first century. It's coming, and lots of things are coming to an end. The human instinct for closure, and the desire for revelation, are once more upon us. *The X-Files* is the expression of that desire. We can look forward, thank goodness, to a party decade in 2001, if previous centuries are anything to go by.

So, with all this in the air, the appearance of a series concerning alien mysteries wasn't really a surprise. The idea would have been floating in many writers' heads. The surprise was that, when it did arrive, this series was actually done so *well*. Each episode seems to be the product of concentrated creative energy, as if it were a tiny feature film. For once, the design, the direction and the writing are all being urged to be the best they can be. Chris Carter has to be congratulated for his single-mindedness in achieving that, and American television can take a bow for its realisation that a single, driven creator at the helm is the best way to run a TV series. Witness *Star Trek* and *Babylon 5*.

And then there are Mulder and Scully, of course. Intelligent, sexy people, who aren't involved with each other. That's us, these days, that is. That's the Internet Generation writ glamorous. If they shag, the show's over: thank goodness Carter knows that, or we'd have another *Moonlighting* on our hands.

Still, he may surprise us. He may have it happen and do it well. That would almost be the obvious thing to do, in a series that thrives on surprises.

This Book

There are lots of books about *The X-Files*, and not all of them are good. This one, we can confidently tell you, is different. We've actually delved into the fiction of the episodes, especially in the conspiracy stories, attempting to make connections, to make sense of what's going on. We theorise about extreme possibilities, and generally pay attention to what the series is trying to say, what it says accidentally, and what it says despite itself. There's a lot of speculation in here, but it's all indicated by words like 'presumably' and 'possibly'. We think we've managed to get a lot of the conspiracy stuff sorted out, but, unlike our heroes, we don't have any sources within the establishment – this is a totally unauthorised book – so much of our theorising will doubtless turn out to be wrong. *The X-Files* is a text which rewrites itself: the latest episodes give new meanings to old ones. We've therefore covered a number of fourth-season episodes – like *Star Trek*, *The X-Files* is now locked in a (seemingly) perpetual cycle of production, and it's difficult to draw the line under one season and say, 'That's your lot.' A word about 'spoilers': because a lot of *The X-Files* is interrelated, this isn't a good book to read if you want to be surprised by a plot twist in an episode that you haven't seen.

The Headings

At the start of each season, we list the number and length of episodes in that season. Then we run down the production personnel for that season, and the regular cast (by which we mean anybody who appears in more than one story, counting multipart episodes as one story).

For each episode, we give the number of the episode, the title, the US and UK transmission dates, the writer and director credits, and list the cast who don't appear in the regular cast list at the start of the season. We summarise the plot, including giving away the ending.

The headings then proceed as follows:

Don't Be in the Teaser: Terrible things happen to people pre-credits in *The X-Files*, this heading documents them.

How Did He Do That?: Recording Mulder's extraordinary leaps to the oddest conclusions, plus plot impossibilities and other anomalous material.

Scully Here is a Medical Doctor: As we're continually reminded. Incidents where she snaps on the latex are reported.

Ooze: Ooze.

Scully's Rational Explanation of the Week: She usually has one, she often has several. Here they all are.

That's a Mouthful: *The X-Files* has developed its own brand of portentous, quasi-philosophical politicobabble, seemingly informed by the writers having seen a David Mamet film once. Imagine a book called: *The Wit and Wisdom of Deep Throat*. That's what this category is like.

Phwoar!: This heading charts Mulder and Scully's relationship, and times when they seem especially close. We also mention scenes of unusually obvious horniness. We are grateful for the help of a number of friends of various sexualities in gleefully adding to this section.

Dialogue Triumphs: We quote the bits that sparkle.

Dialogue Disasters: And a few that don't.

The Conspiracy Starts at Closing Time: We try to work out what the conspiracy's up to, how it works, and who's involved. Big section.

Continuity: This heading keeps track of details concerning Mulder and Scully, their relations, their workmates, their foes and the FBI.

The Truth: This is, as far as we can work it out, exactly what really happened during the episode.

Trivia: We list cultural references, in-jokes (we've tried very hard not to duplicate a single in-joke from any other reference book), cameo appearances by strange people and stuff that doesn't fit anywhere else. But we don't think you're interested in things like number plates and how often Scully fires her gun.

Scientific Comment: Our scientific adviser, Dr Janet Wood of the Astrophysics Group at Keele University, passes comment on things that get her goat concerning the use of science in the episode. Rather than being, like the editors of *The Lone Gunman*, an expert on all things, Dr Wood has consulted many other scientists.

The Bottom Line: The three of us review the episode separately. Partly to show a series of different critical responses, partly to demonstrate that Slouched Man, God-Fearing Man and Geordie Man sometimes disagree rather violently. Each of us took special responsibility for a season, and that person's review comes first.

Boxes: Throughout the text, there are a number of boxes which highlight particular issues, or just take the mickey.

The Episodes

First Season

Note: The order of BBC2 transmission runs: 11, 13, 12, 14 . . .

Second Season

Note: The order of BBC2/BBC1 transmission runs: 41, 44, 43, 42, 45 . . .

Third Season

Note: The order of BBC1 transmission runs: 53, 54, 57, 58, 59, 62, 71, 60, 64, 65 at time of writing, thus messing up the 'tiff' arc and bringing Scully's dog back from the dead. This was allegedly because of the BBC's new guidelines on violence, so future episodes may be severely cut.

Fourth Season

First Season

23 45-minute episodes, 1 40-minute episode

Created by Chris Carter

Line Producer: Joseph Patrick Finn (2–24)
Co-Producers: Larry Barber (11–14), Paul Barber (11–14),
Paul Rabwin (2–24)
Supervising Producers: Alex Gansa (2–24),
Howard Gordon (2–24), Daniel Sackheim (1)
Co-Executive Producers: R. W. Goodwin (2–24),
Glen Morgan (2–24), James Wong (2–24)
Executive Producer: Chris Carter

Regular Cast: David Duchovny (Fox Mulder), Gillian
Anderson (Dana Scully), William B. Davis (Smoking Man, 1,
16,[1] 21, 24), Jerry Hardin (Deep Throat, 2, 7, 10, 11, 16, 17,
24), Doug Hutchison (Eugene Tooms, 3, 21), Sheila Larken
(Margaret Scully, 13), Don Davis (William Scully, 13), Bruce
Harwood (Byers, 17), Dean Haglund (Langly, 17), Tom
Braidwood (Frohike, 17), Mitch Pileggi (Walter Skinner, 21),
Lindsey Ginter (Crewcut Man, 24)

1: 'The X-Files' [a.k.a. 'Pilot']

US Transmission: 10 September 1993
UK Transmission: 26 January 1994 (Sky One)/
19 September 1994 (BBC2)
Writer: Chris Carter
Director: Robert Mandel
Cast: Charles Cioffi, Cliff DeYoung, Sarah Koshoff, Leon
Russom, Zachary Ansley, Stephen E. Miller, Malcolm
Stewart, Alexandra Berlin, Jim Jensen, Ken Camroux, Doug
Abrams, Katya Gardener, Ric Reid, Lesley Ewen, J. B. Bivens

---

[1] His on-screen credit is 'CIA agent': this may or may not be the Smoking
Man. See 'Young at Heart' for details.

Collum National Forest, near Bellefleur, northwest Oregon: four teenagers have been found dead, each with two small marks on their backs. The FBI's Fox Mulder and his new partner Dana Scully order the exhumation of one of the victims and discover an apelike skeleton with a grey metallic implant in the nasal cavity. Later Scully and Mulder 'lose nine minutes' whilst driving along a stretch of open road, and their motel room is burnt, destroying the evidence so far collected. Mulder comes to the conclusion that Billy Miles, another classmate, is responsible for the deaths, despite being in a persistent vegetative state. Billy claims that during a graduation party in the forest aliens kidnapped the youngsters for experimentation, and that once the experiments were concluded he was used to kill his friends. Scully hands over the only surviving piece of evidence – the 'communication device' – to her bosses.

Don't Be in the Teaser: Karen Swinson dies mysteriously.

How Did He Do That?: It is never conclusively explained exactly *how* Mulder works out that Billy is responsible.

Scully Here is a Medical Doctor: Scully states that she went to medical school, but chose not to practise. She performs an autopsy on Ray Soames.

Scully's Rational Explanation of the Week: The young people might be involved in some sort of cult.

Phwoar!: The bathroom scene in which Gillian Anderson strips to her pants and bra is rather nice. When she shows her mosquito bites to Mulder, it's perhaps the start of that legendary parasexual 'thing' between the two agents.

Dialogue Triumphs: Mulder: 'In my line of work the laws of physics rarely seem to apply.'

Scully: 'Time can't just disappear. It's a universal invariant!' Mulder: 'Not in this zip-code.'

Scully to her superiors: 'Agent Mulder believes we are not alone.'

The Conspiracy Starts at Closing Time: Mulder says that there is classified government information that he has been trying to access but someone at a higher level has been blocking him. He is allowed to continue in his work only because he has made connections in Congress.

Smoking Man is seen in Blevin's office. He later stores the 'communication chip' (along with five others) in a box marked '100041' in a store room deep in the Pentagon.

Mulder and Scully lose nine minutes of time when their car is enveloped in a bright light. Since the hidden tracks on the *X-Files* music CD are labelled 'The Missing Nine Minutes', it's possible that the production team still regard this incident as important. Certainly, from this point on, Mulder doesn't seem to regard the fact that, for at least nine minutes, he's been possibly interfered with, as important. Scully, with her knowledge of physics, ought to be jumping up and down in astonishment, but she shrugs it off. Either she simply doesn't believe Mulder, or maybe they've both been got at.

Continuity: Dana Scully has been with the FBI for just over two years. She was recruited out of medical school (her parents still regard this as an act of rebellion). She taught at the FBI academy at Quantico and did her undergraduate degree in physics. Her senior thesis was *Einstein's Twin Paradox: A New Interpretation*. (This is a pretty ridiculous subject for a thesis. Einstein's twin paradox is a simple example of how time dilation affects objects travelling near the speed of light: the twin that's been travelling comes home and meets the twin who hasn't been, and finds that twin is now older. Any 'new interpretation' in the field of physics (as opposed to, say, poetry) would have to present a challenge to the laws of relativity! On the basis that Scully actually passed, we might assume that the thesis itself concerns some small topic of relativity research (a new proof is virtually the only possible area), and that, for some reason, Scully gave it a screamingly over-the-top title that referred to little more than an aside in the introduction. In terms of the series, however, the title is poetically apt, darkly alluding to the fate of Samantha, not to mention Mulder's trick with the two watches.)

Scully is aware of Mulder by reputation. She is assigned to assist Mulder and will write field reports on their activities along with her observations on the 'validity of the work'.

Fox Mulder is an Oxford-educated psychologist who wrote a monograph on 'serial killers and the occult' that helped to catch Monty Props in 1988. He is considered to be the best analyst in the Violent Crime section. His nickname at the academy was 'Spooky'. He describes himself as 'the FBI's most unwanted'. He has 'developed a consuming devotion to an unassigned project outside the Bureau mainstream'. When he was twelve, his eight-year-old sister disappeared from her bed one night. This tore the family apart. Mulder has undergone deep regression hypnosis with Dr Heitz Verber concerning the events surrounding the abduction (see 'Little Green Men').

The X-Files are unexplained cases. Mulder says that at first they seemed to be a garbage dump for UFO sightings and abduction reports.

The Truth: The cover-up perpetuated by Billy's father seems to be a localised rather than a governmental activity. Later episodes '('Nisei'/'731') reveal that Mulder and Scully have actually stumbled upon the work of Japanese scientists, working for the conspiracy, who have been experimenting on the class (either turning one of them into the corpse found in the grave, which is very like those of the little mutants found in 'Anasazi', or substituting for the real corpse a body they had to hand). They use Billy Miles to clean up after them. However, taking Mulder and Scully out of time for nine minutes (if that is, indeed, what happened, and Mulder isn't just exaggerating the consequences of an attack by the sonic weapon seen in 'E.B.E.') is beyond the abilities of the conspiracy as we've seen them. Perhaps a race of genuine aliens has started to take an interest in Mulder's work . . .

Trivia: Chris Carter's wife, Dori Pierson, was born on 21 November. (Pity she wasn't born a day later . . .) As a way of getting her lots of extra birthday cards, the series makes many references to 11.21 (note the US inversion of day and month). We mention them when other publications haven't. In this case, the autopsy is held at 11.21. Carter was born in Bellflower, California, and names the locale here in homage.

The Pentagon scene is a visual steal from *Raiders of the Lost Ark*, and 'We are not alone' was the poster tagline for *Close Encounters of the Third Kind*. When Mulder knocks on Scully's motel room door and she asks 'Who is it?' he answers 'Steven Spielberg!'

The Bottom Line: KT: 'I'm not a part of any agenda. You've got to trust me. I'm here just like you, to solve this.' A fine beginning. The Mulder/Scully dialogue is electric, though the explanations at the story's climax are far too rushed. Little Americana with gothic overtones – chilling and influential.

PC: It's very *Silence of the Lambs* indeed. But it looks different. These dark Canadian forests will soon become as familiar to TV audiences as the dustbowls around LA, but here was where they first made their mark, allowing the series to feel as if it's genuinely moving around the USA, and thus addressing the entire condition of the country. It's as if Canada gives the series an ironic distance.

MD: It's a rattling good yarn, pure and simple. The two key images (the figure standing in a whirlwind of bright light, and the vast storeroom where the communications device is placed) are guaranteed to stick in the memory of the casual viewer. The 'frustration factor' and subversion of expectation – the 'baddies' don't get their comeuppance – certainly marks this out from much American television. I loved this story at the time – it seemed so fresh and vibrant – but it's not surprising that it has visibly aged a bit now, with David Duchovny's performance being a little too mannered. It's very much a pilot script: themes (e.g. familial conflict) that would have been fleshed out in later episodes are briefly sketched here and then pushed to one side. Maybe the extra five minutes subsequent episodes gained is vital to the show's style and success.

The pilot episode lacks the familiar title sequence and theme music. It also features a caption that states: 'The following story is inspired by actual documented accounts.' The end credits of 'Space' feature a detailed NASA disclaimer in addition to the usual one regarding the FBI.

The usual 'The Truth is Out There' caption at the end of the opening credits is replaced by 'Trust No One' ('The Erlenmeyer Flask'), 'Deny Everything' ('Ascension'), 'Éí 'Aaníígóó 'Áhoot'é' ('Anasazi', which is roughly the same phrase – 'Far away from here, the truth is' – in Navajo), 'Apology is Policy' ('731') and 'Deceive Inveigle Obfuscate' ('Teliko').

Certain stories ('Paper Clip', '731', 'Revelations', 'Apocrypha' and 'Pusher') use a shorter version of the title sequence. From the start of the third season, slight changes are made to the theme music.

2: 'Deep Throat'

US Transmission: 17 September 1993
UK Transmission: 2 February 1994 (Sky One)/
26 September 1995 (BBC2)
Writer: Chris Carter
Director: Daniel Sackheim
Cast: Michael Bryan French, Seth Green,
Gabrielle Rose, Monica Parker, Sheila Moore,
Lalainia Lindbjerg, Andrew Johnston, Jon Cuthbert,
Vince Metcalfe, Michael Puttonen, Brian Furlong,
Doc Harris

Ellens Air Base, Southwest Idaho: Mulder and Scully investigate the disappearance (at the hands of the military) of Robert Budahas, an air force pilot. At the base they witness strange lights in the sky, which Mulder

14

believes prove that the air force are using UFO technology. Budahas returns, although his wife says that it's not her husband. Mulder breaks into the base, but is captured and subjected to memory-erasing treatment. Scully overpowers a member of the base personnel and arrives in time to see a dazed Mulder leave the complex, his memory of what he saw gone.

Don't Be in the Teaser: For once, nobody dies. However, Robert Budahas develops a nasty rash and later loses important parts of his memory.

Scully's Rational Explanation of the Week: The pilot's mental instability is caused by stereotypy, a stress disorder that she has studied in zoo animals. The pilots may be the 'washouts' from the government's secret Aurora aircraft project. Budahas's memory loss may be 'selective amnesia'. Oh, and the UFOs are just lasers reflecting off the clouds.

That's a Mouthful: 'You will pack and leave town immediately, or assume the consequences of intense indiscretion.' Or, in English, 'Get lost, or get your arse kicked'.

Dialogue Triumphs: Mulder: 'They're here, aren't they?' Deep Throat: 'Mr Mulder, "they" have been here for a long, long time.'

The Conspiracy Starts at Closing Time: 'I think there's a large conspiracy here,' notes Mulder. No shit, Sherlock? Quite apart from the air force's apparent use of alien technology, there are the first hints of the ongoing government 'you know too much' malarky, and the introduction of Mulder's ally, Deep Throat. Nothing is revealed about Deep Throat, except that he has taken an interest in Mulder's work, and that he is in a 'privileged' position to pass on classified information. On their second meeting, he informs Mulder that Mulder and Scully's lives may be in danger, and that he is interested in 'the truth'. Mulder says that Ellens was one of six bases to which the UFO wreckage from the 1947 'Roswell Incident' was taken.

Mulder has his memory tampered with, but, since he's already been witness to two alien encounters (Samantha's abduction and the car incident in the first episode), this may be part of an ongoing process to, literally, change his mind.

Continuity: Mulder likes guitar rock, is fluent in 'valley speak' ('Later, dude!') and is knowledgeable about American football (discussing the 1968 Superbowl with Budahas). His phone is tapped in this story. Mulder refers to one character as 'Uncle Fester', indicating a knowledge of *The Addams Family*.

The Truth: The US Air Force, or some paragovernmental organisation that exerts an influence on them, has developed the capability to erase parts of a person's memory (Budahas and Mulder). As Scully notes in her report, however, there is no positive proof that the technology they are using is alien (though it is certainly far in advance of known scientific achievement). A triangular craft like those flown here is certainly seen to be an alien vehicle in 'Apocrypha'. What's happening to Budahas physically may be akin to the changes that occur to human beings to make them into mutants (see '731'). (Do the conspiracy need the little mutants to pilot these aircraft?)

Trivia: Budahas's birthday is 21 November 1948, another '11.21' reference. There are also two references to Chris Carter's birthday (after which he named his production company), 13 October 1956: the file number for this case is #DF101364; and the licence number Scully asks about is CC1356. The article on the air base that Scully reads from a microfiche is written by one Chris Carter. 'They're here' was an advertising line for Whitley Strieber's account of alien abduction, *Communion*. When Budahas is first seen after his return he is making a model kit of an F-117A 'stealth fighter'.

The Bottom Line: KT: 'Are you suggesting the military is flying UFOs?' A cracking episode, continuing many of the themes from the pilot (small-town America as a cover for strange doings, etc.). Scully seems more cynical in this story than usual. Some comedy elements don't work (*The X-Files* always seems to have a credibility problem with Generation X), but Duchovny and Anderson are brilliant, developing a sparkling rapport.

PC: Just as well the episode titles aren't shown on screen. This is what I really wanted from this show, a series that would take on all the new American myths presented here. It's bold to take Mulder right into the heart of 'the truth' so quickly, and then pull him away.

MD: 'When does the human cost become too high for the building of a better machine?' This is glorious, and unlike the pilot it's got better with age, now feeling like the entire series in microcosm.

SCULLY'S CROSS

Scully is first seen to wear a small golden cross in 'Deep Throat'. In 'Squeeze' she wears a longer, non-cross necklace, which is stolen by Tooms prior to his attack on her. Maybe this is why she reverts to the cross necklace for 'Conduit' and subsequent stories such as 'Lazarus'. In 'Ascension', we discover that the cross, which Mulder finds, and Mrs Scully asks him to keep, was given to Dana on her fifteenth birthday. After Scully's abduction, Mulder wears the cross, as seen in '3', and gives it back to her when she returns in 'One Breath'. She wears it in several subsequent stories, including 'Revelations'.

3: 'Squeeze'

US Transmission: 24 September 1993
UK Transmission: 9 February 1994 (Sky One)/
3 October 1994 (BBC2)
Writers: Glen Morgan, James Wong
Director: Harry Longstreet
Cast: Donal Logue, Henry Beckman, Kevin McNulty,
Terence Kelly, Colleen Winton, James Bell,
Gary Hetherington, Rob Morton, Paul Joyce

Baltimore, Maryland: one of Scully's old academy classmates asks for her help in catching a serial killer who takes his victims' livers and leaves no obvious signs of entry. Mulder discovers a fingerprint link to an X-File, and a recurring pattern of five murders every thirty years. A man, Eugene Tooms, is arrested, but released after he passes a polygraph test. Mulder and Scully are convinced of his guilt. Tooms attacks Scully at her home, using his ability to crawl through very narrow spaces. He's overpowered and imprisoned.

Don't Be in the Teaser: George Usher has his liver ripped out.

Ooze: Yellow bile, used by Tooms in his 'nest'.

Scully's Rational Explanation of the Week: Ignoring the fingerprint evidence, Scully presents the FBI with a flawless (and completely wrong) profile of the killer. Her explanation of the matching of fingerprints to a crime sixty years before is a convoluted genetics theory (see 'Aubrey'!).

Dialogue Triumphs: Colton: 'Does this look like the work of little green men?' Mulder: 'Grey . . . The Reticulan skin tone is actually grey. They're notorious for their extraction of terrestrial human livers due to iron depletion in the Reticulan galaxy.' 'You can't be serious.' 'Do you have any idea what liver and onions go for on Reticula?'

Scully: 'I think it's bile.' Mulder: 'Is there any way I can get it off my fingers quickly without betraying my cool exterior?'

Continuity: Mulder says he thinks Scully will be running the Bureau by 2023. Tom Colton was in Dana's class at the academy. He is considered a 'high flyer' in the Violent Crime section. Another classmate, Marty Neal, has just received a Supervisory position (he was nicknamed 'J. Edgar junior').

This episode makes it clear that Mulder is not well thought of by many of his FBI colleagues, believed to be incompetent, or an embarrassing crank. As shown in the exchange above, Mulder believes that at least some of the aliens visiting Earth (the 'Greys') are from Zeta Reticuli, the star in the Reticula constellation that Barney and Betty Hill, subjects of one of the first abduction cases, deduced their assailants came from. However, his speech (note the Reticulan *galaxy*, which turns the whole thing into science fiction) is clearly delivered with the sole intention of winding up Colton.

The Truth: Eugene Victor Tooms lived at apartment 103, 66 Exeter Street in 1903, and continued to use the building during each of his awakenings every thirty years. Mulder believes he is a genetic mutation, the livers providing him with sustenance during his hibernation. It is not clear by the end of the episode if this is true or not, although Scully states that his skeletal systems and musculature are abnormal, and that his continually declining metabolic rate dips below that found in deep sleep.

Trivia: Further to Mulder's love of seventies television, he mentions *The Waltons*. Tom Colton mentions the World Trade Center bombing.

The Bottom Line: KT: 'He's building another nest.' A magnificent *Silence of the Lambs* variant, with an outstanding twitchy performance by Doug Hutchison as Tooms. The episode can be faulted for its lack of explanations, but it is dark and nasty with a real sense of evil (though this is almost derailed by Frank Biggs's very obvious speech about death camps and ethnic cleansing).

PC: It's clear that Carter likes the idea that all evil springs from one source, a millennial attitude that says that the horrors of history, in an indirect way, create monsters. That's about the only link between the two sorts of *X-Files* episode: Conspiracy and Monster of the Week. At the time of the first season, I preferred the former, now I'm very much into the latter.

MD: I'm travelling in the opposite direction, but this is certainly one of the strongest simple monster stories. What we have here is an evil Mr Fantastic whose contortions are grotesquely painful and realistic, but we're never shown

Tooms's activities in too much detail, our imaginations doing much of the work. This welcome reticence, and the excellent ending, are particularly dramatic, but it's the little elements that make this story for me – like the outrageously macho way that Mulder shakes Colton's hand.

4: 'Conduit'

US Transmission: 1 October 1993
UK Transmission: 16 February 1994 (Sky One)/
10 October 1994 (BBC2)
Writers: Alex Gansa, Howard Gordon
Director: Daniel Sackheim
Cast: Carrie Snodgrass, Michael Cavanaugh, Don Gibb, Joel Palmer, Charles Cioffi, Shelley Owens, Don Thompson, Akiko Morison, Taunya Dee, Anthony Harrison, Glen Roald, Mauricio Mercado

Lake Okobogee, a UFO 'hotspot' near Sioux City, Iowa: the abduction of Ruby Morris bears chilling similarities to the disappearance of Mulder's sister. The girl's young brother seems fascinated with a static-filled television screen, and produces binary drawings that contain fragments from defence satellite transmissions and other coded information. After investigating the murder of Ruby's boyfriend, which is unconnected to the girl's seeming abduction, the agents go back to the lake and find her returned. However, Ruby's mother is unwilling to allow her to talk about where she has been.

Don't Be in the Teaser: Darlene Morris is hit by falling crockery and burns her hand on a doorknob. Her daughter, Ruby, is abducted.

Scully's Rational Explanation of the Week: A 'statistical aberration' explains the nature of Kevin's binary drawings. Even Scully admits this 'isn't much of a theory'. The stunted trees were caused by an electrical storm.

Dialogue Triumphs: Scully: 'Well, what makes this case any more credible than the hundred-year-old mother with the lizard baby?'

Mulder: 'How can an eight-year-old boy who can barely multiply be a threat to National Security? People call *me* paranoid!'

The Conspiracy Starts at Closing Time: Nothing specific towards the running theme of government cover-up, but the actions of the NSA agents certainly bear the hallmark of their having watched too many spy films. It's interesting that the NSA are involved, considering that they have a stake in this whole business, though we don't quite know whose side they're on (see 'Nisei').

Continuity: Mulder's preoccupation with 'fringe matters' has been 'a major source of friction within the Bureau'. Samantha T. Mulder's case is an X-File opened by her brother. The family address was 2790 Vine St, Chilmarc, Mass. Her date of birth is given as 22 January 1964. (This is flatly contradicted in 'Paper Clip', where her date of birth is given on the medical files as 21 November 1965, and her middle name is Anne. Either Mulder was so upset by her abduction that he got the details wrong when he started the file, or this is a sign that his mind has been manipulated a great deal: there's something ironic and cruel about making Mulder forget his sister's real name . . . Alternatively, when Bill Mulder had that medical file prepared, he either tried to lose Samantha in the bureaucracy, or made a tiny act of rebellion: they'd never get the whole truth about her.) She disappeared twenty-one years ago (1974), when she was eight. The 1965 date of birth would make her closer to seven years old, so perhaps the abduction took place only twenty years ago (1973), which would tie in with Mulder's age at the time of the abduction (as given in 'The X-Files') and with his date of birth (as given in 'Paper Clip'). Mulder states that he used to have a ritual of closing his eyes before he entered his room in the hope that, when he opened them, his sister would be there. Mulder's hypnotic regression 'number 2B' took place on 16 June (year unknown). A 'voice' during the abduction (revealed by the hypnosis) assured him that Samantha would be OK.

Mulder appears to read *The National Comet*. He knows a friend of a friend who he says is able to get tickets for Washington Redskins football games. (Considering his conversation with Deep Throat about this matter in 'E.B.E.', it's possible we know who this friend is . . .)

The Center for UFO Studies is in Evanston, Illinois. Lake Okobogee was the location of four UFO sightings in August 1967, one by a then girl scout, Darlene Morris. Amongst the information contained in Kevin's binary drawings are da Vinci's Universal Man, a DNA double helix, an extract from one of Bach's 'Brandenburg' Concertos, passages from the Qur'an, and a Shakespeare sonnet. (It is worth noting, however, that even a tiny fragment of a DNA helix in binary would require many millions of characters, and that Kevin would have had to have been writing for decades non-stop to achieve this.)

A '302' is an FBI assignment request form. Mulder faxes some of Kevin's binaries to Daniel ('Danny') Bernstein at the Cryptology Section at FBI HQ (see 'The Erlenmeyer Flask', 'Red Museum', 'Avatar' and 'Wetwired').

The Truth: The blackened camper van roof, the sand turned to glass and the bartender who complains of 'killer sunburn in the middle of the night' probably point to the validity of at least some of the UFO sightings around the lake. It certainly seems that Ruby was abducted: when she is recovered her white blood cell count is 'sky high', together with an 'attendant reduction in the lymphocyte population, and a release of glucocorticoids'. All symptoms of prolonged weightlessness. Ruby was told by 'them' to say nothing. Since no medical experimentation that we know of has been attempted on Ruby, and that prolonged zero-g conditions may be beyond their abilities, we might have reasonable cause to doubt that this abduction was the work of Japanese scientists (see 'Nisei'), and believe that it was actually done by (fairly benevolent) aliens.

Kevin appears to have been in contact with these aliens. Could Kevin be a conduit for information taken from the Voyager probes? A lot of the information he receives seems to be akin to what was sent on disk on these missions, including the 'Brandenburg' Concerto. But none of it is useful. Perhaps these aliens are those we see in 'Little Green Men' (who are perhaps those we *don't* see in 'Fearful Symmetry') who have found a Voyager probe and are trying to communicate using the information on it. It could be that, after the initial defence satellite transmissions, which provoked no response, they decided to send something more obvious to the humans receiving the information, and started to raid this cultural storehouse. Kevin trusts Mulder, telling his sister: 'It's OK, he *knows*.' Darlene's fear of ridicule prevents further questioning.

The Bottom Line: KT: 'I *want* to believe . . .' In terms of iconography, one of the strongest ever *X-Files* episodes (the scene in the forest with the wolves, and, particularly, the heart-stopping moment when Scully sees Ruby's face in Kevin's drawings). The plot bears certain similarities to *Close Encounters of the Third Kind* and *Poltergeist* but is none the worse for this. And it contains one of the series' finest episode endings – the first signs that Mulder is less than the wise-cracking Olympian detective of the first three episodes.

PC: The ending is about the only good thing about an absolutely meaningless runaround that steals nearly all its images (bar the central cool binaries idea) from other people.

MD: There *are* problems with plot and structure, but unoriginality is rarely the worst crime *The X-Files* can commit (though the ripping-off of *Poltergeist* is shameless). This is two stories in one: a straightforward, derivative but rather engaging UFO story, and a murder investigation somewhat tacked on via such unexplained leaps as the girl's ability to vanish, Deep Throat-like, from the library, and the pack of almost friendly white wolves. It's interesting to see an early example of how good Mulder is at more traditional FBI activities (such as questioning a suspect), but ultimately it's the back story of Mulder's sister – and that moving ending – that give the story its dramatic root.

5: 'The Jersey Devil'

US Transmission: 8 October 1993
UK Transmission: 23 February 1994 (Sky One)/
17 October 1994 (BBC2)
Writer: Chris Carter
Director: Joe Napolitano
Cast: Claire Stansfield, Wayne Tippit, Gregory Sierra, Michael MacRae, Jill Teed, Tamsin Kelsey, Andrew Airlie, Bill Dow, Hrothgar Mathews, Jayme Knox, Scott Swanson, Sean O'Byrne, David Lewis, D. Neil Mark

Atlantic City, New Jersey: a homeless man is found dead in the Jersey National Park, apparently the victim of a cannibalistic male. Mulder spends a night on the streets and glimpses a creature but is arrested before he can investigate further. Ranger Peter Boulle finds the body of a naked man in the woods, but this vanishes before the anthropologist Professor Diamond can examine it. Despite local law enforcement opposition, Mulder, Scully, Diamond and Boulle track a creature across the city outskirts. Mulder has a confrontation with the 'beast woman', but she escapes back into the woods. Before the 'creature' can be captured she is killed by police marksmen.

Don't Be in the Teaser: An unnamed man in 1947 is killed by having various appendages bitten off.

How Did He Do That?: How does Mulder work out the creature's gender on such slender evidence?

Scully Here is a Medical Doctor: Almost word for word, the excuse that Mulder gives Detective Thompson to explain their gatecrashing his case.

Phwoar!: Scully looks well-foxy with her hair up on her date. It's nice when Mulder and Scully go to the Smithsonian together at the end (without either of them, of course, regarding *that* as a date).

Dialogue Triumphs: Mulder (looking at a magazine centrefold): 'This woman claims to have been taken on board a spaceship, and held in an anti-gravity chamber without food and water for three days.' Scully: 'Anti-gravity is right!'

'You've been spending too much time in supermarket check-out lines.'

'Unlike you, Mulder, I would like to have a life!'

Dialogue Disasters: Scully: 'Mulder, we've put men into space, we've built computers that work faster than the human mind.' Mulder: 'While we overpopulate the world and create new technologies to kill each other with. Maybe we're just beasts with big brains.' Yep, *The X-Files* gets on its soapbox . . . Yawn.

The Conspiracy Starts at Closing Time: The autopsy report from the 1940s disappeared from the police department's files a few years after the original 'Jersey Devil' incident. However, this – and the cover-up faced by Mulder and Scully – is clearly prompted by no more than local concern for the possible impact on Atlantic City's gambling and tourism.

Continuity: Mulder is seen reading the porno mag *Hanky Panky* (with some glee). Scully has a six-year-old godson (Trent), son of her friend Ellen. She has described Mulder to Ellen as 'cute', and says he is not 'a jerk' but is 'obsessed with his work'. She dates a divorcé, Rob, and later turns down a second liaison with him at Circus au Lait.

The Truth: It is *implied*, but never stated, that the woman and her dead mate are descendants of the legendary 1940s Jersey Devil. The male was responsible for the murders; after his death the 'beast woman' was forced to come into town to scavenge for food for her offspring. The woman was twenty-five to thirty years old and she had consumed human flesh. A medical examination of her uterus indicates she has produced children. Both she and her mate are physiologically human. So the menace here is actually . . . poor naked people.

Trivia: This episode sees the first use of the phrase 'extreme possibility'. The policeman mentions Hannibal the Cannibal, so chalk up another *Silence of the Lambs* reference.

The Bottom Line: KT: 'Someone or something out there is hungry.' The first sub-standard *X-Files* episode. Urban myth explanations always have to tread a fine line between cleverness and parody and this episode, full of visual clichés (propeller vents) and bad lighting, falls heavily on the latter. The sub-plot concerning the police cover-up to protect the city's gambling franchises is ham-fisted to say the least. A huge disappointment.

PC: It was at this point that I started wondering if Chris Carter knew what his own series was about. Dull and obvious ecological messages, and a bugbear who is actually just a very poor and uneducated woman who's living wild. (Wouldn't it be the obvious thing for her to have stolen or made clothes?)

MD: Not if she's the descendant of the Jersey Devil! Anyway, this is garbage of the highest order, stuffed full of over-earnest exposition and incredible sub-Freudian sexuality (Mulder describing the 'beast woman' as beautiful). It has all the problems of the pilot episode, only more so, and the ending is just guaranteed to leave you rolling in the aisles.

MULDER AND PORN

In 'The Jersey Devil' Mulder is seen reading *Hanky Panky*, which Scully does not censure him for, and he jokes about a subscription to *Celebrity Skin* in 'Blood'. He finds a porn mag in Oswald's room in 'D.P.O.', and in response to Scully's question says (jokingly?) that he's already read it. In 'Beyond the Sea', Scully comments to Mulder: 'Last time you were that engrossed it turned out you were reading the *Adult Video News*.' At the beginning of 'One Breath', Mulder appears to be watching a porn film (is it an episode of *The Red Shoe Diaries* starring

David Duchovny?) and there are references to his porn video collection in 'Excelsis Dei'. Indeed, it seems that Frohike will inherit these videos on Mulder's death ('Paper Clip'), although it's just possible that they're talking about his collection of UFO and bigfoot vids ('Jose Chung's *From Outer Space*'). The alien autopsy video in 'Nisei' is said by Scully to be 'not your usual brand of entertainment', and Mulder mentions the Playboy Channel in 'Pusher'. His tastes include 'Women of the Ivy League' ('D.P.O.'), so he's into brainy girls.

In addition, there's a directory on Mulder's PC called 'spank' ('Little Green Men'), and we see his office girlie calendar in '3'. Maybe his job drove him to these dubious delights: at the beginning of 'Little Green Men', he is working on an FBI phone tap, listening to two men talking about a stripper called Tuesday; at the end he's listening to a discussion about table and lap dancing. It somehow fits in with his problems with real relationships. The girl on the answerphone in 'Little Green Men' we might take to be one of a whole series of women whom Mulder has the sheer nerve to approach, but not the social confidence to actually date. (Can you imagine what his dinner conversation would be like? 'The shape of this pasta is actually reminiscent of a number of craft seen over Arizona in the mid-seventies. The years of Led Zeppelin and *The Incredible Hulk*. Did I tell you about my sister's abduction?') It fits with the image of a man who sleeps on the sofa with the TV on. Just as well Scully tolerates it, but, if they ever get together, those videos are going out of the window. She may be too late, however. If Clyde Bruckman's comment concerning autoerotic asphyxiation proves to be about Mulder, rather than about himself, then Mulder's hobby may just be the death of him.

6: 'Shadows'

US Transmission: 22 October 1993
UK Transmission: 2 March 1994 (Sky One)/
24 October 1994 (BBC2)
Writers: Glen Morgan, James Wong
Director: Michael Katleman
Cast: Barry Primus, Lisa Waltz, Lorena Gale, Veena Sood,
Deryl Hayes, Kelli Fox, Tom Pickett, Tom Heaton,
Janie Woods-Morris, Nora McLellan, Anna Ferguson

Philadelphia, PA: Lauren Kyte, secretary to the industrialist Howard Graves (a recent suicide victim), is mugged at a cashpoint, but her attackers die mysteriously. Mulder and Scully, contending with the attentions of a covert government agency, question the woman, but are very nearly killed when their car malfunctions. Surveillance photographs of Lauren seem to show that Howard Graves is still alive, although this is soon disproved. Mulder and Scully discover that Graves was killed by his partner Robert Dorlund, and that the company, HTG Industrial Technologies, has been selling restricted military parts to Iranian terrorists. It seems that the 'ghost' of Graves was seeking revenge and trying to protect Lauren.

Don't Be in the Teaser: Lauren Kyte gets mugged. Her Iranian terrorist muggers have their throats crushed from the inside. Just shows that crime doesn't pay!

Scully's Rational Explanation of the Week: 'The mystery isn't psychokinetic energy, it's her accomplice.' Actually she's correct, though in ways she can't imagine. Scully is very sceptical of psychokinesis (sarcastically mentioning 'How Carrie got even at the prom') and poltergeists ('They're here!').

That's a Mouthful: 'If any enquiry about this meeting be made, we request full denial.'

Dialogue Triumphs: Scully: 'You *have* seen it before, I could tell. You lied to them.' Mulder: 'I would never lie – I wilfully participated in a campaign of misinformation.'

Scully: 'I think Howard Graves fabricated his own death.' Mulder: 'Do you know how difficult it is to fake your own death? Only one man has pulled it off. Elvis!'

Security Agent. 'I could make her talk.' Mulder: 'My advice to you: don't get rough with her.'

The Conspiracy Starts at Closing Time: We are never told exactly who the rival agency who call Mulder and Scully into the case are (US Attorney's Office seems the best bet). Mulder speculates 'NSA, CIA, some covert organisation that Congress won't cover in the next scandal'. They have been investigating HTG's links to the Iranian terrorist group Isfahan for a year. Their motives in calling in Mulder seem to be genuine, so if they are CIA or NSA, they're not from the parts of those organisations who are involved with the conspiracy.

Continuity: Scully seems to have a fondness for trashy, big-budget horror films (see Scully's Rational Explanation).

The Truth: This episode appears to conclude that life after death is a fact – unless Lauren possesses genuine psychokinetic powers and is deluding herself.

The Bottom Line: KT: 'He's watching over you, isn't he?' Apparently an unpopular episode with fans, this is a straight ghost story and, if one manages to suspend disbelief, it works very well. There are many memorable set pieces (the scene in Lauren's bathroom), and the effects are terrific (that flying letter opener). As usual, Scully is conveniently out of the room when something genuinely supernatural happens. But what's all that stuff about Mulder wanting to see the Liberty Bell at the end? Something of an oddity – good in parts, but with little substance.

PC: Some nice effects. It's pretty dull, though, and we've seen every single little bit of it before, done better. Hm? Oh, sorry. Fell asleep.

MD: Wake up, this is great! It's a simple story, but it trots along nicely and is well acted. However, it does feature two ridiculous elements that would go on to be *X-Files* staples, namely the weird character who fills in great chunks of background exposition (in this case the graveyard worker who tells us all about the Graves family), and the photograph that features more information than is visible to the naked eye.

7: 'Ghost in the Machine'

US Transmission: 29 October 1993
UK Transmission: 9 March 1994 (Sky One)/
3 November 1994 (BBC2)
Writers: Alex Gansa, Howard Gordon
Director: Jerrold Freedman
Cast: Wayne Duvall, Rob LaBelle, Tom Butler,
Blu Mankuma, Gillian Barber, Marc Baur, Bill Finck,
Theodore Thomas

Eurisko Worldwide HQ, Crystal City, Virginia: Benjamin Drake is electrocuted in his office. Mulder's former partner Jerry Lamana asks for Mulder and Scully's help with the case. Suspicion falls on Eurisko's whizz-kid founder Brad Wilczek and, after Lamana is killed in a Eurisko elevator, Wilczek confesses. However, Mulder believes that the building's computer, the Central Operations System, has achieved a degree of sentience and, acting in self-preservation, is responsible for the deaths. Wilczek creates a virus to destroy the system and, despite the attempts to stop them by the Defense Department, Mulder and Scully succeed. Deep Throat tells Mulder that 'the machine is dead'.

Don't Be in the Teaser: Benjamin Drake is electrocuted in his office washroom.

How Did He Do That?: Mulder displays staggering leaps of logic in working out that the building itself is killing people.

Scully's Rational Explanation of the Week: Brad Wilczek did it.

That's a Mouthful: 'That subpoena has been obviated.' Why does *everybody* in the government engage in this kind of verbal bullshit?

Dialogue Triumphs: Mulder: 'How do you like that, a politically correct elevator?'

Mulder, entering Wilczek's home: 'This is what a 220 IQ and a four-hundred-million-dollar severance settlement brings you!'

The Conspiracy Starts at Closing Time: There's some evidence of a malevolent quasi-government investigation (the Defense Department certainly want to get hold of Wilczek and the COS). Deep Throat's involvement (and knowledge) suggests he is in a position to get information from very high places, and that either the conspiracy are interested in the field of machine intelligence (which doesn't really sound like them), or that he also has access to the military, who are. We still haven't the foggiest as to what he actually *does*. He suggests that Wilczek (despite Mulder's confidence in him) will end up working for the Defense Department when faced with the alternative of life in prison.

Continuity: Scully's home telephone number is (202) 555 6431. Her FBI ID number is 2317-616. (See 'F. Emasculata' for Mulder's badge number, which has a completely different format.)

Mulder knows enough about cars to be able to instantly disable the blaring horn after the attack by the COS.

Jerry Lamana was Mulder's partner in Violent Crimes. He was something of a high flyer until an incident in Atlanta when he misplaced some evidence which resulted in the disfigurement of a federal judge. Since then, his position has been constantly threatened.

The investigation chief Nancy Spiller has the academy nickname 'The Iron Maiden'. A 'Code 5 investigation' indicates defence considerations.

The Truth: This episode suggests that the technological dream of artificial intelligence has been achieved.

Trivia: Microsoft are mentioned by name (Eurisko were two years ahead of them in terms of 'home control' software).

The Bottom Line: KT: 'I'm gonna figure this thing out if it kills me.' A strange episode, with an unoriginal plot (the 'killer building' has been done in several places before, notably the *New Avengers* episode 'Complex') and a lot of seemingly random elements thrown together. But it is quite involving, and the ending is very enigmatic.

PC: An ordinary episode done with a lot of style (the plunge to video in the camera's-eye-view lift scene is very dramatic).

MD: Now, *this* is derivative rubbish (the death of the COS rips off *2001* in a way that transcends mere tribute). It's difficult to detest, but it is dull and heartless. About the best thing here is the character of Wilczek, the untidy-minded software programmer into Zen: for him, the worst part about going to prison is having to wear *shoes* . . .

COMPUTERS

The first clear look at Scully's computer comes in 'Ghost in the Machine', where it's clearly shown to be a PC running DOS 6. (The file WILCZEK.DOC – the document about Wilczek and the COS, in the sub-directory XFILES – is some 2061 bytes in length, which seems a little small!) In 'Little Green Men', Mulder's PC appears to be a DOS/Windows machine (although the production team get it slightly wrong and have a file listed called auto.exec, which is not a valid DOS name), hooked up to a Canon BJC 600. His password is, famously, 'trustno1'. By 'One Breath' he's changed to a Hewlett Packard LaserJet 4+ printer. In 'End Game' Mulder's computer is still running Windows 3.1 (obviously 95 hadn't arrived yet!), a contrast to Scully's Mac-based laptop, as seen in 'Irresistible' and other stories.

8: 'Ice'

US Transmission: 5 November 1993
UK Transmission: 16 March 1994 (Sky One)/
10 November 1994 (BBC2)
Writers: Glen Morgan, James Wong
Director: David Nutter
Cast: Xander Berkeley, Felicity Huffman, Steve Hytner,
Jeff Kober, Ken Kirzinger, Sonny Surowiec

Icy Cape, Alaska: contact has been lost with the Arctic Ice Core Project, where a team of geophysicists working for the government's advanced research projects agency are drilling into the ice for indications of Earth's past climate. Mulder and Scully, along with three scientists, are sent to the base. Scully finds traces of ammonia in the blood of the corpses, along with a single-cell organism – the larval stage of a worm which causes psychotic behaviour in its human hosts. The expedition's pilot and one of the scientists die, but Scully discovers that larvae from two different worms will kill each other and she is able to prevent further loss of life. After the survivors are evacuated the base is destroyed.

Don't Be in the Teaser: John Richter and Campbell kill themselves rather messily.

Scully Here is a Medical Doctor: She performs an autopsy on the five dead physicists.

Ooze: There *is* plenty of blood.

Scully's Rational Explanation of the Week: Severe isolation distress explains the physicists' deaths. The tables are turned, however, when her insistence that the single-cell organism could be the larval stage of a larger animal is dismissed by Hodge.

Phwoar!: Everybody takes their clothes off in this one. The sequence in which Mulder and Scully inspect each other's necks is powerful and edgy.

Dialogue Triumphs: Mulder (when told that they'll need to provide stool samples): 'OK, anybody got the morning sport section handy?' Bear: 'I ain't dropping my cargo for no one!'

Mulder (when stripping off): 'Before anyone passes judgement, may I remind you, we are in the Arctic!'

'It's still there, Scully: two hundred thousand years down in the ice.' 'Leave it there.'

The Conspiracy Starts at Closing Time: Somebody torches the base forty-five minutes after Mulder and Scully have been evacuated. Dr Hodge doesn't know who, though he speculates it was probably the military. Perhaps the conspiracy are aware of, or responsible for, a creature that has a similar effect on human rationality as their television project (see 'Wetwired').

Continuity: Mulder again reveals his extensive knowledge of American football when talking to Professor Murphy. It's a Wednesday when Mulder and Scully arrive at Doolittle Airfield.

The Truth: Mulder speculates that the worms are alien, largely because of their ability to survive very low temperatures. It seems that they came to Earth in a meteorite. The creatures seem to feed on the acetylcholine produced by the hypothalamus, triggering increased aggression in the host body. It is implied (the dog bite suffered by Bear) that they are transmitted via blood or saliva, but this does not seem to account for DaSilva's infection. The worms are almost certainly hermaphroditic.

Trivia: Stunt co-ordinator Ken Kirzinger plays Richter.

The Bottom Line: KT: 'We're not who we are.' A shameless 'tribute' to *The Thing from Another World* (and *The Trollenberg Terror*). Claustrophobic, and very nasty – invasion of the killer tapeworms (mark one, see 'The Host'!). A classic 'base-under-siege', with all of the obvious clichés, but very well written and acted for all that. The first *X-Files* episode to focus on characters rather than concepts.

PC: It's nice to see *Doctor Who*'s old base-under-siege story return to television. Pity it's not very original with its John Carpenter riffs, but it's great fun, anyway, and shows the verisimilitude that was the series' biggest selling point in its first season.

MD: A bit like my old Film Studies teacher's comment on both masturbation and the films of Alan Parker: fun while it lasts, but afterwards you wonder why you bothered. Still, for a few minutes you genuinely think that Mulder must be infected, something that few other programmes could so successfully achieve. It's a shame that the producers have to resort to the old Agatha Christie approach of making the guilty party the most unlikely suspect. (Not only is it never even hinted how DaSilva came to be infected, her character doesn't undergo the expected change of behaviour.) There are other instances of galloping lack of credibility: one moment we're being told that the lack of black spots isn't conclusive, the next Scully uses this as reason enough to believe that Mulder hasn't been infected. Argh!

9: 'Space'

US Transmission: 12 November 1993
UK Transmission: 23 March 1994 (Sky One)/
17 November 1994 (BBC2)
Writer: Chris Carter
Director: William Graham
Cast: Ed Lauter, Susanna Thompson, Tom McBeath,
Terry David Mulligan, French Tickner, Norma Wick,
Alf Humphreys, David Cameron, Tyronne L'Hirondelle,
Paul DesRoches

Houston, Texas: Mulder and Scully are contacted by Michelle Generoo, a NASA worker who believes that the current Space Shuttle programme is being sabotaged. They meet Mulder's boyhood idol, Marcus Belt, a former astronaut who is now project director. He dismisses any suggestion that the programme is being undermined, but the next flight is beset with problems. Belt is haunted by an alien image that he saw in space some twenty years before, an entity seeming to cohabit his body. He states that 'they' have been sabotaging missions for some time because 'they don't want us out there'. The shuttle returns to Earth with Belt's help, but he is hospitalised, and kills himself, much to Mulder's dismay.

Don't Be in the Teaser: Set in 1977, nobody dies, but Lt. Col. Belt (and the audience) get scared witless by the 'face on Mars'.

Scully Here is a Medical Doctor: She aids the medics when Belt suffers his seizure.

Scully's Rational Explanation of the Week: Severe dementia is at the root of Belt's 'possession'.

That's a Mouthful: 'Why would somebody want to sabotage a space shuttle?' asks Scully. Mulder's memorable reply is: 'Well, if you were a terrorist, there probably isn't a more potent symbol of American progress and prosperity. And if you're an opponent of big science, NASA itself represents a vast money trench that exists outside the crucible and debate of the democratic process. Then, of course, there are those futurists who believe that the space shuttle is a rusty old bucket that should be mothballed, a dinosaur spacecraft built in the seventies by scientists setting their sights on space in an ever-declining scale.'

'And we thought we could rest easy with the fall of the Soviet Union,' adds Scully.

Dialogue Triumphs: 'You never wanted to be an astronaut when you were a kid, Scully?' 'Guess I missed that phase.'

And, after the launch: 'I have to admit I've fulfilled one of my boyhood fantasies.' 'Yeah, it ranks right up there with getting a pony and learning to braid my own hair!'

Dialogue Disasters: Mulder: 'You'll get no argument from me, sir, you're a true American hero.'

The Conspiracy Starts at Closing Time: 'The failure of the Hubble telescope and the Mars Observer are directly connected to a conspiracy to deny us evidence,' notes Mulder. 'Evidence of what?' asks Scully. 'Alien civilisation.' 'Oh, of course!' (Every now and then, Mulder's desire to be open to extreme possibilities leads him to go blibber blibber blibber. The Hubble telescope was repaired to enable it to work close to its original specification – and what contribution it might have made to the discovery of alien civilisations is debatable. The loss of the Mars Observer, on the other hand, is rather mysterious. But does even Mulder believe in intelligent life on Mars?) There is some suggestion that Belt may have covered up sabotage on the Challenger disaster in 1986, or been part of the (actual) attempted hushing up of engineering worries concerning the cause of the disaster. Still, since there does turn out to be some alien life around that's associated with the 'face on Mars', then Mulder may be right: after all, evidence of life on any other planet would give the human race a reason for the sort of hope and faith that the conspiracy want to deny them (see 'Talitha Cumi'), and this 'ghost' may be a weapon used by them to prevent further revelations.

Continuity: Lt. Col. Marcus Aurelius Belt was one of Mulder's heroes as a child. Mulder stayed up all night when he was fourteen to watch Belt's spacewalk (this would have been in 1975 or 1976, so presumably Belt was involved in the Apollo/Soyuz link-up). Belt's career included piloting Gemini 8, during which he nearly died, having to make an emergency landing in the Pacific. (The real Gemini 8, piloted by Neil Armstrong and David Scott, made an emergency landing 10 hours and 41 minutes into the flight on 16 March 1966.)

The Truth: Well . . . As Lee Oswald said, 'You work it out.' There is little doubt that the gaseous ghostlike thing seen by Belt in space (and by the shuttle astronauts, and by Generoo before the crash, so it's not just Belt's delusions at work) is not Terran in origin. It may originate from Mars: it certainly looks like the 'face' observed there, but this could be Belt's own fears giving it shape. It appears to be malevolent and opposed to mankind's presence in space.

Trivia: When Generoo sees the face, the night is foggy and wet. The weather clears up remarkably as soon as Mulder and Scully arrive.

Scientific Comment: Mention is made of '. . . solar winds that blow across the surface of Mars at 300 m.p.h. ten months a year'. This isn't the solar wind, which is very weak and would do absolutely nothing to sculpt the Martian landscape. It's just the wind, the same as we have winds on Earth. There would be no reason for the solar wind to act for only ten months of the year. And are we talking about Earth years, Martian years or what? A month relates to Earth's moon, so presumably they are talking in Earth terms.

Even if they couldn't rotate the shuttle to the proper attitude with respect to the sub it would not 'burn up'.

The rotating payload was making a rotating noise when it was released. You wouldn't hear anything, of course. But perhaps one should be charitable and assume that the rotating noise came from the mechanism that spun it, which, since it was attached to the shuttle, the astronauts would hear.

The Bottom Line: KT: 'There's some kind of ghost outside the ship!' For some strange reason this fine episode proved to be vastly unpopular with fans of the series. Apart from the lack of obvious explanation about what the menace actually is (as though *that* were an uncommon fault in *The X-Files*!), there's little one can see that's wrong with the episode. It's superbly acted and covers themes of possession and the problematic nature of hero worship. Maybe the fact that the episode disses the American dream by making the villain of the piece an archetypal modern folk hero ensured that it was poorly received.

PC: Yeah, I like it too. Another area of the American mythos explored – all the stories of NASA encounters with aliens – and a fun use of stock footage.

MD: It's clever, politically literate and perceptive (it comes as no great surprise that by the episode's end Generoo is lying to the media, too). The suicide of Belt is very moving.

10: 'Fallen Angel'

US Transmission: 19 November 1993
UK Transmission: 30 March 1994 (Sky One)/
24 November 1994 (BBC2)
Writers: Howard Gordon, Alex Gansa
Director: Larry Shaw
Cast: Frederick Coffin, Marshall Bell, Scott Bellis,
Brent Stait, Alvin Sanders, Sheila Paterson, Tony Pantages,
Freda Perry, Michael Rogers, William McDonald,
Jane MacDougall, Kimberly Unger

Townsend, Wisconsin: after the discovery of something in the woods the town is evacuated on the pretence of a biological hazard having been found. Deep Throat tells Mulder that it is really a crashed spaceship and that the air force have sent in a reclamation group. He has twenty-four hours before the evidence will disappear. Mulder goes in but is apprehended. Scully arrives to bring him back to Washington for an inquiry hearing, but Mulder persuades her to stay. He befriends Max Fenig, a ufologist, and finds evidence of Max's having been abducted. Max is taken by the aliens, despite the presence of the military team, and Mulder is forced to return to the inquiry. However, he is saved from dismissal by Deep Throat.

Don't Be in the Teaser: Deputy Wright, burnt to death by aliens.

Scully Here is a Medical Doctor: She discusses the finer points of burn pathology with Dr Oppenheim, and is then asked for her help in dealing with the badly injured soldiers.

That's a Mouthful: 'I have my orders and the licence to execute them as I see fit.'

Scully's Rational Explanation of the Week: A downed Libyan jet with a nuclear warhead is the reason for the situation. Max is a delusional schizophrenic (Henderson treats this assertion contemptuously: he, of course, has a fair idea as to what is going on).

Dialogue Triumphs: Max: 'Let me guess, you're with that new group, CSICOP, right? Say no more. You're a cautious man, trust no one, very wise. After what happened to JFK I understand completely!'

Radar Operator: 'Well, sir, the "meteor" seems to be hovering over a small town in east Wisconsin.'

The Conspiracy Starts at Closing Time: Deep Throat's agenda is the focus of this episode: he sends Mulder into the area, then he saves his job just when it looks like Mulder's enemies have the perfect rationale for throwing him out of the FBI ('How can I disprove lies that are stamped with an official seal?'). In a puzzling scene with FBI Section Chief McGrath he seems to be playing both sides off against each other ('always keep your friends close but keep your enemies closer'): from the distance of season four, we can now see exactly what he's doing. McGrath, the head of the Office of Professional Responsibility, and junior representative of the conspiracy in the FBI (Skinner seems to do a flushing out of such moles as the series goes on), thinks he's achieved exactly what his employers want, to have Mulder thrown out of the Bureau, but Deep Throat (his CIA contact and unofficial boss) pulls rank on him to keep Mulder where he is, and uses a truly feeble excuse (backed up by his usual portentous delivery) to do so. From this point on, it could be argued, Deep Throat is dead meat, the subject of much more attention from Smoking Man, and his far more careful actions in 'E.B.E.' are a sign that he's aware that he may have taken a step too far.

At the end, Mulder is once more witness to an abduction. He should start checking himself for implants and radiation burns by now, surely?

Continuity: Scully did her residency in forensic medicine. The National Investigative Committee of Aerial Phenomena (or NICAP), of which Max Fenig is a member, has been following Mulder and Scully's exploits with interest ('your travel expenses are a matter of public record'). Mulder has published an article in *Omni* about the Gulf Breeze sightings under the pseudonym M. F. Luder (an anagram of F. Mulder: he didn't think anyone would notice, but is warned that 'Somebody's always paying attention, Mr Mulder'). He believes most crop circles are fake. There is another reference to the Roswell incident and its 'cover up'.

The leader of Operation Falcon is Colonel Colin Henderson, the air force's top reclamations officer (during the Cold War his job was to prevent the technology of downed US aircraft from falling into enemy hands). Now his mission is to recover crashed UFOs. (These men may also be the Blue Beret team seen in 'Little Green Men', and supply the uniformed gangs of armed men who are at the conspiracy's command, but here Henderson seems to be following a strictly governmental, rather than conspiracy, line.)

The Truth: The episode features a crashed alien spaceship and an invisible and lethal alien on the loose. It appears that Max has already been abducted and subjected to some sort of 'implantation': perhaps the first crashed alien's mission was to retrieve Max. Or maybe we're dealing with two different situations here. Max's implant dilemma is entirely similar to that faced by the various victims of the Japanese scientists (See 'Nisei'). Perhaps, at the end, we see him taken back by them (assuming that they can cause things to levitate, and since that's just what the USAF UFOs do, that's not too big a leap), in order to stop him getting anywhere near, or falling into the hands of, the very real aliens who appear in this episode. All we know about them is that they can become invisible. The invisibility is a trait we associate with the returned zoo animals of 'Fearful Symmetry', and they seem to have been taken by the whiteout aliens of 'Little Green Men', so, with a lot of licence, it seems possible that here we see another battle in the ongoing shapeshifter-and-conspiracy versus whiteout aliens war. At least, that would explain the vast plot holes that appear if Max is being abducted by the same aliens who crash.

Trivia: It's odd that Max assumes that Mulder works for CSICOP (Committee for the Scientific Investigation into Claims of the Paranormal), a group of real-life serious sceptics who wouldn't want Mulder in the same room with them.

The Bottom Line: KT: 'Another intrepid soul in search of a close encounter.' This is a little like biting into a Cadbury's Creme Egg and finding no creamy bit in the middle – a hollow mess with a plot with holes big enough to fly a spaceship through. (What happens to the crashed alien? What is the aliens' purpose in taking Max? Why not take Mulder with him? Is the second spaceship invisible, and, if so, why wasn't the first one?) Despite all of this (and a fairly strong suspicion that Max Fenig is an obvious and pretty insulting parody of SF fans – surely we should be beyond the 'space cadet' stereotypes by now) parts of 'Fallen Angel' are great (particularly Mulder's cool anger at Henderson). Oddly styled, though, with Scully missing for half the episode.

PC: A series of good set pieces put together randomly. The ending is quite meaningless, and a major disappointment.

MD: This left an indelible blank on me when I first watched it, but I quite enjoyed it this time. The complete change of pace was clever, with Mulder thrown straight into a virtual combat zone, and, whatever its flaws, this episode is directed with the brutality of a pop video drenched in testosterone. The little cameos of the harassed doctor who hates fascists and the widow who 'can't afford the truth' are excellent, but one is left with a vague feeling of disappointment after the wordy ending. And, given the deadly nature of the alien, Mulder really shouldn't have survived this episode, either.

11: 'Eve'

US Transmission: 10 December 1993
UK Transmission: 6 April 1994 (Sky One)/
1 December 1994 (BBC2)
Writers: Kenneth Biller, Chris Brancato
Director: Fred Gerber
Cast: Harriet Harris, Erika Krievins, Sabrina Krievins,
George Touliatos, Tasha Simms, Janet Hodgkinson,
David Kirby, Tina Gilbertson, Christine Upright-Letain,
Gordon Tipple, Garry Davey, Joe Maffei, Maria Herrera,
Robert Lewis

Greenwich, Connecticut: a man dies in his back yard from massive blood loss. His daughter (Teena) talks about 'men from the clouds' coming for him. Meanwhile, in Marin County, California, a virtually identical case becomes more of a statistical improbability when it is discovered that the daughter in the California case (Cindy) is the double of Teena. Mulder is told about a forty-year-old eugenics project that created a group of hyper-intelligent psychotic children, one of whom – Sally Kendrick – later worked in the IVF clinic where both Teena's and Cindy's mothers conceived. The girls are kidnapped by Kendrick, but she soon discovers that they are far from innocent eight-year-olds. Mulder and Scully, too, are almost poisoned by the pair, before they are incarcerated with one of their older 'sisters'.

Don't Be in the Teaser: Joel Simmons suffers 75-per-cent blood loss.

Scully Here is a Medical Doctor: Mulder tells *Scully* all about the pumping action of the heart. Similarly, Dr Scully is told (also for the benefit of the viewer) all about *in vitro* fertilisation at the Luther Stapes Center.

Scully's Rational Explanation of the Week: Real bottom-of-the-barrel scraping here. Two serial killers are working in tandem three thousand miles apart, and the likenesses of the clones are random. As Mulder says, 'I'd like to get the odds on that at Vegas!' However, let's not be hard on her: she suspects the girls long before Mulder does, if only in jest.

Dialogue Triumphs: 'Mulder, why would alien beings travel light years to Earth in order to play "doctor" on cattle?' (Good question!)

Mulder: 'One girl was just abducted.' Scully: 'Kidnapped.' Mulder: 'Potato, potahto.'

The Conspiracy Starts at Closing Time: Given Deep Throat's interest in the case, and the fact that the original experiments were sanctioned by the US government, it seems almost certain that the conspiracy has endorsed Kendrick's renewal of the eugenics experiments. Dr Katz's call for an investigation was ignored, and Eve 6 claims that she is still being experimented on. It is possible that this is a facet of a programme that attempted to create the perfect soldier (see 'Young at Heart', 'Sleepless', 'Red Museum' and 'Apocrypha'). Or maybe the conspiracy are interested in what the shapeshifter rebels might be up to with cloning (see 'Colony'). The Eves bear a strong resemblance to the Gregors depicted therein, and might even be the human control group of that experiment, which Deep Throat tells Mulder about in order to have him shut it down.

Deep Throat contacts Mulder via clicks down the phone.

Continuity: Mulder states that, since 1967, thirty-four states have reported unsolved cases of cattle mutilation.

The Truth: According to Deep Throat, the Litchfield experiments were a secret government eugenics project in the early 1950s. A group of children were produced who had 56 chromosomes instead of the normal 46, giving them heightened intelligence (Eve 6 believes her IQ is pushing 265) and strength. However, they were also prone to psychotic behaviour and suicide ('It runs in the family!'). The boys were called Adam, and the eight girls, Eve.

Of the Eves, only three are seen during the story. Eve 6 is held in the Whitfield Institute for the Criminally Insane, and Eve 7 has controlled her psychosis with drugs, becoming Dr Sally Kendrick. She has cloned herself in an attempt to root out the 'Litchfield flaws' (which she characterises as psychotic behaviour beginning at seventeen, and homicidal behaviour starting at twenty). Eve 8 appears at the end.

Cindy and Teena are the progeny of this 'second-generation' experiment, and they appear to be telepathic, which might be a side effect of their unique genetic make-up (although Eve 7 is surprised by this). Their homicidal behaviour starts much earlier, and Teena and Cindy are renamed Eves 9 and 10 by the story's end.

Trivia: As Mulder and Scully question Ellen Reardon, Cindy watches the cartoon series *Eek the Cat*. The cartoon would later return the favour by featuring an animated Mulder and Scully. Eve 6 quotes from the Beatles' 'I Am the Walrus' ('. . . and we are all together!'). There is a mention of the Jones Town massacre.

The Bottom Line: KT: 'We weren't born, we were created.' The best episode so far, a cracking story made more memorable by a series of brilliant set pieces throughout. The pre-titles suggest a simple vampire story – then it gets *really* weird! Many great directorial touches, a breathtaking triple performance by Harriet Harris, and a final scene that's crying out for a sequel.

PC: Indeed, here's a story that's written instead of being thrown together. Where do they find these weird-looking child actors? Can you imagine the auditions?

MD: It's not often that we're allowed to be two steps ahead of Mulder, and here it works well, adding to the suspense of the final scenes. The story's only flaw is that the direction sometimes oversteps the mark, making the first abduction, for example, appear to be a supernatural activity when it is in fact nothing of the sort.

12: 'Fire'

US Transmission: 17 December 1993
UK Transmission: 13 April 1994 (Sky One)/
17 December 1994 (BBC2)[2]
Writer: Chris Carter
Director: Larry Shaw
Cast: Amanda Pays, Mark Sheppard, Dan Lett, Laurie Paton,
Duncan Fraser, Phil Hayes, Keegan Macintosh, Lynda Boyd,
Christopher Gray, Alan Robertson

Bosham, England: another member of the British establishment burns to death. Mulder's ex-girlfriend, Phoebe Green, now an inspector with Scotland Yard, arrives in America and asks for Mulder's help in protecting Sir Malcolm Marsden and his family. A fire breaks out during an important function, the arsonist seeming to target Marsden's children. Mulder attempts a rescue, despite his pyrophobia. An artist's impression of the arsonist is drawn up, and Scully discovers that he is one Cecil L'Ively, currently working as the Marsden's odd-job man. L'Ively's attempt to kill the Marsden children is foiled by Mulder and the man self-ignites. Although horribly burnt, L'Ively survives.

Don't Be in the Teaser: A paint-by-numbers member of the British upper classes spontaneously combusts. Or not, as the case may be. Patronises everyone in sight, including his wife, so probably deserves everything he gets.

Scully's Rational Explanation of the Week: Let's give the girl some credit: her profile of the arsonist is spot on in every aspect other than his means of ignition.

Phwoar!: There's some interesting body language from Scully whenever Phoebe is around. Dialogue, too (Mulder: 'I was merely extending her a professional courtesy.' Scully: 'Oh, is that what you were extending?'). Miaow! Mulder

---

[2] 'Fire' was shown out of order in the initial BBC run, being transmitted after 'Beyond the Sea' and in a late-night slot as part of BBC2's 'Weird Night'.

wanders round Phoebe's hotel room shirtless, and in a robe, and mention must be made of his tuxedo-wearing skills.

Dialogue Triumphs: Mulder on the mysterious tape: 'Ten to one you can't dance to it.'

Phoebe: 'Oh come on, don't tell me you left your sense of humour in Oxford ten years ago?' Mulder: 'No, actually, it's one of the few things you *didn't* drive a stake through.'

Dialogue Disasters: Phoebe: 'Some clever bloke has been giving the aristocracy a scare.'

L'Ively: 'Bloody little cur. I'll skin you alive! See – I'm the caretaker now!'

Mulder: 'Doesn't look like your arsonist is going to make an appearance.' Phoebe: 'That doesn't mean there won't be any fires to put out.'

L'Ively: 'You can't fight fire with fire!'

Continuity: Mulder's pyrophobia dates back to his youth: his best friend's house burnt down and Mulder spent the night in the rubble to keep away looters. Following that he suffered years of nightmares about being trapped in burning buildings. He says he has a photographic memory (we don't see any evidence of this – and it's a very rare ability – so he's probably talking about his acute remembrance of the bad times during his affair with Phoebe). He met Phoebe Green when he was at Oxford and they became lovers. Mulder and Phoebe used to share Sherlock Holmes jokes and Phoebe implies that they once made love atop Arthur Conan Doyle's tomb in Windlesham. (The real tomb is in Minstead in Hampshire. The writer didn't even bother to open a reference book . . .) Phoebe's current lover is Malcolm Marsden.

Scully can do a reasonable British accent (better than most of the actors in this episode anyway . . .). She discovers that there was a child called Cecil L'Ively who died in a ritual murder by a Satanic cult in 1963 in Tottingham Woods near Bath. In 1971 a Cecil Lively apparently died in a London tenement fire.

Phoebe indicates that Scotland Yard believes the 1992 fire at Windsor Castle was the work of the arsonist.

This X-File is given the number 11214893.

The Truth: Whether L'Ively is a genuine pyrokinetic is debatable. He certainly uses the rocket fuel argotypoline as an accelerant, but his power of ignition seems paranormal. Also, his ability to survive massive burning is said to be 'extraordinary' by military experts.

Trivia: Bosham is apparently seventy miles southwest of London, which would place it on the Hampshire coast. The US government, not the British government, issue US visas: the FBI should know that!

Chris Carter's birthday strikes again: Scully's autopsy is at 10.56 (indicating October 1956).

Scientific Comment: You would get a magnesium residue after an exothermic reaction only if there was magnesium present to begin with. It is stated in this episode that fires burning at 7,000 degrees can't be put out with water because it dissociates into hydrogen and oxygen and just adds fuel to the fire, and that rocket fuel burns so hot there are no traces left afterwards. It is true that water would be dissociated at 7,000 degrees, but it wouldn't make any difference to the fire: it would not be like adding fuel. However, you'd never get a fire this hot. Anything based on petroleum or hydrocarbons burns at 700–800 degrees, not thousands. You never get fires hotter than 4,000 degrees from anything. The only way to get 7,000 degrees (which is hotter than the sun's surface) would be to use *real* rocket fuel, that is: hydrogen and liquid oxygen being brought together in a high-compression engine. Not only that, but concrete is a very good thermal insulator, and apparently can be in a fire for days without really being affected. The only thing that happens is that the outside layer flakes off. It would have to be awfully substandard concrete to be affected much at all.

The Bottom Line: KT: 'God, I just love that accent!' Despite a few (no, qualify that: a *lot* of) dodgy British accents, 'Fire' is another fine episode. The script is full of caricatures (L'Ively especially – we know little more about him at the episode's end than at the beginning), but the effects are amazing and it's got enough genuine scares in it to paper over the logic cracks that pop up every now and then. Mark Sheppard is very good as 'Bob'. Amanda Pays chews the scenery.

PC: Written by people who don't know Britain or the British even slightly (Malcolm Marsden is a knight, a lord, and an MP!), this makes you wonder about how accurately the series treats the other communities it visits. Phoebe would be one of the youngest detective inspectors in Britain, and the most upper-class, and she has a very strange choice of current boyfriend. She wears clothes from the 1980s, as if nobody had seen British fashions since Lady Di. Is Cecil L'Ively really the name of a gardener, and Malcolm Marsden the name of a lord? And there's that standard Americanism, the misuse of 'bloke'. It's annoying that, for a series with the depth of *The X-Files*, the approach to Britain is just as rubbish as that of every other American series. Thank goodness they haven't done one set here, or it'd be cricket, tea, thatched cottages and saving the Queen from aliens at Stonehenge.

KT: Sounds like a good story, actually.

MD: My favourite Americanisms were a 'British *Minister of Parliament*' and all that guff about Scotland Yard. Oh, and Sheppard's accent is a hoot, changing from Irish to Aussie to Michael Caine in the blink of an eye (which is a shame because, as Keith points out, he actually puts in a good performance). Still, the episode itself is mostly harmless, and Anderson is great (I love Scully's breezy 'Hello!' to Phoebe).

13: 'Beyond the Sea'

US Transmission: 7 January 1994
UK Transmission: 20 April 1994 (Sky One)/
8 December 1994 (BBC2)
Writers: Glen Morgan, James Wong

Director: David Nutter
Cast: Brad Dourif, Lawrence King, Fred Henderson,
Don MacKay, Lisa Vultaggio, Chad Willett,
Kathrynn Chisholm, Randy Lee, Len Rose

Washington, DC: after a visit from her parents, Scully sees a silent vision of her father shortly before receiving the phone call telling her of his death. Raleigh, North Carolina: a couple are kidnapped a year to the day after a similar crime. A death row prisoner, Luther Lee Boggs, claims to have developed psychic powers which will lead the FBI to the kidnapper. He also claims to be able to communicate with Scully's father. Mulder is, for once, sceptical, but Scully, after further visitations, begins to believe in Boggs's abilities. Tracking the kidnapper, Mulder is shot and badly wounded. The kidnapper escapes with one of the two hostages but is identified as Lucas Henry, Boggs's former accomplice. The victim is rescued and the kidnapper falls to his death. As Boggs is executed, Mulder and Scully are still unsure whether his 'gifts' were genuine.

Don't Be in the Teaser: Captain Scully dies (off screen) from a heart attack. Even our heroes' families aren't immune.

Scully's Rational Explanation of the Week: Having spent nearly an entire episode going Mulder on us, good old Dana ends the story trying to convince herself that Boggs had learnt of her connection to Mulder and researched her, and that her visions of her dead father were grief symptoms (despite the fact that the first occurred *before* she was aware of his death).

Phwoar!: Mulder touches Scully's face as he says how sorry he is to hear about the death of her father.

Dialogue Triumphs: Mulder (on Boggs): 'When he was thirty, he strangled five family members over Thanksgiving dinner and then sat down to watch the fourth quarter of the Detroit/Green Bay game. Some killers are products of society, some act out past abuses. Boggs kills because he likes it.'

Scully: 'Did Boggs confess?' Mulder: 'No, it was five hours of Boggs's "channelling". After three hours I asked him to summon up the soul of Jimi Hendrix and requested "All Along the Watchtower". You know, the guy's been dead twenty years, but he still hasn't lost his edge.'

Mulder: 'Open yourself up to "extreme possibilities" only when they're the truth.'

Scully: 'Well, I came here to tell you that if he [Mulder] dies because of what you've done, four days from now nobody will stop me from being the one that throws the switch and gas you out of this life for good, you son of a bitch!'

Continuity: Scully's father was a navy captain, her mother's name is Margaret. Her father always made the family take the Christmas tree down on Boxing Day. She called her father 'Ahab'; his nickname for her was 'Starbuck' (see 'Quagmire'). Scully's house number is 35. Mulder calls Scully 'Dana' for just about the first time, much to her amusement (or discomfort – it's difficult to be sure). Her father's funeral music is 'Beyond the Sea' by Bobby Darin, which was the music played when his ship returned from the Cuban blockade in 1962 – just before he proposed to Margaret. (Since the Cuban missile crisis happened in October 1962, and Melissa Scully was born in that year, are we to assume that she was born out of wedlock?) The song was also played at their wedding. There are five people at Captain Scully's funeral besides Dana and her mother. Presumably these would include her two brothers (see 'Roland'), though her sister (see 'One Breath') doesn't appear to be there.

Mulder's profile helped to capture the serial killer Luther Lee Boggs. Mulder gives Boggs a piece of cloth which Boggs says belongs to Jim Summers. In reality it is from Mulder's New York Knicks teeshirt (see 'Clyde Bruckman's Final Repose' for an amusing twist on this). Mulder is shot in the upper femur, and seriously wounded.

An X File concerning 'visionary encounters with the dead' is code numbered X-167512. (And, presumably, that's about a particular case, unless Mulder's started to file his library clippings this way, too.)

The Truth: The episode never makes clear whether Boggs is a superb con artist with an accomplice or the genuine possessor of paranormal powers. Initially Mulder believes him to be the former and Scully the latter, but by the episode's end they have switched. As Scully points out, it would have been possible (if difficult) for Boggs to have found out a lot about her and her father. And Scully may have indeed been delusional in her grief at her father's death. But, on the other hand, there is nothing to disprove Boggs's claims: after all, more or less everything he predicts (the shooting of Mulder, Henry falling to his death) comes true.

Trivia: The minister whom Boggs spoke to quoted from 1 John 3:14–15. Max's NICAP cap (see 'Fallen Angel') hangs in Mulder's office.

The Bottom Line: KT: 'Dana, after all you've seen, after all the evidence, why can't you believe?' 'I'm afraid. I'm afraid to believe.' Magnificent, enigmatic and wonderful – the zenith of a superb run of episodes with the performance of the season by Brad Dourif as Boggs. A complex narrative piece, complete with juxtaposed character motivation that could only work if the acting is of the highest quality. A truly great episode.

PC: Still up there with the best episodes of the series. The courage it takes for a series this deep in ratings trouble ('Beyond the Sea' achieved only a 5 rating, the lowest the series has ever sunk, an eminently cancellable position) to do an episode that turns away from the unexplained and denies the audience closure is magnificent. Mind you, there's still that annoying postmodern idea that if you quote from something, then you bring some of the quality of what's being quoted along with you. In this case, the episode takes lots from *Exorcist III*. But it does some original things with the material. Gillian Anderson proves here that she's about ten times better an actor than David Duchovny, by going for restraint and then exploding.

MD: Couldn't agree more with the comments above (except I don't see why it's necessary to praise Anderson by dissing Duchovny!). 'Beyond the Sea' is a remarkable episode, *The X-Files* proving that metaphysical reflection is very much its forte. The monochrome nightmare of Boggs going to the chair – and the souls rushing in – is just terrifying. An incredibly brave story, given that many of the viewing public desire the murder of murderers.

14: 'GenderBender'

US Transmission: 21 January 1994
UK Transmission: 27 April 1994 (Sky One)/
22 December 1994 (BBC2)[3]
Writers: Larry Barber, Paul Barber
Director: Rob Bowman
Cast: Brent Hinkley, Michele Goodger, Kate Twa, Peter Stebbings, Nicholas Lea, Mitchell Kosterman, Paul Batten, Doug Abrahams, Aundrea MacDonald, John R. Taylor, Grai Carrington, Tony Morelli, Lesley Ewen, David Thomson

Germantown, Maryland: Mulder and Scully investigate the latest in a series of five deaths linked by the victims dying during or shortly after sexual intercourse with massive levels of pheromones in their bodies. A security camera witnesses the victim arriving home with a female, but a male leaving. Mulder is convinced that they are tracking 'the ultimate sex machine'. Clues point to a link to a reclusive religious cult, the Kindred. He and Scully travel to Steveston, Massachusetts, where they meet the Kindred. Mulder discovers a secret catacomb area, where a dying man appears to change gender, while Scully finds herself drawn to one of the brothers. The killer is revealed as an escaped member of the sect, 'tainted' by the outside world. After (s)he has killed again, the Kindred arrive to 'take care of their own', and disappear.

[3] 'GenderBender' was originally scheduled for 15 December 1994 but was postponed.

Don't Be in the Teaser: An unnamed New York businessman engages in a wild, passionate bout of sex, then chokes to death. All things considered, *that's* the only way to go!

How Did He Do That?: How does Mulder manage to avoid capture in a tunnel system that he's never been in and his pursuers, presumably, know like the back of their hand?

Ooze: There's some frothy stuff that the victims spew up at various points. And Scully vomits (off screen).

Scully's Rational Explanation of the Week: A transvestite, obviously.

Phwoar!: Scully's reaction to Brother Andrew both includes and transcends the sensual.

Dialogue Triumphs: Scully: 'So, what is our profile of the killer? Indeterminate height, weight, sex. Unarmed, but extremely attractive?!'

Michael: 'The club scene used to be so simple.'

Dialogue Disasters: Cop: 'Cat blew an artery. Must have been some roll in the hay!'

Mulder: 'I know what I saw, Scully, and I saw you about to do the Wild Thing with some stranger!'

The Truth: The killer, Marty, and his Kindred brothers and sisters, are ... er ... Well, the episode's final two scenes (complete with a crop circle – how about that for lack of style?) suggests that they were aliens. Or ghosts. Or something ... They appear to be able to 'vanish' at will (the 'transportation' of the murderer), and use a regenerative gel in the catacomb that also changes gender. The pheromones they release contain human DNA, but their final disappearance does suggest a UFO. Come on, guys, give us a clue! We'd say they were shapeshifters, but their method of changing shape is much more complex than that. Perhaps they're a mutant branch of rebels. Their attitude of wanting to be cut off from the world seems utterly genuine, but rather strange if they've got transport off-planet arranged. Perhaps these are another community of mutated humans (see 'Red Museum') who are taken away at the end against their will by the Japanese.

Trivia: A classic rock fan's dream, Mulder name-checking the Troggs' 'Wild Thing' and Golden Earring's 'Radar Love' and Scully weighing in with a misquote from Lou Reed's 'Walk on the Wild Side' ('she was a he!'). Mulder mentions *The Addams Family* again. The painting that we see Marty standing beside is by H. R. Giger, the designer of *Alien*. Steveston, Massachusetts is named after a real town south of Vancouver, often used by the series for location work.

The Bottom Line: KT: 'Maybe it's the sex that kills.' Difficult to know where to start with this. The episode is a mess, a confusing mixture of about eight different stories all struggling to be understood. Good points first: the juxtaposition of the club scenes with the ordered calm of the Kindred community is well managed, the direction generally being very good. Also, stories about religious cults tend to come over all atheistic and sanctimonious, but this one at least achieves some balance. Yet, for all this, the episode's denouement is a disaster – with seemingly random (and highly implausible) elements thrown in at the last moment to provide a suitably 'enigmatic' climax. The plot has more holes in it than Blackburn, Lancashire. (Who were the Kindred? Aliens? Mutant Hermaphrodites? Bisexuals with a God-complex? How do they 'disappear' from the crime scene?) I'm not in favour of TV spoon-feeding me all the answers, but just one or two would be quite nice. This is also the first episode in which the beauty of the series' initial view of Americana – in which every town has a forest with an alien in it – becomes dissipated. We see the first example of what would soon become the standard *X-Files* visual cliché, a misty inner-city back-alley. For all sorts of reasons, a big disappointment.

PC: Hm? Sorry. Perked up for a bit in the middle of the episode and then dropped off again. Thought that some of the direction and lighting was rather nice, but it didn't keep me awake. Was it any good?

MD: Almost. Some of this actually chugs along quite nicely as a parable on the corrupting influence of the 'World' (Brother Andrew says that he liked some of what he saw in the secular magazine, but that much was 'garish'), but the ending is amateurish in the extreme. What's worse than the lack of explanation is the lack of a conclusion: the narrative just peters out completely.

15: 'Lazarus'

US Transmission: 4 February 1994
UK Transmission: 4 May 1994 (Sky One)/
5 January 1995 (BBC2)
Writers: Alex Gansa, Howard Gordon
Director: David Nutter
Cast: Christopher Allport, Cec Verrell, Jackson Davies,
Jason Schombing, Callum Keith Rennie, Jay Brazeau,
Lisa Bunting, Peter Kelamis, Brenda Crichlow,
Mark Saunders, Alexander Boynton, Russell Hamilton

Maryland Marine Bank: during an FBI operation to capture two bank robbers, Warren and Lula Dupre, Scully's former lover, Special Agent Jack Willis, is critically injured, as is Warren. Willis survives – after thirteen minutes of flatlining in the emergency room – but Warren Dupre dies. After Willis goes missing and Warren Dupre's hand is mutilated to remove his wedding ring, Mulder comes to believe that a psychic transference has taken place. Willis later turns up and appears to be normal, saying he only wants to capture Lula and close the case. However, when he and Scully go to arrest the woman, Willis convinces Lula that he is Warren Dupre and they kidnap Scully. As Mulder and the FBI close in, Lula double-crosses her lover, just as she did before. Willis is slipping into a diabetic coma but he recovers sufficiently to kill Lula just as Mulder arrives.

Don't Be in the Teaser: What a bloodbath! Jack Willis, shot by Dupre, who is promptly shot by Scully.

How Did He Do That?: The mother of all How Did He Do Thats. Mulder, using only two traces on a heart monitor, comes to the conclusion that a transference of souls has taken place! He even finds a loony scientist to back him up! And, for perhaps the first time in the series, this is all so ridiculous that the audience doesn't believe him either!

Scully Here is a Medical Doctor: Something that she reminds an entire emergency team of when they want to declare Jack Willis dead.

Scully's Rational Explanation of the Week: One of her finest forty-five minutes, and this time we're all rooting for her: 'Post-trauma psychosis' explains Jack Willis's disappearance, 'instrument malfunction' the double EEG print, 'stress' for Willis's changing handwriting, and she dismisses near-death experience as 'some sort of dissociative hallucinatory activity'. Then she says she doesn't discount the near-death experience because it can be explained by stimulation of the temporal lobe. 'I sense a big "but" coming,' notes Mulder, dryly!

Dialogue Triumphs: 'My name is Warren James Dupre, and I was born in Clamett Falls, Oregon, in the year of the rat!'

Willis: 'I feel myself getting into their heads and I'm scared by what I'm feeling. The intoxicating freedom that comes from disconnecting action and consequence – theirs is a world where nothing matters but their own needs, their own impossible appetites. And while the pleasure they derive from acts of violence is clearly sexual, it also speaks to what Warden Jackson called their operatic devotion to each other. It's a love affair I almost envy.'

Continuity: Scully and Jack dated for almost a year when he was her instructor at the academy. They share the same birthday (23 February) and used to celebrate it at 'some dive in Stafford that had a slanty pool table'. Jack was born in

1957 (which makes him seven years older than Scully – see 'Paper Clip'). The couple once spent a snowy weekend after Thanksgiving at Willis's parents' cabin, where Jack taught Scully to fish through the ice.

The Truth: Psychic transference? Difficult to say for sure, but Scully's faith in her ex-lover Willis continues long after he has kidnapped her and, frankly, defies belief (but then, this is Scully we're talking about). The pre-title sequence shows some kind of link between the two bodies, and Scully sees (or seems to see) the face of Dupre when held hostage. However, the suggestion that psychic transference extends to tattoos takes some leap of faith. Does it apply to ear piercings? Thank goodness the killer wasn't circumcised . . .

Trivia: There is some confusion over the dating of this episode. Scully says she bought Willis's watch as a birthday present 'three years ago' (c. 1991), but the watch is clearly inscribed 'Happy 35th'. Willis's 35th birthday would have been in 1992, only two years ago, so Scully must be in error. Additionally, when Mulder congratulates Scully on her birthday she says he is 'two months early', indicating that this episode probably takes place in late December.

The FBI aren't able to trace Scully through her cellphone, so obviously Smoking Man (who uses that method to find Mulder in 'Anasazi') has technology they don't.

Scientific Comment: You can't have two heartbeats from a body with one heart. Two brainwaves would have been more believable. Even if it were true that watches worn by people who have had a near-death experience stop because of a release of electrical energy (and cells are dying all the time, anyway), after their strange experience, the effect would surely cease.

The Bottom Line: KT: 'Baby, you ain't gonna believe where I've been!' An unusual approach to an age-old idea, with a potentially difficult theme (Scully's former love life) well handled. Any episode that includes dialogue references to *JFK* ('You're the FBI, you figure it out!') is OK with this author. Once again, however, the 'enigmatic' ending doesn't work as well as it would have with a bit more opinion about what has actually taken place. One gets the suspicion that the production team at this stage seemed to believe that a lack of explanation was exactly what the audience wanted.

PC: Oh, this is crap crap crap crap! A 'psychotic episode' that's 'not an X-File'. This doesn't so much suspend my disbelief as stamp it into the floor. How many times have we seen that 'aircraft sound on tape' scene? And there's the annoying 'execution' quote from *Pulp Fiction* (I can imagine the writers who quote stuff shaking their heads in surprise and saying, 'But fanboys love it when we quote stuff!') This is just silly. And it's nice to know that a nutter can pass the FBI's psychological tests . . .

MD: Some fair criticisms, but I still rather like this story. Maybe I'm just a sucker for those episodes where we get to see Mulder doing something approaching a 'normal' FBI job. 'It means . . . It means whatever you want it to mean.'

16: 'Young at Heart'

US Transmission: 11 February 1994
UK Transmission: 11 May 1994 (Sky One)/
12 January 1995 (BBC2)
Writers: Scott Kaufer, Chris Carter
Director: Michael Lange
Cast: Dick Anthony Williams, Alan Boyce,
Christine Estabrook, Graham Jarvis, Robin Mossley,
Merrilyn Gann, Gordon Tipple, Courtney Arciaga,
David Petersen, Robin Douglas

Washington, DC: a violent bank robbery bears all the hallmarks of Johnny Barnett, a psychopath whom Mulder helped to convict years before. But Barnett apparently died in 1989. Like Barnett, the robber taunts Mulder with threatening notes. After Mulder's friend and former partner Agent Reggie Purdue is killed, Mulder is convinced that Barnett has returned from the grave. The doctor who signed Barnett's death certificate – Ridley – had previously been disbarred for carrying out human experimentation into premature ageing. Ridley turns up at Scully's house and tells the agents that his work has continued, with government backing, and that Barnett, his most successful patient, is alive, and, worse, young again. Mulder sets a trap for Barnett at a cello recital with Scully as the bait. Scully is shot, but is uninjured, wearing a bulletproof vest. Barnett takes a hostage but Mulder rights the wrong of his past by shooting him.

Don't Be in the Teaser: Johnny Barnett, seemingly killed in a sinister medical experiment in 1989, actually comes out of the teaser in better shape than the doctor who's working on him.

How Did He Do That?: Not Mulder this time, but Doctor Ridley. How did he know where Scully lived? Indeed, how did he know who Scully was in the first place, and what her connection to Mulder and, via him, Barnett, was?

Ooze: Barnett's 'Salamander' arm is quite disgusting.

Scully's Irrational Explanation of the Week: Barnett is a ghost. No, hang on, she's probably joking and Mulder, and we, have just failed to get it!

Dialogue Triumphs: Mulder tells Scully that Barnett died in prison. 'You're sure?' 'I *was* paying attention!'

The Conspiracy Starts at Closing Time: The US government has been sponsoring Ridley's latterday research in Mexico and Belize. And, according to Deep Throat, bargaining with John Barnett to buy the research from him once Ridley dies from a rare cerebral-vascular disease. Ridley says that the secret of the US funding goes 'high up the ladder'. A by-product of the original research is a salamander-like ability to regrow injured or severed limbs (which would be of great value to the military? – see 'Red Museum', 'Apocrypha', etc.).

'That guy in the ugly suit is probably CIA,' comments

Mulder while watching the attempts to resuscitate Barnett. 'That guy' is played by William B. Davis, the Smoking Man. Whether he's supposed to be playing the same character as his other appearances is never made clear, as you don't get a very good look at him, but it's a strong possibility. If he is the same character, then Mulder comes to this conclusion by his style and presence, not by recognising him (as he never pursues any CIA connection). Considering Deep Throat's revelations in 'E.B.E.', it's very probable that the Smoking Man does work for the CIA, as well as for the conspiracy, and that he's combining both roles here as the conspiracy continue to use the US military to look into the idea of mutant armies.

Continuity: Mulder's first case for the Bureau, fresh from the academy and aged twenty-eight, was Johnny Barnett, who had killed seven people in a string of complex armed robberies. Mulder's initial partner was Reggie Purdue. Barnett was eventually caught, but agent Steve Wallenburg died because Mulder did not shoot Barnett in the back when he had the chance. (It is against FBI regulations to unnecessarily endanger the life of a hostage: Wallenburg's death explains much of Mulder's subsequent hostility to doing things 'by the book'.) Barnett avoided the death penalty on a technicality and was sentenced to 340 years in prison. He swore revenge on Mulder.

Mulder believes (at least in this case) in capital punishment (as did Scully in 'Beyond the Sea').

Purdue was an amateur author, working on a mystery novel that he often told Mulder about. A friend, and mentor, Purdue always defended Fox against the 'Spooky' nonsense, but was concerned that Mulder's career, which once seemed destined for great things, seemed to be stalled by the cul-de-sac of the X-Files.

The Truth: For once there are no paranormal or supernatural elements present (though Mulder spends half the episode thinking there must be). Fake deaths, obscene Dr Mengele-style medical experiments with government backing, and a massive cover-up, but no ghosts. Thanks to Ridley's work, Barnett has become young again (only his eyes betray his true age). His amputated hand has been 'regenerated' via a technique that derives from research on salamanders.

The Bottom Line: KT: 'Mulder, it's science fiction!' A wildly improbable tale, full of garish set pieces and non sequiturs (who, for example, is the buxom blonde in the cycling shorts and cowboy boots in the last scene? – not that it has anything to do with the plot: I'd just like to know). Fundamentally, however, it's a nice straightforward story of revenge and fear. Includes David Duchovny's best performance of the season and some very good direction. Flawed, but interesting.

PC: Ho hum. Don't you just want Scully to open her door when the incidental music gets operatic to find a male-voice choir out there? I think I get it. This script and the last one were written when it was thought this series was going to be a sort of *Silence of the Lambs* with aliens, and held over into mid-season to get the good stuff up front. You can't see them using ordinary stuff like this in any other season.

MD: It's ordinary only in the sense that 'Aubrey' and 'Irresistible' from the next season are ordinary, i.e. conventional rather than dull. I rather enjoyed it despite its many flaws: the 'salamander arm' seems to be there only for a cheap shock effect, and then there's that ridiculous scene of Scully typing by candlelight. The music is straight from *The Omen*; Barnett's threats make him sound like a minor member of the Corleone clan. The ending, too, is lame, which is unfortunate. Most worrying of all is the fact that Mulder seems to be getting through more (former) partners than Dirty Harry (see 'Ghost in the Machine').

17: 'E.B.E.'

US Transmission: 18 February 1994
UK Transmission: 18 May 1994 (Sky One)/
19 January 1995 (BBC2)

Writers: Glen Morgan, James Wong
Director: William Graham
Cast: Allan Lysell, Peter Lacroix

Lexington, Tennessee: a UFO sighting brings Mulder and Scully running, but their interview with a trucker who claims to have shot at an alien creature is curtailed by the local police force. Mulder visits his friends at the magazine *The Lone Gunman*, and then Deep Throat. He discovers that a UFO was recently shot down over Iraq and that the recovered wreckage, and possibly an alien, are being transported across the countryside in a truck. Despite being under surveillance Mulder and Scully meet in Las Vegas, then follow the truck to Washington state where they find a secret government complex. Once inside, Mulder meets Deep Throat, who explains that the alien is already dead.

Don't Be in the Teaser: An Iraqi pilot shoots down a UFO. Good news for him, but terrifically bad for the alien.

Scully's Rational Explanation of the Week: The trucker shot at a mountain lion. The lights he saw were swamp gas. 'Isn't it more plausible that an exhausted truck driver became swept up in the hysteria and fired upon hallucinations?' The *Lone Gunman* lads are 'self-delusional'. The UFO photo is a fake (which it is, actually). 'Why don't you just admit it, Scully? You're determined not to believe,' says Mulder.

That's a Mouthful: Oceans of politicobabble. Deep Throat says he has been 'a participant in some of the most insidious lies, and witness to deeds that no crazed man can imagine. I've spent years watching you [Mulder] from my lofty position to know that you were the one I could trust.'

Mulder: 'Dangerous? You mean in the sense of outrage: like the reaction to the Kennedy assassination? Or MIAs? Or radiation experiments on terminal patients? Watergate, Iran-Contra, Roswell, the Tuskeegee experiments? Where will it end? I guess it won't end as long as men like you decide what is truth.'

Dialogue Triumphs: Langly: 'Yeah, UFOs caused the Gulf War Syndrome: that's a good one.' Byers: 'That's why we like you, Mulder, your ideas are weirder than ours!'

Scully: 'Those were the most paranoid people I have ever met. I don't know how you could think that what they say is even remotely plausible.' Mulder: 'I think it's remotely plausible that someone might think you're "hot"!'

Scully: 'Mulder, the truth is out there. But so are lies.'

Deep Throat: 'And a lie, Mr Mulder, is most convincingly hidden between two truths . . . If the shark stops swimming, it will die. Don't stop swimming.'

The Conspiracy Starts at Closing Time: Mulder contacts Deep Throat by shining a blue light through his apartment window and awaiting a phone call (since Deep Throat seems to hang up immediately, it is uncertain how they arrange *where* to meet – see 'Eve'). Mulder tells Scully about Deep Throat for the first time. 'All I know is that he's guided us away from harm . . . He's never lied to me . . . I trust him.' Deep Throat promptly lies to Mulder! However, by the episode's climax, we finally know something about the government's knowledge of extraterrestrial life. After the Roswell incident in 1947 there was an ultra-secret conference between the USA, the Soviet Union, the People's Republic of China, Britain, both Germanys and France (see 'Anasazi'). It was decided that should any Extraterrestrial Biological Entities survive a crash, the country that held them should be responsible for their extermination. Deep Throat is one of three men to have exterminated such a creature. He was with the CIA in Vietnam when a UFO was shot down over Hanoi by the marines. The alien's 'innocent and blank expression' as it was shot has haunted Deep Throat. That is why he uses Mulder, to atone for what he has done.

Deep Throat's motivations are reasonably clear in this episode. Realising that Mulder and Scully have met the truck driver, he gives Mulder a little true information to make him trust him, then the lie which he hopes he'll follow, away from the truck. So, while he hopes that Mulder will eventually break the conspiracy, he is terrified by the idea of Mulder going public with the corpse of an alien, right here, right now. His knowledge of Mulder's nature is very subtle: the truck driver has been briefed to appear as an innocent UFO victim, rather than be silent and secret and thus have Mulder follow him. Deep Throat is a rogue CIA man, working for the conspiracy, the 'dark network' that the *Lone Gunman* dudes describe and that is bugging Mulder and Scully. We also, incidentally, meet another alien executioner in this episode, as the truck driver, Ranheim, kills the creature with his gun at the first sight of an alien craft. (Ranheim is really a black beret, Frank Druce.) Will we ever meet the third alien killer?

Presumably the Majestic Project, to which the logs of the Iraqi interception were sent, is an office within the CIA, or within the USAF, who are then reporting to them.

Mulder knew that the Gulf Breeze photos were fakes when he saw them (which was probably the subject of his article in *Omni* – see 'Fallen Angel'). Mulder contacts at least three UFO bodies, including the Center for UFO Studies in Chicago (see 'Conduit'), NUFONT and NICAP (again, see 'Fallen Angel').

Deep Throat says he can get tickets for any American Football game in the country.

Continuity: Scully drinks coffee with cream and no sugar. Mulder has photos of Mars on his walls. He says he has previously investigated multiple UFO sightings at Chesapeake Bay, Okobogee lake (see 'Conduit', although in this story it's 'lakes' plural) and the legendary Area 51, Nevada. None had as much supporting evidence (including anecdotal data, exhaust residue, and radiation levels five times the norm) as this.

Mulder describes the three *Lone Gunman* editors as 'an extreme government watchdog', some of their information being 'first-rate: covert actions, classified weapons', though some of their ideas are 'downright spooky!' Langly – the one wearing the Ramones teeshirt – has recently had break-fast with 'the guy who shot John Kennedy ... Says he was dressed as a cop on the grassy knoll!' Byers states that Vladimir Zironofsky, the leader of the Russian Social Democrats, has been 'put into power' by the CIA, 'the most heinous and evil force of the twentieth century.' (Thankfully Zironofsky is still something of a fringe figure in Russia!) Byers also has some startling theories about the use of metal strips in money to track people's movements. Frohike, meanwhile, thinks Scully is 'hot'! They are quite prepared to lie to Mulder, and don't trust him enough to switch off their telephone tape recorder when talking to him. Gulf War Syndrome is described as 'the Agent Orange of the nineties' and is said to be caused by 'artillery shells coated with depleted uranium' (and not by the 'cocktail' of anti-germ-warfare drugs given to the troops, as is now most commonly believed).

The Truth: For once, there's no second-guessing going on. Aliens exist and governments kill them (ostensibly for their technology, though for the conspiracy that exists within these governments, this is more a matter of warfare: they must be pleased that they've got officialdom to sanction the execution of their enemies as a matter of policy). In future seasons we discover that the conspiracy is actually working with one set of aliens, the shapeshifters. What we may be seeing here is another battle in their continuing war with the whiteout aliens of 'Little Green Men'. The difference between the two sets of protagonists is made manifest in this story: as soon as an alien craft (presumably one piloted by the whiteout aliens, seeking their comrade), appears in the sky, the conspiracy trucker goes to the back of his truck, and executes the alien. The whiteout aliens can bend time and space (as we possibly see in 'Fearful Symmetry'). Here Mulder seems to believe that time/space anomalies are caused by every alien encounter, thus his trick with the two watches, which he thinks is conclusive. Initially this makes sense, because he leaves one watch behind while venturing into the area affected by the alien ship we see at the start. (Note that he isn't scared when he loses a few seconds of time in a short walk!) However, the second time is more ambiguous as it appears that he's kept both watches on him. Nevertheless, it is on this basis that he rejects this 'close encounter': the Japanese scientists working for the conspiracy (we meet them later on in the series), who can simulate all other effects of alien abduction (via sonic weapons in stealth helicopters) cannot manipulate time. Mulder is also surprisingly untroubled by the idea of being unconscious and at the mercy of these abductors: either he's been programmed by them not to worry, or he's merely aware that he can only have been unconscious for moments. There is the possibility that, in this story, both sets of protagonists abduct him!

Whiteout aliens seem to need or like red light: the cell is full of it. And Deep Throat's group have enough of their technology to keep one alive.

Trivia: At the Washington state complex, Mulder and Scully use fake passes supplied by the lads from *TLG*. Mulder is 'Tom Braidwood' (PIN 7593) and Scully is 'Val Stefoff' (PIN 5311). Since they hacked these identities from computer files it's a little scary to find out that an employee of HTG Industrial Technologies (see 'Shadows') is now working at the facility! Somewhere in this building, maybe there's some research into psychokinesis going on . . .

The Bottom Line: KT: 'I'm wondering which lie to believe.' The best episode of the first season, and possibly of the entire series. It really doesn't get much better than this. There are so many good things in this episode – the first appearance of the lads from *The Lone Gunman* (the most interesting semi-recurring characters), loads of background on Deep Throat, a plot that twists and turns but never quite loses sight of its horizons, a marvellous atmosphere of doubt, tension and panic and – best of all – a killer of a script with good lines given to just about everyone. *The* episode to show to non-fans as an example of how good *The X-Files* can be.

PC: I love it, mainly because it needs a lot of work on the part of the audience to figure out what's going on, but, when you get there, there is actually some meat on the bone. One for the video age, then, but it's good to get back to this rough format for what the show is going to be like in the future, which, at this point, they seem to have worked out. It's quite clear that Jerry Hardin has never been given any notes on his motivation: in a certain mood, his fishing for the right note to play his part on is hilarious, but this actually adds to the feeling of imbalance that his character generates.

MD: Everything that Paul says is true, and yet the story actually works because a lot of the time it's using standard cop- or spy-show motifs (Mulder and Scully losing their shadowy pursuers, tracking the truck across country, breaking into a top-security building). It's only the pre-title sequence – and the nature of the disputed cargo – that makes this a recognisable X-File. I love the bit where Scully – in the middle of a rant about how the paranoia of the lads from *TLG* gives them a sense of self-importance – discovers the bug inside her pen.

18: 'Miracle Man'

US Transmission: 18 March 1994
UK Transmission: 25 May 1994 (Sky One)/
26 February 1995 (BBC2)
Writers: Howard Gordon, Chris Carter
Director: Michael Lange
Cast: R. D. Call, Scott Bairstow, George Gerdes,
Dennis Lipscomb, Walter Marsh, Campbell Lane,
Chilton Crane, Howard Storey, Iris Quinn Bernard,
Lisa Ann Beley, Alex Doduk, Roger Haskett

Kenwood, Tennessee, 1983: Samuel Hartley, adopted son of a local preacher, appears to raise a man, Leonard Vance, from the dead. After a string of deaths in the congregation a decade later, the local sheriff, convinced that Hartley and his son are conmen, calls in the FBI. Scully and Mulder attend one of Hartley's services, then help with the arrest of Samuel after a bar brawl. At his arraignment a plague of grasshoppers strikes the court. Hartley tells the agents that he believes his son is innocent, but at the next service a young woman dies moments after Samuel lays hands on her. Convinced of his own duplicity, Samuel is placed in prison, and is beaten to death in his cell. Scully discovers that the girl was poisoned, and she and Mulder realise that Vance was the killer. He has been systematically killing those whom Samuel comes into contact with to discredit him in revenge for bringing him back into a miserable life. Samuel's body disappears from the local morgue and the sheriff is arrested for his part in Samuel's death. Mulder and Scully are left to ponder on the boy's real abilities.

Don't Be in the Teaser: Subversion of the standard opening when Leonard Vance comes back to life. Behold! The miracle of the resurrection.

Scully Here is a Medical Doctor: She is specifically assigned to this case due to her medical background although it is only much later that she is called upon to perform an autopsy on Margaret Homen. She attributes the cause of death to poisoning with potassium or sodium cyanide or with arsenic (the poison actually proves to be cyanogen bromide).

Scully's Rational Explanation of the Week: Scully states she does not doubt the power of God, just the veracity of Samuel's claims ('The Calusari', 'Revelations').

Dialogue Triumphs: Mulder: 'The boy's been performing miracles every week for the past ten years. Twice on Sundays!'

And: 'Wait, this is the part where they bring out Elvis!'

Sheriff Daniels: 'Ninety-nine per cent of people in this world are fools, and the rest of us are in great danger of contagion.'

Dialogue Disasters: Mulder: 'Remember, the boy did rise from the dead. That kind of thing only happens once or twice every two thousand years or so.'

Continuity: Further examples of Mulder's classic-rock background (see 'Beyond the Sea', 'GenderBender'): he has seen the movie *Woodstock*, and he and Scully quote from the Who's 'Pinball Wizard' ('How do you think he does it?' 'I don't know.'). Mulder quotes from the King James version of the Bible (Exodus 10:14); Scully was raised a Catholic and says *The Exorcist* is one of her favourite films (see 'Shadows').

Mulder says that there are 'dozens' of psychic healers in the X-Files, but none are as well authenticated as Samuel.

The Truth: Few answers are forthcoming here. Samuel may or may not have been a genuine healer (Scully clearly thinks his healings are medical anomalies rather than an indication of God at work). He certainly appears to have some insight into Mulder's sister's disappearance. Samuel's appearance to Vance may have been as a ghost, or part of a cyanide-induced hallucination. His body *does* disappear from the morgue, despite being pronounced dead, and the nurse (and others) claim to have seen him walking away. If Vance was really dead in 1983 then we have one of the first documented cases of resurrection since approximately AD 30.

Trivia: More examples of 11.21: it's the time Scully starts her autopsy examination of Margaret Homen, and she mentions 'X-File number 11214893' (Mrs Carter was born in 1948).

The Bottom Line: KT: 'Miracles don't come cheap.' There are many laudable elements on display here. One would have imagined (after 'GenderBender') that the *X-Files*'s look at faith healing would be anything but balanced, but this is not the case. Samuel and his father are treated with some sympathy, the villains (Vance and Sheriff Daniels) have plausible reasons for their actions and Scully and Mulder are, for once, pretty much in agreement about cause and effect. A good episode, with only (again) the lack of a few important answers to spoil the effect. Tremendous pre-title sequence (one of the most genuinely scary moments in the entire series).

PC: Why is Samantha in this episode? As glue to try to keep the two different series (Conspiracy and Monster of the Week) locked together? Keep Chris away from that typewriter! This nothing-special episode is the one I saw with mates in Australia to get them into the series. Of course, it fell victim to Cornell's First Law of TV: 'The forthcoming episode you decide to watch with your friends to persuade them it's a good series is always a crap one.'

MD: At risk of being the first-season apologist, I very much enjoyed this story. For me it's an engaging fable of spiritual pride and redemption, although the 'resurrection' of Samuel is both superfluous and irritating.

19: 'Shapes'

US Transmission: 1 April 1994
UK Transmission: 1 June 1994 (Sky One)/
2 February 1995 (BBC2)
Writer: Marilyn Osborn
Director: David Nutter
Cast: Ty Miller, Michael Horse, Donnelly Rhodes,
Jimmy Herman, Renae Morriseau, Dwight McFee,
Paul McLean

Browning, Montana: something 'not human' has been killing cattle. A rancher, Jim Parker, kills what he believes to be an animal, but it turns out to be a Native American, Joseph Goodensnake. Mulder tells Scully the case has links to the first X-File, and they visit the local Indian reservation. The victim's sister, Gwen, is hostile, and the local sheriff denies Scully permission to carry out an autopsy on Joseph. Jim Parker is killed, and Gwen Goodensnake seems to be the prime suspect. However, an old shaman, Ish, tells Mulder the legend of the manitou, a mythical malevolent spirit with the power to turn men into beasts. Scully is attacked by a beast at the Parker house, but the creature is killed and turns out to be Lyle, Parker's son.

Don't Be in the Teaser: Joseph Goodensnake is shot by Jim Parker after he has badly mauled Lyle Parker. Interestingly, by the end of the story all of these people will be dead, and two of them will die as non-humans.

Scully Here is a Medical Doctor: 'I'm fully qualified,' she tells Sheriff Tscani.

Scully's Rational Explanation of the Week: Goodensnake's enlarged teeth are an abnormal development of calcium phosphate salts. Lycanthropy is 'a kind of insanity', the beast at the end is a mountain lion.

Dialogue Triumphs: Mulder: 'Charlie, do you believe in shapeshifting?' Tscani: 'This is a funeral!'

Ish: 'I sensed you were different, FBI. You're more open to Native American belief than some Native Americans. You even have an Indian name: "Fox". Should be "Running Fox". Or "Sneaky Fox"!'

Dialogue Disasters: 'It was like nature herself was terrified.'

Continuity: The first ever X-File was initiated by J. Edgar Hoover in 1946 (seemingly in the hope of burying an unsolved case). A series of murders occurred during World War II, including seven in Browning, with each victim being 'ripped to shreds'. Police cornered what they believed to be an animal and shot it, but found a human body, one Richard Watkins. Then the murders stopped, but started again in 1954, and continued at intervals ever since (1959, 1964, 1978, 1994). Mulder, however, believes the murders pre-date the X-Files by 150 years.

Mulder says he wears a woman's deodorant (he could, of course, be joking). Scully apparently never gets 'the creeps'. She does, however, mention the 'recent' death of her father (see 'Beyond the Sea').

The Truth: The manitou – an evil spirit of Indian legend whose possession turns people into shapeshifting werewolf-like beasts – is, according to the shaman Ish, behind a string of murders going back hundreds of years. The 'curse' passes from one person to another by a bite, but can also be transmitted to offspring. Thankfully, the episode doesn't bottle it and try to rationalise this: here, a werewolf is a werewolf. Even Scully, shown proof of something paranormally spooky, is left without a get-out clause.

Trivia: The second file Mulder opens is numbered X649176.

Scientific Comment: If you ingest blood, it doesn't alter your own blood. So it would not show up in a blood test.

The Bottom Line: KT: 'There's something "not human" out there.' *A Native American Werewolf in Montana* . . .? Every visual cliché in the book crops up in this episode (full moons, stuffed animals in a thunderstorm, misty woods). There is one terrific transformation scene, although the finished 'werewolf' realisation is less than perfect. But this is one *X-Files* episode without fudged, unclear messages or cop-out endings. Here, the monster is real, and Scully is forced to believe. For that, if nothing else, the episode deserves much praise. The American Indian actors give it their best too.

PC: Ho and Hum. Next!

MD: For once I'm with Paul: this shoddy little tale is so simple and derivative that you lose all interest within minutes. Only the American aboriginal setting gives any hint that there might have been a good story here, desperate to emerge from the clichés and the tedium.

20: 'Darkness Falls'

US Transmission: 15 April 1994
UK Transmission: 8 June 1994 (Sky One)/
9 February 1995 (BBC2)
Writer: Chris Carter
Director: Joe Napolitano

Cast: Jason Beghe, Tom O'Rourke, Titus Welliver,
David Hay, Barry Greene, Ken Tremblett

Olympic National Forest, northwest Washington state: thirty
loggers have vanished and Mulder pulls a few strings to get
himself and Scully assigned to the case, which has echoes of a
similar one in 1934. Travelling to the site with the sheriff
and a representative of the logging company, they find
evidence of eco-terrorism, and capture one of the activists,
who warns them of the dangers of the coming darkness.
They also discover a body cocooned in a shroudlike web in
the trees. Mulder finds evidence of insects in the rings of an
ancient tree, and speculates that the deadly creatures have
been released by tree felling. Although two further attacks
follow, the creatures are repelled by light, the cabin gener-
ator just holding out until dawn. When Scully, Mulder
and Sheriff Moore escape in a jeep they are attacked and
cocooned, but are saved from certain death by the arrival of
a rescue squad, who remove them to a high-containment
facility to recover.

Don't Be in the Teaser: Dyer and Green, two of the loggers,
are killed by a swarm of green insects.

How Did He Do That?: Or, rather, Why? If the 1934 incident
was caused by the same waking of the insects as this one, why
is Mulder so worried about the chances of the insects spread-
ing? They don't seem to have in 1934.

Ooze: There's the brown oily stuff in the log cabin that
Mulder speculates is left by the bugs. And, of course, the
cocoons themselves.

Scully's Irrational Explanation of the Week: Bigfoot!

That's a Mouthful: Clean Suited Man: 'The government has
initiated eradication procedures. They are quite certain that by
using a combination of controlled burns and pesticides they
will be successful.' Mulder: 'And if they're not?' 'That is not
an option, Mr Mulder.'

Dialogue Triumphs: Mulder on the loggers: 'Rugged manly men, in the full bloom of their manhood!'

Mulder: 'I think I'm going to suggest we sleep with the lights on.'

Mulder: 'There's actually this lake where they've discovered a kind of amoeba that can literally suck out a man's brain.' Scully: 'Oh, brain-sucking amoeba!'

Continuity: Mulder refers to the 1980 St Helens volcano eruption in Washington state, and the environmental changes it caused.

The Truth: A mutant bioluminescent micro-organism was released from a volcano some six or seven hundred years ago, and has been dormant within the trees of the forest ever since. The insects, when released, kill their victims by cocooning them and drawing the fluids from the bodies (although how the insects transport a corpse up a tree is never explained!). After the 'attack', Clean Suited Man mentions that the chemical lucipherim was found in Mulder's body, which is normally found in fireflies.

The Bottom Line: KT: 'We're letting ourselves get carried away with this bug story.' A poor, badly plotted episode with a largely artificial atmosphere of tension and two false climaxes before it finally kicks into life in the chilling last five minutes. Good effects and direction are dwarfed by the faults in a plot that staggers through one pointless cul-de-sac after another.

PC: But I really like it! Coming up with a new monster, and then knocking it back and forth through a series of set pieces is something the series does very well. In this case, it's a cottage under siege! Mind you, that isn't a good ending.

MD: The ending is horrid, a woeful cop-out that would be used on more than one occasion in the following season (see 'End Game', 'Død Kalm'). This is a shame, as I really enjoyed the previous forty minutes or so: taut, assured, and let down only by the poor special effects for the luminous insects.

THE TRAILER

Just before the end credits of this story's first BBC2 transmission ('neXt week on *The X-Files*'), a lovely minute-and-a-half trailer for the return of Tooms was shown. It was at this point that BBC2 realised that they had a major crossover hit on their hands, and, the series having survived its trough in the States, that there were a few groovy episodes to go. This was the moment, in fact, when the series moved up a gear and the fans went wild. (As further encouragement, another clip of Scully from 'Tooms' was shown after the end credits: 'Wouldn't miss it for the world!')

21: 'Tooms'

US Transmission: 22 April 1994
UK Transmission: 15 June 1994 (Sky One)/
16 February 1995 (BBC2)
Writers: Glen Morgan, James Wong
Director: David Nutter
Cast: Paul Ben Victor, Henry Beckman, Timothy Webber,
Jan D'Arcy, Jerry Wasserman, Frank C. Turner,
Gillian Carfra, Pat Bermel, Mikal Dughi, Glynis Davies,
Steve Adams, Catherine Lough, Andre Daniels

Druid Hill Sanatorium, Baltimore: Eugene Tooms gets ready for a hearing on his continued institutionalisation. Meanwhile, Scully has a frosty meeting with the Bureau's assistant director and a man who smokes a lot. Tooms is released after Mulder appears to be a ranting maniac at the hearing. Mulder carries out solo surveillance on Tooms whilst Scully (with the help of retired Detective Biggs) goes back over the case, and discovers a previously unknown 1930s victim encased in concrete. They conclude that the corpse was disposed of in this way because it could have incriminated Tooms. Mulder prevents Tooms from killing a couple in their home, but is later framed for an attack on

Tooms, Scully lying to protect him from disciplinary action. Tooms kills his psychologist and prepares for hibernation, returning to his old nest, now under the escalator shaft of a newly built shopping centre. However, Mulder fights and kills Tooms.

Don't Be in the Teaser: In an episode full of subversions of expectation, Tooms totally fails to kill Doctor Monte, his psychologist, in the teaser despite, clearly, longing to (forty minutes of screen time later, however, the deed is done).

Scully Here is a Medical Doctor: Scully, the queen of the autopsy scene, finds a body encased in concrete, then has somebody else carry out the examination.

Ooze: There's sloppy stuff all over the place in this episode, particularly Tooms's nest, and the blood-and-bile finale.

Phwoar!: The car scene between Mulder and Scully is such a sudden narrowing of the emotional gap between them that you expect the format to change radically at any moment . . .

Dialogue Triumphs: Mulder: 'Excuse me, could you help me find my dog? He's a Norwegian Elkhound. His name is Heinrick. I use him to hunt moose!'

Scully: 'My instinct says that burial in cement is murder!'

Dialogue Disasters: Mr Green: 'I hope you'll be comfortable, Eugene. The room in the back is small, but I'm sure you'll be able to squeeze in.' (Groan.)

The Conspiracy Starts at Closing Time: Walter S. Skinner, the assistant director of the FBI, makes his first appearance in this episode, meeting both Scully and Mulder in his office, whilst a man sits and casually smokes a great deal in the background. The Smoking Man's second appearance (or possibly third, see 'Young at Heart') sees him getting his first line of dialogue – 'Of course I do' – when asked by Skinner if he believes Scully and Mulder's story. There is no hint of whom he represents, but Skinner seems to defer to him. (As McGrath deferred to Deep Throat. This is, of course, not the standard relationship between the FBI and the CIA. It's interesting that Mulder and Scully's activities have become such a high-profile matter that the Assistant Director now makes them his personal business.) Skinner tells Mulder towards the end that he was 'close' (presumably meaning, close to having the X-Files shut down on him), and that 'any closer and a thousand friends in the Capitol won't be able to help you'. (As Smoking Man is present in meetings between Skinner and both Mulder and Scully, we can only presume that, since neither knows his name later, he isn't introduced to them. This, perhaps, stretches credibility somewhat, although it is later confirmed (see 'Talitha Cumi') that Skinner doesn't know his name either.)

Continuity: Scully calls Mulder 'Fox' for just about the first time. He tells her that he even made his parents call him 'Mulder'. Skinner says Mulder is 'one of the finest, most unique agents' in FBI history. Most of the FBI, including Skinner and the (unseen) director, feel his talents are wasted on the X-Files. Mulder watches *The Fly* (1958) on TV in his apartment. He seems to sleep on the couch (see 'The Erlenmeyer Flask'). Mulder and Scully have a 75-per-cent 'conviction or conclusion' rate, well above Bureau standard (this is, says Skinner, their only saving grace). Considering the inconclusive nature of the cases we've seen, they must do a lot of hard work off screen! Mulder worked for three years at the FBI Behavioural Science Unit, profiling serial killers.

During his car surveillance of Tooms, Mulder says he has listened to a football game featuring the Philadelphia Eagles and a baseball game with the Baltimore Orioles.

Tooms's X-File is numbered X 129202 (it's now closed!). FBI Article 30, Para 8.7, requires surveillance to be carried out by two sets of agents, one replacing the other after twelve hours.

The Truth: No change from 'Squeeze' – Tooms is still a cannibalistic genetic mutation. Not to mention as mad as toast. Dr Pamela Karetzky has been unable to find any organic or physiological dysfunction in Tooms, although his attorney has blocked further study. At the time of the arrest abnormalities were found in Tooms's striated muscles and axial bones.

Trivia: The names on the two cell doors other than Tooms's that we see in the opening scene are Robbie L. Maier and Scott Schalin.

The Bottom Line: KT: 'Maybe your mind has become too open.' The first thing to say about 'Tooms' is that it's a great *X-Files* episode. The second thing to say is that it's the worst 'great' episode possible. It has flaws that are manifest from the first scene, and it seems to be the beginning of a worrying (and pretentious) stagger into the realms of continuous narrative that the series could well do without (it forms, with 'The Erlenmeyer Flask' and 'Little Green Men', the series' first multipart storyline). There are many fine elements present, however (that entire five-minute sequence of Tooms's entry into a couple's house through the toilet is full of little touches that make the viewer laugh and squirm in equal measure). Again, the performances are top-notch, and for the most part the story carries its message with a thuggish charm that is difficult to criticise. But 'Tooms' is also a sign of difficulties to come, and at its nihilist core, is a mass of 'might have beens'.

PC: Toilets in American TV! One of the ways that the series has been influential is in bringing the little details of real life, left behind long ago at the point of *I Love Lucy*, back to the small screen. This is apt for a show about US mythos, and helps to suspend disbelief. Together with the depictions of different parts of America, it also adds a degree of universality. In what other show, ask yourself, would we be aware, as we are in 'Eve', of one of our leads going to the lavatory? Oh, and 'Tooms' is as good as it has to be, letting us see Mulder as others see him (aren't you just willing him to lie at the judicial review?) and getting the format moving again with the idea that this is one continuous universe and characters can recur.

MD: This contrived and stuttering mess isn't a patch on the original, despite some excellent interplay between the leads (the scene with a tired Mulder in the car is priceless). 'Tooms' seems incapable of making up its mind what sort of story it wants to be, and (er) ends up falling between numerous stools (sorry). I've never seen a lock on a toilet seat before, but perhaps I've led a very sheltered existence.

HAVE THEY ALREADY DONE IT?

Mulder and Scully's relationship is generally acknowledged to be full of sexual tension, but certain signs indicate a different reading. Work partners, no matter how close, don't touch each other in the intimate way that Mulder and Scully have begun to. It's generally frowned upon for FBI agents to get too close to agents with whom they work, but that's a rule that Scully has already broken once. Aware that their colleagues, never mind the conspiracy, are looking out for any disciplinary problem, it's possible that Mulder and Scully have already started an affair, only they've been very discreet, and it's never been shown on screen. The car scene in 'Tooms' appears to show two people finally acknowledging that they're attracted to each other, an attraction we saw developing through the early episodes of the first season. Perhaps, after that, they dated until Scully's abduction, but went no further. Mulder's reaction to her vanishing is that of somebody who's lost a lover, not a dear friend. Upon her return, the relationship becomes deeper. By 'Red Museum', he's wiping her face clean in the way that only people who've been to bed together do. From then on, there are many of these moments, until Mulder's beliefs at the end of '731' add new tension to the relationship, tension which only eases after the cathartic affirmation of their bond in 'Grotesque'. Maybe that *Rolling Stone* cover was just a reflection of our heroes' off-duty hours.

22: 'Born Again'

US Transmission: 29 April 1994
UK Transmission: 22 June 1994 (Sky One)/
23 March 1995 (BBC2)
Writers: Howard Gordon, Alex Gansa
Director: Jerrold Freedman
Cast: Brian Markinson, Mimi Lieber, Maggie Wheeler,
Dey Young, Andrea Libman, P. Lynn Johnson,
Leslie Carlson, Richard Sali, Dwight Koss, Peter Lapres

Buffalo, New York state: Detective Barbala apparently throws himself through the window of a police interview room moments after being left alone with Michelle Bishop, an eight-year-old girl. Michelle states there was another man in the room. Despite her mother's claims that the girl is disturbed, Mulder believes her, although a photofit representation of the mysterious man does seem uncannily like Charlie Morris, a respected police officer killed, apparently by Chinese Triads, some nine years ago. Mulder and Scully visit Morris's ex-partner, Fiore, who is unhelpful and nervous. An ex-policeman, Felder, is killed in a freak accident; again, Michelle is nearby. Discovering that Morris, Felder, Barbala and Fiore were all involved in a drug deal before Charlie Morris's murder, Mulder speculates that the girl may be his reincarnation, seeking revenge, especially against Fiore, who has married Charlie's wife. Michelle goes to Fiore's house but is prevented from killing Fiore by Mulder and by the man's confession to his crimes. Although her mother will not allow the girl to undergo further deep-hypnosis therapy, she appears to be 'cured'.

Don't Be in the Teaser: Detective Rudolph Barbala goes into a room to interview an eight-year-old girl, and ends up getting flung out of the fifth-storey window. Wimp.

How Did He Do That?: All right, so he's seen at one point looking closely at the aquarium diver model, and the autopsy does show that Morris was drowned in a small amount of salt water, but Mulder's recognising the distorted image on the video is still a bit of a leap.

Scully Here is a Medical Doctor: She does the autopsy on Barbala – 'That's your department,' notes Mulder – and discovers what Mulder had suspected: signs of electrocution.

That's a Mouthful: 'Metempsychosis, transmigration, re-embodiment, call it what you will?' Verbal diarrhoea perhaps?

Scully's Rational Explanation of the Week: Scully (more or less correctly) states that the marks on Barbala's body were caused by 'an intense concentration of electrothermal energy'. However, she believes that Michelle is simply disturbed, and that the photofit of Charlie Morris is down to the girl seeing a photograph of the dead man in the police station. As a thoroughly pissed-off Mulder notes, 'Short of her growing a moustache, how much more apparent does it have to become for you to accept it?'

Dialogue Triumphs: Sharon Lazard on Barbala: 'The only time he ever looked at himself was in the mirror. And he always liked what he saw.'

Continuity: Mulder writes his notes on this case (and presumably others) longhand, in a leather-bound field journal (a neat juxtaposition with Scully's use of laptops). This X-File is numbered X-40271. Lazard's brother is a Baltimore cop who worked on the Tooms case, and recommended Mulder and Scully to her.

The Truth: The story appears to support the concepts of reincarnation (with the possibility of the personality from one incarnation being carried into the next) and of continued existence beyond death. Despite the ambiguous nature of the final scenes, there is no doubt, from the evidence witnessed, that Michelle Bishop – conceived at about the time that Morris was killed – *was* Charlie Morris, reborn. She also possesses telekinetic powers, which may or may not be linked to this.

Trivia: Possibly the most staggering coincidence in TV history: in this episode one of the villains is a cop named Tony Fiore, and in the *Forever Knight* episode 'Dead Issue' (first broadcast on 6 October 1992), the main villain is a cop named Tony Fiori.

Maggie Wheeler, the actor who plays Sharon Lazard, appeared with David Duchovny in the movie *New Year's Day*.

The Bottom Line: KT: 'Status: unexplained.' A chilling, well-directed episode, with a lot of memorable set pieces. The climactic scenes are a special-effects tour de force, and the acting is universally good. There are only occasional problems with sustaining the pace of the episode with such slight subject matter (there is only one plot, it doesn't need a genius to work it out, and the fact that it takes Scully and, especially, Mulder so long reduces our faith in them). Great performance by the little girl.

PC: The nadir of the monster/concept-of-the-week stories. It's just dull, darlings! And obvious, and not scary, and bland . . . I could go on.

MD: Please don't – it's lovely, like *Hamlet* with a psychic girl with an origami fixation in the lead role. The image of the underwater diver is memorably bizarre, as is the completed paper menagerie. The only flaw for me is Felder: yet another minor character looking towards *The Godfather* for inspiration.

23: 'Roland'

US Transmission: 6 May 1994
UK Transmission: 29 June 1994 (Sky One)/
2 March 1995 (BBC2)
Writer: Chris Ruppenthal
Director: David Nutter
Cast: Zeljko Ivanek, Micole Mercurio, Kerry Sandomirsky,
Garry Davey, James Sloyan, Matthew Walker,
David Hurtubise, Sue Mathew

Mahan Propulsion Lab, Washington state: a scientist working on a secret project to create a jet engine capable of Mach 15 is killed in his own wind tunnel. The only witness to the death is Roland Fuller, an autistic man employed as a janitor. This is the second death associated with the project, after a car crash in which a brilliant scientist, Arthur Grable, was killed. Soon after Mulder and Scully arrive another scientist on the project is killed with liquid nitrogen. Suspicious of Roland, the agents discover that Grable was Roland's identical twin brother, and that the dead scientist's head has been cryogenically frozen. Mulder speculates that he may have a psychic link with his twin from beyond the grave and that he is 'directing' Roland to kill the others and to complete his work on the project. After Grable's colleague, the sinister Nollette, has sabotaged Grable's cryogenic unit, Roland attempts to kill Nollette, but is prevented from doing so by Mulder and Scully, and by Roland's own personality forcing its way through Grable's faltering hold on him. Despite Mulder and Scully's recommendations, Roland is taken away for psychiatric treatment.

Don't Be in the Teaser: Dr Ronald Surnow, chopped into lots of little bits by a jet-propulsion test propeller in a wind tunnel.

How Did He Do That?: How did Mulder guess the password on the basis of some of Roland's doodles?

Mulder's Rational Explanation of the Week: Arthur Grable faked his own death. (Second time this season for that theory!)

Dialogue Triumphs: Scully (holding a copy of a photo of the car crash in which Grable died): 'By the look of this, he's hamburger!'

Scully (on learning that only the head of Arthur Grable has been cryogenically preserved): 'Wouldn't your client find it somewhat inconvenient to be thawed out in the future only to discover he had no functional mobility?'

Continuity: Scully has two brothers, one older, one younger (presumably the two men seen at Captain Scully's funeral in 'Beyond the Sea').

The Truth: There is a psychic link between the identical twins, one that survived death and cryogenic freezing.

Scientific Comment: The liquid nitrogen is referred to by Scully as being at −320 degrees. All the cryogenic chambers are set at −320 degrees. Whether this is plausible depends on what sort of degrees are intended. Liquid nitrogen only cools to about −180 degrees centigrade. And −273 degrees C is absolute zero − you can't get cooler than that. So this number must be in Fahrenheit, though no scientists (e.g. cryogenicists) would use that system. Minus 320 degrees F is −196 degrees C, which is only a little cooler than one would expect for liquid nitrogen.

The Bottom Line: KT: 'Tell me about your dreams, Roland.' A rather sad, confusing, and somewhat heartless episode, that contains illogical elements, and in which sympathetic characters are treated like scum, and the genuine twenty-four-carat bastard, Frank Nollette, doesn't get his comeuppance at the end. Maybe that's the effect that the production team were going for (hey, life isn't fair), but it's a bit of a choker to find poor old Roland getting carted off to the funny farm at the end. Despite a good climax, and the touching final scenes, 'Roland' is an unsatisfactory mixture of too many ideas, and too little humanity. A real disappointment.

PC: Yeah, but there's lots of good jokes, a real atmosphere, and an interesting, albeit instantly obvious, central idea . . .

MD: 'People die. They go away, and they're not supposed to come back.' How radical *this* is for US TV! Forget toilets, such a moving and distressing episode stands out from the bland soup of much so-called entertainment. While I'm not in favour of stories that pursue miserabilism to the exclusion of all other emotions, this episode does smack of real life to me. Nollette's survival and Roland's institutionalisation are balanced by the joyful finishing of the equation and the tender expression of love at the conclusion: small victories made all the more glorious for being in the face of corporate evil and immoral prejudice. Nods towards *Rain Man* (Roland counting items in the blink of an eye), and a wicked sense of humour (I love the headless scene-of-the-crime corpse outline!), only add to the satisfaction derived from this simple story.

24: 'The Erlenmeyer Flask'

US Transmission: 13 May 1994
UK Transmission: 6 July 1994 (Sky One)/
9 March 1995 (BBC2)
Writer: Chris Carter
Director: R.W. Goodwin
Cast: Anne DeSalvo, Simon Webb, Jim Leard, Ken Kramer,
Phillip MacKenzie, Jaylene Hamilton, Mike Mitchell,
John Payne

Deep Throat rings Mulder and tells him to watch Channel 8, currently carrying a news report about a fugitive evading police capture after a lengthy chase. Mulder and Scully investigate what seems to be a routine case, but discover some puzzling anomalies concerning the car at the scene. They trace the car to a Dr Berube at the Emgen Corporation, Gaithersburg, Maryland. However, there doesn't seem to be anything worth investigating, and Mulder is ready to give up until Deep Throat tells him he has 'never been closer'. After Berube's apparent suicide Scully checks the contents of a flask found in his lab, whilst Mulder follows a lead to a storage facility and finds several live bodies stored in liquid. He takes Scully to the site but the evidence has been removed. Mulder finds the fugitive – Dr Secare, a human-alien hybrid – but is overcome by toxic fumes given off by Secare when shot. All traces of the investigation begin to disappear, and the doctor whom Scully worked with on the flask dies in a car crash. Deep Throat arranges for Scully to gain access to a secret facility and steal an alien embryo for use in a trade to get Mulder back. This succeeds, but Deep Throat is killed during the exchange. Later, Mulder tells Scully that the X-Files have been closed down.

Don't Be in the Teaser: Dr William Secare, chased by the police, shot and apparently drowned.

How Did She Do That?: Of thousands of possible passwords (and on the basis only of a labelled flask), Scully plumps for the correct one in the containment facility.

Scully Here is a Medical Doctor: Scully's medical background enables Deep Throat to get her into the Fort Marlene High Containment Facility. This kind of thing happens a lot in *The X-Files*, and often it's pretty baffling: if they can forge her credentials for the containment facility they could just as easily forge her original qualifications.

Ooze: Green toxic blood. Lots of it.

Dialogue Triumphs: Mulder and Scully discuss Deep Throat's cryptic nature: 'Do you think he does it because he gets off on it?' 'No, I think he does it because you do.'

Scully after Mulder has asked her to find out what the contents of the 'Purity Control' flask are: 'If this is monkey pee, you're on your own.'

Crewcut Man: 'Your cellular phone's been ringing off the hook.' Mulder: 'I'm a popular guy!'

The Conspiracy Starts at Closing Time: 'Inside the intelligence community,' notes Deep Throat, 'there are so-called "black organisations", groups within groups, conducting covert activities unknown at the highest levels of power.' (An absolute definition of how the conspiracy functions, and one that definitively separates them from 'the government' as a whole.) He confirms that 'they have had alien DNA since 1947' and tells Mulder that the Roswell incident was 'just a smokescreen' and that 'they've had half a dozen better salvage operations than that.' (It was probably a smokescreen only in terms of the subsequent furore: both the word 'better' and statements made in 'E.B.E.' imply that the incident was a real one.) The DNA is held at the Fort Marlene High Containment Facility under a project codenamed 'Purity Control'. This is also what's written on the flask itself (the conical one of the title, which isn't the vessel containing the foetus, as many people suppose).

Deep Throat states, as we've long suspected, that Mulder is 'too high-profile' to kill. However, his motivations here are complicated. It's as if, finally compromised, he decides to throw aside all caution (including meeting Scully) to preserve the life of his pawn, Mulder. Perhaps he feels partly responsible for Mulder's involvement. And he is the son of an old friend (see 'Paper Clip'). Deep Throat doesn't feel able to walk into the facility to get the alien foetus himself, but, perhaps with all his business taken care of (and X fully briefed?), he is able to present it to his colleagues in exchange for Mulder's life. Maybe he's counting on his clout and the surprise of his presence to have some effect. His final words, 'trust no one', seem to indicate that he was shot by, or that the car containing the killers was sent by, somebody who he knew was a friend or somebody he knew shared his doubts. (The 'friend' in the former case might have been X, forced to order the killing of Deep Throat rather than compromise his own position, or more likely the Smoking Man, who possibly spent enough time with Deep Throat when they were both younger to regard him as a friend (see 'Apocrypha'). The killer was Crewcut Man (see 'Red Museum').)

However, surely Deep Throat knows that his appearance will indicate that he's compromised the secrecy of what his colleagues are doing. In that sense, being killed will have been no surprise. The only alternative was for him and Mulder to have gone public with what they'd found out: and there'd certainly have been no going back to the conspiracy for him then. It's touching that such a duplicitous figure dies protecting pawns that he'd previously felt able to lie to. In the end, they *could* trust him.

Whatever the background, Deep Throat is shot, and Scully clearly believes him to be dead.

At the end of the episode Mulder says that Skinner rang him to tell him of the closure of the X-Files, and that the decision had come from 'the highest level of government'. (It is hinted that Skinner, and even the unseen Director, did not agree with this decision, but could do little about it. Presumably, the conspiracy has clout above the FBI's level of command, and are thus allowed to intrude down into the FBI command structure. The conspiracy – which we know is international in nature (see 'E.B.E.', 'Anasazi', etc.) – seems to have become part of a number of security agencies and governmental bodies.) Scully and Mulder are reassigned to other duties.

Continuity: Again we see that Mulder sleeps in his front room with the television on (see 'Tooms'). (This is almost certainly a reaction to his sister's abduction. If electromagnetic disturbance is a sign of alien incursion, then it's a great early warning. Duane Barry shares the TV habit.) This time *Journey to the Centre of the Earth* (1959, starring James Mason) is the film that has sent him to sleep (probably Pat Boone's performance). He also makes an oblique reference to *Star Wars*, further establishing his 'classic SF fanboy' credentials. Mulder speaks to 'Danny' again (see 'Conduit'). Skinner is mentioned, but not seen.

The police captain makes a scathing reference to *The Silence of the Lambs* in connection with what law enforcement does for a living as compared with the FBI.

This episode is the first indication that the blood of certain aliens (and alien/human hybrids) is toxic (with horrific results for Mulder).

The Truth: Under Dr Berube's project, six volunteers (all terminally ill) were injected with alien DNA and became hybrids. Deep Throat tells Mulder that 'they' have possessed alien DNA since 1947, without the technology to do anything with it. However, from 'Colony' we might conclude that he's lying, since 'they', in this case, are probably a similar group of rebel shapeshifters to those seen in that story, who have been on Earth since 1947. Their human assistants are found and eliminated by Deep Throat's fellow conspirators before Mulder can expose them, but Deep Throat has at least been able to show Mulder the effects of shapeshifter blood. However, there is another interpretation: Purity Control is an apt name for the conspiracy's project: later episodes reveal that they're against human/alien DNA experiments, and aim to preserve the purity of the shapeshifter race. But it's odd that the rebels who are doing the experiments in this episode also adopt that name: perhaps it's an ironic joke. Or maybe, since these experimenters are definitely human, and not aliens, Dr Berube was once part of Purity Control and absconded with the flask, deciding to experiment with the shapeshifter DNA for his own reasons.

Trivia: This is the first episode in which Deep Throat is referred to by that name (sarcastically, by Scully).

The ending of this episode mirrors the ending of 'The X-Files': Mulder calls Scully at 11.21 (she takes the call at 11.22), and the Smoking Man puts the alien embryo in the Pentagon storage facility (in a box marked '6604' along with other embryo jars).

The door numbers at Zeus storage (1013 and 1056) are both references to Chris Carter's birth date (see 'Deep Throat'). Zeus Storage is at 1616 Pandora Street (quite applicable considering what's 'in the box', as it were).

The Bottom Line: KT: 'Trust no one!' A fine, tense episode, from its *Bullitt*-style car chase in the pre-title sequence to the shocking execution of Deep Throat. But . . . we still know *nothing* at the end of it. Again, there are more questions than answers (chiefly, who are the 'they' that Deep Throat has been banging on about all season?). And the final scene, for all its terrific impact, seems to have been tacked on as an afterthought. Memorable for all the right reasons, but a few of the wrong ones, too – the pacing of the episode is hopeless, beginning like a runaway train and getting slower and slower. Mulder's investigation of the Zeus warehouse is one of the best scenes ever, awesomely lit and chillingly realistic. But it's a shame that this and other undeniably great moments aren't followed through to a logical conclusion. Good effort but, ultimately, no cigar.

PC: Like a lot of the conspiracy episodes next season, it does leave you unsatisfied.

MD: Any episode that has Scully saying 'There's just one thing I don't understand . . .', and features a hitman who looks like a satanic hybrid of Peter Schmeichel and Stephen Berkoff, can't be all bad. Although the first two-thirds of 'The Erlenmeyer Flask' are splendid, the implausible stealing of the embryo and the horribly contrived exchange to free Mulder threaten to derail proceedings entirely.

Second Season

25 45-minute episodes

Created by Chris Carter

Line Producer: Joseph Patrick Finn (25–27)
Co-Producer: Paul Rabwin
Producers: Rob Bowman (38–49), Paul Brown (25–33),
Joseph Patrick Finn (28–49), Kim Manners (43–49),
David Nutter (27–37)
Supervising Producer: Howard Gordon
Co-Executive Producers: R.W. Goodwin,
Glen Morgan (25–38), James Wong (25–38)
Executive Producer: Chris Carter

Regular Cast: David Duchovny (Fox Mulder), Gillian Anderson (Dana Scully, 25–30, 32–49), William B. Davis (Smoking Man, 25, 28, 30, 32, 46, 49), Bruce Harwood (Byers, 27, 32, 42, 49), Dean Haglund (Langly, 27, 32, 49), Tom Braidwood (Frohike, 27, 32, 42, 49), Mitch Pileggi (Walter Skinner, 25, 26, 28, 30, 32, 40, 41, 46, 49), Raymond J. Barry (Senator Richard Matheson, 25), Nicholas Lea (Alex Krycek, 28–30, 49), Steven Williams (X, 28, 30, 32, 39, 41, 47), Sheila Larken (Margaret Scully, 30, 32), Tegan Moss (Young Dana Scully, 32), Melinda McGraw (Melissa Scully, 32), Don Davis (William Scully, 32), Lindsey Ginter (Crew-cut Man, 34), Peter Donat (Bill Mulder, 40, 41, 49), Brian Thompson (The Pilot, 40, 41), Rebecca Toolan (Mrs Mulder, 40)

25: 'Little Green Men'

US Transmission: 16 September 1994
UK Transmission: 21 February 1995 (Sky One)/
28 August 1995 (BBC2)
Writers: Glen Morgan, James Wong
Director: David Nutter

Cast: Mike Gomez, Raymond J. Barry, Les Carlson, Marcus Turner, Vanessa Morley, Fulvio Cecere, Deryl Hayes, Dwight McFee, Lisa Anne Beley, Gary Hetherington, Bob Wilde

The X-Files have been closed down, Mulder and Scully reassigned and prohibited from meeting. While working on electronic surveillance as part of a fraud investigation, Mulder is informed by a friendly senator that the Arecibo ionospheric observatory in Puerto Rico – although officially closed – has been picking up possible extraterrestrial signals. Mulder travels there and finds evidence that aliens are transmitting information found on one of the Voyager spacecraft back to Earth. Mulder confronts an extraterrestrial, but Scully's arrival is soon followed by a truckload of Blue Berets. Although Mulder and Scully escape with their lives, the one piece of evidence they have – a reel of tape – proves to be completely blank.

Don't Be in the Teaser: It features only Mulder's voice and the machines in the observatory kicking into life.

Scully Here is a Medical Doctor: Scully is seen teaching students how to perform an autopsy. Mulder gets to do his own (non-invasive) post-mortem later.

Scully's Rational Explanation of the Week: An electrical storm wiped the tape – she's probably right.

Phwoar!: Mulder and Scully hold hands as he tells her, 'I still have you.'

Dialogue Triumphs: 'We wanted to believe, we wanted to call out . . . We wanted to listen . . . I wanted to believe, but the tools have been taken away, the X-Files have been shut down. They closed our eyes. Our voices have been silenced, our ears now deaf to the realms of extreme possibilities.'

Mulder's greeting to Scully in an underground car park: 'Four dollars for the first hour of parking is criminal. What you've got better be worth at least forty-five minutes.'

The Conspiracy Starts at Closing Time: By implication, the lack of follow-up to Voyager and the abrupt ending of NASA's high-resolution microwave survey of the universe might be down to the conspiracy (who wouldn't want their own signals to the shapeshifters, or those of the whiteout aliens, to be heard).

Mulder may or may not go through a period of missing time in this story. Previously, the whiteout effect has been used to indicate this. He doesn't seem concerned about this, but would he be? The Blue Berets are an elite crash retrieval unit (similar to or the same as the one seen in 'Fallen Angel') who are authorised to kill civilians (and act this way, astonishingly, outside US territory in convoys in broad daylight). The whiteout aliens (whom we may take to be the 'greys' of popular myth) have not actually been seen clearly anywhere in the series, though Mulder knows the shape of their faces well enough to scare his witness with a drawing of one. They are, for some reason known only to them, broadcasting material from the Voyager space probe back to Earth (as we have already seen in 'Conduit'?). Is this their rather complicated way of saying hello? Showing up at the Arecibo project is also a very odd thing to do, unless they wanted to erase the data that was sent there (if it's an ionosphere research lab, the data could have bounced there accidentally off the ionosphere, so what we're witnessing isn't an attempt at contact, but at hushing up the material we saw being passed along in 'Conduit').

Mulder's memories of his sister's abduction are different in this episode from when he recalled them in 'Conduit'. In that version, they were both asleep when she was taken. Either this is the result of the fuzzy nature of hypnotic regression, or Mulder's memories are being tampered with. (Perhaps to forget the aliens' assurance that Samantha would be OK, to set him more against them? Certainly, firing his gun at them would previously seem most out of character . . .)

Continuity: When Mulder's sister was abducted, on 27 November 1973, their parents were out and he and Samantha were playing Stratego – a very apt game, considering the way Mulder's life went. (Stratego involves finding out what the nature of the pieces on the other side is, which ones are dangerous, and where the most vital piece of information is being hidden.) Aptly, an item concerning Watergate was on the news. (Mulder was in fact waiting for *The Magician* at 9 o'clock – a further example of Mulder's love of tack TV, as is a later reference to the quiz show *Jeopardy* – see 'Deep Throat', 'Squeeze' and 'Jose Chung's *From Outer Space*'.) He saw his sister floating away, and then a 'stickman' at the door. (Similar to the stickman who appears at Arecibo.) There is a message on Mulder's answerphone from a nameless (and husky-voiced) female who complains that, after his constant attempts to get her to have lunch with him, he has stood her up. In the absence of Deep Throat, Mulder is fed information by Senator Richard Matheson (see 'Ascension', 'Piper Maru'), who seems only to have the aims of an interested and empowered amateur, and doesn't play both sides as Deep Throat did. Skinner seems annoyed by the Smoking Man's use of an illegal phone tap. He doesn't smoke. Mulder can recognise one of Bach's 'Brandenburg' Concertos (though he gets the precise passage wrong), yet he seems not to know that this was the first selection of music on the Voyager spacecraft. He speaks very little Spanish. Deep Throat was buried at Arlington Cemetery (Mulder watched this from a safe distance). The Smoking Man smokes Marlboro cigarettes here (he changes to Morleys later on).

The Truth: Unless Mulder imagined all the events in the observatory (and he is emotionally unstable in this story), there is a definite encounter with the whiteout aliens: an experience which seems similar to the abduction of his sister. We know from later stories that the conspiracy were at least planning to take her: is it conceivable that the whiteout aliens acted first, grabbing Samantha before the Japanese could? Could it be that the only thing those on the conspiracy side who tell Mulder they have information about her location actually know is that the other lot have got her? Or is the truth simply that the conspiracy have based their whole abduction scenario around the real abductions carried out by the whiteout aliens, these being already entrenched in folk tales? Once more, a line is drawn between the whiteout aliens and the conspiracy: the Blue Berets arrive, presumably on conspiracy orders, to *stop* Mulder from contacting them. Mulder and Scully are left with no proof, however.

Trivia: It seems that Mulder is travelling as Betty Grant (is Scully's finger meant to be pointing at Charles Grant?). He actually boards the plane under the name of George E. Hale, who was mentioned earlier in the episode as having been chasing Elvis all his life.

Scientific Comment: Voyager 1 did not pass the 'orbital plane' of Neptune, but the 'orbit' of Neptune.

The episode implies that the only thing that Arecibo Observatory ever did was search for extraterrestrial signals. They have done some of that, but their main job is proper radio astronomy. The place would not be closed up if the SETI project was no longer funded, so having Mulder find a deserted control room is totally wrong. It would not be isolated in the middle of the jungle, either. There really was a high-resolution microwave survey started on 12 October 1992, and terminated after only a year.

The Bottom Line: MD: From the extraordinary Voyager sequence to the downbeat ending, this is a cracking opener, albeit not quite what most fans were probably expecting. It's even darker than average – and I don't just mean the lighting – with a sense of pessimism permeating much of the dialogue. Chinks appear in Mulder's self-belief, and the whole thing – with its limited number of characters and dingy observatory location – becomes an exercise in separation. Mulder – on his own, but 'narrating' for Scully – is forced to ponder the nature of reality and the proof that has eluded him ('Even if I could see them, would they really be there?'). Despite everything we might have expected, but very much in keeping with our humanity, when Mulder is finally confronted by the alien creature of his childhood, he is terrified and tries to shoot it.

KT: 'What if they come?' I found this episode a staggering disappointment on first broadcast, but it has aged quite well. The underground car-park scene is a shameless tribute/parody of *All The President's Men*, but after this the episode picks up, with the balletic Shakespearean Matheson/Mulder sequence and Scully's brilliant losing of her 'shadows' at the airport. And there's the mother of all cross-country car chases at the climax. Skinner's protection of Mulder is the first sign of depth in his character, too. Not the classic it could have been, but worthy of a second chance.

PC: Not from me. This is the episode that convinced me at the time that Fox had decided to shove the series back into the shape of a generic TV show. The unexplained plot lapses, the idiocies (why is part of the vast Arecibo telescope complex out in the jungle, and why is it abandoned, and just what the hell are the aliens up to?), and the cartoon nature of the opposition (look out, it's the Blue Beret UFO team, headed by that crusty soldier type who's always going to be growling, 'I'll get you, Fox Mulder!') make this firmly the Saturday-morning version of the show. I still can't watch it without a little shudder, and wonder how they managed to recover from it.

DATING THE STORIES

As a rule of thumb, *X-Files* episodes are supposed to take place close to the date of their first US transmission. However, in the first season we don't get any positive confirmation of this until 'Squeeze', when it is stated that it is 1993. Scully's journal in 'Ghost in the Machine' is dated 24 October 1993. 'Lazarus' is probably set in December 1993. In 'Young at Heart' Barnett's apparent demise (his death certificate is dated 16 September 1989) was (approximately) four years ago, according to Mulder. By 'Shapes' it is definitely 1994. 'Tooms' takes place 'months' after 'Squeeze'. 'Born Again' takes place in April (the final scene being on the 19th). 'The Erlenmeyer Flask' begins on Sunday, 8 May 1994, covers the events of several days, and concludes (according to another on-screen caption) '13 days later'.

In '3' – with the X-Files now reopened – Mulder flicks over the pages of his girlie calendar from May to November, suggesting the passage of time between this episode and 'The Erlenmeyer Flask'. Thus, the first six episodes of the second season take place over a period of some six months or so, with Mulder doubtless spending a lot of time on very routine assignments (as seen in 'Little Green Men' and 'The Host'). 'Firewalker' takes place between 11 and 13 November 1994 (which means that '3' and 'One Breath' must have taken place in the first ten days of that month). After this adventure, Mulder and Scully spend a month in quarantine, and we see three more investigations. It is therefore physically impossible that the autopsy seen in 'Irresistible' can take place on Monday, 14 November 1994, as stated by Scully. 'Die Hand die Verletzt' (see the last date stamped into the library book on witchcraft) is probably (and more sensibly) set in late January (or early February) 1995. 'Anasazi' is set between 9 and 16 April (on-screen captions).

The Thinker was killed on 16 April; when Scully meets Frohike in 'The Blessing Way' it is two days later. Scully's (unfinished) autopsy in '2Shy' is on 29 August. Most of 'Syzygy' takes place on 12 January (on-screen caption). 'Piper Maru' is said to take place some five months after the murder of Melissa Scully (actually, it's more like nine). 'Avatar' begins on 7 March 1996. 'Wetwired' runs between 27 April and 10 May.

26: 'The Host'

US Transmission: 23 September 1994
UK Transmission: 28 February 1995 (Sky One)/
4 September 1995 (BBC2)
Writer: Chris Carter
Director: Daniel Sackheim
Cast: Darin Morgan, Matthew Bennett, Freddy Andreiuci,
Don Mackay, Marc Bauer, Gabrielle Rose, Ron Sauve,
Dmitri Boudrine, Raoul Ganee, William MacDonald

Mulder is assigned to another case that he thinks is meaningless and insulting: a corpse found in the sewers of New
Jersey. However, when Scully comes to perform the autopsy
she finds a fluke worm within the body. A worker is later
attacked in the sewerage system, the bite mark on his back –
although much too large – seeming to have come from a
fluke worm. A human/worm creature becomes trapped in the
sewage processing plant, but tries to head back to sea. Scully
discovers that the original corpse came from a Russian ship
that had been used in the Chernobyl clean-up operation.

Don't Be in the Teaser: The poor young Russian has to clear
a blockage from the ship's tanks, and you just know he's not
gonna make it . . .

How Did He Do That?: Mulder spends the entire episode
making brilliant (and completely irrational) guesses about
where the flukeman is heading for or can currently be found,
the most staggering being his convenient spotting of a passing sewage tanker in Betty Park when all leads have failed.

Scully Here is a Medical Doctor: She gets to do an autopsy
on the dead sailor, complete with wriggling fluke worm.

That's a Mouthful: 'Reinstatement of the X-Files must be
undeniable!'

Ooze: Some serious goo after the workman cleans his teeth.

Scully's Rational Explanation of the Week: Scully pins the blame for the fluke/human creature on Chernobyl, and she would appear to be correct. For once everyone agrees with her assessment, including Mulder and Skinner.

Dialogue Triumphs: Scully: 'Is this seat taken?' Mulder: 'No – but I should warn you I'm experiencing violent impulses.'

Mulder, after Scully has said that some 40 million people are infected with flatworm worldwide: 'This isn't where you tell me some terrible story about sushi, is it?'

The Conspiracy Starts at Closing Time: Mulder is told (during an anonymous phone call) that he has a friend in the FBI who considers it imperative that the X-Files be reopened. Subsequent episodes point to that friend being Skinner, despite his claims just to be following orders. He accepts that this case should have been an X-File and that Mulder and Scully's full involvement might have saved the workman's life.

Scully is passed a copy of *National Comet* (see 'Conduit' – there's a half-hidden headline concerning 'Nirvana stars' and a teddy bear!) containing a story about a monster on a Russian ship. Both this and Mulder's two phone calls are subsequently shown to have been the work of X (see 'Sleepless'). Creatures mutated by radiation are very much his stock-in-trade, but here his main aim is probably to begin contact with Mulder in a way that doesn't relate directly to the conspiracy.

Continuity: Mulder has recently considered leaving the Bureau.

The Truth: A genetic mutation triggered by abnormal radiation levels – a fluke worm with humanoid physical characteristics.

Trivia: Scully's autopsy is on John Doe number 101356, case no DP112148: references to Mr and Mrs Carter's birthdays again.

Scientific Comment: Scully says that an animal with no sex organs is a hermaphrodite. But a hermaphrodite has both sets of sex organs.

The Bottom Line: MD: 'You know, they say three species disappear off the planet every day. You wonder how many new ones are being created.' Terrifying (if predictable) scenes on the ship and in the sewers add up to B-movie homage that just pulls back from being the ultimate 'monster-in-the-bog' fable. The story briefly grapples with the difficulty one has prosecuting such a creature through normal channels of law and justice, but suffers from too many endings. The exchanges between Mulder and Scully continue to make up for any shortcomings, and the scene where he bursts into Skinner's office is delightfully under-played.

KT: 'It looks like I'll have to tell Skinner that his murder suspect is a giant blood-sucking worm after all!' Gross! In fact mega-gross, with terminal potential! Do not, under *any* circumstances, watch this immediately after eating. There's more good work on Skinner on display, whilst Duchovny (denied Anderson's presence for most of the episode) gets to display quite a decent range of acting. The ending is *very* messy.

PC: A decent monster story in a series still shaken up by the change of format (I was very scared that this situation was going to last a long time). Mulder on his own is really a bit too morose to be enjoyable. The partial escape of the flukeman means that there's another monster out there in S&M's own version of Arkham Asylum (Tooms is about the only one they've finished off). And the monster suit is pretty terrible, so terrible that I was worried at the time that the monsters were being standardised and rationalised too. It's good to know that it's my hero, Darin Morgan, in there, though.

27: 'Blood'

US Transmission: 30 September 1994
UK Transmission: 7 March 1995 (Sky One)/
11 September 1995 (BBC2)

Writers: Glen Morgan, James Wong,
from a story by Darin Morgan
Director: David Nutter
Cast: William Sanderson, John Cygan,
Kimberly Ashlyn Gere, George Touliatos, Gerry Rosseau,
Andre Daniels, Diana Stevan, David Fredericks,
Kathleen Duborg, John Harris, R.J. Harrison

Mulder investigates an outbreak of 'spree killings' in the town of Franklin, Pennsylvania. The murderers were perfectly normal individuals with no previous history of violence or antisocial behaviour, although Scully's postmortem reveals abnormally heightened levels of adrenalin (each person seeming to have suffered from a phobia) and traces of an artificial substance, LSDM. LSDM is an experimental synthetic insecticide that releases pheromones to scare away flies, and Mulder believes that it is having a similar effect on certain people. He is sprayed by a helicopter working under cover of darkness, but seems to be unharmed. He and Scully track down the remaining phobic individual suffering from exposure to LSDM and prevent a massacre.

Don't Be in the Teaser: A soon-to-be-unemployed postal worker, Edward Funsch, not only survives the teaser but the whole episode (completely against the viewers' expectations).

How Did He Do That?: Mulder's sudden deduction that the town is also the subject of some weird subliminal-message experiment, which remains unproved until his phone 'message' at the end. But can we trust him? Is he barking up the wrong tree or simply barking? (After what he's sprayed with in this episode, the latter is quite possible – if only temporarily).

Scully Here is a Medical Doctor: She performs an autopsy on Mrs McRoberts.

Scully's Rational Explanation of the Week: The LSDM seems to be at the root of the problem, although Scully would appear to lack the evidence she needs to be 100 per cent certain of even this.

Dialogue Triumphs: Frohike: 'So, Mulder, where's your little partner?' 'She wouldn't come. She's afraid of her love for you.'

And: 'You know, Frohike, it's men like you that give perversion a bad name.'

Mulder on the local cop: 'He's probably one of those people that thinks Elvis is dead.'

The Conspiracy Starts at Closing Time: Somebody is sending the messages that cause people to start killing, and that same somebody may be responsible for covering the townsfolk with LSDM in the first place. Is this a 'controlled-release' experiment such as those we hear of in 'Apocrypha', or an attempt at mind control such as we see in 'Wetwired'? Mulder is certainly exposed to the same substance (which somehow allows you to perceive messages which other people don't see), and those who controlled this experiment wanted him to know that, so here's yet another occasion when his poor, besieged brain has been got at, with, this time, possibly fatal results. It would be nice to see the return of the subliminals someday, if only because that would make such a neat cliffhanger.

Continuity: Mulder played right field at baseball. The April edition of *The Lone Gunman* featured details of the CIA's fibre-optic micro-video camera, which is small enough to be carried by a fly(!); the August edition described LSDM. Frohike is very keen on Scully (see 'E.B.E.'). Scully makes a sarcastic comment about 'Reticulus' (see 'Squeeze').

The Truth: Fear-inducing insecticide, possibly in conjunction with (probably subliminal and visible only to those affected by the chemical) messages via electronic devices.

Trivia: A few seconds of a Basil Rathbone Sherlock Holmes movie are glimpsed just before the 'Do It!' advert. The nurse buzzing on the door is buzzing the word 'kill' in Morse code.

The Bottom Line: MD: Strangely gripping. The script extends far beyond its initial interest in (and disgust at) the use of DDT in the 1950s, featuring subtle nods towards Middle American decline and a critique of US gun culture. The direction, too, is top-notch: look out for a Charles Manson/Waco montage on television and a memorable tracking shot over the photos of the victims. Only Mulder's barmy theory about subliminal messages jars, but this is easily forgotten when it's so swiftly followed by Fox seeing 'Do it!' on a TV screen – which turns out to be an advert for a fitness club.

KT: 'A forty-two-year-old real-estate agent murders four people with his bare hands. That's not supposed to happen *anywhere*.' OK, I'm the one who usually engages in hyperbole, but this is *magnificent*. A horrifying central concept (suburbia goes psycho) chillingly played. The 'subliminal messages' are by turns terrifying and hilarious, particularly the astonishing sequence in the garage involving Mrs McRoberts ('He'll rape you. He'll kill you. Kill him first!'). One great set piece after another, full of elegant touches and iconography (though there is one silly element, namely the first examples of 'Ask the *Lone Gunman* Editors', as Byers, Langly and Frohike display amazing expertise on the most obscure subjects – here the common fly). The clock-tower finale with its visual links to Hitchcock's *Vertigo*, and echoes of the real-life 1966 Charles Whitman murders, is dazzling. And this is one occasion when an underplayed, enigmatic ending actually works.

PC: At the time, I thought the ending was a real cop-out (I get nostalgic about this period of the show, when everybody I knew had given up on it as having bottled out, because it came through it all so wonderfully), but, in retrospect, this is a very well-realised episode, dealing with some really sticky stuff about guns, university towers and grudges that America is still nervy about coming to terms with. A jolly good source of screensavers too.

Nicholas Murray Butler is alleged to have described an expert as someone who 'knows more and more about less and less', until eventually they know 'everything about nothing'. This seems not to be true of the three editors of *The Lone Gunman*. They appear to know everything about *everything*! Initially introduced in 'E.B.E.', Langly, Byers and Frohike were described as 'an extreme government watchdog', which explains their interest in and knowledge of political conspiracies like the Kennedy assassination, UFO sightings and government agencies – particularly the CIA – and their covert operations. However, their knowledge seems to extend into areas that are, frankly, staggering. Some of the areas they display expertise on include species of fly ('Blood'), the mating habits of zoo animals ('Fearful Symmetry'), Japanese shipping routes ('Nisei'), the technology used to heighten the impression left by writing on paper ('Apocrypha') and television broadcast signals ('Wetwired'). Given his undoubted friendship with them, one might wonder why Mulder doesn't simply ask them the nature of the conspiracy. On their previous track record, they would probably be able to give him an answer within minutes.

28: 'Sleepless'

US Transmission: 7 October 1994
UK Transmission: 14 March 1995 (Sky One)/
18 September 1995 (BBC2)
Writer: Howard Gordon
Director: Rob Bowman
Cast: Jonathan Gries, Tony Todd, Don Thompson,
David Adams, Michael Puttonen, Anna Hagan,
Mitch Kosterman, Paul Bittante, Claude de Martino

Mulder receives a newspaper report on the demise of a prominent doctor specialising in sleep disorders and an audio cassette of the man's final 911 call before his death. Although the man claimed that his apartment was on fire, no evidence for this was found by the fire crew, although Dr Grissom had discharged his fire extinguisher. Mulder and his new partner Alex Krycek investigate, Scully performing an autopsy on the corpse, which shows secondary physiological responses to having been in a fire ('as if his body believed that it was burning'). In a similar case, a man is 'shot', but no bullets are found. The common link seems to be that both men were involved in (or subjects of) experiments on an elite group of soldiers during the war in Vietnam. One of only two survivors of that group – Augustus Cole, 'the Preacher' – seems to have developed an ability to physically influence other people, even to the point of 'suggesting' that they are dying. Mulder tracks the man down, but just as he is becoming rational, Krycek shoots him, thinking the Bible he was holding was a gun.

Don't Be in the Teaser: Dr Grissom fights a fire (that doesn't exist) in his apartment, and dies as a result.

How Did He Do That?: Mulder jumps from the Vietnam sleep experiments to Cole's ability to project his unconscious with little real explanation (beyond a vast amount of sub-Jungian guff about building a bridge between the conscious and unconscious worlds). Also, as Salvatore Matola seems to still be alive at the episode's conclusion, why doesn't Mulder simply use him as proof of the experiments?

Scully Here is a Medical Doctor: Another two autopsies (one interrupted!).

Phwoar!: The phone calls between Mulder and Scully in this episode have a certain charge to them.

Dialogue Triumphs: Krycek: 'You don't know the first thing about me.' Mulder: 'Exactly!'

The Conspiracy Starts at Closing Time: The newspaper report, 911 tape and (later) a file concerning the sleep experiments come from X, a man who is aware of Mulder's dealings with Deep Throat. He says he has no intention of making the same 'sacrifice' as Deep Throat (indicating that Deep Throat knew, when he confronted the conspiracy, that his actions would probably be fatal): 'The truth is still out there – but it's never been more dangerous.' (He seems to be a follower of Deep Throat with the same connections, thus probably CIA. (In 'Wetwired' we see that he's a close lieutenant of the Smoking Man.) He appears to owe his old mentor something, and is thus prepared to risk his life for Mulder: only not as much.) Krycek – who claims to be open to 'extreme possibilities' – is actually working for the Smoking Man, stealing Mulder and Scully's copies of the Vietnam files (the conspiracy seems to be interested in anything that involves altering human capabilities, as 'Nisei' shows). It's also typical of the Smoking Man, as we discover later, to underplay the abilities of his enemies, both to underlings like Krycek and to his bosses.

Continuity: Mulder uses the pseudonym George Hale when contacting Scully at Quantico. Krycek claims that many at the academy admire Mulder and follow his career (however, this may be, along with much else that Krycek spouts, a load of bollocks).

The Truth: Cole and the others were part of an elite group (J7) of Vietnam soldiers who volunteered for sleep 'eradication' experiments on Paris Island. Absence of sleep – made possible by an operation and use of antidepressant drugs – was supposed to make the soldiers more aggressive. However, they stopped obeying orders and went on a killing spree, murdering hundreds of civilians. Cole – who like the other vets hasn't slept for twenty-four years – discovered a way of psychically affecting other people's sense of reality. There is the problem of whether the gun/Bible Cole is holding is real or not to Krycek. Perhaps Cole was making Krycek see a gun because he wished to die (as he, sort of, indicates to Mulder).

On the other hand, what we see may be Mulder's subjective view and Krycek, with his own agenda, may have killed Cole without any help from the veteran himself.

Trivia: Dr Grissom may be named after the astronaut Gus Grissom, who also died in a fire, on board Apollo I in 1967.

The Bottom Line: MD: *The X-Files* does *First Blood*, only better! Gripping stuff, with wonderful splashes of surrealism, most notably the dead Vietnamese people 'haunting' the ex-soldier. 'Sleepless' is a rare example of a story that mixes strange goings on and the conspiracy-based back story without either element suffering.

KT: 'Scully's . . . a much larger problem than you indicated.' 'Every problem has its solution.' A story with a load of references to the American psyche, and the guilt complex surrounding Vietnam (My Lai is mentioned). The template for this seems to have been Adrian Lyne's *Jacob's Ladder* (with a couple of nods at *Apocalypse Now*). Another fine, dark, complex, multi-layered episode.

PC: Erm, a bit dull, but Krycek is initially very convincing as a cool little follower for Mulder (and, with what the fans knew was going to happen concerning Scully, the expectations set up by television are used cleverly to make us, initially, trust him).

29: 'Duane Barry'

US Transmission: 14 October 1994
UK Transmission: 21 March 1994 (Sky One)/
25 September 1995 (BBC2)
Writer: Chris Carter
Director: Chris Carter
Cast: Steve Railsback, C. C. H. Pounder, Stephen E. Miller,
Frank C. Turner, Fred Henderson, Barbara Pollard,
Sarah Strange, Robert Lewis, Michael Dobson,
Tosca Baggoo, Tim Dixon, Prince Maryland, John Sampson

Mulder is flown to Richmond, Virginia, to take part in a hostage negotiation. Duane Barry, who believes he is regularly abducted by aliens, has escaped from a psychiatric institute. Mulder talks to Barry, and recognises the man's use of FBI terminology. Duane Barry left the FBI in 1982. When one of the hostages is shot Mulder goes in, disguised as a paramedic, and continues to gain the man's trust, talking about his abducted sister. He gradually encourages Barry to release his hostages, but Scully discovers that Barry was shot in the head in 1982 and might well be a delusional pathological liar. Barry is shot, bringing the situation to a satisfactory close, but X-rays reveal metal fragments in the man's gums, sinus cavity and abdomen, and holes in his molars, which would seem to back up what he said about being abducted. Scully discovers that one of the metal fragments has a barcode-like marking on it, but Barry escapes from hospital and attacks and kidnaps her.

Don't Be in the Teaser: The eponymous Duane Barry has a *very* bad time in his home having an 'encounter'. Allegedly.

Scully's Rational Explanation of the Week: The metal items in Barry are shrapnel from Vietnam. Yeah, right.

Phwoar!: The scene that is, for many people, the most pivotal moment in *The X-Files*. Mulder swims in Speedo trunks (actor's own). Also, it must have been quite a warm swimming pool . . .

The Conspiracy Starts at Closing Time: From the Smoking Man's words at the end of the previous episode, we gather that Barry is, at the end, directed to Scully's home via his implants, and sent to a prearranged site where she can be collected by the Japanese scientists.

The Truth: 'The government knows about it, you know. They're in on it sometimes, right there in the room when they come. They work together,' says Duane. And, as we see from later episodes, he's absolutely right. Apart from the bit about aliens. Duane's been abducted on to an advanced USAF craft, meets either USAF staff disguised as aliens, or alien/human hybrids, and, having had his memory wiped, is experimented on by Japanese scientists. It's difficult to know how much of what Duane says is real (or what reality is for him – his speech about aliens experimenting on children seems to be entirely for Mulder's benefit), but he's correct about a lot of things.

Scientific Comment: The barcode is only ten microns across. It is doubtful that supermarket barcode readers could detect this.

The Bottom Line: MD: 'Duane Barry is not what Mulder thinks he is.' A gripping hostage scenario – almost free of generic trappings – is intercut with Barry's memories of the aliens and a 'dentist-from-hell' scene. Pared to the bone, and all the better for it. Marvellous.

KT: 'There's a situation going down.' Yes, this one's got pretty much everything too. Startling pre-title sequence (and an even more impressive cliffhanger), and a lot of classic one-room, dialogue-heavy drama. Somebody's clearly been given a strobe machine for Christmas, however . . .

PC: Yes, it's brilliant, mainly because it succeeds in turning all this murky back-story stuff into pointed, dramatic, encounters, something the conspiracy stories very rarely manage. This is indeed good drama. This particular siege scenario is actually going to happen one of these days.

30: 'Ascension'

US Transmission: 21 October 1994
UK Transmission: 28 March 1995 (Sky One)/
2 October 1995 (BBC2)
Writer: Paul Brown
Director: Michael Lange
Cast: Steve Railsback, Sheila Larken,
Meredith Bain Woodward, Michael David Simms,
Peter Lacroix, Steve Makaj, Peter Lapres, Bobby L. Stewart

Mulder replays his answerphone message from Scully, and is shocked to hear the sounds of an attack. He rushes over to her house to find the police already there. Scully is missing, and Skinner orders Mulder not to get involved with the FBI's attempts to track her down. However, Mulder realises that Barry is taking Scully to Skyland Mountain in Virginia, hoping that the aliens will take her rather than him. He persuades Krycek to accompany him, in contravention of Skinner's orders, and races to the summit in a cable car, only for Krycek to turn off the machinery. When Mulder does reach the summit, Scully is nowhere to be seen, Duane Barry claiming that the aliens have taken her. Barry dies, and Mulder is blamed. However, Krycek vanishes just as Mulder is about to make a claim against him, having finally realised that the young agent is part of the conspiracy. Skinner can't do anything, but says he will order the reopening of the X-Files. 'That's what they fear the most.'

Don't Be in the Teaser: It's just a recap, via Mulder listening to his answerphone message, intercut with images of Scully's abduction by Barry.

How Did He Do That?: Mulder seems to have psychic 'flashes' at the scene of the crime. (Probably just a dramatic way of showing how his thought processes zap their way over clues: we see the way he does it, but we still don't quite follow how . . .)

Dialogue Triumphs: Krycek: 'You know Chernobyl, Valdez, Three Mile Island, they were all linked to sleep deprivation. The US Department of Transportation estimates that over a hundred and ninety thousand fatal car crashes every year are caused by sleeplessness.' Mulder: 'Do they estimate how many people are put to sleep listening to their statistics?' (It's cool that Krycek, who's obviously quite similar to Mulder, has that cute way with hard data too . . .)

The Conspiracy Starts at Closing Time: The Smoking Man is in on the discussion about Scully's absence (he *still* isn't introduced by name to Mulder despite this being their second – possibly third – meeting), and continues to direct Krycek's actions. Barry either tracked Scully down via the implant or was informed of her address by the conspiracy (the latter seems reasonably plausible, given the speed with which the authorities arrive on the scene of the abduction – indeed, the look that Krycek gives the Smoking Man when Mulder asks how Barry knew where Dana was speaks volumes). Obviously, the conspiracy decided that putting an implant in Scully would be a good idea, because, as later episodes show, it would allow them to monitor everything that she and Mulder did. Which is why she's given back so quickly. Mulder goes to see Senator Richard Matheson, but is intercepted by X (the conspirators have something with which they could incriminate the senator). Mulder believes that Krycek killed Duane Barry, and that the military pathologist's autopsy was incomplete, with no toxicological analysis.

Continuity: Margaret Scully had a dream that her daughter would be 'taken away'. (Did a faceless man come to her and talk in iambics? See 'The Blessing Way'.) She describes Dana as a sceptic.

At the end of the episode, angered by Scully's abduction, Skinner takes his first overt action to disobey the conspiracy, and reopens the X-Files, allowing Mulder to continue his work more easily.

The Truth: Scully is certainly abducted. (We see a glimpse of her on an operating table having her stomach enlarged for some reason. At the time, various official materials made it clear that this was Mulder's imagined view of what was happening to her (the weirdo!), but in '731' Scully remembers the scene herself, so it happened, unless . . . but no, that's just too paranoid a conclusion for words.) The second 'UFO' that so frightens Barry is a helicopter. (Mulder seems to believe that the first one was also a helicopter, and, judging by later episodes, he may well be right. A helicopter fitted with a sonic weapon was certainly enough to fake just the same kind of event in 'E.B.E.'.) What the Japanese scientists were doing to her stomach, a mission separate from putting an implant in her, is a matter for lurid speculation, but it, erm, might result in her immortality! (See 'Clyde Bruckman's Final Repose'.) It's interesting that Skinner already knows of an existence of a 'they'. He's been an unwilling but knowledgeable accomplice to the conspiracy, and we might assume that, once it became clear that they were on the same side, Mulder grilled him off screen for all the (limited) information he had.

Trivia: Mulder receives Scully's call on his answerphone at 11.23 (so, does Duane break in at 11.21?). Duane Barry's reported reference to a 'Stairway to Heaven' is more likely to be about the 1946 Michael Powell and Emeric Pressburger film (UK title: *A Matter of Life and Death*) than that song by Led Zeppelin. The song on the radio in his car is 'Red Right Hand' by Nick Cave and the Bad Seeds.

The Bottom Line: MD: 'They only have one policy: deny everything.' Despite being just about the only mainstream US TV show to feature the music of Nick Cave this is a tremendous disappointment, largely because it has twenty minutes of plot stretched over twice that time. It's exciting up to a point, but then peters out completely, having about ten possible endings leading into each other.

KT: The lack of plot is the most annoying thing here. The episode is full of great moments (the final shot is staggering), but it's too bitty to be fully effective. A somewhat disappointing end to a fine run of episodes.

PC: I thought it was OK, and it was brave to have Scully taken away, but it's just an excuse to have a scene on top of a cable car, isn't it? Actually, thinking about it, it is a pretty good cable-car-top scene, and we need more of those, so what the hell?

31: '3'

US Transmission: 4 November 1994
UK Transmission: 4 April 1995 (Sky One)/
9 October 1995 (BBC2)
Writers: Chris Ruppenthal, Glen Morgan, James Wong
Director: David Nutter
Cast: Justina Vail, Perrey Reeves, Frank Military,
Tom McBeath, Malcolm Stewart, Frank Ferrucci,
Ken Kramer, Roger Allford, Richard Yee, Brad Loree,
Gustavo Moreno, John Tierney, David Livingstone

Mulder reopens the X-Files, and is almost immediately called to Los Angeles. The LAPD are investigating a murder in which the body was drained of blood, which Mulder links to murders committed in other states by the self-styled 'unholy trinity'. He apprehends John ('the son') in a blood bank, and thinks that the man is suffering from a mental illness. However, when exposed to sunlight John immediately suffers fourth-degree burns and dies. A stamp on the man's hand leads Mulder to Club Tepes, where vampire fetishists and young people into 'blood sports' gather. He meets Kristen, who is involved with John, 'the father' and 'the unholy spirit'. John returns to life, but Kristen destroys the trinity of vampires.

Don't Be in the Teaser: Garrett Lorre – a rich family man – becomes food and drink for the vampires.

How Did He Do That?: Mulder arrives at the crowded Club Tepes and (incredibly) goes straight up to Kristen. If (as John claims) the vampires believe they cannot be seen in mirrors, then how do they shave?

Phwoar!: It's odd to see Mulder getting off with a woman. It's as if, without Scully, he's throwing himself into things head first (in 'Grotesque' we see that, before he met her, this is how much of a bulldozer he was). When he's distant from her, or hurt, as we see in the 'tiffing' story arc of season three, he also tends to throw himself at women (and 'throw' is about all Mulder can do in the field of the chat-up), as if daring fate to hurt him. In this case, what with the shaving and the blood sports, he's got to his most cliff-teeteringly self-destructive. And, with the former, his most toe-curlingly sexy. He spends quite a bit of time with his shirt hanging half off as well. And all this while still wearing Scully's cross.

Dialogue Triumphs: Does Mulder want to live forever? 'Not if drawstring pants come back into style.'

Dr Browning after Mulder has admitted he is beginning to believe in vampires: 'You're really upsetting me . . . on several levels.'

Continuity: Mulder says he hasn't slept since Scully's disappearance. He uses the alias 'Marty Mulder' when investigating the Hollywood Blood Bank. Scully's personal X-File is numbered 73317.

The Truth: Mulder has been tracking the 'Trinity Killers' (FBI file number: X256933VW) for a year. They have previously killed six times in two states (Tennessee and Oregon). This presumably means that Mulder and Scully worked on the case as an X-File during the period covered by the first season. In each instance the corpse is drained of blood and every mirror on the scene is smashed. The perpetrators are, to all intents and purposes, vampires. They can be seen in mirrors (although John thinks he can't) and don't react to crucifixes, but suffer burns when exposed to sunlight and need to ingest large amounts of blood. John 'dies' of his burns, but comes back to life: beyond that, their claimed longevity is not proved, and Kristen's sacrifice seems to kill the 'unholy trinity'.

Trivia: The writing on the wall in the victim's blood is 'John 52:54', which Mulder claims is the biblical passage 'He who eats of my flesh and drinks of my blood shall have eternal life, and I will raise him up on the last day.' However, this should be John 6:54 (there are only 21 chapters in John's gospel).

The Bottom Line: MD: 'I'll do things with you no one's ever done.' *The X-Files* rips off, well, just about every modern vampire variant, and adds little to the genre, although there is a clever allusion to the shaving scene in the original *Dracula*. Instead of making vampirism an AIDS allegory, '3' has the two running in parallel (Mulder enquires if Kristen is afraid of catching AIDS through her interest in 'bloodsports'). As an *X-Files* episode it's not unacceptable, however, especially for the poignant scene where Mulder puts a folder concerning Scully's disappearance into the filing cabinet. The chemistry between Duchovny and his then girlfriend Perrey Reeves is remarkable, and the atmosphere and iconography – the forest fires, the loaf filled with blood – are vivid. Also memorable is the scene where John describes a terrifyingly humanist universe where death is the end and only grotesque vampires can achieve immortality. The conclusion, though, is too muddled for words.

KT: 'Are you going to ask what a normal person like me is doing in a place like this?' With a list of roots as long as a very long arm (*Forever Knight*, *Count Yorga, Vampire*, *Scream and Scream Again*, *Near Dark*, the works of Anne Rice, the *Kolchak* episode 'The Vampire', the Blacula films, etc. . . .) this veers haphazardly from schlock to brilliance (often with little stopover in between). There's some good stuff here, but the Sadean abuse subplot seems disturbingly out of place in this fantasy setting, and the finale is a right mess. One gets the impression that the entire episode was written purely as a device to keep Scully's crucifix on display and therefore provide a link between the previous episode and the next one.

PC: Tough assignment, this one, and it doesn't quite make it, despite some awesome photography and design. It's truly weird to see Mulder in a sexual encounter (again, at the time – and I know I do go on – I saw this as another bit dropping off the format). The vampires are just so . . . ordinary, that it's hard to believe there isn't some kind of technological twist on the legend coming up. Though the idea of having a delve through the goth club thing is interesting, it isn't pursued, leaving this a very unbalanced and weird episode.

32: 'One Breath'

US Transmission: 11 November 1994
UK Transmission: 11 April 1995 (Sky One)/
16 October 1995 (BBC2)
Writers: Glen Morgan, James Wong
Director: R. W. Goodwin
Cast: Jay Brazeau, Nicola Cavendish, Lorena Gale,
Ryan Michael

Northeast Georgetown Medical Center, Washington, DC: Scully has been found in unknown circumstances. She is unconscious and is being kept alive artificially. Mulder notices that a phial of her blood has been stolen from the hospital, and chases the thief. X rescues Mulder and shoots the assailant, but refuses to tell Mulder what happened to Scully. Her medical records show that her immune system has been decimated by very advanced genetic experimentation. Mulder receives details of the location of the Smoking Man via a message in a packet of Marlboro cigarettes, and tries to interrogate him. X arranges for Mulder to kill some individuals who are involved in Scully's disappearance, but, instead, Mulder chooses to stay by Scully's bedside. Scully eventually recovers.

Don't Be in the Teaser: Young Dana Scully murders a poor little snake.

Scully Here is a Medical Doctor: On Scully's 'living will': 'Dana is a doctor. Her criteria for terminating life support is quite specific.'

That's a Mouthful: X: 'At eight seventeen tonight, they will search your apartment. They will be armed, you will be waiting . . . to defend yourself with terminal intensity.'
'This high-capacity compact . . . high calibre weapon is pointed at your head to stress my insistence that your search for whoever put your partner on that respirator desist immediately.'

Phwoar!: Scully's unfeasibly large bosoms. Mulder smiles in such a wonderful way when she wakes up, and weeps as he gives her back her cross.

Dialogue Triumphs; The Smoking Man: 'Don't try to threaten me, Mulder. I've watched presidents die.'

Frohike explains how he stole Scully's medical records: 'Stuck 'em in my pants.' Mulder: 'There's plenty of room down there.'

Langly: 'We're all hopping on the Internet to nitpick the scientific inaccuracies of *Earth 2*.'

The Conspiracy Starts at Closing Time: X says that he used to be like Mulder. (Presumably, his own investigations took him to the heart of the conspiracy.) He knows (but cannot explain) why Scully was taken, indicating that, like Deep Throat before him, he is actually privy to the nature of the conspiracy, but doesn't want to reveal all of it (possibly because the information could only have come from him: Krycek's use of secrets in later episodes may change that position). Later, we see that he does actually do real work for the conspiracy (or the CIA – and is there much of a difference?) on occasions ('Soft Light'). He is, however, prepared to allow Mulder to kill off some of the agents who participated in Scully's abduction. (That's got to be a pretty unique situation: the agents in question must be freelancers like Cardinal from 'Apocrypha': they can't be members of any intelligence organisation or there'd be too many questions. And X must have come across the knowledge of their impending break-in in such a way that the conspiracy doesn't know he knows. And he must be confident that these agents don't know enough about anything to give the game away if Mulder just injures them. All in all, it seems that he's either trying to keep Mulder sane, by giving him some revenge in anticipation of Scully's death, or maybe just settling some scores of his own.) X himself can (just about) kill a junior agent of the conspiracy and get away with it. (One wonders if the conspiracy think that Mulder killed the blood thief.)

Having had Scully for some time, why do the conspiracy

need to take a blood sample now, anyway? Is it that they know her DNA will soon be back to normal, and they want to conceal the evidence, or that the demands of getting her back with Mulder (so that the implant can start to pass or record information) overcame the need to take data at the end of an experiment?

Skinner slips Mulder the note about the Smoking Man. Good lad! Odd that he knows his home address, though. The Smoking Man is willing to die, not for the cause, but seemingly out of a sense of ennui. What his bosses plan to do to him, judging by his fear of them, must be much, much worse than being shot . . .

Ultimate paranoia corner: the *Lone Gunman* lads' screensaver *just happens to be* a picture of Richard Nixon, similar to the one on the television when Samantha Mulder was abducted. You don't think . . . No, actually. Of course not.

Continuity: Dana was a 'tomboy' as a girl. One of her brothers is called Bill jnr, which indicates that, like Mulder's, her father is named William. She was (and presumably still is) afraid of snakes. Her middle name is Katherine, and this episode confirms she was born in 1964. Scully's gravestone bears the inscription 'The Spirit is the truth', attributed to 1 John 5:07 (with an unusual use of a zero in the verse number). It should be 1 John 5:6 ('. . . the Spirit is truth'), with no definite article. Perhaps the mason got it wrong? Mulder signed Dana's will as her witness. He buys the recovered Scully a Superbowl video as a present (presumably as a joke). Skinner volunteered for service in the marines in Vietnam when he was eighteen (he had an out-of-body/near-death experience and says he is afraid to explore further extreme possibilities – see 'Avatar'). He makes an oblique reference to *The Godfather* ('Then what? He sleeps with the fishes?') The Smoking Man (called 'Cancer Man' by Mulder) has no wife or family. He drinks bottles of Budweiser. Mulder attempts to contact X by taping an 'X' in his window (so is someone always watching his apartment?). Frohike appears at the hospital with a bunch of flowers for Scully.

Melissa, Dana's older sister, is a bit of a hippie. The Smoking Man's address is: 900 West Georgia Street. (It's reasonable to assume that he moves after this episode! See 'Talitha Cumi'.)

The Truth: Scully has certainly been experimented on by a superior technology, and has had her genetic material altered. (More evidence towards that immortality business (see 'Clyde Bruckman's Final Repose')?) What were the conspiracy up to? Perhaps the original intention was to keep her and mutate her, but somebody, perhaps X, persuaded the conspiracy to send her back with an implant. The nature of the mysterious Nurse Owens – who helped Scully through her coma but doesn't in fact work at the hospital – is never explained.

Trivia: The Thinker is modelled after an Internet fan, Yung Jun Kim.

The Bottom Line: MD: Hospital drama, conspiracies and suspense, plus splashes of dreaming surrealism: an atypical X-File, but a strangely beguiling one.

KT: Beguiling, certainly. There are many great (and tremendously vivid) scenes, particularly Mulder's confrontation with 'Cancer Man' and his attempted resignation with Skinner. And the symbolic Dana-on-the-river sequences are worthy of considerable praise. But all the stuff about branch DNA seems to be a complete red herring. And why does every *X-Files* episode of this era seem to end up in a dark underground car park?

PC: This is a weird combination of dullness and 'too much, too soon'. Now that Mulder knows the Smoking Man's address, why isn't he round there every night? It's genuinely touching to see Mulder and Scully back together, though.

33: 'Firewalker'

US Transmission: 18 November 1994
UK Transmission: 18 April 1994 (Sky One)/
23 October 1995 (BBC2)
Writer: Howard Gordon

Director: David Nutter
Cast: Bradley Whitford, Leland Orser, Shawnee Smith,
Tuck Milligan, Hiro Kanagawa, David Kaye, David Lewis,
Torben Rolfsen

Mulder and Scully investigate recent events at a volcanic
research post at Mount Avalon in the Cascade mountains.
They find the brilliant but erratic leader has gone AWOL and
appears to be killing the remaining members of the research
team, and that the Firewalker robot seems to have videoed the
shadow of a lifeform that can exist at impossibly high temperatures. It transpires that all the members of the expedition
– except the leader, Trepkos – have been infected by a fungus
brought back by Firewalker, and that Trepkos is striving to
ensure that the infection does not spread further. With the
infected team members dead, Scully and Mulder are rescued,
and spend a month in quarantine.

Don't Be in the Teaser: The folk at the California Institute of
Technology manage to activate Firewalker remotely, reveal-
ing the body of a team member, Pil Erikkson, and the shadow
of . . . something.

Scully Here is a Medical Doctor: She just can't wait to whip
out her test tubes and analyse those spores. Mulder even feels
the need to inform Tanaka of her 'medical doctor' credentials
when his cough gets worse.

Scully's Rational Explanation of the Week: Post-traumatic
stress.

Phwoar!: Mulder risks being shot to go and warn Scully. He
touches her neck when he gets to her.

Dialogue Triumphs: Mulder: 'I'm going to find Trepkos.'
Scully: 'What if he's already dead?' Mulder: 'Then he'll have
a lot of trouble answering my questions.'

Continuity: There are references to recent events, including
Scully saying, 'I'm back, and I'm not going anywhere.'

The Truth: The parasitic fungus seems to be a silicon-based lifeform that is resistant to high temperature. Sand (silicon dioxide) found in the lungs of one of the victims would seem to indicate respiration.

Scientific Comment: The temperature in the caverns is stated as being 130 degrees, but people go into them during the episode. They must therefore mean 130 Fahrenheit, a system which scientists don't use.

What's the point of charting all the crevices and fissures so Firewalker doesn't trip? The robot is meant to go where people can't go.

The Bottom Line: MD: 'Mulder, that is science fiction!' This season's hot equivalent of 'Ice' proves to be another undemanding adventure. It's not the richest nor most engrossing of episodes, although an interesting contrast is established between Mulder and Trepkos, a man obsessed with 'truth' almost to the point of insanity. The gross body effects and the gripping conclusion – as Scully strives to evade being covered with spores – are quite capable of diverting one's attention, however.

KT: 'The truth is an elephant described by three blind men . . .' A quite rubbishy remake of 'Ice' without an original idea anywhere on display. No poetry. No soul. Just line after line of great dialogue ('You still believe you can petition heaven to get some penetrating answer . . . If you found that answer, what would you do with it?') that doesn't mean a damn thing. Quite depressingly lacking in even the most basic emotion. And the way in which Scully's recent adventures are dismissed casually in two minor scenes and about five lines of dialogue stinks of tokenism.

MD: But that's two more scenes than it would get in most US series!

PC: At the time (OK, that's the last time I'm going to say that) I thought that this was the point when the series got back on form. A solid, tight series of set pieces in the base-under-siege format are one of the things the show should never forget it's good at (though, in the conspiracy stories, it often has). I'm quite happy to lack depth once or twice in return for moments of original horror. That is one of the things this show is designed to do, after all . . .

34: 'Red Museum'

US Transmission: 9 December 1994
UK Transmission: 25 March 1995 (Sky One)/
30 October 1995 (BBC2)
Writer: Chris Carter
Director: Win Phelps
Cast: Paul Sand, Steve Eastin, Mark Rolston,
Gillian Barber, Bob Frazer, Robert Clothier,
Elisabeth Rosen, Crystal Verge, Cameron Labine,
Tony Sampson, Gerry Nairn, Brian McGugan

Mulder and Scully investigate a number of cases in Wisconsin involving hysterical teenagers who the local sheriff believes have been possessed. Suspicion initially points towards the Church of the Red Museum, a New Age vegetarian sect in the heart of 'cattle country'. After a further attack the leader is arrested, but an old farmer takes Mulder and Scully out to see livestock being injected with genetically engineered growth hormone. It is this that he blames for the escalating violence and unease in the town. Later a plane containing Gerry Larsen, the local doctor, crashes. The man was carrying details of various families and what proves to be a phial of alien material similar to that in the Erlenmeyer flask. He has been conducting illicit experiments on the children of the town, and the 'abductions' were the attempt of a local man (a paedophile who was watching and videoing the members of a particular family) to draw attention to them. The assassin who shot Deep Throat appears on the scene, trying to tidy away the loose ends, but is himself shot before Mulder can question him.

Don't Be in the Teaser: Gary Kane survives, despite being found in his underwear in the woods with 'He is one' written on his back in marker pen.

Phwoar!: Mulder wipes barbecue sauce off Scully's face in a very fond way.

Dialogue Triumphs: Mulder: 'You know, for a holy man, you've got quite a knack for pissing people off.'

Scully: 'Kind of hard to tell the villains without a scorecard.'

The Conspiracy Starts at Closing Time: It seems that Larsen, the local doctor, has been paid to inject certain children with regular doses of alien genetic material, which seems to render them immune to disease (a plan duplicated many times in many places, as we see in 'Nisei). The conspiracy, as always, object to the mixing of shapeshifter genes with those of humans (meaning that 'Purity Control' (see 'The Erlenmeyer Flask') is a knowingly ironic codename for the alien rebels to give their substance), and send Deep Throat's killer (Crewcut Man) to stop it. The death of Kane snr some years previously – after he expressed worries about his son's growth – would seem perhaps to be more than a simple 'accident'.

Continuity: Once again, Mulder talks to Danny at the FBI (see 'Conduit', 'The Erlenmeyer Flask'). According to Scully's voiceover at the end, this is file number XWC060361.

The Truth: The disappearing teenagers are down to Gerd Thomas, the voyeur/paedophile who has been spying on the Kane household for some years. It's not clear how he came by the drug used to sedate the young people, which is also responsible for their nightmarish visions, but there is no suggestion that Gary and the others were psychically attacked as initially suggested. Thomas wanted to expose Dr Larsen's experiments – thus the cryptic messages on the teenagers' backs. The Church of the Red Museum believe in soul transference (or 'walk-ins' as Mulder describes it), but are ultimately innocent of any wrongdoing. Indeed, it's only the nature of Larsen's injections – alien antibodies in an experiment with the Red Museum people as a control group – that makes these events an X-File at all. The aggression of the locals is, apparently, genuinely down to what's being (in a quite everyday fashion) pumped into their meat. (It's worth noting in passing, however, that Larsen's experiments stretch back to when these children were born, but according to Mulder, Oden and the others have been in the area for only three years.)

The Bottom Line: MD: The excellent and diverse introduction – switching from the meat factory to a Peeping Tom to the young man being found by policemen – gives something of the flavour of this story. The galloping change of emphasis – it's really like watching four or five stories rolled into one – at least keeps the viewer's interest, although this does lead to a lack of explanation and a desperately contrived plane crash which is there purely to get our heroes one step closer to the solution. Still, there's a marvellous confrontation between Mulder and the local jocks – it almost looks like he's spoiling for a fight – and the return of Deep Throat's assassin leads to a marvellously tense conclusion. A great episode to watch while munching a burger – especially if it's made with 'safe' British beef!

KT: 'I'm a sick man.' Gorgeous to look at (the colours are so vivid – the entire episode is streaked with images of red, from the car Mulder and Scully drive, to the turbans worn by the Museum), if a bit paint-by-numbers. And, as noted above, there is so much going on it's difficult at times to remember which one of the eighteen subplots you're supposed to be concentrating on at any given moment. There are a few staggering coincidences, too (not only the plane crash, or the fact that Mulder and Scully are in town on an unrelated case, but that 'they' seem to have chosen this exact moment to pay Dr Larsen for his work).

PC: It's cool that this script suddenly becomes a conspiracy story out of nowhere, and that the two plots blend very well, but this is one of those *X-Files* stories that aren't really 'about' something, that can't be summed up in twenty-five words or fewer, like a *Friends* episode title: 'The one with the Werewolf'. When the show loses focus like that, it's often in trouble, but that's not very evident here.

One of the most impressive things about *The X-Files* is the way that the merchandise of the series has been kept up to such a high standard. The comic is a case in point. Written initially by Stefan Petrucha, and drawn by Charlie Adlard, it has managed on many occasions to be better than the series itself. While the TV series sometimes suffers from the need to explain itself to the greater mass of the audience, the comic scripts remain determinedly highbrow, dealing with the deeper ramifications of paranoia, socially constructed reality and the nature of truth. This approach reached its peak in 'Trepanning Opera', in which the story is told from the point of view of various characters, some of whose perspectives are very unreliable, leading to a final questioning of whether any point of view can be trusted. The comic maintains an arc of its own, rather more all-pervasive than that of the TV series, and rather more subtle. (The return of Samantha was one subject handled better in print than on screen.) Petrucha also tends to use paranormal icons that the TV series hasn't explored yet (such as suggesting that all religious and paranormal experience is the result of temporal lobe disorder, a subject that, while absolutely within the territory of the series, lends itself rather better to the descriptive power of comics). The feel of the series is maintained, however, through using similar storytelling techniques (including pre-titles sequences) and camera angle art, plus dialogue that really sounds like the leads could be saying it. Recent stories such as 'Home of the Brave' have even adopted the series' recent swing into black comedy and satire. It could be said that Adlard's art doesn't capture the facial appearance of the characters very well, but when the body language, gestures and speech are so perfect, who's complaining? The *X-Files* comic is that rarest of things, a TV adaptation that transcends its source and has managed to become a classic in its own medium.

THE COMICS UNIVERSE

35: 'Excelsis Dei'

US Transmission: 16 December 1994
UK Transmission: 2 May 1995 (Sky One)/
6 November 1995 (BBC2)
Writer: Paul Brown
Director: Stephen Surjik
Cast: Sheila Moore, Jerry Wasserman, Tasha Simms,
Jon Cuthbert, Paul Jarrett, Ernie Prentice

A nurse working with the elderly claims she was the victim of a violent rape – and that her attacker was invisible. Scully and Mulder's arrival at the Excelsis Dei nursing home in Worcester, Massachusetts, is swiftly followed by the deaths of a patient and of an orderly, seemingly pushed to his death from an upper window. One of the female patients claims to see 'spirits' patrolling the building. The autopsy on the old man shows traces of poison in his blood stream, and Mulder concludes that the patients are taking other medication in addition to that supplied by Grago, the nursing home's doctor. The culprit is a Malaysian staff member, who has been growing mushrooms in the cellars. Although the drug made from the fungus appears to combat Alzheimer's disease, it is also to blame for the manifestations of the 'angry spirits' and is, ultimately, a poison. Mulder is saved from death by drowning, and the old people – now deprived of the mushroom-derived tablets – succumb to Alzheimer's once more.

Don't Be in the Teaser: Michelle Charters, patronised by male colleagues, has her butt pinched by a septuagenarian, and then gets raped by an invisible entity (she says . . .). Death would, perhaps, have been kinder.

Scully Here is a Medical Doctor: She tries to resuscitate Hal, and checks the (lack of) pulse on the orderly.

Scully's Rational Explanation of the Week: The woman was either raped by an elderly patient in a semi-schizophrenic state brought on by Dr Grago's Alzheimer's treatment, or (more accurately, as it turns out) there must be some fungal or other environmental factor causing delusional and violent behaviour.

Dialogue Triumphs: Mulder, finding Scully watching a video in his office: 'Whatever tape you've found in that VCR, it isn't mine.' Scully: 'Good, because I put it back in that drawer with all those other videos that aren't yours.'

'Are you saying that the building's haunted? Because if you are you've been working with me for too long, Scully.'

Scully: 'Mushrooms aren't medication. They taste good on hamburgers, but they don't raise the dead.'

Continuity: Mulder says he has several X-Files concerning alleged 'entity rape'. This is one phenomenon he seems pretty sceptical about.

The Truth: Difficult to say for sure, but it seems that Gung's mushrooms have in some way 'reactivated' the angry spirits of those who died in the nursing home. The connection between the old folk's ability to see the 'ghosts' and their ability to cause damage isn't really explained, unless either the patients are exhibiting psychic abilities, or everyone's perceptions are at fault.

Trivia: This episode is sometimes erroneously known as 'Excelsius Dei'.

Scientific Comment: Nobody would ignore a cure for Alzheimer's just because it used an illegal mushroom.

The Bottom Line: MD: This strange mixture of *Ghost*, *Cocoon* and *One Flew Over the Cuckoo's Nest* proves, ultimately, to be a simple *X-Files* story about ghosts. Or something. Although hampered by a complete lack of explanation (why do the 'spirits' depart at the end?), it's atmospheric stuff, and an interesting examination of filial responsibility and of different cultural attitudes towards ageing. The 'ghosts' are really quite spooky, and there's a nice shot of the building at the end, moving from darkness to light with an echo of the malevolent spirits. Only the scenes with Mulder about to drown prove to be unexciting and poorly executed.

KT: 'They've taken revenge for their mistreatment.' Influenced largely by the films *Awakenings* and *The Entity*, this rumbles along without much point for a long time before bursting into life with the brilliant scene of Mulder and Michelle trapped in a bathroom that is filling with water (let's not, for the moment, consider how long it would take a room of that size to fill from a couple of burst pipes . . .). The concepts look good on paper (growing old is horrible and the young don't help), but the realisation is disappointing. And, can anybody explain the motivation behind murderous attacks on Mulder and Scully (who haven't done anything to anybody at the home) while both Doctor Grago and Mrs Dawson (a memorably dodgy pair of hypocritical gangsters) seem to go through the entire episode untroubled?

PC: No for the water scene, yes for the theme and the atmosphere. It's interesting to note that, originally, the rape victim was going to be a lesbian, but, in the final cut, she's just surly. OK, so let's give them some credit, maybe they didn't like that juxtaposition either. Mind you, I'm uncomfortable about a fantasy show, even one as committed as *The X-Files*, dealing with rape. At least the victim doesn't get happy by the end of fifty minutes, but we are left with the vague impression (because this episode only does vague impressions) that (a) the event was somehow unreal, and (b) she 'deserved' it for being nasty to the patients. Ick.

36: 'Aubrey'

US Transmission: 6 January 1995
UK Transmission: 9 May 1995 (Sky One)/
13 November 1995 (BBC2)
Writer: Sara B. Charno
Director: Rob Bowman
Cast: Terry O'Quinn, Deborah Strang, Morgan Woodward,
Joy Coghill, Robyn Driscoll, Peter Fleming,
Sarah Jane Redmond, Emanuel Hajek

Aubrey, Missouri: the remains of an FBI agent are discovered – some fifty years after his murder – by B. J. Morrow, a woman police officer whose visions appear to be giving her glimpses of events in 1942. The agent seems to have been a victim of the very killer he was investigating, the word 'brother' having been carved into his chest. A similar attack took place in Nebraska, Harry Cokely having raped a woman and cut the word 'sister' on to her chest with a razor. He was never accused of the similar murders in Missouri. Now the 'sister' attacks seem to be happening again. Cokely, although released, is an old man, but Morrow accuses him of attacking her. Scully and Mulder interview Mrs Thibodeaux, the woman who survived Cokely's attack in the forties, and she reveals that she was pregnant as a result of the rape. The boy – who turns out to be B.J.'s policeman father – was given up for adoption. Morrow seems to have inherited her grandfather's violent impulses, and is responsible for the modern-day murders.

Don't Be in the Teaser: Technically, it's just B. J. Morrow discovering a body, but we also witness, in flashbacks, the murder of Special Agent Sam Chaney, whose body it is that she finds.

How Did He Do That?: Scully and Mulder discuss the latter's amazing leaps of logic in a joking manner: 'I seem to recall you having some pretty extreme hunches.' 'I never have.'

Scully Here is a Medical Doctor: She confirms that the two X-rays of the teeth match, examines the unearthed bones, and pronounces Cokely dead towards the end.

Ooze: Plenty of blood. B.J. is sick at one point.

Scully's Rational Explanation of the Week: B.J.'s 'psychic flashes' are events she heard her father discussing emerging through her unconscious.

Dialogue Triumphs: Mulder: 'I'd like to know why this policewoman would suddenly drive her car into a field the size of Rhode Island and, for no rhyme or reason, dig up the bones of a man who's been missing for fifty years . . . unless there was a neon sign saying "dig here!" '

Scully: 'The man we're talking about is seventy-seven years old.' Mulder: 'George Foreman was forty-five when he won the heavyweight crown. Some people are late bloomers.'

Continuity: Mulder says he has always been intrigued by women named B.J. In the 1930s, Special Agents Sam Chaney and Tim Leadbetter used their spare time to work on so-called 'stranger killings' (what would these days be referred to as the work of serial killers). They were pioneers of behavioural science. There are hints that they were regarded as pariahs in the FBI of their era in the same way that Mulder is today. They disappeared in 1942 working on the 'slasher' murders.

The Truth: Mulder proposes that Morrow has inherited her grandfather's psychotic 'gene', which skipped a generation but has now been triggered by her pregnancy.

Trivia: Mulder's fascination with women named 'B.J.' might be down to his then-girlfriend, Perrey Reeves, playing a woman named B.J. on *Doogie Howser M.D.* at the time. Cokely seems to be watching *Bringing Up Baby* (1938) on TV during the final scenes. Exactly twenty-six minutes into the episode, in the scene where B.J. is in the cellar discovering Leadbetter's skeleton, keep your eyes on the staircase behind her. Whilst descending, Gillian Anderson trips and almost falls, steadying herself, with some help from David Duchovny.

The Bottom Line: MD: A little cracker, this. A twisting plot, some fine suspense, and peerless performances. The script and direction are inspired, and one can almost imagine this story working as a 'weird' episode in a 'straight' cop show. And that's a compliment, not a criticism.

KT: 'Someone's gotta take the blame, little sister, and it's not gonna be me!' It's a pity this is so close in the season to 'Red Museum', as both episodes concern strange messages left on people's bodies. This is a nasty little piece that works largely because every sympathetic character has a dark secret (Tillman's insistence on B.J. aborting their baby, Mrs Thibodeaux's hatred of her own son conceived out of rape). The scene of B.J. attacking Mrs Thibodeaux is one of the best of the season.

PC: Ordinary, good, and solid, and sets the standard for these 'filler' episodes – that is, the ones that could marginally sneak into other series and are generally written by outside writers. It is, thematically, a bit of a mess, though.

SEEDS

In 'Deep Throat' Mulder is seen eating seeds of some sort while driving the car. He offers Scully some in 'Squeeze' ('Seeds?' he asks: she declines). In 'Eve', 'E.B.E.' and 'Miracle Man' he's seen eating them again; in the third story they're obviously sunflower seeds. He also eats them in 'Little Green Men' when doing the 'bugging' job, and in 'Hell Money' and 'Wetwired', amongst others. In 'Aubrey' we get a kind of explanation: he used to have nightmares as a child that he was the only person left alive, and when he awoke his father would always be in the study eating sunflower seeds. (Extreme paranoia department: since Mulder's dad knew so much, did he know something about the protective biological effects of

---

SEEDS

sunflower seeds, and has Mulder been inadvertently protecting himself all these years?) In 'The Blessing Way', the Navajo give Mulder a pouch of seeds; in 'Teso dos Bichos' Dr Lewton's small intestine reveals that he had been eating sunflower seeds ('A man of taste,' comments Mulder).

37: 'Irresistible'

US Transmission: 13 January 1995
UK Transmission: 16 May 1995 (Sky One)/
20 November 1995 (BBC2)
Writer: Chris Carter
Director: David Nutter
Cast: Bruce Weitz, Nick Chinlund, Deanna Milligan,
Robert Thurston, Glynis Davies, Christine Willes,
Tim Progosh, Dwight McFee, Denalda Williams,
Maggie O'Hara, Kathleen Duborg, Mark Saunders,
Ciara Hunter

An FBI agent in Minnesota investigates a desecrated grave and, thinking it the work of extraterrestrials, he calls in Mulder and Scully. Mulder believes that the cutting away of nails and hair points instead to a human fetishist, and he is concerned that the man will escalate towards killing in order to satisfy his cravings. A prostitute is murdered, and Scully takes the corpse to Washington for further analysis. A fingerprint of the murderer – Donnie Pfaster – is found on the body, but when Scully returns to Minneapolis she is forced off the road by the man and captured. However, Mulder and Agent Bocks find Pfaster's location in the nick of time.

Don't Be in the Teaser: The story begins with a funeral . . .

Scully Here is a Medical Doctor: Yet another autopsy. She says that in medical school she developed a clinical detachment from death.

Phwoar!: Having found Scully, Mulder holds her as she cries, and kisses her hair.

Dialogue Triumphs: Agent Mo Bocks: 'You're saying some human's been doing this?' Mulder: 'If you want to call them that.'

Mulder: 'Some people collect salt and pepper shakers. Fetishists collect dead things – fingernails and hair. No one quite knows why, though I've never understood salt and pepper shakers myself.'

Mulder: 'You know, people videotape police beatings in darkened streets, they manage to see Elvis in three cities across America every day, but no one saw a pretty woman being forced off the road . . .'

Continuity: Mulder has really come to Minneapolis to watch the Vikings play the Washington Redskins, for which he has a pair of tickets. He seems quite annoyed that he and Scully will have to miss the match. Scully says she trusts Mulder with her life. She has never seen a case of grave desecration before, though she has read about them.

The Truth: Pfaster is just a psychotic death fetishist. Or is he? Scully (without any explanation) sees him morph into other human 'shapes' and into some sort of alien creature. However, given that no mention is made of this in the dialogue, and that Scully also sees the alien thing in a nightmare, it is difficult to state categorically that Pfaster isn't human (and it must be said Scully is pretty disturbed during this particular episode).

Trivia: The music being played at the funeral is *Trios Gymnopedies* (first movement) by Erik Satie.

The Bottom Line: MD: 'It is somehow easier to believe . . . in aliens and UFOs than in the kind of cold-hearted inhuman monster who could prey on the living to scavenge from the dead.' The theme of this episode in a nutshell (although somewhat ruined by attempts to make the human killer some sort of 'creature' from Scully's point of view). Unfortunately, coming hard on the heels of another fairly 'straight' episode, it doesn't provide the ideal juxtaposition (it would be lovely to have this episode following after, say, 'The Host'), though it still gives an idea of what *The X-Files* might have been like, had it not so firmly placed itself in a fantasy milieu. It's nice to see Mulder acting as a 'normal' agent (we've been told that he was very successful before getting involved in the X-Files, and here we see why), and Pfaster – Norman Bates's spookier cousin – is far creepier than any number of weird aliens or half-human hybrids. Mind you, it's difficult to understand how a man so strange he almost makes Eugene Tooms look normal is so easily given a delivery job and accepted by the unsuspecting middle-class family on his rounds – still less why his strange behaviour (and insistence on returning to his apartment) doesn't start any alarm bells ringing in the prostitute's mind. As well as featuring a tiny homage to *Taxi Driver* ('You talking to me?') and an ending photo montage somewhat reminiscent of *Peeping Tom*, 'Irresistible' is one of the very best Scully stories. But do people in Minnesota really leave their doors open?

KT: 'The conquest of fear lies in the moment of its acceptance.' This story of 'the devil in a button-down shirt' by the middle of the following season would become somewhat commonplace in *The X-Files*, which is a pity as, taken in isolation, they work really well. But, week after week, they become clichéd. 'Irresistible' is great, though, with vague necrophiliac undertones (that's got to be a first for mainstream US TV!) and some good performances, chief amongst them being Gillian Anderson who, again, proves she's the best actor on this show *by miles*. Scully's nightmares are brilliantly staged, and her scene with the FBI psychologist is one of the highlights of the season (although it's rather sad that, after a brilliant set-up, there's no concrete reason given for why this case should upset her any more than any other – after all, she's seen some weird shit over the last couple of years). There's also a fine performance from Bruce Weitz (late of *Hill Street Blues*), who makes an oblique reference to the real-life serial killer Jeffrey Dahmer at one point.

PC: So what does this killer want, exactly? Too bowdlerised

by a long way. It's a bit disturbing, as well, that having Scully tied up and helpless is now a recurring motif. And why do that crap morphing business just to let us know we're watching *The X-Files*? All these factors insult the audience in a big way, and it's nice to know that they're all addressed and turned around during season three, when the scripts allow us to deal with the realities of violent abuse ('Oubliette'), Scully as a professional (notably '2Shy' but generally all round), and stories without supernatural elements ('Grotesque').

38: 'Die Hand die Verletzt'

US Transmission: 27 January 1995
UK Transmission: 23 May 1995 (Sky One)/
27 November 1995 (BBC2)
Writers: Glen Morgan, James Wong
Director: Kim Manners
Cast: Dan Butler, Susan Blommaert, Heather McComb,
Shaun Johnston, P. Lynn Johnson, Travis MacDonald,
Michelle Goodger, Larry E. Musser, Franky Czinege,
Laura Harris, Doug Abrahams

A teenager is killed in Milford Haven, New Hampshire, an area associated with witchcraft, and nervous police officers call in Mulder and Scully. Despite Scully's scepticism, toads fall from the sky, water runs down basins anticlockwise, and Shannon Ausbury, a friend of the dead boy, makes claims of ritualised abuse when she was young. The girl appears to commit suicide, but the focus of the investigation moves from her father to the mysterious woman teacher whom no one can remember appointing. Jim Ausbury is consumed by what appears to be an enormous snake; Mulder and Scully are captured by the remaining adherents of the dark religion practised by some of the schoolteachers, but are saved from ritual sacrifice by the psychic intervention of Mrs Paddock, the mysterious temporary teacher. Paddock vanishes from the scene, leaving a taunting message.

Don't Be in the Teaser: No deaths, but a remarkable sequence as we realise that the Nice School of Christian Bigots is actually the Spooky School of Nutter Diabolists. (The 'pre-title' sequence actually takes place immediately after the credits, with the death of Jerry Stevens after the summoning of dark forces.)

Scully's Rational Explanation of the Week: The falling toads are due to tornadoes in north Massachusetts. She does at least concede that the man with the gun looked as if someone else was controlling him. Why can nobody remember hiring Mrs Paddock? 'A bureaucratic oversight.'

Phwoar!: Mulder puts himself between Scully and the gun in the shower.

Dialogue Triumphs: Mulder to Scully after the local cop has been dribbling on about 'Heavy Metal bands that influence kids': 'Better hide your Megadeath albums.'

Continuity: Scully's expertise on snake digestion leads Mulder to suspect that she watches the Learning Channel.

The Truth: Paddock – presumably a human acolyte with incredible evil powers, although this is never made clear – can influence others, especially if she has an item that belongs to the person, and controls a (supernatural?) snake of vast proportions. It's quite possible that she's the cause of the power cut (the lights come back on after she has left) and other phenomena seen during the course of the episode (including the toads?). She has presumably come to the area to punish the followers of the 'forces of darkness' who have lost their faith, and is somehow summoned by the teenagers' invocation, attacking a teacher with 'flesh-eating bacteria' so that she can take over his position for a while.

Trivia: The title is German for 'The Hand, The Pain' – presumably a reference to Mrs Paddock's burning of her hand on a candle to control the actions of others, translated by the cultists as 'His is the hand that wounds'. Paddock is an old English word for toad. The Ausbury family is named after a fan, Jill Ausbury, and Jerry for another fan, Jerry Jones. Pete Calcagni is the husband of another fan.

Scientific Comment: It is true that Coriolis forces in the northern hemisphere would make the water go down clockwise, but this can be disturbed by other forces. For instance, if you get out of a bath in such a way as to create vorticity, that could overcome the Coriolis forces. If the water fountain was asymmetric, it could go the other way. It's not necessarily evidence of Satanism!

The Bottom Line: MD: 'Did you really think you can call up the Devil and ask him to behave?' The themes raised – loss of faith (in 'evil' rather than 'good' forces), ritual abuse, repressed memories – are a tad more interesting than the somewhat lumpen execution. The (rather nice) lack of closure and (more annoying) lack of anything resembling an explanation (just what was the nasty old woman with the pet snake?) means that it's exciting and frustrating in equal parts. Still, there are great set pieces aplenty, and the plot executes just enough twists to prevent it being a complete retread of old *Omen*-type ground.

KT: 'So . . . lunch?' 'Mulder, toads just fell from the sky!' Another good mixture of small-town American myths, and pseudo-something-or-other horror. Love Mulder's description of Paper Lace's 'The Night Chicago Died' as 'devil music'. The naming of High School Crowley is a good in-joke, as is a genuine line of Aleister Crowley lore ('Do what thou wilt'). Great music, too (hugely influenced by *The Omen*, but, given the subject matter, that's pretty inevitable!).

PC: Again, it's a pity that the show is allowing itself time off from closure. The nature of the evil teacher is a vast unanswered question, and one that's very troubling in a show that's concerned with seeking the truth. In the second season, all the rules about how far from the rational the show is going to go seem to have been suspended, leading to a number of episodes where, to put it bluntly, bizarre things happen for no reason. Groovy set pieces, though.

39: 'Fresh Bones'

US Transmission: 3 February 1995
UK Transmission: 30 May 1995 (Sky One)/
4 December 1995 (BBC2)
Writer: Howard Gordon
Director: Rob Bowman
Cast: Bruce Young, Daniel Benzali, Jamil Walker Smith,
Matt Hill, Callum Keith Rennie, Kevin Conway,
Katya Gardner, Roger Cross, Peter Kelamis

The FBI are called in after the second suicide in under a month at an immigration processing centre in North Carolina. Although there is no evidence of foul play, the widow of Private McAlpin is convinced that he would not take his own life. A voodoo symbol was found on the tree which McAlpin crashed into, and suspicion focuses on Bauvais, the leader of the Haitians who make up most of the immigrants. As Mulder and Scully investigate, McAlpin's body vanishes from the morgue, the man later being found – alive – beyond the camp perimeter. Although McAlpin appears to murder his friend Harry Dunham, the real instigator of all the violence is the brutal camp commander, Colonel Wharton. He lost men during the US invasion of Haiti, and is systematically beating the immigrants as revenge, using voodoo to stop the two soldiers testifying against him. Bauvais – killed by the colonel – is 'resurrected', and ensures that Wharton receives a suitably grotesque punishment for his crimes.

Don't Be in the Teaser: Jack McAlpin steps into a scene straight from *Poltergeist*, then crashes his car into a tree.

Scully Here is a Medical Doctor: She is about to perform an autopsy on McAlpin, but the corpse has been replaced by that of a dog.

Ooze: Some nasty pale stuff flows from Scully's palm. McAlpin vomits off screen, and there's a cereal bowl full of maggots.

Scully's Rational Explanation of the Week: Voodoo works purely on suggestion and fear. Bauvais has switched Mc-Alpin's body for the dog despite his being in a cell. And this is the first episode in which the phrase 'old wives' tale' is used!

The Conspiracy Starts at Closing Time: X turns up (contacting Mulder via a playing card – the ten of diamonds) and sketches in the political dimension to the events at the processing centre, basically saying that everything will soon be swept under the carpet. Mulder says he is surprised to see the man again (after disobeying his orders in 'One Breath'). Maybe this encounter is simply to re-establish contact with Mulder, or maybe, for X, this case is personal (has he got a Haitian background, or is he an illegal immigrant, like that other agent of the conspiracy, Luiz Cardinal of 'Apocrypha'?). It doesn't seem likely that the conspiracy would have an interest in this matter, although they might be interested in a chemical which turns people into zombies . . . There is a suggestion that the military are sanctioning Wharton's actions in retaliation for the death of three soldiers in Haiti.

The Truth: Wharton 'went native' in Haiti to such an extent that he returned to the US conversant with voodoo. A poison (possibly extracted from frogs) can induce a zombie-like state in small quantities. The nature of Chester Bonaparte – who died during the riot ten weeks previously but seems like a normal kid (albeit one who can change into a cat!) to Mulder and Scully – is unclear, but his 'new life' is presumably also linked to voodoo.

Trivia: Doesn't Private Dunham seem a little short for a marine? He's not much taller than Scully. The card that X leaves Mulder appears to be a coded reference to where they should meet (County Road 10).

The Bottom Line: MD: Darker than Dracula's underpants. The whole thing romps along, blessed with some lovely direction (there's a nice zoom into the cracked face of the statue in the pre-title sequence, later mirrored by the rotten face glimpsed in the car mirror). A grotesque scene with Scully's hand ripping open leads into a lovely double-twist ending.

KT: 'They will only warn you once. After that, no magic can save you.' As Kenny Lynch said in *Doctor Terror's House of Horror* (1964), 'You don't want to mess with that voodoo!' Partly objectionable because it takes every Caribbean folk myth and mixes them up without much intelligence (as if just mentioning the words 'voodoo' and 'zombie' will make the audience happy), there are good things on offer (Daniel Benzali – a year before *Murder One* and stardom – is excellent), and the candle-filled graveyard finale is effective. There are a few nods at Edgar Allan Poe, too (notably *The Premature Burial* in the final shot).

PC: Eek! Scary! The last bit is really scary! It's all done so terribly well that you don't realise until a few days after that it's basically a load of set pieces glued together with expectation. Which could be one of the secrets of this show's success: do the lighting and design well, and the rest will follow (as *Doctor Who*'s best script editor, Andrew Cartmel, once noted).

40: 'Colony'

US Transmission: 10 February 1995
UK Transmission: 6 June 1995 (Sky One)/
11 December 1995 (BBC2)
Writers: Chris Carter,
from a story by David Duchovny, Chris Carter
Director: Nick Marck
Cast: Dana Gladstone, Megan Leitch, Tom Butler, Tim Henry,
Andrew Johnston, Ken Roberts, Michael Rogers,
Oliver Becker, James Leard, Linden Banks, Bonnie Hay,
Kim Restell, Richard Sargent, David L. Gordon

Arson attacks on abortion clinics have claimed the lives of three doctors who were unrelated but apparently identical. Mulder and Scully try to track down the other clones, but during the course of their investigation an FBI agent is killed, as is the doctor they were trying to protect – although, as with the others, no corpse remains to be analysed. Despite being 'grounded' by Skinner, Mulder and Scully are contacted by a CIA agent who claims that the cloned men are the result of Soviet cold-war experiments, and that they are being systematically destroyed by a Russian assassin at the behest of the US authorities. Suddenly Mulder is forced to return home on important family business: his sister has reappeared after all these years. Scully continues the investigation and eventually finds the remaining clones. However, the protection she organises for them proves inadequate. Samantha Mulder – now the adopted daughter of one of the doctors – explains to Fox that the assassin is in fact a shapeshifting alien. Mulder tries to contact Scully, but it is too late: she has just let another Mulder into her room.

Don't Be in the Teaser: Mulder's heart stops in the Arctic.

Scully Here is a Medical Doctor: She reads the autopsy of the dead agent: his blood seems to have coagulated.

Ooze: Lots of it as the clones and the assassin are stabbed or shot. Scully steps in some ooze at one point and it ruins her shoe. And there's whatever is in that blood bag she's holding in the warehouse (looks suspiciously like an alien embryo that's been stamped on!).

Scully's Rational Explanation of the Week: The arsons are the work of militant pro-lifers. Nevertheless, in a great subversion, she's less than willing to believe the moronic state-sanctioned-murder nonsense that 'Chapel' spouts.

Dialogue Triumphs: Mulder: 'I have lived with a fragile faith built on the ether of vague memories from an experience I could neither prove nor explain . . . What happened to me out on the ice has justified every belief. If I should die now it would be with the certainty that my faith has been righteous, and if through death larger mysteries are revealed I will have already learned the answer to the question that has driven me here: that there is intelligent life in the universe, other than our own, that they are here among us, and that they have begun to colonise.'

'You've got to wonder about a country where even the President has to worry about drive-by shootings.'

Scully: 'Whatever happened to "trust no one"?' Mulder: 'I changed it to "trust everyone". Didn't I tell you?'

Continuity: Mulder's parents are separated. Samantha mentions Stratego (see 'Little Green Men'). Both Mulder and Scully are on the Internet, and receive anonymous e-mail tip-offs. Mulder's father now lives in West Tisbury, Massachusetts.

The Truth: According to 'Agent Chapel', the cloned doctors are the result of the Gregor programme in the former USSR, and they entered the States in the 1970s on German passports, infiltrating medical establishments in case of war. However, 'Chapel' is a shapeshifting alien killer, with green, toxic blood, so this simply isn't true: see the next episode.

Trivia: Scully is woken by 'Mulder' at . . . You've guessed it, 11.21. Ambrose Chapel is named after a church in the Hitchcock movie *The Man Who Knew Too Much*. In that film, the name is wrongly believed to be that of a person. Exactly Mulder and Scully's mistake!

The Bottom Line: MD: Uneven but good, despite the contrived events (a broken pencil, Scully taking a shower) that work towards that breathtaking cliffhanger.

KT: Impossible to like because it cheats for just about the first time in the series' history (the lie about Samantha returning being unresolved until the next episode). The episode features several great set pieces (the UFO crashing into the sea); the CIA stuff is well played, even if it is a complete red herring; and the *Terminator* influence that marbles the opening scenes becomes less obvious as the episode progresses. But it's still chock-full of dark back-alley chases that smack of a lack of ideas. A series is usually in trouble when it allows the actors to start thinking that they're writers!

PC: A mate of mine who'd given up on the series because of its nebulous and unresolved nature asked another friend what was happening these days. 'Oh, an alien bounty hunter has arrived to kill the clones of Mulder's sister' was the reply. And that's just the trouble. After all these shadows and grey areas, a dirty great, large-as-life, shapeshifting, alien bounty hunter takes some swallowing. It's a tightrope walk the series loves to do: have they gone too far? And in season three, they manage to totter their way along quite well. But here they fall right off and plummet to the floor screaming, 'But it's true!' And why does the bounty hunter's craft hit the water with an explosion?

41: 'End Game'

US Transmission: 17 February 1995
UK Transmission: 13 June 1995 (Sky One)/
18 December 1995 (BBC2)
Writer: Frank Spotnitz
Director: Rob Bowman
Cast: Megan Leitch, Colin Cunningham, Garry Davey,
Andrew Johnston, Allan Lysell, J. B. Bivens, Oliver Becker,
Beatrice Zeilinger, Bonnie Hay

Scully is captured by the alien, 'disguised' as Mulder, who wants to exchange her for Samantha. Skinner arranges for a sniper to shoot the alien during the hostage swap, but the plan fails and both Samantha and the assassin tumble over a bridge. Fox tells his father about Samantha's death, and he gives his son a note from her, encouraging him to travel to an abortion clinic in Rockville. Although Scully is on the scene when Samantha's body is recovered from the river Mulder meets other 'Samanthas' in the clinic. They are alien clones, just like the other Samantha, and are being hunted down by the assassin. Mulder cannot save them, but pursues the killer to the Arctic sea, where his ship originally came down. Left for dead by the bounty hunter, Mulder is saved by a rescue team. He has been contaminated by the alien's blood, but Scully oversees his recovery.

Don't Be in the Teaser: A recap, and then the USS *Allegiance*'s abortive attempt to destroy the bounty hunter's craft.

Scully Here is a Medical Doctor: Scully's conclusions regarding the retrovirus that killed Agent Weiss save Mulder's life. She does the electrocardio treatment on Mulder.

Scully's Rational Explanation of the Week: 'Several aspects of this case remain unexplained,' she concludes with characteristic understatement. Her rant at the end about science winning over belief smells strongly of a desperate need to believe in something other than belief itself. One gets the impression this is going to get worse before it gets better.

Dialogue Triumphs: Mulder: 'How was the opera?' X: 'Wonderful, I've never slept better.'

X: 'Is the answer to your question worth dying for?'

The Conspiracy Starts at Closing Time: X says that a fleet has been dispatched from Anchorage to make sure the bounty hunter doesn't leave. This raises the question of who sent that fleet. The conspiracy have surely just made use of the services of the bounty hunter to kill a bunch of rebels who are misusing the technology of the aliens they are allied with (the conspiracy afterwards employ the bounty hunter again). Is there a section of the military who are interested in and know about aliens, but are not allied to the conspiracy? (Maybe the NSA men who talked to the boy from 'Conduit' are involved: they must know of the whiteout aliens' attempts to communicate with Earth, and, considering that an NSA man is sent to stop the mutant on the train leaving the USA in 'Nisei' and '731', perhaps they're involved with those rebel shapeshifters who want to merge their DNA with humanity's.) Alternatively, it's possible that X is just not being careful with his language. Perhaps the fleet has been sent to investigate the loss of the submarine, which will merely have the *result* of making sure the bounty hunter doesn't leave, or the fleet is deliberately hunting the craft that downed the sub, without knowing what it is. Scully later reports that no trace of it or the submarine USS *Allegiance* was ever found. Skinner appears to be aware of X's connection to Mulder, or perhaps he just realises that whoever he meets in the building is going to be the contact. The detail of the bounty hunter's cover story while he's Ambrose Chapel indicates the depth to which the conspiracy (through the Smoking Man) have penetrated the CIA. (And he's either got enough knowledge from government sources to pilot a nuclear sub, or he finds the technology simple; or he has some method of stealing knowledge from those whose appearances he duplicates.) His knowledge of Mulder includes the information that he's been shot before, which indicates a day-to-day knowledge of Mulder's life (presumably, the Smoking Man has been reading the reports that Mulder submits to Skinner). If Scully's implant is actually recording her experiences, then X is going to find himself in deep water if the conspiracy ever recover it. It's likely that he knows about it at this point, hence his reluctance to deal with Scully, but he must, in the end, settle for the knowledge that it doesn't transmit the information, but rather saves it, and is hoping that it will never be recovered. Either that, or he arranged for her to get a dodgy one, because the conspiracy are often surprised by Mulder and Scully's presence and actions in the episodes before she has the implant removed.

Shapeshifters can survive leaps from great heights, and can recognise each other no matter what face they're wearing. The phrase 'bounty hunter', unless Sam is simplifying the concept for Mulder, implies a system of commerce and mercenaries. The alien ship is 800 metres across, and emits radio noise all across the spectrum (indicating, as does 'Apocrypha', that these ships can communicate with their owners). It can hover, and zap human hearing and communication systems with what is, apparently, a sonic weapon (of the type referred to in 'E.B.E.'? – maybe that's one of the things that the shapeshifters have given the conspiracy).

Mulder doesn't usually have to get authorisation or do (much of?) the normal paperwork on X-Files cases. But the death of a fellow agent is enough to put Skinner's place as his protector in jeopardy from quite ordinary sources. Would Skinner normally call Mulder into his office for a 'family emergency', or does he know how weighted this particular event is? But Bill Mulder knows better than to trust telephones . . . (This story reveals that he's also a 'smoking man'. Must be the company he keeps.)

Continuity: The alien killer says that (the real) Samantha is still alive. The female aliens also indicate that they know where Samantha is, but, since they've just admitted that they're manipulating Mulder, this could be taken with a pinch of salt. However, they do know a lot about the original woman, and we know that the conspiracy, the shapeshifters' allies on Earth, abducted Samantha in the first place. It's hardly a surprise that other shapeshifters know where she is.

The Truth: These aliens came to Earth in the 1940s, and, since their genetic material is the sort that the US government holds, and their foetuses look like the one seen in 'The Erlenmeyer Flask', it seems that one of the first such arrivals was at Roswell. They have established a 'colony' of clones based on the two original visitors (presumably the originals of the 'doctor' and 'Samantha'). This 'Samantha' may look nothing like the real woman. Although they believe that they will one day inherit the Earth (and they seem to think this will happen naturally, without military action), they have been forced to scatter as the clones are identical to the two sources. Work at the abortion clinics has given rise to a way of combining human and alien DNA which will make future 'generations' non-identical. However, the experiments weren't sanctioned (the shapeshifters seem to be into racial purity, which indicates that the conspiracy's own experiments with humans don't involve alien DNA, and explains why they seem to spend a lot of time killing off those who do meddle with it), and a bounty hunter was dispatched to wipe out the 'colony' (as an aberration in their colonisation programme). The aliens can be killed only if the base of the back of the skull is pierced. Their blood is fatal to humans as it contains a retrovirus that triggers an immunological response to produce excess amounts of red blood cells. The virus becomes dormant at low temperatures, however.

Trivia: In this episode we see that the number of Mulder's apartment is 42 – either a brilliantly conceived Douglas Adams in-joke, or a complete coincidence. At the top of the e-mail Scully receives we see: 'To: Dana Scully, 001013'. Another hidden 1013.

The Bottom Line: MD: Poor Scully – another day, another lunatic (what's that, her third psycho/alien weirdo this season?). This is the closest the show gets to 'straight' SF thriller (alien bounty hunter tries to kill another group of extraterrestrials who are colonising the Earth hardly sounds like *The X-Files*), and if anything it's a notch up from the previous episode. I love the scrap between Skinner and X, and the incredible descending sub tower!

KT: 'It's a good story. I've heard a lot of good stories lately.' There are actually about six stories here (some of them *very* good, some less so), and the episode ends up with so much going on that it's often difficult to keep track of what, exactly, we're supposed to be concentrating on at any one time. The bridge sequence is great, and Skinner's got a couple of brilliant little cameos, but the whole thing is so complicated that this was the point I began to guess at how much of a corner the production team had painted themselves into with this whole conspiracy malarky. And, can somebody please tell them to turn the bloody lights on once in a while?

PC: I concur about the conspiracy, if not the lighting. It was at this point that you started to need not only to have seen the previous conspiracy episodes, but to have studied and discussed them at length, in order to enjoy the latest ones. Fortunately, between, I suspect, this season and the next, Frank Spotnitz (who has *the* most apt name) sat down with Chris Carter and got all the conspiracy stuff sorted, leading to the run of coherent (if still somewhat audience-shredding) conspiracy episodes in the next season. These episodes,

however, are a mess. They seem to go on forever, because
there are many slow-paced threads all continuing at once.
Worse, the conspiracy distracts us from the human drama.
Bill Mulder's bizarre reaction on hearing that his daughter has
vanished again alienates us from the whole thing, because it's
just not how a human being would behave. Later information
backs up his apparent insensitivity (it's doubtful that he ever
believed that this was the real Samantha, since he could have
phoned up the conspiracy and asked). But the moment is
sacrificed for a backstory that we don't yet know about,
resulting in what's almost an anti-drama.

42: 'Fearful Symmetry'

US Transmission: 24 February 1995
UK Transmission: 29 June 1995 (Sky One)/
23 January 1996 (BBC1)
Writer: Steve de Jarnatt
Director: James Whitmore, Jr
Cast: Jayne Atkinson, Lance Guest, Jack Rader,
Jody St Michael, Charles Andre, Garvin Cross, Tom Glass

The death of a construction worker and the mysterious escape
of an elephant from a nearby zoo bring Mulder and Scully to
Idaho. Although much damage was caused in the town of
Fairfield, no one saw the creature, and there is no sign that the
cage was tampered with. However, Scully remains convinced
that the WAO – a radical anti-zoo group stationed in the area
– are to blame, and she follows a man as he breaks into the
zoo. He is killed, seemingly by a tiger, but video footage of
his death reveals no attacking animal. Mulder discovers that
no pregnancy at the zoo has ever successfully come full term,
and an autopsy on the elephant shows that it was pregnant.
Mulder postulates that extraterrestrials are harvesting the
animals for embryos and returning the creatures to the wrong
location.

Don't Be in the Teaser: A construction worker is killed by an invisible elephant. Honest.

Scully Here is a Medical Doctor: She performs an autopsy on the elephant (which involves stepping into the corpse!), despite it being beyond her 'job description'. She also examines Kyle Lang's body and finds evidence of manslaughter.

Scully's Rational Explanation of the Week: The lights used by the workers affected their night vision, and the video cameras were of such poor quality that they couldn't pick out a grey elephant in the dark. About as plausible as Mulder's invisible elephant.

Dialogue Triumphs: Mulder: 'I'd be willing to admit the possibility of a tornado, but it's not really tornado season. I'd even be willing to entertain the notion of a black hole passing over the area . . . but it's not really black hole season, either.'

The Conspiracy Starts at Closing Time: Mulder is once more present during an alien whiteout, and may thus have lost time again. (It's becoming a way of life for him.) If the aliens featured here are also the ones who abduct people with whiteouts, then they continue to be portrayed in a relatively benign way: they want to save the planet's animals. There would be many easier ways for the conspiracy and their Japanese scientists to nick animal DNA if they wanted it. Besides, this lot can warp spacetime and make things invisible, two attributes which define the whiteout aliens and seem beyond the abilities of the shapeshifters and their conspiracy allies.

Continuity: Mulder once saw a David Copperfield show (possibly on TV – see 'Little Green Men') in which the magician made the Statue of Liberty disappear. Frohike was arrested at a 'Free James Brown' rally. Langly has a 'philosophical' problem with having his image bounced off a satellite.

The Truth: Animal embryos are being harvested by extraterrestrials. It's not explained, however, what causes the 'invisible creatures', or the animals' return to the wrong place (Mulder blathers on about disruption in the spacetime continuum, but he's clearly been watching too much *Star Trek* recently) or – given the aliens' poor map-reading – how they manage to locate Sophie, the ape having been moved.

Trivia: Blake Towers seems to have been named after the author of the poem ('The Tyger') from which the title comes.

Scientific Comment: When Mulder says that the aliens are suffering from 'an astrological variation, a trouble with the spacetime continuum', at the very least he should have said astronomical, not astrological!

The Bottom Line: MD: 'Man save man.' Marvellous, a great example of how rich a brew *The X-Files* can be, with a quite different example of alien interaction with our planet from that seen in the previous story. Presumably this is why the BBC showed this one out of sequence, as they didn't want to start their BBC1 run with something so atypical. But what makes a classic X-File anyway? OK, so this is a 'message episode', but who cares? It's a great message, and the opening sequences are wonderfully bizarre.

KT: 'Unless it's trick photography, that kid was killed by some kind of phantom attacker.' A hell of a pre-title sequence; in fact, a hell of an episode. Apart (again) from the lack of a clear motivation for the animal abductions (three or four theories are put forward, but most seem like Mulder grabbing at straws), this is a really good episode. There's an anger in the writing that is unusual in *The X-Files* (which is normally much more cynical – even when it's getting on its soapbox).

PC: Oh come on! Let me get this straight: these aliens, who have been scaring the hell out of our heroes with their abduction stuff, have now started abducting gorillas to save our planet's wildlife from humanity. The reason the BBC showed this one out of order was, I suspect, that it's bloody ridiculous. I mean, what next, the gorilla abduction support group? Otters with implants? Can we be sure of the safety of Mulder's poor goldfish? This whole grey-alien/snatched-from-your-bed business started out as a hard, scared, response to all that hippie space brothers nonsense. Shoehorning abduction mythology back into green crystal dolphin politics is just a ridiculous, rabbitlike response to the new mythos, both in 'fact' and in fiction like this. *The X-Files* should be more cynical than this, but with the hippie Indians on the horizon, it got worse before it got better. This was just an excuse for an elephant autopsy, wasn't it?

43: 'Død Kalm'

US Transmission: 10 March 1995
UK Transmission: 27 June 1995 (Sky One)/
16 January 1996 (BBC1)
Writers: Howard Gordon, Alex Gansa, from a story by
Howard Gordon
Director: Rob Bowman
Cast: John Savage, David Cubitt, Vladimir Kulich,
Stephen Dimopoulos, Claire Riley, Robert Metcalfe,
Dmitry Chepovetsky

The only survivor of the USS *Arden*, which went missing in the Norwegian sea, appears to have aged prematurely, and Mulder and Scully decide to investigate. They charter a ship to the area – which has seen an unusually high incidence of disappearing vessels over the years – and find the rusted remains of the *Arden*. Stranded on board the prematurely aged ship, they find one survivor, who soon dies, and a pirate whaler, who has not aged. The FBI agents discover that the water supply has become infected, and that only the recycled sewage water is safe to drink. This supply is dwindling, and Mulder and Scully begin to age. However, they are rescued and, thanks to Scully's detailed notes, even Mulder recovers fully.

Don't Be in the Teaser: The men of the USS *Arden* mutiny

152

in a desperate attempt to escape the ageing, but by the time of their rescue it's already too late for them.

Scully Here is a Medical Doctor: Mulder is able to get her a clearance code to see Lt. Richard Harper, the only survivor of the *Arden*. Later, her notes help to save Mulder's life.

Scully's Rational Explanation of the Week: Free radicals – highly reactive chemicals containing extra electrons that can attack DNA and cause body tissue and cell membranes to oxidise, thought to be at the root of natural ageing – are being released as the ship is drifting towards a large metallic source (e.g. a meteorite), with the ocean acting as a battery.

Phwoar!: Neither of them will drink the last water. Aww . . .

Dialogue Triumphs: Mulder: 'I always thought when I got old I'd take a cruise . . .'

The Conspiracy Starts at Closing Time: According to Mulder, scientists involved in the Philadelphia Experiment, which attempted to make battleships invisible to radar, were not, as is commonly believed, moved to the Manhattan Project. They continued their work at Roswell, New Mexico, utilising alien technology, and less than nine months later caused the USS *Eldridge* to disappear from the Philadelphia Naval Yard and reappear minutes later in Northwick, Virginia.

Continuity: Mulder gets seasick; Scully doesn't. Scully refers back to the events of 'One Breath', and says that she no longer fears death.

The Truth: Your guess is as good as ours. Mulder knows of nine unexplained cases of ships vanishing as they passed through the 65th parallel, dating back to 1949, which suggests a long-standing phenomenon. No explanation is made for the problems with instrumentation (particularly radar) in the area, and suggested causes of the ageing moves from wormholes and the Philadelphia Experiment to free radicals released because the ship is drifting towards a large metallic meteorite, to a water supply infected with what Scully calls 'heavy salt'. This seems to be at the root of the human ageing at least, as her theories are proved correct when Mulder is treated in the naval hospital, but it's difficult to see how infected water would cause the entire ship to degenerate. No explanation is given for how or why the water was infected or for the disappearing vessels in the past or for the true role played by the crashed meteorite (if indeed that's what the recent light in the sky was). And why, exactly, was Olafsson unaffected?

Trivia: Leeds isn't on the coast, so how can a Royal Naval ship disappear between there and Cape Perry? There is a port of Leeds, but it's a canal port, so a warship wouldn't be sailing from there. (Given the destination, Hull, or New-castle-upon-Tyne, would seem the likely port of origin.) The life raft the crewmen jump into in the teaser is numbered 925 (25 September is the birthday of Gillian Anderson's daughter).

Scientific Comment: The battery theory wouldn't work. The positively charged meteor, the sea and the battleship wouldn't form a circuit.

The Bottom Line: MD: 'Time got lost.' A triumph of style over substance and the shaggiest of shaggy-dog stories, 'Død Kalm' is a bit of a mess. It's atmospheric, and well-directed, and the enclosed survival play that it becomes is well acted by the regulars, but the complete lack of explanation, the gross contradictions and the cop-out ending (echoing that of 'End Game', only two episodes previously) relegates this to an also-ran amongst 'X-Files without monsters'. No amount of Norse mythology and fog can disguise the fact that the story simply hasn't been thought through properly.

KT: 'I think I hear the wolf at the door.' I'd forgotten just how bad this one was. Boring isn't a word normally used in connection with *The X-Files*, but this is a terrible, bland, mindless episode full of culs-de-sac and blind alleys. It grabs on to any passing horror movie clichés (rats, the 'bleeding' ship) and waves them in the air saying 'be afraid'. No thanks,

I was too busy laughing. Even the much-admired make-up isn't really very good (that's when you can see it – turn the lights on please).

PC: My God, are we anywhere near the end of the season yet? The best *X-Files* episodes trip their way lightly through all the possibilities, and then settle on one, even if they don't tell us which it is. This story is based on the 'throw enough phenomena at the wall, and some of them will stick' theory. As usual, everything looks great, but having our heroes just escape from things, instead of settle them, is always unsatisfactory, and wasn't regarded as fair play before the second season. This story, by the way, seems heavily influenced by *Miss Smilla's Feeling for Snow* by Peter Høeg which, incidentally, has a suspended ending too, only that's a literary masterpiece, and this isn't.

44: 'Humbug'

US Transmission: 31 March 1995
UK Transmission: 3 July 1995 (Sky One)/
9 January 1996 (BBC1)
Writer: Darin Morgan
Director: Kim Manners
Cast: Jim Rose, Wayne Grace, Michael Anderson,
The Enigma, Vincent Schiavelli, Alex Diakun, John Payne,
Gordon Tipple, Alvin Law

The murder of an 'Alligator Man' (the forty-eighth such attack in twenty-eight years across America) brings Mulder and Scully to Gibsontown, Florida, a town populated largely by former circus 'freaks' and sideshow artists. After another savage killing the FBI agents become suspicious of Sheriff Hamilton – who used to be Jim-Jim the Dog-Faced Boy – and Dr Blockhead, whose blood matches that found at the scene of the second murder. However, the real culprit seems to be an atrophied Siamese twin, who can detach from his brother and is searching out a more suitable carrier. He finds this in the form of the jigsaw-tattooed man who can eat anything – including, it seems, the murderous twin.

Don't Be in the Teaser: Jerald Glazebrook, the alligator man, killed in his swimming pool.

How Did He Do That?: Or, perhaps, why? Why suddenly start a hunt for the Fiji Mermaid on the basis of a drawing on a restaurant menu?

Scully Here is a Medical Doctor: She does the autopsy on Lanny, the 'normal' twin.

Phwoar!: That remarkably clever scene with Scully's semi-exposed breast and Lanny's deformed stomach/brother.

Dialogue Triumphs: Mulder (after the bizarre interruption to the funeral): 'I can't wait for the wake.'

Mr Nutt: 'I've taken in your all-American features, your dour demeanour, your unimaginative necktie design, and concluded that you work for the government . . . An FBI agent.'

Dr Blockhead (after removing a bloody nail from his nose): 'For instance, did you know that through the protective Chinese practice of Tubu Shon, you can train your testicles to drop into your abdomen?' Mulder: 'I'm doing that as we speak.'

Mulder: 'I could be mistaken – maybe it was another bald-headed, jigsaw-puzzle-tattooed, naked guy I saw.'

Mr Nutt: 'Not all women are attracted to overly tall, lanky men such as yourself. You'd be surprised how many women find my size intriguingly alluring.' Mulder: 'You'd be surprised how many men do as well.'

Dr Blockhead (with numerous hooks in his chest): 'If people knew the true price of spirituality there'd be more atheists.'

Sheriff Hamilton (having found Mulder and Scully hanging around in his garden): 'Investigation isn't going too well, is it?'

Continuity: Scully's uncle was an amateur magician who

taught her sleight of hand. Seemingly Mulder also had an uncle with similar abilities.

The Truth: Just as Scully says: it's Lanny's brother (not the Fiji Mermaid!).

Trivia: This episode was aired in the USA on the day before April Fool's Day. The trailer park is named Gulf Breeze, after the place where those sightings that Mulder doesn't believe in occurred.

The Bottom Line: MD: 'We're exhuming . . . your potato.' *The X-Files* does *Basket Case*! Having been wobbling on for ages about the diversity of the format, I must begin by saying that I'm not sure such an obviously surreal and *Twin Peaks*-y episode really does *The X-Files* any favours. When everything is strange, it's difficult to take anything seriously (but then I expect that is the point). Even Scully is wildly out of character: far from being the rationalist foil to Mulder, here she's swapping bizarre one-liners, pulling off sleights of hand and coming up with a theory so weird that no one believes her ('Now you know how I feel,' remarks Mulder). And the plot is almost non-existent. Still, with a script this clever, I'm not complaining too much. The sequences in the wonderfully named Hepcat Helm's 'Tabernacle of Terror' are especially memorable.

KT: 'You recall what Barnum said about suckers?' Now *this* is funny! Quite why, at this stage in its history, a series as po-faced as *The X-Files* should attempt a comedy episode (even one as surreal and in places downright nasty as this) is interesting. The reducing of one of the series' most important sacred cows (Mulder) to a straight man is inspired. There are loads of brilliant characters, set pieces and plot devices (Michael Anderson excels as Mr Nutt, a dwarf made angry by society's stereotyping). There's also a great little rant against genetic engineering towards the end that is out of place, but strangely compelling. Less impressive than later exercises in this field ('Clyde Bruckman's Final Repose' and 'Jose Chung's *From Outer Space*' especially), but only because, after three or four of this type of episode, we've grown used to its style. 'Humbug' was the first, and a diamond of a trailblazer for others to follow.

PC: Never mind the comedy aspect, this is simply the best-written show of season two. Morgan, as always, has some weight behind his parody, and the many syntheses between the normal and the not, not to mention the simple and solid ending (an ending! *The X-Files* this week had a proper ending!) make this very satisfying indeed.

45: 'The Calusari'

US Transmission: 14 April 1995
UK Transmission: 11 July 1995 (Sky One)/
30 January 1995 (BBC1)
Writer: Sara B. Charno
Director: Michael Vejar
Cast: Helene Clarkson, Joel Palmer, Lilyan Chauvin,
Kay E. Kuter, Ric Reid, Christine Willes, Bill Dow,
Jacqueline Dandeneau, Bill Croft, Campbell Lane, George Josef

A photograph taken just before the mysterious death of two-year-old Teddy Holvey at the Lincoln amusement park, Virginia, apparently shows the boy following a balloon moving against the prevailing wind. When the image is enhanced there seems to be a childlike figure holding the balloon. Scully is sceptical, and is particularly suspicious of Mrs Holvey's superstitious Romanian mother, Golda, who began living with the family soon after Teddy's birth. She seems both protective and afraid of Teddy's older brother, Charlie. Mr Holvey is killed in a freak accident, and Golda dies when trying to perform a protective ritual, her eyes apparently pecked out by birds. Charlie blames events on Michael, his stillborn brother. The poltergeist/spirit of Michael takes on physical form to masquerade as Charlie and is taken home by Maggie Holvey, although when she tries to perform a Romanian rite over the 'boy' he attacks her and

Scully psychically. They are both saved by the Calusari, Romanian religious elders who sever the link between Charlie and 'Michael'.

Don't Be in the Teaser: Teddy Holvey, killed by a fairground train while following a balloon.

Scully's Rational Explanation of the Week: The moving balloon is blamed on the wind (despite moving in the wrong direction), and Teddy's escape from his harness is down to two-year-olds being 'slippery'. (Mulder says that it would be impossible for the boy to free himself, unless he were the reincarnation of Houdini – 'and that would be an X-File in itself'.) Scully blames everything else on the old woman, accusing her of Munchausen's-by-proxy and of wielding a pretty vicious garage-door remote-control unit. This is one of those episodes in which the viewer gets perverse satisfaction from watching Scully thrown about like a rag doll towards the end. Explain that away, then!

The Truth: 'Michael' – the 'spirit' of Charlie's stillborn brother – is the root cause of the mayhem. Exactly how Golda and the Calusari open the garage door, however, is never explained (or maybe it was Charlie who opened it).

The Bottom Line: MD: 'This programme contains scenes that some viewers may find upsetting,' said the BBC announcer before the initial terrestrial transmission of this episode, and certainly the opening sequences are horrifying for any parent or, indeed, any normal human being. Hugely derivative (chiefly *Damien – The Omen II* and *The Exorcist*), but there's just enough pace to keep your interest, and the audience's changing attitude to the grandmother (who moves from bogeywoman to tragic heroine) is well handled.

KT: 'There were three strange men. They were performing some kind of ritual.' I like this episode a lot, chiefly because it plays with audience expectations and then throws the expected climax back in the viewer's face with a gigantic 'Stuff you!' A bottle Hammer movie, in other words. Mind you, if Scully seeing Mrs Hovley dangling ten feet in the air isn't final concrete proof of the existence of some form of supernatural phenomenon, then ... Ah, what's the point? Almost certainly the first *X-Files* story to use the word 'diarrhoea'.

PC: But not the last! The opening scenes are so deeply scary that reducing it all to mumbo-jumbo seems a bit of an anticlimax. Again, for the umpteenth time this season, Mulder and Scully just stand around watching the climax.

46: 'F. Emasculata'

US Transmission: 28 April 1995
UK Transmission: 18 July 1995 (Sky One)/
6 February 1996 (BBC1)
Writers: Chris Carter, Howard Gordon
Director: Rob Bowman
Cast: Charles Martin Smith, Dean Norris,
John Pyper-Ferguson, Angelo Vacco, Morris Panych,
Lynda Boyd, John Tench, Alvin Sanders, Kim Kondrashoff,
Chilton Crane, Bill Rowat, Jude Zachary

Mulder and Scully are somewhat confused by their latest assignment from Skinner: to liaise with the police searching for two escaped convicts. They notice that the prison from which they absconded is quarantined, and when one of the inmates is found dead his corpse is taken away by men in protective suits. Scully learns that the epidemic at the prison is highly contagious, and that it was a botched experiment by a large American pharmaceutical company. The government, as Mulder discovers when he confronts Skinner and the Smoking Man, are now actively suppressing information and destroying all the evidence, hoping to prevent the spread of infection without causing a panic. Mulder and the police track the remaining prisoner to a bus depot, but the infected man is shot before Mulder can question him in detail.

Don't Be in the Teaser: Dr Robert Torrence comes to a sticky end in the jungle. Literally.

Scully Here is a Medical Doctor: She uses this as justification to muscle in on the contagion investigation.

Ooze: Oh, just gallons of it.

Dialogue Triumphs: US Marshall: 'FBI run out of crooked politicians to sting?'

The Conspiracy Starts at Closing Time: The Smoking Man states that there was an outbreak of haemorrhagic fever in Sacramento, California, in 1988, which was covered up. 'The truth would have caused panic. Panic would have cost lives. We controlled the disease by controlling the information.' In this instance, the pharmaceutical company were performing experiments in prison, and the government are now trying to cover things up. Dr Osbourne says, 'Don't believe for a second that this is an isolated incident.' Pink Pharmaceuticals have covered every move, even to the extent of finding a prisoner with the same name as Torrance so that the entire episode can be passed off as a postal error. The conspiracy, or perhaps the government, ensure that Mulder and Scully's 'evidence' is discredited (indeed, it's perfectly possible that this was an attempt to do away with the agents). At the end of the episode Skinner warns: 'Agent Mulder, I'm saying this as a friend – watch your back. This is just the beginning.'

Assuming that the Smoking Man doesn't also have an everyday government agenda (and we never see evidence of his doing anything but for the sake of the conspiracy), then we can assume that the outbreak of contagion in the prison is the result of a conspiracy-sponsored experiment. Indeed, this episode fits in utterly with the revelation in 'Apocrypha' that the conspiracy are trying to develop a hardier, germ-warfare-resistant strain of humanity. The occupant of the railway car in that episode is even reputed to be infected with haemorrhagic fever, so it's a good bet that the case the Smoking Man refers to was that of a previous escapee.

Continuity: Mulder's badge number is JTT047101111.

The Truth: *F. Emasculata* is a beetle that carries a parasite that attacks the human immune system, usually causing death in thirty-six hours. The disease is transmitted via exploding pustules that contain the beetle larvae.

Trivia: Another 11.21 and DP reference: the package mailed to the prisoner is package number DDP112148, and another 925, the house number of the escaped prisoner's wife.

The Bottom Line: MD: 'There'll be a time for the truth, Mulder, but this isn't it.' An X-File only because it smacks of conspiracy (the disease has nothing to do with aliens or the supernatural), 'F. Emasculata' is a great take on the apocalyptic speculation that swept the world after the outbreak of the Ebola virus in Africa. It's chilling but somehow lifeless, and it was probably a mistake to split Mulder and Scully up so early. The moment Scully tells Mulder that there is no evidence left at the prison, and that he must take a statement from the remaining prisoner, you just know that the episode is going to end with a whole lot of fresh air as 'proof'. The special effects are gross, and I swear I'll never complain about zits again.

KT: 'You can't protect the country by lying to it.' 'It's done every day.' Echoes of *The Satan Bug*, *The Andromeda Strain* and even the *Survivors* episode, 'The Last Laugh'. Good fun this, although at heart it's a hoary old B-movie full of ciphers and clichés. Somewhere in the middle of a procession of obvious (if effective) set pieces is a smashing little story about disinformation struggling to get out. There's a great scene with Skinner towards the end ('Where do *you* stand?' 'Right on the line that you [Mulder] keep crossing!').

PC: For once, we don't get all the set pieces we expect. There are loads more good disease moments to be had, but, instead of pushing them to the maximum, the script falls back on the conspiracy to provide drama in what seems to be frantic desperation. Sorry to be so negative, but I really think that this season has problems.

HAEMORRHAGIC FEVER

Haemorrhagic fever, rather than being an ailment in its own right, is better described as a symptom of acute tropical viral diseases such as dengue and Ebola. In western Europe there have been outbreaks of Ebola – originally known as 'green monkey disease' – in Marburg, Frankfurt and Belgrade (giving rise to Marburg disease as an alternative name), where a virus of the green monkey (*Cercopithecus aethiops*) infected human laboratory workers and scientists. The virus is known to be transmitted via infected blood (or, in one instance, sexual intercourse), but, despite recent and well-publicised outbreaks in Africa, it is not a disease likely to spread in more affluent countries. The outbreak of 'haemorrhagic fever' in California that Deep Throat mentions in 'F. Emasculata', therefore, must be the result of laboratory experimentation with green monkeys, or with Ebola itself. Perhaps the conspiracy hope to use a re-engineered version of the virus as a weapon, or want their mutant army to be immune to such a weapon. The paranoia of the character in 'War of the Coprophages' who warns of an imminent outbreak of Ebola might well be justified.

47: 'Soft Light'

US Transmission: 5 May 1995
UK Transmission: 25 July 1995 (Sky One)/
13 February 1996 (BBC1)
Writer: Vince Gilligan
Director: James Contner
Cast: Tony Shalhoub, Kate Twa, Kevin McNulty,
Nathaniel Deveaux, Robert Rozen, Donna Yamamoto,
Forbes Angus, Guyle Frazier, Steve Bacic, Craig Brunanski

Detective Kelly Ryan, an ex-student of Scully's, asks for the FBI agent's help on her first case: a man has vanished from within a locked room, in a Virginia hotel, leaving behind only a black shadowlike stain. Clues gained from two similar disappearances, and the deaths of two policemen at the railway station, eventually point to Polarity Magnetics, a research lab. Dr Chris Davey explains that his partner, Dr Chester Banton, was subject to a massive quantum bombardment some weeks previously in a freak accident. He's been missing since then, but Mulder and Scully apprehend the man at the station. He claims that since the bombardment his shadow has become dark matter – a deadly black hole – and that the government are after him. The people died when his shadow accidentally touched them. Moved off the case by the local police force, Mulder contacts X, who attempts to rescue Banton. Another death in the Polarity Magnetics lab seems to indicate that Banton killed himself, but Mulder instead suspects that Dr Davey – who was secretly working for the government – has been disposed of. X and his associates embark on a programme to investigate Banton.

Don't Be in the Teaser: Patrick Neuwith, a tobacco company executive, is reduced to a pile of carbon.

How Did He Do That?: How did Mulder so swiftly notice the 'killer' on the video tape?

Scully's Rational Explanation of the Week: Despite all that she's seen recently, Scully is still so sceptical you can almost write the dialogue yourself. Mulder says that he suspects that it's all down to spontaneous human combustion; Scully says that there's no scientific proof for this. (Meaning that she hasn't read *Bleak House* recently?) By the time she comes round to this theory, Mulder has moved on to a new idea.

Dialogue Triumphs: Scully: 'Nonsensical repetitive behaviour is a common trait of mental illness.' Mulder: 'You trying to tell me something?'

Mulder: 'As a favour, we just handed over an A-bomb to the boy scouts.'

The Conspiracy Starts at Closing Time: Davey was working for the government; Banton fears a 'brain suck' that will reveal all his secrets. With good reason: X, too, is interested in the man. (Why, though, does he let him go after the initial botched attempt? Do they recognise each other, and has X already decided to kill Davey?) X is still annoyed that his identity has been revealed to Mulder's associates (presumably meaning Scully and Skinner – see 'End Game'), although Mulder says that he can trust them. X claims not to have killed Banton (which is true: though it seems he kills Davey), but his sinister agenda means that Mulder won't contact him again. 'You're choosing a dangerous time to go it alone, Agent Mulder,' says X, who also talks about his 'loyalty' to his predecessor. Mulder suspects that X is merely using him as his 'stalking horse', that is, relying on his ability to find the mysterious and supernatural so that X can steal it for his masters. Either X also has a workaday agenda of CIA activity – of which taking Banton and handing him over (for what looks like just the 'brain suck' he feared) is a part – or he has to do some actual work for the conspiracy every now and then to keep up an appearance of loyalty. A personal weapon such as Banton's shadow seems like just the sort of thing the conspiracy would be into, but then, any government would be, too. The 'brain suck', while it resembles the conspiracy's ability to record people's memories or erase them, isn't something we've seen them use before. Scully's definition of 'dark matter' is so wrong that, once again, we have to question her physics credentials, or wonder if she's been programmed with misinformation to mislead Mulder.

Continuity: There's a lovely moment in homage to Eugene Tooms when Scully looks at the ventilation grille in the dead man's room. ('You don't think anybody could squeeze in there?' 'You never know!') Scully says she intends to buy Mulder a 'utility belt' for his birthday, indicating a knowledge of *Batman* (either the comics or, more likely, the

TV series). She implies that she has been on the receiving end of sexual discrimination within the Bureau.

The Truth: Thanks to Banton's 'two-billion-megawatt X-ray', his shadow – thrown by harsh light – is deadly dark matter that kills humans on contact (but oddly it has no effect on inorganic matter).

Trivia: The cigarette company executive worked for Morley's, the brand that the Smoking Man finally favoured.

Scientific Comment: Probably the worst episode scientifically because they were trying to be scientific. It's stated that quantum particles, neutrinos, gluons, mesons and quarks are dark matter and that no one knows if these really exist.

Problems with this:

a: Everything obeys quantum mechanics so everything is a quantum particle. It's a meaningless description.

b: Neutrinos and mesons can be detected, so definitely do exist. The presence of three quarks in a particle has been seen through diffraction, so there's very strong evidence that they exist.

c: The nature of dark matter has not been determined. It's known to exist because the behaviour of galaxies and galaxy clusters does not fit with the gravitational forces you'd expect for the amount of mass that you can see. The dark matter must be there to provide the mass, but must be dark so we can't see it. Suggestions for what it is range from massive black holes, brown dwarfs, white dwarfs, mini black holes and massive neutrinos, to as yet undiscovered elementary particles, e.g. Weakly Interacting Massive Particles (WIMPs). It's the elementary-particle explanation that *The X-Files* seems to be going for.

Also, there are problems with burning the man's shadow into the wall:

a: If the elementary particle hasn't been discovered yet it must be difficult to detect. That means its interaction with matter would be very weak and it would go straight through objects (including people) without affecting them (like a neutrino).

b: Even if the particles would produce an effect like this, why didn't the chairs, desks and so forth get their shadows burnt in as well?

Also, it's stated that the shadow is like a black hole, splitting molecules into atoms, unzipping electrons from their orbits and changing matter to energy. Problems with this:

a: A black hole doesn't do any of that. A heat source would split the molecules and ionise the atoms.

b: If the shadow is like a black hole it should have a strong gravitational attraction and pull things towards it. You wouldn't have to be touching it.

c: Why don't non-organic things fall in?

The Bottom Line: MD: A great central idea – a reverse on Peter Pan with a deadly rather than an absent shadow – is somewhat marred by its bland execution, although there is still much to enjoy here. The scene where Ryan and her 'boss' stop Mulder and Scully questioning Dr Banton is great: while Scully makes a valid point about Ryan's struggle for survival in 'the boy's club', you just want to punch Detective Ryan's lights out ('We'll call you if there's any more you can do,' she says, patronisingly, after Mulder and Scully have just solved her case for her). And then, of course, she dies in tragic circumstances, and you feel really bad ... The ending is superb.

KT: 'My shadow isn't me ...' The 'forgotten' X-File (I didn't remember this at all when rewatching it for this review). There are a few oddities here (Scully's line 'You don't have a clue, do you?' suggests she believes that Mulder often makes up his investigations as he goes along, which may be true (see How Does He Do That?) but it is not the impression she normally gives). There are some powerful scenes, but the episode does have something of a feeling of going through the motions.

PC: Very bland, but with a nice and odd twist on X to stop us from trusting him too much. I really hate it when the series gets scientific things like 'dark matter' so wrong, though, especially when they could have made something up so easily.

48: 'Our Town'

US Transmission: 12 May 1995
UK Transmission: 1 August 1995 (Sky One)/
20 February 1996 (BBC1)
Writer: Frank Spotnitz
Director: Rob Bowman
Cast: Caroline Kava, John Milford, Gary Grubbs, Timothy Webber, John MacLaren, Robin Mossley, Gabrielle Miller, Hrothgar Mathews, Robert Moloney, Carrie Cain Sparks

Mulder and Scully's latest case is the disappearance of an inspector at Chaco Chicken's poultry processing plant. Despite a strange fire witnessed on the night of the man's disappearance, the case seems nothing out of the ordinary, and the local sheriff believes that he was leaving his wife for another woman. However, the man was about to recommend the closure of the plant on health and safety grounds, and a young woman working there suffers a psychotic episode and is shot. An autopsy reveals that she was suffering from Creutzfeldt-Jakob Disease, while her records show that she should be forty-seven years old. Mulder orders the dredging of the local river, which reveals numerous skeletons stretching back many years. Scully is almost the next victim of the area's cannibalistic cult, but she is saved by Mulder.

Don't Be in the Teaser: George Kearns is in for more than a bit of rumpy-pumpy in the foggy woods.

How Did He Do That?: If it weren't for the truck driver having a fit just as Mulder is driving along it is doubtful that he would ever have thought of getting the river dredged.

Scully Here is a Medical Doctor: Her autopsy on Paula Gray shows conclusive evidence of CJD, which is, er, as rare as hen's teeth. Do you think the people who abducted her were actually British farmers?

Scully's Rational Explanation of the Week: Bonfires explain the scorch marks in the field (the sheriff suggests an 'illegal trash burn').

Phwoar!: Mulder strokes Scully's hair after he rescues her from the headlock.

Dialogue Triumphs: Scully: 'She claims that she saw some kind of a fox-fire spirit. I'm surprised she didn't call Oprah as soon as she got off the phone with the police.'

Mr Chaco: 'Not many people I know are as useful as these chickens!'

Continuity: Mulder says that a documentary on an asylum he saw in college gave him nightmares (Scully: 'I didn't think anything gave you nightmares.' Mulder: 'I was young . . .').

The Truth: All the guff about fire spirits is a complete red herring. Walter Chaco has been educating the townsfolk in the delights and benefits of cannibalism, chief of which amongst the latter seems to be the absence of ageing. He lived with a cannibalistic tribe in New Guinea in 1944; since moving to Dudley, Arkansas, some eighty-seven people within a 200-mile radius have 'disappeared'. After consuming the corpse stew, Walter and his friends disposed of the bones in the river. Chaco himself kept the heads of his victims in an ornate cupboard. George Kearns – about to try to close down Dudley's chief employer, Chaco Chicken – was killed but seems to have been suffering from CJD. Presumably the presence of the CJD prion in his spinal tissue spread it to the other townsfolk. Chaco Chicken (slogan 'Good People, Good Food!') seems not to be implicated, despite the fact that the creatures are being fed on the ground remains of the unusable bits from dead hens.

Scientific Comment: CJD doesn't develop in ten weeks; it's certainly not time for an epidemic to develop. During the autopsy, Mulder looks at a slice of Paula's brain, but her head is still intact. Wasn't aware you could do that!

The Bottom Line: MD: An explicit take on the BSE crisis. It starts brilliantly, but peters out just a tad towards the end: what works well via innuendo and suggestion (cannibalism, small-town niceness) just looks plain daft when presented unblinkingly. The spectacle of townsfolk queuing up for their spoonful of human stew from the big pot seems silly, and the ending reeks of *Scooby Doo*. You're just dying for Mulder to say 'Sheriff Arens!??!' after ripping his mask off. Plus, we've got Scully in jeopardy again. Oh, and for a series that prides itself on its gruesome special effects, the head Paula sees on a spike is rubbish beyond description.

KT: 'Who knows, Scully? This could turn out to be even more interesting than fox-fires.' I don't think this has *anything* to do with BSE (despite Scully's throwaway line about cows being burned to stop the spread of 'mad-cow disease'). I'm not convinced that this worry had reached the American consciousness yet and the winter 1995 CJD panic was still months away when this episode was first broadcast. On the contrary, it's actually an age-old variant on the 'small town with hidden secrets' strain of writing (is a town of cannibals any more ridiculous than a town full of Satanists? Discuss . . .). Taken as a piece of modern gothic Americana, it works on most levels (I *love* the bit where Scully looks at the skeletons, thinks about what Mulder has been suggesting regarding what's in the food supply, and elects not to eat her family bucket of Chaco Chicken!).

PC: I agree with Marty: cannibalism's one thing, but all the ritualistic trappings are another. It'd be scarier if they ate people blandly and coolly, as real cannibals (not that anybody's ever proved there ever were any such people) probably did.

49: 'Anasazi'

US Transmission: 19 May 1995
UK Transmission: 9 August 1995 (Sky One)/
27 February 1996 (BBC1)
Writer: Chris Carter,
from a story by David Duchovny, Chris Carter
Director: R. W. Goodwin
Cast: Floyd 'Red Crow' Westerman, Michael David Simms,
Renae Morriseau, Ken Camroux, Dakota House,
Bernie Coulson, Mitchell Davies, Paul McLean

A hacker nicknamed the Thinker has gained access to a classified Defense Department file which details the international conspiracy that has kept the existence of extra-terrestrials a secret since the 1940s. The file has been encoded into Navajo. Mulder, who complains of not having been able to sleep, attacks Skinner and risks being thrown out of the FBI. Meanwhile, the Smoking Man discusses developments with Mulder's father, who is implicated in the cover-up. Bill Mulder asks Fox to come to see him, but before he can tell his son of his involvement he is shot by an assassin. Scully, hoping to clear her partner's name, takes Mulder's gun away for ballistics analysis, but this leaves him vulnerable to attack by the assassin – Krycek. Scully is forced to shoot Mulder to prevent him from killing Krycek, and reveals that LSD or amphetamines have been pumped into Mulder's water supply in an attempt to induce psychotic behaviour. Scully takes a recovering Mulder to New Mexico, where Albert Hosteen, a Navajo, translates the Top Secret files. Mulder is shown an old boxcar, revealed by a recent earthquake, which is full of seemingly alien corpses. However, the Smoking Man locates Mulder, and troops under his command torch the enclosed metal carriage with Mulder inside . . .

Don't Be in the Teaser: The box car is uncovered. Amazingly, no one dies.

That's a Mouthful: The Smoking Man: 'As always, maintain plausible denial. The files are only as real as their possible authentication.' And: 'I strongly encourage you in that event . . . to deny everything.'

Phwoar!: Scully starts taking Mulder's clothes off and tells him to lie down on her bed . . . because he's ill. Plus, an interesting shot of Mulder in his boxers, complete with suspicious bulge.

Dialogue Triumphs: Mulder (after the lads from *TLG* tell him about the 'trained killers' who are following them): 'You boys been defacing library books again?'

The Thinker: 'I don't want you to know my real name – I just don't think it's that important that you know.' Mulder: 'Sounds like a line I used in a bar once.'

Mulder on the fourth commandment and alien life: 'The part where God made heaven and Earth but didn't tell anyone about his side projects . . .'

The Conspiracy Starts at Closing Time: From what we see, the Smoking Man's alien cover-up conspiracy involves the governments of Italy, Japan and Germany. It probably includes many more. Bill Mulder is certainly implicated, his involvement probably stretching back to the 1940s. He has kept this secret from his son ('Forgive me,' he says, as he dies in his son's arms), he and the Smoking Man having agreed never to meet again. The Smoking Man claims to have protected Fox Mulder until now. (He's telling the truth in a sense, in that he's decided, or been told, not to kill Mulder to prevent him becoming a martyr, but in the third season it's the Smoking Man who always opts for violence, and his bosses who want him to use more subtle methods. Perhaps the Smoking Man's relationship with Bill Mulder is such that the 'martyr' line is one that he's convinced his superiors of in order to avoid having to kill his friend's son.)

When Mulder calls for X he does not turn up (see 'Soft Light'). Scully's name is in the Top Secret file, along with Duane Barry's. It has something to do with 'a test' (see 'Nisei' and '731'). The Smoking Man – a 'black-lunged son of a bitch', according to Mulder – says that Fox's father was the originator of the project, but this is not substantiated. (By the end of the trilogy, it's clear that, if he did originate the project, he must have been very quickly seized by ethical doubts and tried to stop it.) The Smoking Man also tells Mulder that he did not authorise Bill Mulder's murder. (In the light of the attempted elimination of Krycek as a loose cannon later on, that may very well be true. Perhaps somebody else in the conspiracy wanted Bill Mulder dead, and was getting tired of the Smoking Man protecting his friends. So the assassination attempt on Krycek was either the conspiracy covering the fact that they and the Smoking Man sometimes have different ends, or the Smoking Man taking revenge.)

After the War, Axis scientists, granted amnesty, experimented on 'merchandise', i.e. the 'aliens' that Mulder finds so many remains of (see 'Paper Clip'), or alien/human hybrids, or deformed human subjects ('Apocrypha'). Mulder notices a smallpox vaccination scar on one of the corpses, so it's probably the last, meaning that the secret railroad and human experimentation camps of that episode have been running for decades.

The aliens who took the Anasazi six hundred years ago, and 'come here still', seem to have a similar preservation instinct to that of the ones who took the animals in 'Fearful Symmetry', and these whiteout aliens may be the enemy against which the conspiracy is building a (similar-looking) army of human mutants.

Continuity: Scully's father told his daughter about the use of Navajo in World War II codes. The Thinker was briefly mentioned in 'Colony'. The Smoking Man speaks fluent German. (Was he, perhaps, the liaison officer responsible for the Nazi scientists smuggled to the States at the end of the war? If he was Werner Von Braun's case officer, then he might, indirectly, be behind the entire American space programme (bet that would blow Mulder's mind!) and still have good enough contacts to effect the cutbacks mentioned in 'Space'.)

The Truth: See The Conspiracy Starts at Closing Time above.

Trivia: The Thinker is seen reading a book called *50 Greatest Conspiracies of All Time*. Chris Carter appears as one of the FBI agents interrogating Scully. R. W. Goodwin appears as a gardener.

The Bottom Line: MD: Plotted more tightly than a gnat's naughties, this is just marvellous, and the pinnacle of the *X-Files*' unique line in 'aliens-as-absence' episodes. The twists and turns (how cleverly the woman who shoots her husband further down the corridor turns from being a piece of dramatic fluff into an intrinsic component of the plot) keep one on tenterhooks, and the sudden presentation of Mulder as a nutter is compelling.

KT: 'What is this?' 'The Holy Grail!' Like 'Little Green Men', I *loathed* this when it was first transmitted (how odd that the bookends of a slightly disappointing season should have been those that set my teeth on edge, rather than rubbish like 'Død Kalm'). Now, rewatching it, I can't believe how wrong I was. The episode is a bit cluttered (Krycek seems only to be there for Mulder to beat up – poor Nick Lea hardly gets to utter a word), with far too many plot strands being laid down for a conclusion that could never hope to deliver all of the answers. But, for all that, the idea of turning daddy Mulder into a dark figure, the sight of Fox going to pieces, the first example of 'Skinner Baiting' as a sport (see 'Piper Maru', 'Pusher' and others), and the amazingly well-handled climax mark the episode out for praise.

PC: Yes, this sets things up nicely for the next season. You can almost hear the clunk of the series moving up a gear as decisions start to be made regarding the nature of the aliens and the conspiracy. In many ways, that gear is reverse, because things we've assumed concerning Scully's abduction and the aliens are overturned in order to give the series a more distant sell-by date. The mysteries are taken further away, and we're told that what we've seen so far is horrid, but actually quite ordinary. I like that a lot, and I like the final coherence of this trilogy. If it had gone wrong, though, it could have smelt worse than those poor humans in the boxcar.

Third Season

24 45-minute episodes

Created by Chris Carter

Co-Producer: Paul Rabwin (51–73)
Producers: Joseph Patrick Finn, Kim Manners,
Rob Bowman
Supervising Producer: Charles Grant Craig
Co-Executive Producers: Howard Gordon, R.W. Goodwin
Executive Producer: Chris Carter

Regular Cast: David Duchovny (Fox Mulder), Gillian Anderson (Dana Scully), Jerry Hardin (Deep Throat, 50, 73[4],), William B. Davis (Smoking Man, 50, 51, 59, 65, 70, 72, 73), Bruce Harwood (Byers, 51, 58, 65, 72), Dean Haglund (Langly, 51, 58, 65, 72), Tom Braidwood (Frohike, 50, 51, 58, 65, 72), Mitch Pileggi (Walter Skinner, 50, 51, 58, 63–66, 70, 72, 73), Raymond J. Barry (Senator Richard Matheson, 58), Nicholas Lea (Alex Krycek, 50, 51, 64, 65), Steven Williams (X, 58, 59, 72, 73), Sheila Larken (Margaret Scully, 50, 51, 72), Tegan Moss (Young Dana Scully, 64), Melinda McGraw (Melissa Scully, 50, 51), Peter Donat (Bill Mulder, 50, 51, 73[5]), Brian Thompson (The Pilot, 73), Rebecca Toolan (Mrs Mulder, 50, 51, 73), Ernie Foort (FBI Gate Guard, 50, 66), Lenno Britos (Louis Cardinal, 50, 51, 64, 65), John Neville (Well-Manicured Man, 50, 51, 65), Don S. Williams (Elder, 50, 51, 59, 65[6]), Jaap Broeker (The Stupendous Yappi, 53, 69), Brendan Beiser (Pendrell, 58, 59, 65, 70), Tyler Labine (Stoner, 61, 71), Nicole Parker (Chick, 61, 71)

---

[4] Here playing an image of, and not the actual, Deep Throat.
[5] Here playing an image of, and not the actual, Bill Mulder.
[6] Credited as 'Elder 1' in this episode, but still the same character.

50: 'The Blessing Way'

US Transmission: 22 September 1995
UK Transmission: 5 March 1996 (Sky One)/
12 September 1996 (BBC1)
Writer: Chris Carter
Director: R. W. Goodwin
Cast: Floyd 'Red Crow' Westerman, Alf Humphreys,
Dakota House, Michael David Simms, Forbes Angus,
Mitch Davies, Benita Ha, Ian Victor

Mulder has apparently died in the boxcar fire. Scully is ambushed and forced to hand over her copy of the MJ files, and is suspended on her return to Washington. Her back-up tape is missing. The Smoking Man informs the conspirators that Mulder is dead and that the files are recovered. Frohike tells Scully that the Thinker has been killed. Albert Hosteen and his Navajo comrades find Mulder in a hole in the desert, and set up a healing ceremony for him, during which he has visions of Deep Throat and of his father. Scully discovers an implant in the back of her neck, but gets only partway through a hypnotherapy session intended to establish how it got there. She visits Bill Mulder's funeral, where the Well-Manicured Man warns her that her life is in danger: she'll be killed either by somebody she trusts or a pair of assassins. She tries to stop her sister from coming to her apartment, but is intercepted by Skinner. Melissa is shot by Krycek's partner, who mistakes her for Dana. Meanwhile, Scully – distrustful of Skinner – tricks him into being held at gunpoint. He pulls out his gun too.

Don't Be in the Teaser: Albert and his relatives are roughed up. Mulder seems to be dead.

How Did He Do That?: Mulder gets out of the burning boxcar and into the rocks surrounding it! (To be fair, we know that two of the little mutants managed this in the past, so presumably there's a hole in the wall of the boxcar, with a narrow rock tunnel.)

Scully Here is a Medical Doctor: And like all good doctors, she doesn't try to treat herself.

That's a Mouthful: Even after he's dead, you can't shut Deep Throat up. 'Moving backwards into the perpetual night. It consumes purpose and deed, all passion and will. I come to you, old friend, with the dull clarity of the dead . . .' Dull, yes, clear, no. They should have called him 'Big Mouth'.

Isn't it interesting that all of the 'dead' people in this episode talk in a mannered, poetic and thoroughly bizarre fashion (Deep Throat, Bill Mulder, even Fox himself in Scully's dream: 'I have returned from the dead to continue with you')? Maybe this is a device the dead use to convince the living that when they are speaking to them in dreams, it is illusion rather than reality! Or, maybe it's just that somebody wants, desperately, to win an Emmy.

Phwoar!: Scully's purple pyjamas are . . . sort of sexy in that they're designed to be incredibly unsexy, and that's her all over. This episode sees an awful lot of Mulder undressed, being bathed and generally looking gorgeous.

Dialogue Triumphs: Mulder, on being told he must not change clothes or bathe for four days: 'That's really going to cut into my social life.'

The Well-Manicured Man: 'We predict the future. The best way to predict the future is to invent it.'

The Conspiracy Starts at Closing Time: The conspirators are a kind of consortium, representing global interests (so Scully's continuing reduction of them to 'the government' is very naïve). They meet in what seems to be a club, and have been working together for at least forty years. They include the Elder and the Well-Manicured Man, with at least six others. They have always handled the FBI 'internally' (through the Smoking Man, who is scared enough of the conspiracy to lie and make excuses to them). They can sway (but not, seemingly, control) federal judges. They have two standard ways of having somebody killed. One: one or two men do the killing, with an unregistered weapon, which they leave at the scene; they have false documents and immediately leave the country. Two: somebody the victim trusts kills them. (These are an exact description of the working methods of human and alien agents, the person of trust almost certainly being a shapeshifter.) The Well-Manicured Man seems to think such killings unnecessary or, at least, that they have been poorly handled recently (by the Smoking Man). In 1972 (or 1973, according to the next episode), William Mulder was pictured with several members of the conspiracy (including Deep Throat, the Smoking Man, the Well-Manicured Man and Klemper). They often used to visit the Mulder household. Bill was with the State Department (but that covers a multitude of sins).

Vultures won't eat the corpses of the little mutants, presumably because of their infected and/or radioactive nature. It's interesting that they're buried in a boxcar, which is still the chosen method of transportation for them these days ('731'), and near Los Alamos, where radiation releases would be harder to detect. The mutants were killed by hydrogen cyanide.

Continuity: Scully has an implant in her neck (a computer chip), of which she has no recollection (we can assume it was put there during her abduction). Under hypnosis she says that she was afraid that she'd die, but she was cared for by a man. (Was this one of the Japanese scientists ('Nisei'/'731')? Or maybe she's talking about Mulder looking after her in hospital ('One Breath').) Her memory of the sounds is 'all screwed up' (a reaction to the drugs used to wipe her memory, or is this the effect of a 'sonic weapon', which in 'E.B.E.' Mulder suggests are used to fake an abduction experience?). During Scully's abduction an alarm sounded (a test, something routine, or was the place she was taken under attack from some enemy?). Scully says that she's not wearing her necklace today (see 'Deep Throat', 'Tooms', etc.).

William Mulder is buried in Parkway Cemetery, Boston, Massachusetts.

Scully is brought before the Office of Professional Conduct Articles of Review. She's given a leave of mandatory absence, with no pay or benefits, for direct disobedience, and has to hand in her weapon and badge. We see her key to Mulder's apartment (it's labelled 'Mulder').

Frohike describes Mulder as a good friend, 'a redwood among mere sprouts'.

The Truth: 'There is truth,' Deep Throat says about the afterlife, but then adds that there is 'no justice', without which the truth is meaningless. Then he paraphrases Nietzsche. So, are Mulder's experiences a genuine near-death glimpse into the afterlife, or a load of hallucinations? Mulder hears from his father, who tells him that he, Fox, will find the truth that will destroy him (Bill, that is, and he's presumably talking about having his sense of worth, or, since this is in Mulder's mind, his son's sense of his father's worth, destroyed, since he's already dead). This indicates (since, as far as Mulder is concerned, it turns out to be untrue) that all these visions really are from his imagination. Certainly, they all talk with the heightened language Mulder uses for his reports. Deep Throat is pontificating as always, and, as we have seen, represents the place as having truth, but not justice or judgement. (In other words, Mulder feels that, even though they're dead, this bunch of, literally, faceless men, to which his father and Deep Throat belong, have not been brought to justice.) His sister isn't there (this is death, and Mulder has faith that she's alive). It's interesting to speculate, however, that, beyond its archetypal and psychological reality, this place Mulder finds himself in may also be a physically real place. It's described as being a bridge between two worlds, having no time, and being a point of origin. We know that at least one sort of alien in this series can take people out of time quite literally (the missing nine minutes being one of the few concrete instances), and they must come from somewhere. The Holy People of the Navajo are summoned along this path, and the Anasazi are hinted to have been taken by aliens. Is this the wormhole where Scully's going to end up, if Clyde Bruckman's prophecy of her immortality proves correct? (See 'Clyde Bruckman's Final Repose'.)

Certainly, this space is real enough for Mulder to communicate with Scully from it. (But that's the trouble with being reductionist about mystical experiences. The whole thing is subjective.) All of this isn't helped by Albert's non-committal answer to Mulder's question: 'It wasn't a dream?' 'Yes,' he says. What, does he mean, 'yes it was' or 'yes it wasn't'?

The Bottom Line: PC: The least satisfactory part of the trilogy, because not a lot happens, and what does looks alarmingly like the writer has lost control of the plot – a sort of giddy veer away from a through line. The crap second-hand poetry in the near-death experience doesn't help. Krycek's angst at killing the wrong person is a nice touch: he still believes in what he's doing at this point. And it's interesting how Scully's chat with Mulder's mum is a reflection of Mulder's chat with her mum in the previous season. There's also a great dissolve from spacey death to the Stars and Stripes. Oh, and the new version of the title music (and the shortened opening credits used for the next episode) is fab, a pulling in of the hems and cutting away of flab that reflects the new discipline this season was to impose upon the series.

MD: Another slow and reflective season opener, albeit one blessed with a wonderfully silly ending. The dream dialogue and Navajo narrative – you can tell this is a Chris Carter script, can't you? – do indeed wobble close to being purple prose of the worst kind, but for me this is an enjoyable and engrossing attempt to turn American TV into something more lyrical.

KT: 'These sons of bitches, they're rigging the game.' This is OK – another one where it seemed disappointing on first broadcast because we had all had six months to get worked up and expect a masterpiece. Terrific cliffhanger, and a good double bluff in making the audience briefly think that Skinner is Scully's would-be assassin. And we have John Neville, another *great* actor, given a part without any motivation and trying, desperately, to find a character in there. And succeeding. Worst bit: Dana using the phase 'freaked out'. It's OK

when Julian Cope's saying it, love, but it sounds dreadful
coming from you!

51: 'Paper Clip'

US Transmission: 29 September 1995
UK Transmission: 12 March 1996 (Sky One)/
19 September 1996 (BBC1)
Writer: Chris Carter
Director: Rob Bowman
Cast: Walter Gotell, Floyd 'Red Crow' Westerman,
Robert Lewis

Mulder arrives and halts the stand-off between Scully and
Skinner. Skinner says he has Scully's copy of the tape.
Scully's mother finds Melissa in hospital. Mulder takes the
photograph of his father and the conspirators to the editors of
The Lone Gunman, who identify one of the men as the war
criminal Victor Klemper. Mulder and Scully visit Klemper,
who directs them to a disused mine, but then informs the
Well-Manicured Man that Mulder is still alive. Klemper
meets his death in suspicious circumstances shortly after.
Albert Hosteen comes to the aid of Melissa, but when Skinner
visits the ward he is attacked and the tape he is carrying is
stolen. The Smoking Man, realising that the conspirators are
becoming aware of his bungling, violent methods, tries to kill
Krycek with a car bomb, but it fails to destroy him or the tape.
At the mine, Mulder and Scully find thousands of records of
American citizens, complete with tissue samples. Mulder
finds that a file on his sister was planned to be his. Scully
encounters some small grey humanoids, while Mulder sees a
vast spaceship overhead. Gunmen rush in, but the agents
escape. Skinner tells them that he's come to an arrangement
with the Smoking Man: he gets the only copy of the tape
back, and Mulder and Scully are in the clear. Although the
Smoking Man knows that Skinner no longer has the tape,
Skinner says that Hosteen and twenty other Navajo have

memorised the contents of the tape. Melissa Scully dies.

Don't Be in the Teaser: Native Americans, bears, buffalo, all unscathed. It turns out that there's trouble in store for the buffalo's immediate family, though.

How Did He Do That?: How does Albert memorise the contents of the tape when Skinner loses it moments after meeting the guy for the first time? This is obviously part of an elaborate bluff on Skinner's part, as the Smoking Man guesses, but can't take the risk of trying to prove it so.

Scully's Rational Explanation of the Week: It's the Nazis. There were no experiments on aliens, just on humans. (She may be right: see 'Nisei'/'731'.)

That's a Mouthful: Skinner hangs out with the Smoking Man far too much in this episode: 'I just thought you should know of certain potentialities' and 'I'm quite aware of your policies in those regards.'

Phwoar!: It's lovely that Mulder can embrace Scully at the end and comfort her.

Dialogue Triumphs: Scully: 'I've heard the truth, Mulder. Now what I want are the answers.'

Skinner (relishing his escape from the power of the Smoking Man): 'This is where you pucker up and kiss my ass!'

Dialogue Disasters: Klemper's Dr Von Scott moment: 'Progress demands sacrifice!'

The Conspiracy Starts at Closing Time: There are at least eight conspirators, who meet in a room, perhaps in a club, in New York City. One of them, the apparently English Well-Manicured Man, seems to dislike the Smoking Man's violent methods of getting things done, because he sees them as inefficient and gaudy. The Smoking Man is certainly a servant of this group, willing to lie to them to avoid exposing his failures. He's been handling 'security' for them, not very well.

Skinner calls the Smoking Man 'sir', contemptuously, in

this instance, but thinks that it would be hard for the conspiracy to have him killed. They can, apparently, arrange
deaths by botulism, heart attack or plane crash. (They almost
certainly bump off Klemper for saying too much.) The Well-
Manicured Man tells Mulder and Scully that in 1947 a
body was recovered from the Roswell UFO crash, and that
Klemper was using the knowledge gained there to try to
create human/alien hybrids. (This may not be the whole truth:
it becomes clear towards the end of this story that the 'aliens'
seen in the corridors and the boxcar are altered humans, but
the technology used to alter them, and their intended final
form, may well be alien.) William Mulder collected information on American citizens for use in disaster management
after a nuclear war (the medical database covers almost every
US citizen born since 1950). He objected to the use of the
data in selecting citizens to be abducted and mutated. As a
result, his daughter was abducted to keep him silent. (It's a
mark of the power the conspiracy has that they were actually
able to ask him to choose which of his children was to be
taken. Bill Mulder was obviously aware that running to the
authorities for help would be impossible. Or maybe he was
aware that, with future events impending, Samantha would
actually be better off where she was, or even as a mutant.)
Whatever, since the shapeshifting aliens were revealed to be
concerned with racial purity, and against mixing their genes
with humans (if we believe the fake Samantha in 'End
Game'), then perhaps the Well-Manicured Man is encouraging Mulder to believe that the 'baddies' he's up against are
those who mix human and alien DNA, that is, the rebel
faction amongst the shapeshifters, rather than those who are
trying to mutate human beings into something resembling
'Greys' (that is, his own side).

When the Elder, having despaired of the Smoking Man's
latest Principal-Skinner-like excuse, calls up some 'friends'
to help, he either summons the armed men in CIA fleet
Sedans (who would, presumably, be usually under the Smoking Man's control), or the dirty great spaceship that hovers
over the old mine. The former seems the more likely, if only

because the presence of a single, tentatively exploring stick-man (the one Scully sees in silhouette, the distinction from the human grey mutants who run past her being underlined) is hardly strong action. The whiteout aliens seem to have learned about this place, and popped in to have a look, just at the moment that the conspiracy (who are working for the shapeshifters) order it closed down. (Alternatively, the skinny alien has come to take away the little mutants, in which case perhaps the Elder called both the UFO and the CIA to the mine.) It boggles belief that the human grey mutants are actually still living down there, but maybe we're dealing with a colony of escaped lab subjects.

Continuity: Scully has a recent tissue sample in her file (taken during her abduction experience?). There is no file on Fox Mulder (suggesting that, if he has been abducted during the series, it's always been by genuine aliens rather than the conspiracy). Samantha Ann Mulder is here stated to have been born on 21 November 1965, and her ID number on the file is 378671. The birth date flatly contradicts the one that Fox wrote down for her when he opened her X-File (see 'Conduit'). Since Bill Mulder created this database, it's probably his lie on display here. (It's pretty naff, actually, to turn over established continuity for the sake of an in-joke. Fox and Samantha are now regarded as being born on the same days as Mr and Mrs Chris Carter.) Fox William Mulder was born on 13 October 1961, his (unused) ID number being 292544 (the numbering system would seem, then, to be based on date of birth, or date of abduction). The hatred that Mrs Mulder feels towards her husband, which hasn't diminished, extends directly from his choosing Samantha rather than Fox to be 'abducted' (although she herself was unable to choose between the two of them). This, rather than the abduction itself, as Fox had always believed, was the reason for the break-up of the Mulders' marriage.

The Truth: Operation Paper Clip, the US plan to offer Nazi scientists sanctuary in return for their skills, was the project that brought Werner Von Braun to the USA and started the space programme. (All this is real-world true, astonishingly. In 1945, the British wanted Von Braun, the inventor of the Vl and V2 rockets, to be arrested for war crimes, but he was spirited out of Germany by the Americans.) But it continued after the 1950s. Victor Klemper, who had conducted medical experiments on Jewish subjects (it is implied that he was working either with or under Josef Mengele), arrived as part of the project, and, using the information on American citizens assembled by Bill Mulder, he started to abduct humans and experiment on them. (Any security breach, as seen in the previous two episodes, was settled by the gassing of the mutant subjects.) Bill Mulder was apparently against these experiments, but, as we see later, as a close friend of Deep Throat and the Smoking Man, he's implicated up to his neck, despite Mulder's cosy decision that he was acting under duress ('731').

Trivia: (Well, extreme seriousness, really . . .) A white buffalo is born on the farm of a northern tribe of Native Americans, indicating great changes coming. The mother buffalo dies, seemingly sacrificing herself for her child in (yes!) a clunking great metaphor.

Scully knows Napier's constant off the top of her head: the Lisa Simpson of the FBI.

Scientific Comment: Napier's constant (e, as in log to the base e) is used as the door code. However, the writer screwed up. First of all, Scully is asked if she knows the formula for Napier's constant. It's a number, not a formula. Then Mulder asks Scully if 27828 is right and she says it is. But $e = 2.71828$, not 2.7828. The writer missed out the 1 (or at least David Duchovny did). But why have a coded door at all since there's an unlocked one at the other side of the hill?

Using tissue samples for post-apocalyptic IDs is obviously crazy. Who on earth would bother going around ID-ing anyone, dead or alive? They'd have more to worry about than that.

The Bottom Line: PC: The closing coup by Albert is very satisfying, but, as with many of the conspiracy episodes, that closure is partly a sigh of relief that next week they might get back to some monsters. *Sophie's Choice* is an original choice as this week's cultural poach/rip-off. When I originally saw these three episodes, I was incredibly pissed off by them, thinking that Carter and Co. were deliberately sacrificing narrative coherency for a vague sense of paranoia, that they were never going to be able to tie all these threads together in a satisfactory way. In other words, that they'd decided the show was *Babylon 5*, but had improvised a master plan after the fact. In retrospect, seeing the conspiracy episodes again for this guide, I've found them to be linked much better than I'd thought, the kind of intelligent, video-age television that I'd always argued for, where you have to look back over the page to understand. But that doesn't stop them from being very alienating for the casual viewer who's trying to follow the plot. Their success with the casual viewer suggests that, worryingly, it's possible to get by in series TV by just presenting a lot of atmosphere and gravitas in place of drama. In terms of fiction, it's nice to see Mulder so driven, and Scully acting on a leap of faith. The problems of the conspiracy stories, and many other weaknesses in the format, were about to be dealt with in great style, in the best season of the series so far.

MD: A satisfyingly hectic conclusion to the trilogy.

KT: 'I don't work deals.' This is great; right up there with 'E.B.E.', 'Blood' and 'Beyond the Sea' as classic examples of *The X-Files'* original format. It's full of unanswered questions, though, which is a pity: why do Mrs Scully, and later Skinner, place such trust in this strange Navajo Indian they have only just met (especially as Skinner surely knows that nothing should be taken at face value)? There's a fine example of the 'Skinner-baiting' trend that would become almost farcical by the end of the season, with Krycek and mates kicking seven grades out of poor old Walter, but, again, why doesn't Krycek just kill Skinner? He must realise that he'll be identified by his former boss. And Klemper has all of the menace of American television's previous Nazi creation, Colonel Klink of *Hogan's Heroes*. There's a huge 'but' coming here though! The scene of Mulder seeing the spaceship is one of *the* moments on *The*

X-Files. Final proof that everything he has always believed in is for real, and Scully's not with him! Of course, she's busy having her own close encounter. Great lighting, for once.

From the beginning, there has been a hidden agenda at work both within the series *The X-Files*, and in its production. In the pilot episode Mulder talks of classified information that he cannot gain access to because he is being blocked 'at a higher level'. By 'Deep Throat' he is confident enough to state that 'there's a massive conspiracy here'. At this point, the series' main prop shuffles blinking into the light and hides behind a convenient plot device. By the beginning of the third season it is eating mad pie, drinking straight vodka, listening to Oasis at volume 11, and shouting 'LOOK AT ME, I'M THE CONSPIRACY BACK-STORY' at the top of its voice.

Unlike other successful US telefantasy series of recent years, including *Quantum Leap* (which celebrates the American dream – and works precisely because of that) and *Star Trek: The Next Generation* (which takes American liberalism to the brave frontier of the future), *The X-Files* seems somewhat embarrassed by being an American series. It's got the same outsider, fundamentally European viewpoint on America that earlier writers of American Gothic (such as Poe and Lovecraft) had. This genre covers two great fears. Firstly: this new land is supposed to be really great, but what if we've been fooled, what if it's not? That, broadly speaking, is what 'Monster of the Week' stories are about. Secondly: what if, secretly, those evil old rulers, barons and aristocrats that we thought we'd left behind in Europe followed us to America and are still in control?

Take a bow, the conspirators.

Due, perhaps, to the archetypal nature of *The X-Files'* origins ('Let's do something inspired by

Kolchak, Project UFO and *The Outer Limits'*), the series' 'Monster of the Week' credentials had never been in doubt. (By episode three, they're doing mutant serial killers with great confidence.) However, the conspiracy thread took longer to establish itself, probably because conspiracy stories often have no monsters, big effects or obvious formats. This got to be such a problem by the end of the second season that *X-Files* fans (and, more importantly, the general public) were starting to say that they didn't like the series when it became all talky, when there wasn't an obvious fantastical schtick going on. It was also being said that 'the conspiracy story' could never be satisfactorily concluded, because any logical explanation would end the series.

But things change. Efforts were made not only to put big effects and monsters into the conspiracy stories (such as the oil alien in 'Piper Maru'), and to integrate the two strands of the series into one (such as in 'Wetwired', a very necessary thing to do if you want to keep those viewers who hate the conspiracy stories watching), but to make sense of what the conspiracy stories were about. By halfway through the third season, it became clear that the production team hadn't, as the viewers had previously suspected, been making it up as they went along, painting themselves further and further into a corner with one revelation after another, until there was nowhere left to go. Rather, there did seem to be some sort of a specific idea of where the series was headed, an actual hidden back-story, which presumably has an end.

The story arc's not quite as all-encompassing as that of *Babylon 5* yet, and sometimes we wonder if it was always meant to be there (Morgan and Wong, for instance, don't seem to stick to the rules as closely as the other writers), but at least, these days, it's definitely out there.

52: 'D.P.O.'

US Transmission: 6 October 1995
UK Transmission: 19 March 1996 (Sky One)/
26 September 1996 (BBC1)
Writer: Howard Gordon
Director: Kim Manners
Cast: Giovanni Ribisi, Jack Black, Ernie Lively, Karen Witter,
Steve Makaj, Peter Anderson, Kate Robbins, Mar Andersons,
Brent Chapman, Jason Anthony Griffith

A series of probable electrocutions bring Mulder and Scully to the countryside around a lightning research centre. They find a local car mechanic who survived a strike, and was near one of the fatal ones. Darren Peter Oswald proves to be a frustrated kid with a crush on his former remedial teacher and an ability to conduct lightning and manipulate electrical objects. He restarts his boss's heart after causing him to have a cardiac arrest, and Mulder and Scully have Oswald arrested, although he is released by the sceptical local sheriff. Oswald kidnaps his teacher, having killed his best friend in a fit of pique. Cornered, he summons the lightning again, but this time it hits him. Oswald survives, and is locked up, his electrical powers apparently returning.

Don't Be in the Teaser: Jack Hammond, who makes the crucial *X-Files* error of 'Shoving the Weird Kid Around', gets zapped in his car.

How Did He Do That?: Mulder takes some tiny anomalies and makes a case out of them. When he begins to guess that Oswald can conduct or control lightning he does at least admit that 'It's a leap'.

Scully Here is a Medical Doctor: 'Based on my opinion as a Medical Doctor . . .' She does an autopsy on the charred body of one victim.

Ooze: Mulder's melting cellphone appears to exude treacle!

Scully's Rational Explanation of the Week: Erm, no: the first sign that this season they're trying to get away from the comedic inevitability of her doubts. She highlights the statistical improbabilities of lightning striking so many times, and challenges the police chief's rational explanation.

Phwoar!: Scully has used that vast FBI fashion budget to get herself some vampy sunglasses.

Dialogue Triumphs: Scully: 'I hope you're not thinking this has anything to do with government conspiracies or UFOs?'

Mulder (admiring Scully's plaster cast of a boot print): 'That's great. Now can you make me a little cherub that squirts water?'

Continuity: Mulder is familiar with T.S. Eliot ('April is the cruellest month').

The Truth: Darren Oswald, having survived being struck by lightning, gains an electrolyte imbalance and a conductive body (unless these qualities were latent in him already), can affect all manner of electrical systems, and attract lightning.

Trivia: For a story that depicts a Stephen King community, there's appropriately a lot of pop music involved, including james's 'Ring the Bells' on the jukebox, Filter's 'Hey Man, Nice Shot', the under-car view set-up from Bruce Springsteen's 'I'm On Fire' video, and teeshirts celebrating the Vandals (whose memorable song is 'Live Fast, Diarrhoea'). The Rosemarys play 'Mary Beth Clark I Love You' on TV, which is actually an excuse to name her, J. Hartling and Deb Brown, all Internet fans. The Astadourian Lightning Observatory is named after Chris Carter's PA, Mary Astadourian.

Scientific Comment: It's stated that lightning emits radio waves at a particular frequency: 8 cycles/sec. It does emit radio waves, but not just at one particular frequency.

The Bottom Line: PC: Mulder and Scully's version of Arkham Asylum continues to fill up with weird kids. The atmosphere of small-town yuck is very nicely drawn, and it's good to get back to weird kids and monsters, though the ending is (necessarily this time, I think) arbitrary. Chris Carter's credit is shown inside the drama itself at the end, on a television set that Oswald is watching, which says all sorts of things about how the series has become a defining and limiting factor in exactly the sort of mythology that Mulder investigates (an idea which it would later take Darin Morgan to mine effectively). One of these characters really should say: 'This is like an episode of *The X-Files*!' But Carter probably just thought it looked cute.

MD: I thought this was lame and bland in the extreme, with many ridiculous elements (the cop who knows all about lightning because there's a research station nearby, which we never see and has no bearing on the story) and a plot that's so slight it threatens to vanish without trace at any moment. Instead, events limp along via such contrived notions as the sheriff releasing the kid from jail. The fact that from the outset the audience knows what's going on ensures that 'D.P.O.' has about as much tension as an average episode of *George and Mildred*.

KT: 'Bummer!' As far back as 'Deep Throat' (episode two!) I discovered the series had a real problem with presenting Generation X as anything other than a joke. Here it is turned into full-blown paranoia of the worst middle-aged, middle-class bollocks imaginable. And yet, for all that, the episode is quite tasty in places. Even the groan-inducing 'He *is* lightning, we have to get to him before he *strikes* again' line (think about it!) doesn't blow it. It's *Son of Firestarter* of course, but with a mad, stressed-out quality that grows on you.

53: 'Clyde Bruckman's Final Repose'

US Transmission: 13 October 1995
UK Transmission: 26 March 1996 (Sky One)/
3 October 1996 (BBC1)
Writer: Darin Morgan

Director: David Nutter
Cast: Peter Boyle, Stu Charno, Frank Cassini,
Dwight McFee, Alex Diakun, Karin Konoval, Ken Roberts,
David MacKay, Greg Anderson

Fortune tellers are being murdered by a serial killer. A mystic, the Stupendous Yappi, is called in to psychically trace the killer, but Mulder is sceptical of the man's abilities. Another body is found by an insurance salesman, Clyde Bruckman, who seems to be cursed with the ability to know how people are going to die. Bruckman foresees Mulder's murder by the killer, and predicts that Scully will hold his hand in bed. The killer comes after Bruckman, as he had expected, but Mulder chases and, thanks to Bruckman's warning and Scully's intervention, emerges unscathed. Bruckman, however, has taken an overdose, Scully holding his hand as he dies.

Don't Be in the Teaser: Madame Zelda fails to foresee being murdered.

How Did He Do That?: Mulder leaps to the conclusion that Bruckman is precognitive, rather than the more obvious one that he's the killer. He's 'got a feeling' about it.

Scully Here is a Medical Doctor: She performs an autopsy off screen.

Ooze: Blood, entrails, eyeballs, mud, putridity and liquescence.

Scully's Rational Explanation of the Week: She and Mulder think that Yappi is just playing the odds. People see what they want to see, and Clyde is just lucky. 'I'm not one who readily believes that kind of thing.' Understatement of the decade, surely?

Phwoar!: Scully deals with Bruckman's pass with sublime calm: 'There are hits, and there are misses, and then there are misses.'

Dialogue Triumphs: Scully to Mulder, after the latter has been expelled from the room by Yappi because of his scepticism: 'I can't take you anywhere.'

Mulder: 'Mr Yappi, read this thought: –'

Bruckman reading Mulder's badge: 'I'm supposed to believe that's a real name?'

Mulder's wonderful reaction to Bruckman's apparently precognitive opinion of auto-erotic asphyxiation: 'Why are you telling *me* that?'

Bruckman to the killer: 'You do the things you do because . . . you're a homicidal maniac.'

Continuity: Scully refers to Ahab, who died, like Macbeth, because he misinterpreted a prophecy. (In 'Quagmire', we're hammered over the head with a Mulder-as-Ahab metaphor, but here he successfully interprets the prophecy, so is Mulder someday going to fall into this trap again?) Scully, asking how she's going to die, is told 'You don't.' Does this mean that Scully is going to get lost in 'missing time' forever? Or that she is not the ordinary human woman we think she is? (Did we get the real Scully back after the abduction?) Or is Bruckman just being very nice to the object of his desire?

Mulder isn't convinced by the reading of tealeaves, and claims not to be a Freudian (despite the possible Oxford degree in psychology), but he does believe in psychic ability (if not Yappi's!). He's had prophetic dreams (possibly it's just déjà vu). Bruckman misidentifies a bit of cloth as having come from Mulder's New York Knicks teeshirt, in a neat reversal reference to 'Beyond the Sea'. Satanists usually take the eyeballs and leave the body, according to Mulder, which indicates that he has investigated Satanic cults before. Scully gets to keep Mrs Lowe's dog at the end of the episode (see 'War of the Coprophages', 'Quagmire').

The Truth: Ever since he reflected on the circumstances of the Big Bopper's death in 1959, Clyde Bruckman can calculate how anybody is going to die. The universe thus seems preordained. But then a chaotic element suggests that that may not be completely true. If Bruckman was talking about himself, and not Mulder, when he referred to auto-erotic asphyxiation being an undignified way to die, he commits suicide in a more dignified way as soon as he realises that there actually is such a thing as free will.

Trivia: Bruckman's non-winning lottery numbers (if anybody fancies trying this) are 9, 13, 37, 39, 41 and 45. (The winners are all one digit lower.) *Midnight Inquisitor* is a tacky national tabloid. References are made to J.D. Salinger, Madonna and Kato Kalin, and to Buddy Holly returning from the dead to do the Lollapalooza tour with the Crickets. Mulder (inevitably!) quotes from 'Chantilly Lace' ('You *know* what I like').

Jaap (pronounced 'yapp') Broeker is actually David Duchovny's stand-in.

When playing cards with Scully, Bruckman holds 'dead man's hand' (aces and eights), the poker hand that Sheriff 'Wild Bill' Hickok was holding when he was shot in the back. Interestingly, it is said that carrying a (real) dead man's hand will ensure a restful night's sleep.

Several of the character names in this episode are drawn from the silent comedy film era, including Clyde Bruckman himself, who directed films by Laurel and Hardy and W.C. Fields amongst others. (One of his films plays in the *Space: Above and Beyond* episode 'R&R', in which David Duchovny appeared, which was written by Darin Morgan's brother Glen.) The hotel the killer works at is El Damfino, a nod to Buster Keaton's boat *Damfino* in *The Boat*. Detective Cline is named after the silent movie director Eddie Cline. Detective Havez is named after Jean C. Havez, a collaborator with the original Clyde Bruckman. The dead man under the car is Claude Dukenfield, which was the real name of W. C. Fields (another Bruckman associate). Scully watches the Laurel and Hardy movie, *The Bullfighters* (1941), their final movie for Fox during their twilight years. (It's interesting that old comedy, with all the alienation of time passing that it implies, and its contrast with the glossy production on display here, is used as a metaphor for mystery and the occult in this series ('Syzygy').)

The Bottom Line: PC: What an extraordinary piece of work. The story concerns the nature of freedom of choice, following two men who see reality as predetermined. One becomes a psychotic killer (because he can?) while the other becomes resigned and sells insurance. There are all sorts of sidelong commentaries on the nature of free will, from the dog's ghoulish actions, for which he can't really be blamed, to Bruckman's oddly beautiful view of his own destruction. But a custard pie shows that the future is actually up for grabs. The usual ghoulish and comedic, as well as deeply insightful, joys of a Darin Morgan episode are all evident, and this story shows off something he's particularly good at: an ordinary person is the centre of the story, even favoured by the direction, and Mulder and Scully are seen from his distant, slightly alienated, point of view. Altogether gorgeous.

MD: Duller than a dull thing with dull knobs on. I mean, yes, it's all very clever and well acted, but it's extremely tedious, like watching metaphysical paint dry. What actually happens here, dramatically or literally? There's a constant undercutting of tension (Bruckman being more concerned by the nature of the pie than Mulder's fate) and even the *A Zed and Two Noughts*-style surrealism seems thrown in to make up for the complete absence of plot.

KT: '. . . And so was your father!' I'm with Paul all the way on this one. A little gem that benefits from the funniest opening in *The X-Files* (the scene immediately after the opening credits is astonishing) and loads of great little asides (Bruckman trying to sell Mulder insurance, 'Say "Hi" to the FBI', etc.). However, 'if coincidences are just coincidences why do they feel so contrived?' The episode runs entirely on coincidences, from Bruckman and the killer almost meeting in the pre-titles, to the 'highly improbable' safehousing of Bruckman in the very hotel where the killer works. I suspect Darin Morgan might be having another joke on his audience with this, but it reduces the impact of a brilliant episode.

EMMY AWARDS

At the 1994 Emmy Awards ceremony *The X-Files* won a single award, that for Individual Achievement in Graphic Design and Title Sequences, won by James Castle, Bruce Bryant and Carol Johnsen. The next year was barren, despite seven nominations, but 1996 brought something of a bounty. This was the season that the series won *five* Emmys . . .

Writing, Drama Series: Darin Morgan, for 'Clyde Bruckman's Final Repose'.

Guest Actor, Drama Series: Peter Boyle, for 'Clyde Bruckman's Final Repose'.

Sound Editing for a Series: for 'Nisei'.

Sound Mixing, Drama Series: for 'Nisei'.

Individual Achievement in Cinematography for a Series: for 'Grotesque'.

54: 'The List'

US Transmission: 20 October 1995
UK Transmission: 2 April 1995 (Sky One)/
10 October 1996 (BBC1)
Writer: Chris Carter
Director: Chris Carter
Cast: Bokeem Woodbine, Badja Djola, John Toles-Bey,
Ken Foree, April Grace, J.T. Walsh, Greg Rogers,
Mitchell Kosterman, Paul Raskin, Denny Arnold,
Craig Brunanski, Joseph Patrick Finn

Taken to the electric chair, Napoleon 'Neech' Manley vows revenge. Days later, a prison guard is found murdered. Mulder and Scully discover that Neech had a list of five persecutors he was going to kill. Danielle, his widow, now has a new lover, having promised Neech that she would never love another. As more bodies are found, and all other explanations exhausted, Mulder and Scully fail to prevent the deaths of Danielle's lover and the brutal prison governor, Neech's revenge precisely concluded.

Don't Be in the Teaser: Neech Manley is executed, and we are spared none of the horrors of the electric chair. Mr Simon appears for only about thirty seconds, but he's dead meat, too.

Scully Here is a Medical Doctor: She questions the prison doctor about his autopsy, as though only her autopsies count.

Ooze: Maggots and peeling skin.

Scully's Rational Explanation of the Week: It's a conspiracy amongst prisoners and guards, with an uncaught accomplice.

Dialogue Triumphs: Scully, asked who would be on her hit list: 'I only get five?' (Which isn't like her at all, really.) Mulder responds, 'I remembered your birthday this year, didn't I, Scully?'

Scully, on Neech's wife's new partner: 'A woman gets lonely. Sometimes she can't wait around for a man to be reincarnated.'

Continuity: Scully mentions being taught by catechism, the first strong indication (beyond her cross necklace) that she was raised a Catholic (see 'Miracle Man', 'Revelations').

The Truth: Neech has, somehow, returned to life, possibly in the form of various animals ('transmigration of the soul' as he calls it). The governor and the guards are involved in systematic abuse.

Trivia: The chaplain in the teaser is played by the series producer Joseph Patrick Finn.

The Bottom Line: PC: The series isn't good at doing heat: Vancouver doubles for Florida mostly using interiors. Carter raids the media cupboard again: *The Silence of the Lambs* (again), *Candyman*, *Shocker*, and *Pulp Fiction*. The pace is slower than a sloth watching county cricket, and the twist is that the supernatural shtick is . . . exactly who and how we thought it was, right back to the teaser. The sheer professionalism of the series by now stops it being as dull as a dull first-season episode, but it's still pretty damn dull. At least Carter's social conscience is on display: capital punishment is shown as barbaric, the governor is keen to beat up his prisoners (killing them if necessary), and death row is the place where the US puts its black male prisoners.

MD: What Paul says about the good stuff is true, but what's saddest about this episode isn't so much its sampling of other texts, but its cannibalism of its own, being little more than a retread of 'Fresh Bones' (with a hint of 'Beyond the Sea' thrown in for good measure). As with the previous story, there's a crushing lack of drama, and a feeble ending that beggars belief. I'm really not sure that this is in any form an improvement over the less exciting first-season stories. Mind you, any actor with a name like Bokeem Woodbine deserves an Oscar or something in my book.

KT: 'I will return!' This is rubbish. Like all of the worst bits of every bad horror film you've ever seen stitched together into a long, disorganised, nasty mess. Good social themes and conscience, bad drama. Dreadfully incoherent ending too. Why are Mulder and Scully in this episode? They solve nothing, they achieve nothing. All that happens is that a lot of men die (some deservedly, though that's not really the point) and, at the end of the episode, Mulder and Scully leave town none the wiser – not only is there no closure, there's no point either.

55: '2Shy'

US Transmission: 3 November 1995
UK Transmission: 9 April 1996 (Sky One)
Writer: Jeffrey Vlaming
Director: David Nutter
Cast: Timothy Carhart, Catherine Paolone, James Handy,
Kerry Sandomirsky, Aloka McLean, Suzy Joachim,
Glynis Davies, Randi Lynne, William MacDonald

A man on a blind date kills his companion in a car, covering her in a dissolving ooze. Scully discovers the nature of the ooze, and meets a sexist cop, while Mulder traces a suspect from similar previous killings, theorising that the man needs fatty tissue. The man kills again, and Mulder and Scully reason his identity from the poetry he quotes from to lure victims to dates. They find his computer files, and alert every woman named in them. While Mulder is sidetracked, Scully protects the latest target and captures the killer.

Don't Be in the Teaser: Don't finish a date in a car overlooking Cleveland. You'll get cocooned like Lauren MacKelvey.

How Did He Do That?: For once, Mulder takes longer to reach the silly conclusion than the audience does.

Scully Here is a Medical Doctor: 'You're a medical doctor?' 'You sound surprised.' For once there *isn't* an autopsy, much to Scully's relief.

Ooze: Viscous hydrochloric acid plus traces of pepsin. It sucks the fat out of you, apparently.

Phwoar!: Mulder puts his arm around Scully in the police station, for no reason other than he likes it.

Dialogue Triumphs: Mulder: 'It's not the finely detailed insanity that you've come to expect from me . . .'

Dialogue Disasters: Reaction of a man with a prostitute on discovering a corpse: 'Uh-uh, forget this!'

Continuity: Wendy Sparks, the Cleveland police department FBI liaison, knew of Mulder's expertise in serial killings (and weird stuff?).

The Truth: Virgil Encanto is a 'genetically different' human who needs fatty tissue to survive, and has been getting it in the most horrid way.

Trivia: Another 10.13, the time when Mulder is telling Scully about the test results.

The Bottom Line: PC: Despite several dodgy moments (the

world's most gorgeous hooker, a villain called Virgil Encanto, the idea that being a 'freelance translator of Italian literature' is a good living and that sixteenth-century Italian poetry would turn anybody on), this is a highly effective, and rather gooey, examination of the darker areas of the patriarchy. If the sexist cop is very clichéd, the further examination of a female nightmare is very subtle. Encanto's message that his victims don't have to do what's expected of them is extremely seductive, but it's a feminist message used to a sexist end. This monster preys, literally, on those with body-image problems (although, typically, Lauren is hardly somebody with 'a weight problem'). Scully is ambushed in a bathroom (again), but this time wins the bout, part of the third season's empowering of the character, and also apt for the story. The actor playing the killer is fab, he's given a great theme by Mark Snow, and the script is realistic about the frailty of human desire. At the end, Mulder and Scully's personal Arkham Asylum gets another inmate. Odd moment: Duchovny's weird and bad reaction shot on 'There is not going to be an autopsy'.

MD: Looks fine to me. Anyway, I like the feminism that runs through this story, as Paul indicates (most notably Scully and the 'victim' defeating the masculine manipulator), but it is a shame to watch *The X-Files* treading water so. This reminds one of an unused Tooms script, and it's not even that good.

KT: 'I don't know too many scorpions who surf the Internet.' It's a nice idea, using an Internet background to the murders, though only a technophobe would seriously suggest (as this episode seems to) that the medium is populated by ugly fat girls and psycho-killer men. And there's that cock-and-bull back-story about that annoying woman who wants the killer to read her poems (her death doesn't come a minute too soon for *this* writer), and her blind daughter. Your point being, Jeffrey? OK, now, here's the Major Inconsistency: Encanto requires fat to replace a chemical imbalance in his body. An imbalance he has, presumably, had since birth (he tells Jesse as much). So, how did he survive until he discovered that he could suck fat from others? How old was he when he started killing? At least with Tooms there is a plausible explanation for why he's never been caught (he hibernates for thirty years between murder sprees). Encanto is an academic, which suggests a long period spent in education of one sort or another. How on Earth hasn't he made a mistake before now? (As a friend of mine pointed out shortly after this episode was broadcast, his school life must have been a laugh and a half: 'Now I'd like the person who sucked all of the fat out of Jennifer Smith in form 2B to own up . . .')

56: 'The Walk'

US Transmission: 10 November 1995
UK Transmission: 16 April 1996 (Sky One)
Writer: John Shiban
Director: Rob Bowman
Cast: Thomas Kopache, Willie Garson, Don Thompson,
Nancy Sorel, Ian Tracey, Paula Shaw, Deryl Hayes, Rob Lee,
Andrea Barclay, Beatrice Zeilinger

Mulder and Scully investigate a number of apparent suicide attempts at an army veterans' hospital, and find their way blocked by General Callahan. The ghost of a soldier seems to be haunting the place. After more deaths, Quinton Freely, a meek nurse, is arrested, since he delivered mail to all the victims' homes. But it turns out that he's working for Sergeant Leonard Trimble, an amputee who has killed all the victims remotely through some kind of telekinesis. Quinton is suffocated, and, his wife and child having been attacked, the general goes to execute Trimble, stopping when he realises that that's just what Trimble wants. One of Trimble's former victims, badly burnt, suffocates Trimble.

Don't Be in the Teaser: Lt. Col. Victor Stans *fails* to die by boiling himself; his third failed suicide in as many weeks ('He won't let us die').

How Did He Do That?: Mulder accuses a quadruple amputee of murder. Talk about committed!

Ooze: Stans's face.

Scully's Rational Explanation of the Week: Shell-shock, post-traumatic stress syndrome, and (she's getting a bit more open-minded) she won't rule out Gulf War Syndrome. The general is protecting his men from prosecution for the murder of their families.

Dialogue Triumphs: Mulder: 'Sometimes the only sane response to an insane world is insanity.'

Trimble (to Scully): 'If I could leave my body right now, I could think of something else I'd rather be doing!'

Continuity: Scully is familiar with how to get her way in a military bureaucracy, doubtless a family life skill. Mulder is still writing his reports longhand into his journal.

The Truth: Trimble can use astral projection to affect objects at a distance, send backwards phone messages, and appear as a remote image. He receives some help from Roach, stealing mail to provide Trimble with a 'psychic connection'.

Trivia: Trimble mentions Fred Astaire, while watching a Fred and Ginger movie.

Scientific Comment: If a dental X-ray plate was exposed to radiation it would be fogged all over, not show stripes; although, if it was covered by something like a comb, you'd get a picture of the comb.

The Bottom Line: PC: It's good to see Scully taking Mulder's side so much by now, as the third season's subtle character arcs get under way. There's a nice *Cat People* quote in the pool scene, which works because it surprises with a menace from another direction: inside the pool. It is also a surprise that dental X-rays can pick up astral projection, but a pleasant one that the series' only use of 'back-masking' is for a cool sound effect. This is, however, one of those stories in which the cause of the problem is obvious straight away, with an ending full of mock weight, and ends up being oddly dull.

MD: A definite improvement on previous stories, with a newish modus operandi and an age-old hatred of war on display.

KT: 'He kills our wives and children, but he won't let us die.' Hmmm ... The swimming-pool scene, and little Trevor's death in his sandpit, are terrifying. But I can't help thinking this is just a series of nice set pieces strung together for effect. Mind you, a touch of Gulf War Guilt Syndrome (like Vietnam Guilt Syndrome but less defeat-orientated!) gives the episode a nice edge. And I love that line about people sitting at home watching the war on cable as if it was a video game. Which is *exactly* what I did and, I suspect, most of the rest of the audience did, too. Part of an ongoing hidden agenda by the producers to get the viewer to confront his/her own demons (see also the next episode).

57: 'Oubliette'

US Transmission: 17 November 1995
UK Transmission: 23 April 1996 (Sky One)/
17 October 1996 (BBC1)
Writer: Charles Grant Craig
Director: Kim Manners
Cast: Tracey Ellis, Michael Chieffo, Jewel Staite, Ken Ryan,
Dean Wray, Jacques LaLonde, David Fredericks,
Sidonie Boll, Robert Underwood, Dolly Scarr, Bonnie Hay,
David Lewis

Amy Jacobs is kidnapped, and Lucy Householder, who was held for five years in similar circumstances, seems to know too much about the case. The blood from her nosebleed is of Amy's rather than her own blood group, and she becomes a suspect, despite Mulder's sympathy for her and his conviction that she's experiencing Amy's plight directly. Mulder and Scully track down the real kidnapper, Karl Wade. Lucy goes to the oubliette under Wade's house, where she was imprisoned long ago. Wade has already fled with Amy, but, from Lucy's reaction, Mulder realises where they are. Mulder shoots Wade in a nearby river. Amy stays underwater too long, but Lucy 'drowns' in her place, thus saving her and ending the trauma.

Don't Be in the Teaser: Amy Jacobs gets snatched from her bed, and, at the same time, Lucy falls into a mumbling trance.

How Did He Do That?: Mulder doesn't leap to the obvious weird conclusion in front of the others if it means that Lucy's a suspect. But the idea that, having been in front of dozens of witnesses when Amy was taken, she is a suspect at all strains credibility.

Scully Here is a Medical Doctor: She investigates the blood types of Amy and Lucy.

Scully's Rational Explanation of the Week: Mulder's identification of Lucy with his sister stops him acting rationally. Lucy is Wade's accomplice in a reverse abused/abuser scenario.

Phwoar!: Mulder is very huggable and vulnerable when he introduces a slight stutter into the line about his sister. The geek beneath the cool exterior is revealed.

Dialogue Triumphs: Mulder (in response to Scully's assertion about Samantha): 'Not everything I do and say and think and feel goes back to my sister . . .'

Continuity: Mulder doesn't hesitate to kill Wade to save Amy. (He's clearly learnt the lesson of his early indecision ('Young at Heart'), although, to be fair here, Amy is being drowned and is in little danger of being inadvertently shot.) Mulder seems to have a good working knowledge of resuscitation technique (standard FBI training?). Neither Mulder nor Scully seems to smoke.

The Truth: Lucy gains an instant empathy with Amy when

she is kidnapped by the same man, to the extent of seeing what she sees, bleeding for her, and transporting water from her lungs into hers, breaking all sorts of physical laws. Mulder's explanation, 'empathic transference', is logically impossible, but seems to fit.

The Bottom Line: PC: This looks great, and manages to create another female nightmare without a hint of exploitation. The wet, leafy countryside becomes a character, as it does in all the best episodes. Just a hint of the paranormal, and it doesn't detract from Amy's terrible situation in the slightest.

MD: Indeed, one of the better 'almost normal' episodes, though the pace is somewhat pedestrian. It's fascinating to observe that initially Scully is shown as pursuing a theory based on 'coincidence' (the second blood type found on Lucy's clothes) and Mulder is more interested in compassionately protecting a former victim.

KT: 'I've got my own set of problems now, thank you.' Kidnapping is a federal crime, so it's surprising that it has taken Mulder and Scully two years to get invited on to a case. Then again, this is a *strange* kidnapping. There's another *JFK* reference (the 'photo-cutting' scene). It's difficult to know exactly what the writer was trying to say here, except that no one is innocent. In a nutshell, this disturbing episode forces the viewer to focus on their own dark corners. Scully's normal persona of disbelief can be very irritating (e.g. 'The Calusari'), but here it would be downright insulting if the persecuted Lucy were a slightly more sympathetic character. But here is the problem: this poor woman has every reason to be pissed off given what she had been through. However, viewer expectation requires that she accept her fate without complaint. Which makes her sacrifice all the more upsetting. Not one to watch after a few beers if you're looking to get cheered up. Amy seems to be wearing her socks in bed. Hasn't anybody told her that they get covered in fluff when you do that?

58: 'Nisei'

US Transmission: 24 November 1995
UK Transmission: 30 April 1996 (Sky One)/
24 October 1996 (BBC1)
Writers: Chris Carter, Howard Gordon, Frank Spotnitz
Director: David Nutter
Cast: Stephen McHattie, Robert Ito, Gillian Barber,
Corrine Koslo, Lori Triolo, Paul McLean, Yasuo Sakurai

A group of Japanese scientists examine an apparent alien in a railway car, and are killed. Mulder buys a video of the autopsy, and investigates the supplier, only to find that he's been murdered. At the scene, a Japanese agent is captured, but is freed when it is discovered that he is a high-ranking diplomat. His briefcase contains satellite photos of a ship and a list of local members of a UFO group, MUFON. Scully meets a group of former abductees, who recognise her as one of their number, and Mulder searches the shipyard, seeing a strange craft at the docks, apparently brought in on the ship. He is visited by Skinner, who says that the Japanese man has been murdered and that his briefcase is being sought. Mulder turns to Senator Matheson, who tells him to give the photos from the case back, for his own safety. Scully gets her implant examined, and remembers some details of her abduction, enough to recognise that one of the men who took her was a Japanese war criminal, who was in the railway car. Mulder finds a train carrying another apparent alien, and, despite Scully and X's pleas not to do so, boards it.

Don't Be in the Teaser: A group of Japanese scientists are shot down by armed men.

How Did He Do That?: How did Steven Zinzer get hold of a video copy of the autopsy and the murder of the scientists? That story about pulling it off the satellite at 2 a.m. sounds false, and, even if it is true, who was broadcasting it to whom? And why?

Dialogue Triumphs: Scully, on the video: 'This is even hokier than the one they aired on the Fox network.'

On the green substance: 'Olive oil, snake oil . . . I suppose you think it's alien blood.'

The Conspiracy Starts at Closing Time: X knows exactly what Mulder is up to, indicating that he is under surveillance most of the time. Skinner is still acting suspiciously in wanting to recover the Japanese agent's briefcase, but, having broken ties with the Smoking Man, he probably just wants to avoid a diplomatic incident (and to protect Mulder and Scully – though when he realises the extent of the hot water they've got themselves into he backs off like a scalded cat). Scully remembers a bright, white place, a drill bit, and her stomach being distended (which, in previous episodes, we were encouraged to believe was only Mulder's imagination working overtime). She bears a mark on the back of her neck from where the implant was extracted. Many of the abductees suffer from cancers (from radiation exposure? – see '731').

Continuity: Senator Richard Matheson is on the Intelligence Committee, and can't tell Mulder everything he knows (a significant step up on his earlier position, where he seemed to be in the dark and trying to discover the answers: see 'Little Green Men') – although there are, in turn, things that he is not aware of. Scully has told Mulder of her experiences in the deserted mine, and a reference is made to her attempted regression hypnosis in 'Paper Clip'. Mulder carries a second gun in an ankle holster (the implication being that this is a recent development – 'I get tired of losing my gun'). Mulder says that it's widely held that aliens don't have blood (an ironic comment, considering his own plight at being exposed to it – see 'The Erlenmeyer Flask'). Scully seems to have moved since 'The Blessing Way'. She now lives in an apartment (number 5).

The Truth: The commander of Japanese Medical Corps unit 731, who experimented on human captives during the war, was Dr Ishimaru. He was brought to the USA as part of Paper

Clip, and was one of the humans who presided over Scully's abduction.

Trivia: The series' only mention of Vancouver. There's a rather crap indication that all villains adjust their hair after violence, as Krycek does in 'Ascension'. (Let's hope it's just mining a joke once too often, and not a plot-related motif like the Smoking Man's cigarettes . . .) Agent Pendrell is named after Pendrell Street in Vancouver.

The Bottom Line: PC: The revelation that Scully was abducted by human beings is very shocking, and pulls the tablecloth from under one's expectations so much that one is tempted to forgive the conspiracy episodes all their other flaws. A step back from the mystery was needed, and, while leaving the audience going 'but . . . but . . .', this is a brilliant coup. The investment in this episode is huge: trains and boats, all there before our eyes, and there's a wonderful camera pan in the teaser. That said, this episode emphasises that the icons and design of the conspiracy episodes are all the same: cases in car boots; helicopters; running gunmen; McGuffin pieces of evidence; boxcars; war criminals; lengthy speeches in the series' patent form of Diet David Mamet. There are also the trademark Stupid Moments, those images that work only because of the utter commitment of all concerned. Why, for example, does Skinner come all the way to Pennsylvania for three lines? How do the *Lone Gunman* editors make out the name of a ship with their magnifying glass? And isn't the scene of all the abductees sitting in the lounge wonderfully silly? ('Why are you all at her house?') Oh, and Paul McLean, who plays the Coast Guard Officer, turns in a truly horrible performance.

MD: This starts well but tails off a little, although there's always enough going on to keep the viewer pleasantly entertained.

KT: 'Monsters begetting Monsters!' A very confusing episode, albeit one that seems to have an idea where it's going. Some great touches (the first scene with a man waving at passing children from the Boxcar of Death! or that great bit where all of the abductees get out plastic bottles containing their implants and rattle them at Scully!). The Japanese diplomat Mulder tackles is the worst Kung Fu ninja in the history of US television (Mulder beats him, for goodness' sake!). Visually stunning, however.

59: '731'

US Transmission: 1 December 1995
UK Transmission: 7 May 1996 (Sky One)/
31 October 1996 (BBC1)
Writer: Frank Spotnitz
Director: Rob Bowman
Cast: Stephen McHattie, Michael Puttonen, Robert Ito,
Colin Cunningham

Mulder hunts for Ishimaru on the train. Scully, investigating her implant, finds that a shipment of them were sent to a Dr Zama, at an institute in West Virginia. The place is a camp for deformed people, victims of Hansen's Disease, who were experimented on by Zama. Recently, these victims were all killed, their bodies thrown into a pit. Mulder sees a similar creature on the train, in a separate boxcar. He's attacked by the NSA agent who has already killed Zama (who is in reality Ishimaru). The man's mission was to stop Ishimaru getting the creature out of the country. He tells Mulder that there's a bomb on the train. Scully, meanwhile, meets the Elder from the conspiracy, who tells her that the Hansen's Disease victims were, along with various other minority groups, exposed to diseases and radiation. Scully manages to deduce the exit codes for the boxcar, but the NSA man attacks Mulder again. The agent leaves, but is shot by X, who saves Mulder from the ensuing explosion. Mulder has Ishimaru's journals, but he discovers that they're useless, having been rewritten. The Smoking Man has the real ones.

Don't Be in the Teaser: Hundreds of apparent Hansen's

Disease sufferers are herded into vans, taken out and shot by the US military.

Scully Here is a Medical Doctor: She knows that Hansen's Disease is the proper name for leprosy.

Scully's Rational Explanation of the Week: 'There is no such thing as alien abduction.' In this case at least, she's probably right.

Phwoar!: Agent Pendrell has a boyish crush on Scully.

Dialogue Triumphs: Mulder, pointing a gun at the NSA man: 'As an employee of the National Security Agency, you should know that a gunshot wound to the stomach is probably the most painful and the shortest way to die. But I'm not a very good shot, and when I miss, I tend to miss low.'

'Scully, let me tell you, you haven't seen America until you've seen it from a train!'

The Conspiracy Starts at Closing Time: The NSA man says that the 'leper' in the boxcar is suffering from haemorrhagic fever, although by the end it seems pretty clear that the man is a soldier 'prototype', immune to radiation poisoning and the effects of biological warfare. However, given that this is the very disease that the Smoking Man mentioned he'd been involved in preventing the spread of ('F. Emasculata'), is it possible that this earlier incident involved an experimental 'victim' too? Haemorrhagic fever is a disease transmitted through blood, so is the conspiracy attempting to mimic the shapeshifters' blood in humans (which had some very powerful effects in 'The Erlenmeyer Flask')? If the conspiracy is creating soldiers (see 'The Red Museum' for further experimentation into disease resistance, and 'Sleepless' for other experimentation on military personnel), presumably it is preparing to fight a war. But against whom? Will this army fight for them in conquering the Earth, or are they preparing to battle a foe like the whiteout aliens? Or is their military thinking simply that they need to develop this new weapon (the ultimate soldier) before another power (Japan?) does?

Scully's computer chip is a neural network that replicates her thoughts and possibly transmits them (although this is unlikely, given the fact that the conspiracy remains ignorant of X's subversion). It's made by a Japanese company. X knows about the shooting of Scully's sister, but says he doesn't know everything (he's not one of the Elders). He seems fascinated by the mutated human: perhaps he hasn't seen one this close before. It's almost certain that he hands Ishimaru's journals over to the Smoking Man (the price of going undetected).

Continuity: Scully was brought to the boxcar during her abduction (and had what done to her?). Mulder studied French (and not Japanese!) at high school.

The Truth: The President apologised for radiation releases over the public, which ended in 1974. (Again, scary real-world stuff!) But these experiments continued, the victims being the great American underclass: the insane, the homeless, the diseased. One of the survivors at the camp tells Scully that those who were exterminated were not genuine Hansen's Disease sufferers, but rather had Hansen's-type disfigurements (presumably as a result of the experiments that Ishimaru carried out on them). What Mulder still believes to be an alien/human hybrid is more likely a human leper, a victim of this experimentation. The fat Elder is erasing the whole project, including the victims, because of the security implications involved in leaking information about it to the Japanese government. The conspiracy is (oddly) equated with the US government here. It's probable that a project this vast was acknowledged at the highest levels of government. There are also the possibilities that (a) the aliens with whom the conspiracy are involved have ordered these killings because they're against experimentation with their DNA, preferring that the purity of their race be maintained; and (b) that this forms, along with various other killings in 'The Erlenmeyer Flask', 'Red Museum', 'Colony' and 'Paper Clip', an ongoing policy of eliminating all of those involved in such work. If this is true, then Mulder is right, and that is a hybrid in the boxcar. But it's worth noting that, in those other cases, the experimenters are killed along with their work, and here it's only the victims that get exterminated.

Trivia: Mulder's home telephone number is 550199. Another 10.13 reference: the combination Scully gives Mulder to free him from the boxcar is 101331.

The Bottom Line: PC: A triumphal rabbit-out-of-hat trick. Not only do we now have a solid plot under the conspiracy stuff, but it's one with an incredible moral potency. What other series would dare suggest that the American government is actually following a Nazi eugenics policy? Can you imagine the British equivalent? (Tony Clark of *Between the Lines* stumbles across MI5 systematically exterminating Pakistanis.) It takes both a fantasy series, and the decay of the American Union (and the resulting death of rationality and trust), to make such a vast fictional accusation seem vaguely credible. It's such a brave and left-wing thing to do (although, in the USA, such beliefs are the nadir of right-wing isolationism) that it's scarcely credible they could have got away with it. Scully, quite rightly, thinks that this is the central problem that they should from now on concern themselves with, and starts to see Mulder's preoccupation with aliens as simply decadent. That message, from a series that used to have its head in the clouds, is astonishing.

MD: The background story does indeed become ever more fascinating, but I'm not sure that '731' works as well as some of the other conspiracy stories, although there are nice touches (notably the Scully–Pendrell interchange).

KT: 'What was he exposing those people to?' 'Terrible things.' A huge, allegorical fascist nightmare (anybody who doesn't think 'Belsen' when Scully looks into the open grave clearly isn't following where this storyline is going). A complex narrative that, in its final moments, suddenly, and quite without warning, changes the focus of the series forever. The *Between the Lines* simile suggested by Paul is interesting in that it is possibly the only other series recently to get into the grey areas of government and disinformation that *The X-Files* is playing with here. A work of terrible beauty.

Those of us who were reading *Fortean Times* before *The X-Files* came along became happily certain of what sort of cases Mulder and Scully would be covering very quickly. The world they inhabit is broadly the world that Charles Fort, collector of strange tales and anomalous stories, described in books such as *Lo!*. Fort's legacy is *FT*, a magazine that takes the viewpoint of neither Mulder nor Scully, but settles for something in between, a kind of entertained uncertainty and willingness to learn more. Episodes of the series that seem to be influenced by the real-world cases that the magazine describes include 'Deep Throat' (the USAF technology, including the wedge-shaped craft, previously unseen in media SF); 'Space' (which reflected the magazine's tales of astronaut encounters with aliens, and its fascination with the 'face on Mars'); 'E.B.E.' (a feast of Fortean references, including stealth helicopters, the Roswell incident and captured aliens) and the Duane Barry episodes (in which we see the whole myth of alien abduction). Images from Fortean folklore crop up too, like the mutant being led along in 'Nisei', a near-copy of a famous Fortean photo. It's true that the comic strip seems more willing to take on the mythos of the Fortean world (the shapeshifters, for instance, which are a staple of the TV series, are a pure invention, owing nothing to modern mythology), but with episodes such as 'Jose Chung's *From Outer Space*', even the TV series has started to ponder the nature of truth and the paranormal experience. Once, *Fortean Times* was the leading journal of a minority group, those who thought that the entire truth about the world was not evident, or was even secret. Now, thanks to *The X Files* and the paranormal culture it's revived, such beliefs are more plausible, and even fashionable. Episodes such as 'Jose Chung' examine the idea that the traffic between TV series and perceived reality is two-way, that *The X-Files* has shaped the mythology that *FT* is now reporting. That cross-fertilisation of folklore is an area of great interest to Forteans. Case in point: a drawing of a UFO in issue 92, a wedge-shaped craft with the detailing of one of the models seen in the series. One wonders if it would have looked that way five years ago . . .

60: 'Revelations'

US Transmission: 15 December 1995
UK Transmission: 14 May 1996 (Sky One)/
27 November 1996 (BBC1)
Writer: Kim Newton
Director: David Nutter
Cast: Kevin Zegers, Sam Bottoms, Kenneth Welsh,
Michael Berryman, Hayley Tyson, R. Lee Ermey,
Lesley Ewen, Fulvio Cecere, Nicole Robert

Mulder seeks the killer of eleven fake stigmatics. Kevin, a boy who is a real stigmatic and has a religious maniac for a father, looks like being the next victim when he's kidnapped by a man called Jarvis. Mulder and Scully find Kevin, but Jarvis escapes, and is murdered by the real killer, Gates, a man with hands that can burn. Mulder and Scully try to protect Kevin, but the killer abducts him again, and takes him to a recycling plant where he intends to kill him. Scully, based on the merest hint from Kevin's father, intuits that she needs to go there, and she saves the boy.

Don't Be in the Teaser: A (false) stigmatic priest is killed by a member of his congregation.

How Did He Do That?: This time, he doesn't. Mulder is rational in the face of Scully's leaps of faith, going so far as to allege, with a straight face, that the killer used an acetylene torch to melt the bars, and that the man is being driven by the 'Jerusalem Syndrome'. One gets the feeling that he's enjoying showing Scully how it feels to be on the receiving end of unbreakable rationalism.

Scully Here is a Medical Doctor: She does an autopsy on Jarvis, and comes to the unmedical conclusion that the body isn't decaying and smells of roses. (Mulder appears not to agree, at least on the latter point.)

Scully's Leap of Faith: 'I believe He can create miracles.'

Mulder's Rational Explanation of the Week: Kevin, disturbed by his father's institutionalisation, wounded himself. Religious stories are 'hagiographic fabrications, not historical truths', and, 'parables, metaphors for the truth'.

Phwoar!: Scully getting all maternal is strangely arousing. Mulder complains that she never runs a bath for him after she does this for Kevin.

Dialogue Triumphs: Mulder: 'Looks like Kevin was abducted by Homer Simpson's evil twin.'

Scully (during the autopsy): 'Mulder, would you do me a favour? Would you smell Mr Jarvis?'

Mulder on the 'fanatics': 'They give bona fide paranoiacs like myself a bad name.'

Continuity: There's another mention made of catechism (see 'The List'). Scully believes in Armageddon, was raised a Catholic (see 'Miracle Man'), but it's been six years since her last confession. She says she's not sure why she drifted away from the Church. Mulder thinks that the Bible is metaphorical, not the truth itself, and he doesn't get out of bed on Sundays (which, if Duchovny is right and Mulder is Jewish, isn't entirely a matter of being without faith).

The Truth: Simon Gates, a rich executive, returns from Jerusalem with the ability to heat things with his hands. His quarry, Kevin, can (intermittently) appear in two places at once, and can disappear from sight (as, it seems, can Jarvis!). He seems to suffer from genuine stigmata (although, as with much real-world stigmatism, one is somewhat puzzled by the positioning of the 'nail wounds': in the palms, as per tradition but at variance with biological possibility, rather than in the wrists, as attested archaeologically). From their behaviour, one might assume that Kevin is some religious deity, and Simon an agent of a dark force, but this is never made explicit. Gates may be trying to bring on Armageddon (an odd aim for an agent of Satan, considering that the Bible has the Devil losing that final battle), or avoid it and usher in a 'New Age'.

Scientific Comment: The sun turning to darkness and the moon to blood are references to solar and lunar eclipses.

The Bottom Line: PC: The tension in Mulder and Scully's relationship becomes greater, the wisecracking muted, along the same issue as last week: are Mulder's obsessions really what an intelligent person should concern themselves with? Or are there even more things in heaven and earth? This episode very neatly reverses their roles, managing to make Scully's scepticism understandable, open her up and increase her role. The episode also succeeds in mining the vast divide between religious belief and paranormal belief, exploring why the two can't sit together comfortably. One such titbit thrown up is the delicious question of whether antipsychotic drugs can prevent religious experiences. Amidst such depth and subtlety, it's sad that, because of fears about offending the audience, we're not actually allowed to discover what the nature of the battle represented here is. If the villain is working for the 'New Age', then that's the whole of the New Age community (and what percentage of the viewers would that be?) branded as Satanists. If it's the other way round, and Gates is trying to bring on Armageddon, then we've actually had the Antichrist and the Messiah in this week's episode, struggling in a recycling plant. Hmm, I begin to see the problem. Whatever, it's still an extraordinary episode.

MD: I wouldn't worry too much about the New-Agersas-Satanists thing, Paul. One nutter does not a blanket generalisation make (and if I had a pound for every time that Christians are presented as bigots, busybodies, puritans or simply insane by the media ... I'd be quite rich by now, actually). Still, as you say, this is the episode's major flaw: you're not left with any option but to see Gates as a loony and Kevin as a lad who, by the episode's end, is beginning to believe his mad father's 'hype'. Despite the unusual abilities on display, the episode is purposefully shorn of any biblical power or symbolism, making the whole thing somewhat lifeless. It works reasonably well as an X-File, but Scully's character changes beyond all recognition, and you've got to be worried by any writer who thinks St Ignatius is a character in the Bible.

KT: 'You must come full circle to find the truth.' If *I* had a pound for every time *The X-Files* has shagged up its religious position, I'd have almost enough to buy a copy of this book. This is halfway towards being a great episode (*The X-Files* doing the second coming is a delicious idea – even if the Son of God is known as Kevin this time around). But then they ruin it, and they ruin it through a very unlikely source. Mulder. Having Mulder 'go Scully' on us (and her) in 'Beyond the Sea' was inspired because it had conceptual depth. Here it's just an angry rant from a writer who seems to have gained all of her understanding of religion and the religious from an afternoon in Sunday school. That apart, visually influenced by *The Dead Zone*, and conceptually by *The Omen II* (well, sort of!), and with a good ending, 'Revelations' works on most levels. And, even for a series that seems to delight in hiring weird-looking actors, this episode takes the biscuit.

61: 'War of the Coprophages'

US Transmission: 5 January 1996
UK Transmission: 21 May 1996 (Sky One)
Writer: Darin Morgan

Director: Kim Manners
Cast: Bobbie Phillips, Raye Birk, Dion Anderson, Bill Dow,
Alex Bruhanski, Ken Kramer, Alan Buckley, Maria Herrera,
Sean Allan, Norma Wick, Wren Robertz, Tom Heaton,
Bobby L. Stewart, Dawn Stofer, Fiona Roeske

Mulder stumbles across a series of killings apparently caused
by cockroaches with very hard exoskeletons. He visits a
Department of Agriculture building that turns out to be a
replica of an ordinary house, given over to studying cockroaches. There he meets Bambi, an entomologist. He goes to
see an inventor of robot insects, who speculates that the metal
bugs might be alien probes. Scully arrives amidst panic in the
town. The director of the local methane plant, where Mulder
thinks the bugs might be refuelling on dung, goes crazy
because of the infestation, and fires his gun, blowing the place
up. Bambi and the inventor walk off into the twilight, the
bugs having flown away.

Don't Be in the Teaser: To full-on horror-movie music, Dr
Bugger (!) the exterminator is killed by cockroaches! If you
have lunches, prepare to lose them now.

Ooze: Oh no! Ick! Grooooo! Apart from the bugs themselves,
there's a continuing meditation on the theme of dung. Scully
even eats Choco Droppings.

Scully's Phone-In Rational Explanation of the Week: The
whole idea of alien life is, apparently, anti-Darwinian
(what?) and astronomically improbable. The victims have (in
order) an allergy to cockroaches (anaphylatic shock), died as
the result of a psychotic drug-induced delusion (Eckbalm
Syndrome), and have, erm, been straining too hard on the
toilet.

That's a Mouthful: Scully: 'I'm not going to ask you if you
just said what I think you just said because I know it's what
you just said!'

Phwoar!: Mulder is fascinated by Bambi, who thinks UFOs

are nocturnal insect swarms. They manage about a quarter of a kiss, nodding their heads towards each other invitingly. 'Does my scientific detachment disturb you?' He's obviously into weird sceptics, but that doesn't stop Scully getting a bit snappy. As she tells Bambi, loading her gun in a very professional manner, 'This is no place for an entomologist.'

Dialogue Triumphs: 'Dr Bugger', on freezing roaches: 'Where's the fun in that?'

Mulder: '. . . just because I work for the federal government doesn't mean I'm an expert on cockroaches.'

Mulder to Bambi: 'What's a woman like you doing in a place like this?'

Mulder hangs up on Scully while he's with Bambi: 'Not now.'

Scully: 'Her name is Bambi?' Mulder: 'Both of her parents were naturalists.'

Mulder on his close encounter with the praying mantis: '. . . as a result I screamed – *not* a girlie scream . . .' (See 'Jose Chung's *From Outer Space*'!)

Bambi (on the cockroach under the microscope): 'He's hung like a club-tailed dragonfly.'

Scully (watching Bambi and Dr Ivanov going off together): 'Smart *is* sexy.'

Continuity: Scully's exciting weekend at home involves eating a plate of greens and a tub of ice cream, with a glass of water, reading *Breakfast at Tiffany's*, and defleaing her dog (see 'Clyde Bruckman's Final Repose', 'Quagmire'). She always assumes it's Mulder on the phone (so much for that life she claimed to want a couple of seasons back). Mulder hates insects, having had a 'praying mantis epiphany' in a tree, although he's quite happy to handle them. (The head of a mantis *does* look very like the head of a little grey alien . . .) Mulder spends his time chasing lights in the sky. But then, everybody knew that anyway. This case is given the file no. 667386 (Mulder puts the file to good use at the episode end).

The Truth: There may have been some robot insects feeding on dung, and they may have been alien probes. But the deaths might well have been incidental, exacerbated by hysteria.

Trivia: Five seconds of *The Seven Year Itch* is glimpsed as one of the characters in the hotel is changing TV channels. (We suspect a joke, but, aside from the 'itch' bit, we don't get it.) The movie *Planet of the Apes* is quoted from. Twice! (A cool sidelong glance at another species inheriting the Earth.) On the subject of invasion, there are lots of visual references to *The War of the Worlds* (and the town's name, Miller's Grove, is derived from Grover's Mill, the location of the first Martian landing in Orson Welles's radio version). *Breakfast at Tiffany's* was the answer (or, to be exact, question) that cost David Duchovny the game when he appeared on *Jeopardy*. The TV news reporter, Skye Leikin, is a reference to fan Leikin Skye, who won a trivia contest to be named on screen. The name A. Ivanov is a nod to I. Asimov, who devised the Three Laws of Robotics. Dr Bambi Berenbaum is named after Dr May R. Berenbaum, Head of Entomology at the University of Illinois, and an authority on insects.

Scientific Comment: It is impossible to agree with Scully when she dismisses the possibility of extraterrestrial life on grounds of anti-Darwinianism. Given the size of the universe, it's almost inconceivable that there would be no other life out there. Once you have life, Darwinian evolution implies that it will become intelligent through survival of the fittest. And keeping beer in liquid nitrogen would freeze it solid.

The Bottom Line: PC: Wa-hey! Not only an honest-to-goodness monster story that has viewers crawling up the walls (the 'bug across the lens' gag is fab), but a hilariously ironic commentary on Mulder and Scully's relationship (they're trying to get back to their friendship, but they're physically separated, and Mulder wants to demonstrate to Scully that he's a single man), and an inquiry into the nature of mystery to boot. You get the feeling that Morgan would have liked to have his insect protagonists vanish into mist completely, and that only the concrete nature of the typical *X-Files* plot stopped him.

Still: there's only one Darin Morgan. In any other series, his literate, passionate, scatological and ironic ventures into sheer style would stick out like a sore backside. Here, to the series' credit, he seems to be at home.

MD: The best Darin Morgan script so far: the balance is flawless, and the running gag about Scully not coming to Massachusetts is gorgeous. I love the scene of Scully in the supermarket, encountering the woman who's not seen roaches 'but they're everywhere', and the man fearful of the Ebola virus ('We're all going to be bleeding from our nipples!'). The ensuing chaos when she tries to reassure everyone says a lot about most people's attitude to authority when it comes to matters of health and safety. The direction is flawless, although – and despite the horrible toes of the man who dies in the motel! – for once I'm not sure it's nasty enough. And as I typed those words a shield bug landed on my monitor. Spooky.

KT: I think this might be one we all agree on! This is an *Avengers* episode on acid. Flawlessly researched (every character seems to be an expert on something – except Scully who's an expert on *everything*), and with a neat line in 'bugs' jokes (that roach-crawling-across-the-screen sequence made me fall out of my chair the first time I saw it). And we've got two of the grossest moments in TV history (the dude with cockroaches in his arm, and, even worse, the guy on the toilet). It seems churlish to criticise any aspect of this, though they've done Generation X up the Khyber again. *Star Trek: The Next Generation* hire Steven Hawking. *The X-Files* takes the piss. A necessary difference, I think! Can I skip the next few episodes and go straight to reviewing 'Jose Chung'?

62: 'Syzygy'

US Transmission: 26 January 1996
UK Transmission: 28 May 1996 (Sky One)/
13 November 1996 (BBC1)

Writer: Chris Carter
Director: Rob Bowman
Cast: Dana Wheeler-Nicholson, Wendy Benson,
Lisa Robin Kelly, Garry Davey, Denalda Williams,
Gabrielle Miller, Ryan Reynolds, Tim Dixon, Ryk Brown,
Jeremy Radick, Russell Porter

Three high-school boys are killed, the townsfolk blaming
Satanic cultists. Two girls, Terri Roberts and Margi Kleinjan,
who were with the last victim, have confirmed the involvement of dark rituals. The boy's coffin combusts at the funeral,
and, against Scully's protests, Mulder and his new friend,
Detective Angela White, visit a local astrologer. The two girls
psychically trap a boy who offends them behind seating in the
gym, killing him. The local people dig up a field and find
some bones, but they turn out to be those of a dog. Terri and
Margi terrorise and murder another girl. While Mulder and
Scully are distracted by Mulder's out-of-character tryst with
White, the girls fall out over a boy, who gets killed in the
crossfire, and accuse each other of the murder. They confront
each other in the police station as the mob arrives, causing
havoc, but, as midnight passes, their powers pass with it.

Don't Be in the Teaser: Jay de Boom falls into the clutches
of Shampoo's psychotic twin sisters and gets well hung.

Scully Here is a Medical Doctor: She investigates the coffin
in gloves.

Scully's Rational Explanation of the Week: Embalm-
ing fluid combusts, and the people are subject to 'rumour
panic'.

Phwoar!: 'I was hoping you could help me solve the mystery
of the horny beast . . .' Mulder, in the middle of a vast lovers'
tiff with Scully (continuing their alienation following the
train incident), goes after Detective White, allowing her to
leap on top of him. Of course, it's because everybody's acting
out of character, Mulder drinking rough vodka and orange

while Scully smokes (and paces like an alley cat) in the next room. When she bursts in on him, it's as if the ghosts of Hattie Jacques and Kenneth Williams have entered the building. She's certainly upset that he's still trying to display his sexuality: 'the big macho man . . .'

Mulder sniffs Scully at one point.

Dialogue Triumphs: According to Mulder, Scully is 'Rigid in a wonderful way.'

Mulder to Scully on the plastic gloves: 'I know how much you like snapping on the latex.'

Mulder on why he usually drives: 'I was just never sure your little feet could reach the pedals.'

'That's a bad thing?' 'Bad like an Irwin Allen movie!'

The continuing mantra of disaffection between the two agents: 'Sure. Fine. Whatever.'

Continuity: Mulder says he doesn't normally drink (compare 'Deep Throat'). His credit card is good for three hundred dollars.

The Truth: An alignment of Mercury, Mars and Uranus on the day that the girls were born in 1979 focuses the energy of the cosmos through them on their birthday, and causes everybody else to act out of character too. Especially when they're in the house of Aquarius. Or something.

Trivia: The Keystone Kops on television, with Aram Khachaturian's 'Sabre Dance' on the soundtrack, seem to be a symbol of the occult at work (see 'Clyde Bruckman's Final Repose' for more silent-movie chaos motifs). There is a mention of the federal government being unable to pay its bills. The high school is named Grover Cleveland Alexander after another of David Duchovny's incorrect *Jeopardy* answers. (Can't they leave him alone? One day he'll just snap.) The name of the town, Comity, means courtesy, and we see signs on the way in and way out of town that indicate (perversely) that Mulder and Scully are now leaving and then now entering that state of mind. A birthday number, this time month and year: Mulder brings one of the girls to the police station at 11.48.

Scientific Comment: Oh no – astrology. One can suspend one's disbelief for liver-eating mutants, UFOs, invisible elephants . . . but not astrology. However, leaving that aside: the girls' strange behaviour was supposedly caused by a conjunction of Mercury, Mars and Uranus. At the end of the episode a full moon with three planets next to it is shown. Presumably, this was meant to be the conjunction. However:

a: Since Mercury is very close to the sun, the only way you can get those planets aligned is to look from the Earth to Mercury then Mars and Uranus with your line of sight going very close to the Sun. So you'd only be able to see it, if at all, at dawn or dusk. To see a full moon, the moon must be on the far side of the Earth from the Sun, so you have to look directly away from the Sun to see one. Therefore, you can't possibly see that conjunction next to a full, or even quarter, moon.

b: There have been murders for three months. A conjunction with Mercury involved wouldn't last long, since it's got a short orbit. Even the Earth has moved a lot in three months. The effect switched off miraculously at 12.00 on the girls' birthday, which is not consistent with the three-month lead-up.

The mention of a geological vortex or high-intensity meridian is total junk. A meridian is a line of longitude, like the Greenwich meridian, a line on a map. So how can you have a 'high-intensity' one?

The Bottom Line: PC: This is more like it, Chris! The subtle character arc of Mulder and Scully's falling out continues, played, unlike everything else in this series, at a level where the casual viewer wouldn't be disturbed by it. True, the script suffers from Carter Syndrome: the menace is . . . exactly what we're told it is in the teaser. But there's lots of fun to be had in this cut-price *Carrie*. The character play more than makes up for the silly astrology plot, and who cares if a gun going off in your holster would leave you maimed for life? There are moments of Darin Morgan charm around the discovery of the dog. Things are spoilt a bit, though, by what is, even for Mulder, a very silly summing up.

MD: Silly is the word. From the ridiculous idea of an 'upright' school with a demonic goat for a logo to the excruciating dancing-tables ending, this is a stinker. What was doubtless intended as being a witty parody of the True Love Waits campaign and Satanic-abuse stories spiralling out of control comes unstuck because the dialogue lacks any of the sparkle that Morgan would have brought to it. And I'll swallow some pretty incredible concepts in the cause of watching *The X Files*, but, as with our scientific friend, the reality of astrology is not one of them!

KT: 'Did you hear who the cult is supposed to be going after next? A blonde virgin.' *Heathers*! Or not. Interesting mention of the (real-life) McMartin pre-school trial. This is good fun in small doses (I *love* the 'Mr Tippy' sequence), with a healthy slice of self-aware dialogue. But, as for Mulder's bollocks speech at the end . . . Hated it.

BAD ACTORS

The telefantasy writer Nigel Kneale, interviewed in the magazine *SFX*, complained about *The X-Files*, particularly citing 'those two non-actors' as a reason for his dismissal of it. This seems to suggest he has missed the point completely. David Duchovny and Gillian Anderson aren't bad actors at all – Duchovny is a fine actor, Anderson a *brilliant* one – rather, they are playing characters who are, themselves, *very* bad actors, characters who have suppressed their emotions for years due to the nature of their work, and their relationship with each other, and others, has suffered accordingly. 'Syzygy' may give us a hint at what the real Fox Mulder and Dana Scully are like under their cool façades. Then again, maybe it just shows them 'acting' in a different sense.

63: 'Grotesque'

US Transmission: 2 February 1996
UK Transmission: 4 June 1996 (Sky One)
Writer: Howard Gordon
Director: Kim Manners
Cast: Levani, Kurtwood Smith, Greg Thirloway, Susan Bain, Kasper Michaels, Zoran Vukelic

A serial killer claims that he was possessed by a spirit, then another killing occurs after he's been arrested. Mulder's old teacher, Bill Patterson, resents Mulder's involvement in the case and his support for the man's claims that the spirit has inhabited a new killer. Mulder finds a roomful of the killer's victims, made into gargoyles. It turns out that, baffled, Patterson actually requested Mulder's involvement. Mulder becomes very involved, decorating his apartment with the killer's art and sleeping in the man's room, during which time he's disturbed by an attacker. Scully finds the killer's blade, with Mulder's fingerprints on it, stolen from evidence, and becomes afraid for her partner's sanity. Patterson's lieutenant is killed. It turns out that Patterson is the killer, driven mad by the case, and crying out for Mulder to catch him.

Don't Be in the Teaser: A life model is attacked and facially mutilated, and an artist is brutally arrested.

How Did He Do That?: Mulder's leap to Patterson's being the killer is very intuitive: but that's the whole point. However, in the scene where Mulder moves his thumbs across the gargoyle's eyes, don't you think that the gargoyle looks very like Patterson? Maybe he left a big clue under Mulder's nose.

Ooze: Clay!

Scully's Rational Explanation of the Week: Mostow, the killer, has an accomplice.

Phwoar!: Scully's having a go at Patterson for pushing Mulder too far is incredibly sexy: she really cares for Mulder.

And here we see what he was like before he had her to save him all the time: driven, consumed, going right to the edge and then just teetering back when he can see over it. He turns his mobile phone off: in this series, that's like becoming a hermit. You could say that, hurt by the distance that's now between him and Scully, Mulder deliberately throws himself into this self-destruction, crying out for Scully to save him in exactly the way that Patterson cries out to him. The difference between the two, ultimately, is that Mulder will always have Scully there for him.

Continuity: Bill Patterson runs the Investigative Support Unit at Quantico, a behavioural science guru. Although he was a good student, Mulder 'couldn't worship' Patterson, and so quit the ISU eight years ago.

The Truth: If we assume that Patterson had a gargoyle mask, then there's no supernatural element whatsoever, just a psychologically acute picture of what battling monsters and staring into the abyss do to you. There's an extraordinarily realistic look at the human psyche going on here. Patterson taught Mulder about how to become a monster in order to catch them, but these days he's in complete denial of that side of himself, saying that the killer says this stuff 'because he's insane', refusing to look into the pit any more. He tells stories about Mulder when he's drunk: on one level, he's deeply in love with his former student, because he's transcended his teachings. The two things came together in his need to call Mulder in to solve this case: to punish Mulder for leaving him, to baffle this bright boy, to turn him into something like what Patterson has become, and, as the just bit of him wants, to capture and stop him.

Trivia: The gargoyle art is reminiscent of Clive Barker's drawings. And at least one gargoyle is very like Davros in *Doctor Who*. Mostow is said to have come to the US 'during perestroika' (glasnost – openness – would be the better term, as perestroika refers to internal reconstruction). Agent Nemhauser is named after the post-production supervisor,

Lori Jo Nemhauser. (All this naming of characters after production staff ought to seem too cute for words, but the effect is actually to give the series a great variety of ethnic and everyday-strange character names, making it actually seem the most realistic TV series in this regard.)

The Bottom Line: PC: Utterly magnificent: a script that could have been a movie or a novel, represented just as well in series television. There are echoes of *Manhunter*, certainly, but nothing that the format itself doesn't demand. Otherwise, bar the old cat-leaps-out gag, this is completely original, with psychological depths that, these days, only *The X-Files* explores. It also looks gorgeous, designed and lit in many shades of grey. Mind you, Skinner is in it only to remind us that he still exists.

MD: An American Gothic *Cracker*, indeed. The themes explored here remind me very much of a factual book I read on criminal psychiatry and psychological profiling, which had the effect of making the 'real world' seem a very frightening and potentially insane place. 'Grotesque' makes the cartoon killings of 'Syzygy' fade yet more into insignificance.

KT: 'Why didn't it kill me like it killed the others?' A mature, thoroughly bewildering step into the heart of darkness. A miniature Thomas Harris novel with echoes of Dostoyevsky and *From Hell* into the bargain.

64: 'Piper Maru'

US Transmission: 9 February 1996
UK Transmission: 11 June 1996 (Sky One)/
4 December 1996 (BBC1)
Writers: Frank Spotnitz, Chris Carter
Director: Rob Bowman
Cast: Robert Clothier, Jo Bates, Morris Fanych,
Stephen E. Miller, Ari Solomon, Paul Batten, Russell Ferrier,
Kimberly Unger, Rochelle Greenwood, Joel Silverstone,
David Neale, Tom Scholte, Robert F. Maier

A French diver, investigating a crashed aircraft on the ocean floor, is surprised to see a human form inside. He becomes possessed, and transfers that possession to his wife. The rest of his crew suffer from radiation burns. Scully sees an old navy friend of her father, who was sent on a submarine mission to retrieve a downed atom-bomb-carrying B-52 many years ago. Mulder, still on the trail of the 'craft' he saw in the dockyard after his previous investigation into the alien autopsy video, follows Krycek to Hong Kong, where he, together with his salvage company partner, Jerry, has been selling secrets from the MJ Files on the DAT (digital audio tape). The diver's possessed wife follows Mulder to Hong Kong, and attacks a squad of French agents with a burst of radiation. Skinner is shot in what seems to be a coffee-shop argument. The possessed woman passes her alien infestation on to Krycek.

Don't Be in the Teaser: Gauthier, a French diver, gets ambushed by an alien ooze.

Scully Here is a Medical Doctor: 'I'm a medical doctor,' she tells the doctor examining the crew of the *Piper Maru*.

Ooze: Inside victims' eyes.

Phwoar!: This sees the end of the Scully/Mulder tiff arc, marked by a rather self-conscious affirmation of their respect for each other at the start. She was, after all, there for him last episode, and he doesn't seem to need to test the bounds of their relationship again. She seems to have forgiven him for his obsession with aliens at the cost of the real truth, and this two-parter unites their points of view again. Mulder's reaction to Scully's instant aircraft knowledge: 'I just got very turned on.'

Dialogue Triumphs: Scully to Mulder: 'They could drop you in the middle of the desert and tell you the truth is out there, and you'd ask them for a shovel.'

The Conspiracy Starts at Closing Time: The men who threaten Skinner are from 'the intelligence community'. We might speculate the CIA. The coffee shop in which they meet him seems to have the most unobservant staff imaginable. Perhaps they're just 'discreet' ... Krycek says he didn't kill Mulder's father, but, since there would be little point in sending a shapeshifter to do it in a disguise that Bill Mulder wouldn't recognise, we can only assume he's lying. The digital tape containing the MJ Files is in a locker in Washington, DC.

Continuity: Commander Johanson used to be a friend of Scully's father. The Scullys lived three doors away from the Johanson house at Miramar naval air base. Scully went to school with his son, Richard (who was recently killed in the Gulf). Scully watched her dad and brothers building model aircraft, and has an unfeasible amount of knowledge about aircraft. There are continuity references to 'Colony' and 'End Game' (the UFO recovery). Skinner's secretary here is Kimberley Cook.

The Truth: Allegedly, a B-52 crashed at coordinates 42 North, 171 East, during World War II. It was carrying the third nuclear bomb (to follow the Hiroshima and Nagasaki weapons) to be dropped on Japan. The submarine *Zeus Faber* was sent on a mission to recover the bomb, but the crew of the sub suffered from what appeared to be radiation burns. This is a cover story, pure and simple (see 'Apocrypha'). Submarine Captain Sanford was the first victim of an alien ooze.

Trivia: There's a mention of (real-life) French nuclear testing in the Pacific, and there are possible oblique references to the Oklahoma City bombings. Piper Maru is the name of Gillian Anderson's daughter. Another 11.21 reference: the number of the flight Mulder and Krycek take back to Washington is 1121. Gauthier is named after the effects supervisor, Dave Gauthier.

Scientific Comment: How did the oil get into an airtight suit, and out of an airtight submarine? How could the crew be irradiated without their ship being irradiated?

The Bottom Line: PC: Another wild lurch along the tightrope.

This episode is a mess, using all the regular conspiracy episode props one after the other, seemingly in desperation. One gets the feeling of this cookie jar being raided once too often, but then, next episode, miraculously ... It's really strange that anybody should suspect the French of wanting to nick a forty-year-old nuclear weapon when they have modern ones of their own. Gauthier and his wife had their photo taken in front of a crap backdrop of the Eiffel Tower, and the model shot of the submarine is truly awful, sub (sic) *Blake's 7*. Somebody on the production team is still reading *Miss Smilla* . . .

MD: Preferable in many ways to 'Nisei', this is really a rather jolly exercise in compulsive storytelling, although the switch to Hong Kong seems little more than a desperate attempt to paint parts of the episode with international colours.

KT: 'We bury the dead alive, don't we?' On first broadcast, this was the first conspiracy episode since 'The Erlenmeyer Flask' that I had (a) fully understood, and (b) enjoyed. With hindsight, I was as wrong about this as I was about 'Paper Clip', '731' et al. This is an episode that sees the series treading water. Literally. Some good set pieces, though (Scully's visit to Johanson, Skinner's shooting). Although rather obvious attempts are made to soften Dana's 'navy brat' past with soft lighting and mood music, the effect isn't badly handled. The fact that Skinner's secretary calls Scully when he is shot says much about how far Scully and Mulder have climbed in the FBI hierarchy.

65: 'Apocrypha'

US Transmission: 16 February 1996
UK Transmission: 18 June 1996 (Sky One)/
11 December 1996 (BBC1)
Writers: Frank Spotnitz, Chris Carter
Director: Kim Manners
Cast: Kevin McNulty, Barry Levy, Dmitry Chepovetsky, Sue Mathew, Frances Flanagan, Peter Scoular, Jeff Chivers, Martin Evans

Skinner is taken to hospital, while Mulder rides with Krycek, hoping to retrieve the DAT from its hiding place. Their car is ambushed, but Krycek attacks the assailants with a radiation burst. The Smoking Man orders these victims destroyed. Scully finds out that the man who shot Skinner also shot Melissa, and petitions the FBI to pursue Krycek. Mulder believes that the alien is inhabiting oil, and gets the *Lone Gunman* editors to open the safe-deposit box where the tape is meant to be, only to find it has gone. Krycek has it. The conspiracy, meanwhile, want the Smoking Man to get the man who shot Skinner out of the country before he's caught. Mulder arranges a meeting with the Well-Manicured Man, and swaps the knowledge that Krycek has been selling secrets from the tape for a warning that Skinner is still in danger. Scully protects Skinner, and apprehends his assailant, but he offers Krycek's destination in return for his life. Krycek is heading for a North Dakota missile site, to which the recovered UFO has been moved. Mulder, Scully, the Smoking Man and a squad of his troops arrive there. The Smoking Man stops Mulder and Scully entering, and the alien ooze leaves Krycek, returning to the craft. Skinner's assailant dies in his cell. Krycek is left trapped in the silo.

Don't Be in the Teaser: On 19 August 1953, a survivor of the submarine crew tells his story to Bill Mulder, the Smoking Man and, possibly, Deep Throat, who are very much a unit at this point. They seem to be investigating in exactly the way that Mulder does now . . .

Scully Here is a Medical Doctor: She checks on Skinner's condition.

Ooze: Fifty-weight diesel oil, a medium for an alien creature that inhabits bodies.

Phwoar!: Scully's passionate confrontation with Louis Cardinal. And Agent Pendrell still has a crush on her. Her assertiveness with two junior agents at the hospital is way cool. It's good that Mulder puts his arm around Scully beside Melissa's grave.

Dialogue Triumphs: Langly: 'We show a talent for these G-men activities.'

The Conspiracy Starts at Closing Time: The conspiracy don't appear to know what the ooze is (they don't seem to feel that they've missed anything in their retrieval of the craft), and the ooze makes no effort to contact them, having to establish for itself the location of the craft. The alien may be an enemy of theirs in an unusual form (perhaps one of the whiteout aliens: the radiation burst is akin to their whiteout effect). The Smoking Man has seen the effects of the burst before (thanks to his and Mulder snr's investigation in the 1950s), and seems worried about them. Alternatively, since the craft the alien arrived in is of the triangular kind that the conspiracy have been developing with the US Air Force – and given that radiation bursts and the capacity to inhabit any medium would be logical abilities for a creature that could change its shape – perhaps this is one of the rebel shapeshifters (who did arrive on Earth in the 1940s) surprising the conspiracy with a new technique. The creature's ability to (partially) carry on pursuing Krycek's agenda while it inhabits his body indicates (as does its ability to make human bodies walk and talk English) that it can access his memories. This is perhaps further evidence that this is a shapeshifter, since these may have a way to access memories from those they resemble. Indeed, it is possible that the dangerous blood of the shapeshifters is the real nature of the creature, and that oil, a human body or a 'morphing' fleshy container are all suitable 'media' for them. The alien can clearly survive for fifty years with no food, water or air (that we're aware of). The groove in the craft seems to be a 'door' for the liquid to enter, but since the current nature of the alien seems to be a thing of desperation rather than normal procedure, perhaps it's safe to say that the groove is normally used for something else. The ooze was obviously able to traverse the sea bed during its time on Earth, so it must have chosen to enter the corpse in the Mustang in order to ambush the diver, having left its craft when the conspiracy raised it. One wonders what it hopes to gain from re-entering its craft now: perhaps it's hoping to take off soon.

The conspiracy meet on New York's 46th Street. They view the Smoking Man as their 'associate' in Washington. They've just discovered that he's prepared to lie to them. The Well-Manicured Man seems to want to frustrate and end the Smoking Man's violent activities. The conspiracy used to keep UFOs at a base in Nevada (the famed Area 51?), but this place has recently become unviable (probably due to all the public attention). They now keep them in a disused missile silo site. The French action can perhaps be best explained if they have been excluded from the conspiracy and, acting on Krycek's information, they want a slice of the UFO action now!

Continuity: Melissa's murder is FBI case number 621517. Krycek and the craft are entombed in silo 1013 (of course). The epitaph on Melissa's gravestone reads 'Melissa Scully, beloved sister and daughter, 1962–1995.' The man who shot her and Skinner was Louis Cardinal, a Nicaraguan, formerly involved in the Iran/Contra scandal. (True to the conspiracy's methods, he left an unregistered gun at the scene of Skinner's shooting.) There are continuity references to 'Colony', 'End Game', 'Paper Clip' (Krycek's attack on Skinner) and a possible oblique reference to 'Revelations' ('Other than a sign from God.' 'I've seen stranger things, believe me.').

The Truth: During World War II an alien craft was shot down as a 'Foo Fighter', almost certainly in the same incident which downed the Mustang. A submarine crew were sent to this area of the Pacific to recover what they were told was a Flying Fortress carrying a nuclear weapon. Instead, the captain was attacked by an alien entity, and many of the crew died from a form of radiation sickness. When the captain was locked away from the controls of the ship the alien presence returned to the water, realising that it couldn't use the sub to get to the land. In 1953 Bill Mulder and the others investigated the fate of the submarine (they don't seem to have encountered or been used by the conspiracy at this point). In 1996 the conspiracy (see 'Colony', 'End Game') recovered the alien craft from this area. Later, the French vessel, also acting on information from the MJ Files, found the P-51 – and the alien. It was now inhabiting the 'dead' pilot of the P-51.

Trivia: The conspiracy's phone number is 5551012, one short of 1013. (Can you imagine their answerphone message? 'Hello, conspiracy. We're not here. We never were.') The number of the missile silo is also 1013. The music at the Ice Rink is Strauss's *The Blue Danube*.

The Bottom Line: PC: Isn't it odd that the conspiracy say 'UFO' when they know exactly what these things are? It's good to see the Smoking Man telling his bosses that his pawn 'acted alone', one of many delights in a script that actually saves this two-parter completely, mainly through the refreshing device of throwing us some solid bits of information to hang on to. This idea of early closure as a remedy for the misty and intangible nature of the conspiracy works quite well throughout the third season. In this case, we're quite surprised and pleased that Scully actually lays her hands on the man who killed her sister, a motif which looked like it would be with us for all time.

MD: The pre-title sequence is excellent (the chap who plays the young Smoking Man is staggeringly accurate, even down to vocal inflections), and much of what follows does not disappoint.

KT: 'You can't bury the truth.' Oh yes you can, matey. The 1950s RCA Victor tape recorder sets the tone for this marvellous episode: style, and astonishing attention to detail. One tiny point of query, however: the Assistant Director of the FBI is shot and only three agents turn up at the hospital, two seemingly very inexperienced, and the third (Scully) there only because he's gone out on a limb for her and Mulder so often. You would have thought the place would have been crawling with middle management eager for promotion.

THE THIRD MAN

In 'Apocrypha' a sequence set in 1953 shows the young Bill Mulder working with the young Smoking Man (their relationship had been commented upon as early as 'Anasazi') and a third man. Although this character isn't given a line, several clues point to his being Deep Throat. The early-seventies photos seen in 'The Blessing Way' and 'Paper Clip' establish that the three men worked together along with Klemper and the Well-Manicured Man. Deep Throat's motivation in helping and protecting Fox before his death seems to be that he is the son of an old and trusted friend whom he had chosen as his conscience. Indeed, it seems that Bill Mulder and Deep Throat shared similar disquiet over the way in which their work was progressing. Perhaps most tellingly, in 'Talitha Cumi' when Smith, the shapeshifting alien, confronts the Smoking Man with his personal demons, the forms he assumes are those of Deep Throat and Bill Mulder, the implication being that the ghosts who haunt the Smoking Man are his two former partners and friends, both of whose deaths he was (perhaps indirectly) responsible for.

Byers: well.
Frohike: middling.
Langly: badly.

66: 'Pusher'

US Transmission: 23 February 1996
UK Transmission: 25 June 1996 (Sky One)
Writer: Vince Gilligan
Director: Rob Bowman

Cast: Robert Wisden, Vic Polizos, Roger R. Cross,
Steve Bacic, Don Mackay, Brent Sheppard, D. Neil Mark,
Meredith Bain Woodward, Julia Arkos, Darren Lucas

Detective Frank Burst goes to Mulder and Scully about a
man who calls himself 'Pusher', who has admitted to several
'suicide' killings, and escaped him. The agents track him to a
golf range, where he makes a trooper set himself on fire, but
they catch him. He's freed because of Mulder's testimony and
Pusher's ability to convince the judge of his innocence. He
walks into the FBI, and accesses private files, causing Skinner to
be attacked by a secretary. It turns out that Pusher is dying of a
brain tumour. After he talks Frank Burst to death over the phone,
Mulder corners him in a hospital, where he plays Russian
roulette with the FBI agent. Scully, about to be shot by Mulder
at Pusher's request, pulls the fire alarm, breaking Mulder's
concentration and allowing him to shoot Pusher instead.

Don't Be in the Teaser: Pusher sends a car carrying him,
Burst and a deputy into a collision with a lorry. The deputy is
killed.

How Did He Do That?: Mulder jumps at exactly the right
magazine advert as being Pusher's. Pusher, for his part,
instantly realises that Mulder and Scully aren't, actually,
potential customers, but the FBI. Pusher, despite his many
gifts, isn't psychic, so how does he know that the oncoming
truck is from the Cerulean Blue Hauling Company? Lucky
guess? Coincidence?

Scully Here is a Medical Doctor: She gives Burst mouth-to-
mouth resuscitation and assesses Pusher's brain condition
over a video link.

Ooze: Collins's self-inflicted burns.

Scully's Rational Explanation of the Week: 'Please explain
to me the scientific nature of "The Whammy".' The cir-
cumstantial evidence is enough, in this case, to make Scully
(eventually) agree with Mulder.

Phwoar!: Mulder looks gorgeously shaken after he shoots Modell. Scully sheds a tear when Mulder's about to shoot her, and they hold hands at the end, playing with each other's fingers. If they were ever close to going home and shagging like bunnies, this is the point. Mulder doesn't seem strong enough not to shoot Scully (after all, she's the one with the balls in this relationship), but there is a suggestion that Mulder subconsciously wants revenge for her shooting him.

Dialogue Triumphs: Pusher: 'You must be Frank Burst? You know, I've got to tell you, you got the greatest name.'

Mulder: ' "Mango Kiwi Tropical Swirl"! Now we know we're dealing with a madman.'

Continuity: There's another example of Mulder's T.S. Eliot fixation when he (mis-) quotes *The Hollow Men* with the phrase 'Not with a whimper but a bang'. Doubtless, thanks to the events of 'Nisei', he now has a Japanese dictionary.

The Truth: Pusher was an army supply clerk who wanted to be in the special forces, an anti-authoritarian who wanted to be in authority. He failed the FBI psyche test several years ago (he should have waited: by the time of 'Lazarus' they were letting anybody in . . .) and, until a cancer developed in his temporal lobe, was a failure. The cancer brought on epilepsy, and the power to make people obey his will, but it was also killing him.

Trivia: The *World Weekly Informer* is a tacky tabloid. As well as the headline FLUKEMAN FOUND WASHED UP IN MARTHA'S VINEYARD, it has further headings: DEPRAVITY RAMPANT ON HIT TV SHOW (with a photo of what must be two of the series' creators, one in suspenders), and GIRL RAISED BY SQUIRRELS FOR 15 YEARS FOUND BEGGING FOR PEANUTS IN PARK. There are apt references to *Yojimbo* and *Svengali*. Dave Grohl, of the Foo Fighters and formerly Nirvana, and his wife, Jennifer Youngblood-Grohl, make a cameo appearance as Pusher attempts to enter the FBI building. (He should have been in last week's episode . . .)

The Bottom Line: PC: Not very well received amongst US fans, possibly for one of two reasons. One: we'd all have preferred it if Mulder had had the mental strength to break Pusher's control; but, two: the villain is actually a dark version of many viewers of the show. That reaction is a pity, because he's actually fabulous, a bulky, rude bully with 'Samurai' stylings so obviously fake that his use of them is obscene. Robert Wisden does an amazing job with the man's odd mix of charisma and ugliness. For him to be a discontented militiaman, with that outsider fascination for the things of government such morons claim to hate, is very subtle characterisation. Mind you, the script does have its failings, such as none of our heroes even trying to defend themselves against a menace the nature of which they're all well aware. Earplugs would have helped, and couldn't Frank Burst just have held the phone away from his ear? Scully really should stop Mulder from telling so much of the truth in court, and his shooting of Pusher at the end is probably grossly unlawful. Final proof, also, that actors just can't look natural shopping.

MD: I love the sequences with the fake pass, and the production team really seem to have it in for poor old Skinner this season (why him in a building full of hundreds of people?). The image of the chap setting himself on fire is terrifying, and much of the episode has a similar grotesquely hypnotic appeal.

KT: 'Bet you five bucks I get off!' Sometimes when I see lists of least favourite episodes on the Internet, I want to smash up my computer and go and live in Papua New Guinea. That this episode (and 'War of the Coprophages' and 'Jose Chung's *From Outer Space*' and 'Space') regularly comes below tripe like 'The Jersey Devil' and 'GenderBender' in such polls makes me want to resign from the human race in protest. A classic example of the age-old truism that, if you try to be daring in TV, the fans will spit at you. 'Pusher' is a masterpiece. It's about 'a little man who wishes he was big'. What does this remind us of? Poor Skinner gets maced and chinned by the local YTS-trainee. After being shot two weeks ago, somebody is *clearly* trying to tell him something. Excellent ending. In fact, excellent episode.

67: 'Teso dos Bichos'

US Transmission: 8 March 1996
UK Transmission: 2 July 1996 (Sky One)
Writer: John Shiban
Director: Kim Manners
Cast: Vic Trevino, Janne Mortil, Gordon Tootoosis, Tom
McBeath, Ron Sauve, Alan Robertson, Garrison Chrisjohn

The grave of a female shaman is found in Ecuador. The
urn containing her body is taken to a museum in Boston,
and becomes the centre of controversy as the Ecuadorians
demand its return. Several academics vanish: one, having
discovered a dead rat in his car, is identifiable only by his
intestine, found in a tree. The curator's assistant, Belack, falls
under suspicion, seeming tired and washed out after taking
Ecuadorian tribal drugs. His friend, Mona, finds the museum
toilets full of rats, and then vanishes. Mulder and Scully read
Belack's journals and arrest him, but he disappears. The
agents go into the sewers in pursuit, and find the bodies of all
the vanished people, but, rather than the jaguar or the rats
they expected, they're attacked by a horde of cats. They
escape and the State Department decide to send the urn back.

Don't Be in the Teaser: Dr Roosevelt gets killed by something nasty and feline created by a nearby tribal ceremony.

How Did He Do That?: A human killer is the most obvious
thing in the world, so Mulder opts for death by Ecuadorian
jaguar spirit.

Scully Here is a Medical Doctor: She plays 'Whose Intestine Is It Anyway?' by examining its last lunch.

Ooze: Yahey, the Vine of the Soul.

Scully's Rational Explanation of the Week: Belack is the
killer, the rat climbed into the car to keep warm, lots of old
buildings have rats ... Mulder may have been drinking
yahey.

Dialogue Triumphs: Mulder: 'If someone digs me up in a thousand years, I hope there's a curse on them, too.'

Scully to cop: 'Label that.' 'As what?' 'Partial rat body part.'

Continuity: Scully: 'A possessed rat? The return of *Ben?*' Another example of her love for big-budget, tacky horror films (see 'Shadows', 'Miracle Man').

The Truth: The shaman's soul transmigrated into a host of killer cats.

Trivia: Dr Lewton is named after Val Lewton, who produced the movie *Cat People*.

The Bottom Line: PC: What could have been a very routine episode is saved by a cool series of audience expectation bluffs as to the real nature of the killer, using media references to send us guessing this way and that. It consciously uses the 'cat-leaps-out' gag more than once, and Ecuadorian viewers will be pleased to find out (in a 'Fire' kind of way) that their countrymen all wear quaint native costume, with not a pair of Levi's in sight, but for what could be a filler episode, it's cracking. The script raids *Altered States*, Pharaoh's-curse movies and *The Rats* before settling on a riff from *The Uncanny*. I'll now make way for the others to make the obvious joke. Go on.

MD: Er, what joke would that be? This is a fair-to-middling episode, although the entire plot is so hackneyed and predictable that the viewer is left feeling 'Been there, seen it, bought the officially licensed poster magazine . . .' The silly ending is a bit of an added bonus, though.

KT: 'Invasion of the Killer Pussies . . .' Sorry, couldn't resist it. The body count in this episode is *astronomical*! The cats are brilliant (notably in their shocking first appearance). Anyone wanting to go to the toilet during, or immediately after, this episode . . . Well, think twice, that's all.

68: 'Hell Money'

US Transmission: 29 March 1996
UK Transmission: 9 July 1996 (Sky One)
Writer: Jeffrey Vlaming
Director: Tucker Gates
Cast: B.D. Wong, Lucy Alexis Liu, James Hong,
Michael Yama, Doug Abrahams, Ellie Harvie, Derek Lowe,
Donald Fong, Diana Ha, Stephen M.D. Chang, Paul Wong

A Chinese man is found dead, burnt in a crematorium oven in San Francisco. With him is a fragment of hell money, ceremonial cash used to placate the dead. Chinese characters are painted on the door of his house, labelling it as a haunted house. Meanwhile, a man loses a secret lottery, and is buried in an as-yet-unused grave. Mr Hsin, a carpet layer, has lost an eye in that same lottery, trying to win to pay for his daughter's operation. Mulder and Scully's Chinese detective contact, Chao, is attacked by the 'ghosts' who buried the earlier victim. Mulder and Scully track a rogue doctor to the place where the lottery is held, and also find Chao there. Mr Hsin has lost the lottery, and is due to forfeit all his organs. Chao was working for the game, but, sickened by it, he rebels, and shows that the game is fixed. Mulder and Scully save Mr Hsin, but nobody will talk about the lottery, and the perpetrators go free. Chao is killed for his transgression.

Don't Be in the Teaser: A kid on the run is ambushed by masked 'ghosts', who burn him in a crematorium oven.

How Did He Do That?: Mulder and Scully instantly suspect Chao, for no good reason.

Scully Here is a Medical Doctor: She does an autopsy on the burnt man, and on an organ donor who turns out to have a (living) frog inside him.

Scully's Rational Explanation of the Week: Ritual Triad killings.

Dialogue Triumphs: Scully: '. . . if I'm right this is one man who left his heart in San Francisco.'

The Truth: The losers of the lottery have certain body parts removed, which are sold by the lottery organisers. If we accept certain perceptual problems concerning the 'ghost' enforcers, then no supernatural elements are present.

Trivia: Mulder refers to *Ghostbusters* ('Who you gonna call?').

The Bottom Line: PC: Incredibly nihilistic, this episode upset me more than any number of Monsters of the Week could. No good is done, nothing is achieved, futility is all. I've always been disturbed by self-sacrifice, the tendency of people to form an orderly queue for the firing squad. At the centre of it is the way that the heroes' traditional foreknowledge of who the bad guy is (a cliché that a series as good as this shouldn't stoop to) translates in this case into sheer (and, as it turns out, accurate) prejudice on the part of Mulder and Scully, as they harshly interrogate and suspect Chao, who, in terms of the plot, isn't acting suspiciously at all. Add to that the question of why, if nobody is ever seen to win this lottery, anybody still plays it, and what the frog was about, and you've got an alienated and disturbing evening's viewing. That might be good or bad: but I suspect this is scary for all the wrong reasons.

MD: I loved this episode – I don't think it's nihilistic so much as realistic, the acute poverty and the (real-life) trade in human organs being almost impossible to watch in a fantasy fiction about little green men. This central concept is strong enough to carry the episode, as long as we ignore possible cultural stereotyping and the unexplained frog (nice image, though, given its apparent symbolism in Chinese culture). I suppose it's a critique of all lotteries, with the majority paying to make a tiny minority grotesquely rich (and thus the ultimate right-wing parable), although it is indeed worrying that we get only one hint that anyone has ever been seen to win before. There's now two million dollars in the pot, for crying out loud! I have no problem with the ending: Chao saves Hsin and his daughter, and puts a stop to the exploitative game. The perpetrators go free – but then, as I say, life can be like that . . .

KT: 'It's definitely not Chinese food I'm smelling . . .' No, I don't like this one either. My main problem with the episode (which, as Martin notes, is full of terrific images) is exactly the same as Paul's – good people die (notably Chao), whilst evil seems to win (or, at least, get a fighting draw), which might be realistic, but in a series as life-affirming as *The X-Files* doesn't work at all well. And there are some very dodgy (if, no doubt, unintentional) racist attitudes on display. Nowhere near as bad as *Big Trouble in Little China*, though, so that's all right then.

69: 'Jose Chung's *From Outer Space*'

US Transmission: 12 April 1996
UK Transmission: 16 July 1996 (Sky One)
Writer: Darin Morgan
Director: Rob Bowman
Cast: Charles Nelson Reilly, William Lucking,
Daniel Quinn, Jesse Ventura, Sarah Sawatsky, Jason Gaffney,
Alex Diakun, Larry Musser, Alex Trebek, Allan Zinyk,
Andrew Turner, Michael Dobson, Mina E. Mina

Scully relates the story of one of her cases to the novelist Jose Chung, whom Mulder has refused to see. Recently, Mulder had a girl who was apparently the victim of an abduction hypnotised, and she told the standard abduction story. But the story of the boy who was with her was different: he said he was imprisoned with an alien smoking a cigarette. A watching telephone engineer saw the aliens, and then had a series of experiences with 'Men in Black'. Hypnotised again, the girl remembered USAF men instead of aliens. Then a dead alien was found: he turned out to be a USAF major in an alien suit. Mulder met another USAF man who told him a tale of USAF abductions, their men pretending to be aliens, but, according to Chung's other interviewees, this interview did not take place. Mulder and Scully met the 'Men in Black' in Scully's hotel room, and one of them was revealed to be (or resemble) a game-show host, Alex Trebek (later Scully is unable to recall the meeting). Mulder and Scully were shown the supposed crash of a secret USAF aircraft. Among the dead was the pilot whom Mulder says he spoke to. Chung's research finished, he is visited by Mulder, who asks him not to go ahead with the book as it will make the whole business look foolish, but *From Outer Space* is published, and everyone is left just as confused as before.

Don't Be in the Teaser: Two unconscious humans, two freaked-out 'greys' and . . . Lord Kinbote.

Scully Here is a Medical Doctor: She performs the 'alien autopsy' and finds a zip. 'It's so embarrassing.'

Scully's Rational Explanation of the Week: The girl is suffering from stress and sexual trauma, the hypnotist is leading her on, hypnotism doesn't enhance memory (despite her own experience to the contrary), the witnesses have fantasy-prone personalities, and the abduction scenario is now culturally entrenched. 'Mulder, you're nuts!'

Phwoar!: Scully's sober hero-worship of Chung is charming, and her fictional 'You tell anyone, you're a dead man!' just makes us want her to boss us about. And, of course, Mulder and Scully wake up in the same room, but Scully doesn't remember anything about the night before (which is a cool comment on the initial boy/girl problem). Mulder lying on his bed at the end certainly looks like a ticking timebomb of some sort.

Dialogue Triumphs: Blaine's description of Scully and Mulder: 'One of them was disguised as a woman, but wasn't pulling it off, like her hair was red, but it was a little too red . . . And the other one – the tall, lanky one – his face was so blank and expressionless.'

Man in Black: 'Even the former leader of your United States of America, James Earl Carter junior, thought he saw a UFO once. But it's been proven he only saw the planet Venus.' Roky: 'I'm a Republican!'

'Yep, that's a bleeping dead alien body if ever I bleeping saw one!'

Pilot: 'You ever flown a flying saucer? Afterwards, sex seems trite.'

Scully: 'I know it doesn't have the sense of closure that you want, but it has more than some of our cases.'

The Conspiracy Starts at Closing Time: Memory loss after 'UFO' encounters is attributed to nerve gas or (again) a sonic weapon.

Continuity: Mulder may (or may not) like lots of sweet-potato pie. The Stupendous Yappi has hosted a video based on Blaine Faulkner's camcorder footage, entitled *Dead Alien: Truth or Humbug?*. Scully never considered the paranormal much before working with Mulder. She thinks Chung's *The Caligarian Candidate* is one of the greatest thrillers ever written (Chung's *The Lonely Buddha* is also one of her favourite novels). Mulder also considers Chung 'a gifted writer'.

Sleep difficulties, muscle problems and nose bleeds are all (according to Mulder) signs of 'post-abduction syndrome'.

The Truth: 'How the hell should I know?' It goes against the whole spirit of the episode to do this, but ... The USAF, disguised as aliens, has been systematically abducting American citizens. The abductees are subjected to memory erasure. (All this we've seen before in previous episodes.) The pilot's explanation to Mulder is new: that this is a test of new reconnaissance aircraft, and the folk myth of UFOs is being built up worldwide to ensure that these craft won't be shot at. However, this is revealed to be a rather naïve point of view (it doesn't include any knowledge of human experiments). He and his fellow pilot were abducted from the scene of their latest abduction by 'Lord Kinbote', who resembles a

Japanese comics character. This, like several turns of this story, seems to be a device to make sure that witnesses to weird events aren't believed, because their stories are too bizarre. That 'Lord Kinbote' is also a creation of the USAF is underlined by the fact that he appears from one of the triangular UFOs flown by them in 'Deep Throat'. The pilot, on being found by his bosses with Mulder, says that he's dead meat, and refers to Lord Kinbote very casually, giving the impression that he's told the truth as far as he knows it, and that, rather than make him appear ridiculous, now that he's talked to Mulder, his superiors will have him killed. And they do. The sincerity of his story is underlined by the fact that the cook who would have witnessed this conversation tells Chung that Mulder just sat there alone eating sweet-potato pie all evening, asking him stereotypical questions about UFOs. (The cook presumably had his memory wiped and altered into a series of images taken from the media, in this case vaguely echoing *Twin Peaks*.) Chrissy's story of alien abduction is very similar to Duane Barry's and Scully's, and, indeed, has been carried out by the same forces. Mulder and Scully encounter two 'Men in Black' who look like celebrities. But Scully seems very out of it during this encounter and later claims not to remember it all. At some point, then, we must assume that Scully's been got at by the memory-erasing device (in the form of a sonic weapon?) and forced to forget the encounter. (The best way to break the two of them up – or to have one doubt the other and thus expose them to the authorities – would be to cause the two of them to have different experiences of the same event, especially with one account being so ridiculous. This is, in effect, the first attempt to do to our heroes what is later attempted with Skinner in 'Avatar'.) It's also possible that Scully's been preconditioned not to be able to perceive these two shapeshifters. They're carrying out a plan of making witnesses seem laughable that's much too subtle for the Smoking Man, but seems to be just the sort of thing that the Well-Manicured Man would think up. The hypnotherapy employed in this story, and the USAF's implied memory-wiping, act to make sure that virtually every version of the truth on show here is suspect. Chung's final book makes the whole field look ridiculous, but it's significant that he's become jumpy enough to draw a gun when he thinks he sees an alien: maybe he's quite aware of what he's just done. There, it was a nasty job, taking a script apart like that, but we had to do it. We were just conforming to the needs of an episode guide.

Trivia: The Mulder and Scully characters in Chung's book *From Outer Space* are called Reynard Muldrake and Diana Lydsky. There's a *Close Encounters* mashed potato allusion. At the end of the episode Roky goes to live in Ej Cajon, California, the town where Darin and Glen Morgan grew up. Blaine Faulkner wears a *Space: Above and Beyond* teeshirt (in an episode first shown on the night when David Duchovny guested on that show) and also has Mulder's 'I Want To Believe' poster. Alex Trebek hosts the American game show *Jeopardy*, the effect being rather like the sudden entrance of Bob Monkhouse. The other 'Man in Black' is the former wrestler Jesse 'The Body' Ventura, also a famous face. Jimmy Carter's real-life UFO 'encounter' is mentioned, and it is implied that the Angels of Mons were actually German projections of images of the Virgin Mary over French lines in order to protect themselves. Roky Crikenson's name is a play on Roky Erickson of the 13th Floor Elevators (his next band was Roky Erickson and the Aliens). Klass County is named after Philip J. Klass, a UFO debunker (and a great proponent of the Venus-as-UFO theory); Robert Vallee, Jack Schaffer and Sergeant Hynek all have the surnames of UFO experts. Detective Manners is named after the producer Kim Manners. Judging by his description of CIA hypnosis experiments in the 1950s, Chung's *The Caligarian Candidate* seems to be a close cousin of Richard Condon's *The Manchurian Candidate*, and also includes a nod to *The Cabinet of Doctor Caligari*. Mulder is seen watching the famous Bigfoot footage on TV. Reference is made to 'the military/industrial/entertainment complex', of which the Fox Network would be a leading part. The opening, as with most of Darin Morgan's stories, is pure *Star Wars*, but the Star Destroyer turns out to be a phone engineer's crane. (This story all over.) Lord Kinbote is named after David Kinbote, a character from Vladimir Nabokov's *Pale Fire*. The novel concerns the way people interpret experience to conform to their opinions.

The Bottom Line: PC: 'Roswell!' What an astonishing script. This is the first script to deal with the fact that the material Mulder and Scully investigate has become part of the American psyche, and that the series itself is responsible for shaping and projecting that material. (The 'alien autopsy' footage is a brilliant pastiche, its musical score a rather obvious take off of . . . *Theme from The X-Files*.) The story is constructed like a series of Russian dolls: versions of the truth buried inside one another. There's a powerful commentary on the nature of subjectivity going on here: Scully edits the crude detective's swearwords out of what she tells Chung; Blaine's narrative is wildly at odds with her own (and it's fun to see Mulder and Scully reconstructed into the 'Men in Black', that, in the mythos, they would be cast as); Mulder won't even play this game, he sees it as so treacherous. There are also numerous delightful moments and catchphrases in a ferociously entertaining episode, from the mapping of the hypnotherapist and the other humans into aliens, to 'Men in Black' lore recast as wrestler braggadocio (underlining how what the world currently believes is, basically, what it sees on TV), to Mulder's girlie scream when he sees the alien. That's a moment of genuine feeling, though, as is the ending, when we see that natural emotion has been completely replaced by the conditioned responses and demands of television. That's the scariest *X-Files* episode for you. The funniest. And the best.

MD: 'I know how crazy this sounds . . .' Just imagine that your first sight of *The X-Files* was that intentionally daft pre-titles sequence, complete with badly animated Ray Harryhausen-type monster! There are great things going on here – I especially liked the character of Blaine, desperate to get abducted to avoid having to find a job, who says he learnt a little something about courage from playing Dungeons & Dragons. The little flashes of reality are very enjoyable – from Mulder's mention of prison rape to Chung's interest in hypnosis as proving the power of mere words – and the Mulder-like summing up at the end is great. But . . . When I first watched this I thought it was by far the worst Darin Morgan script, the clever ideas and smart direction lost beneath a diabolically obscure narrative structure that was trying to be too clever by half. Now I'm not so sure. Maybe I'm just too thick to really enjoy Morgan's work.

KT: 'This is not happening!' This is *so* good it almost defies logic. Morgan, with this and his previous three scripts, has, effectively, taken the series to pieces, and reconstructed it as a parody of the original. But it's so much more than a mere clever pastiche; Roky's 'testimony', all that stuff about Venus being mistaken for UFOs, Mulder's reaction to the discovery of the 'alien' (*positively* the greatest single moment in the history of the programme), the 'alien autopsy' . . . There are many magical moments. Fantastic – in every sense of the word.

PARODIES

One of the episodes of the final season of *Spitting Image* in 1996 featured a clever parody of *Scooby Doo – Where Are You?* that dragged Mulder and Scully into the plot, solving the crime much to the chagrin of a very cheesed-off Velma, who complains that *The X-Files* has done nothing more than rip off the cartoon series' format and plots. (Mulder notes that *The X-Files* is 'grown up' and 'scary', but still gives his partner a 'Scully-snack'!) There are times when that has a ring of truth to it. We haven't quite got to the Smoking Man being led off in handcuffs screaming 'I would have got away with it, too, if it hadn't been for you meddling FBI agents', but there's always next season . . .

Another TV series to successfully parody the *X-Files* aesthetic is its Fox stablemate, *The Simpsons*. In the episode 'Grampa vs. Sexual Inadequacy', Bart's reading of a book on UFOs, combined with a spate of child abandonment in Springfield, leads Bart, Milhouse and their friends to speculate that an elaborate government conspiracy involving 'the Rand Corporation' and 'the Saucer People' is responsible. When Lisa, playing a Scully-type sceptic, pours scorn on the idea, suggesting sarcastically that they should also include 'the Reverse Vampires' in their theory, Bart apes Mulder by taking her seriously. Rumours abound that *The Simpsons* is shortly to *do* a specific *X-Files* parody episode featuring the voices of Gillian Anderson and David Duchovny.

Often lampooning aesthetics can prove a critical summation of real problems. In a January 1996 issue of *NME*, the comedy column 'Oi! Bullshitter! With Grant Mitchell' focused on Scully, or, as she will forever afterwards be known, 'bird off *The X-Files*'! Many people were, by this stage, getting thoroughly sick of Scully's lack of belief in what is in front of her eyes (see 'The Calusari'). Here it is taken to ridiculous (if obvious) extremes: 'You reckon you're an FBI agent out to find out about UFOs and all that shit? Well aincha? What does it take, eh?' The rant continues with the memorable opinion: 'Every week Mulder rings up and says: "Oi! Bird off *The X-Files*, I've got a crashed spaceship/werewolf/vampire/conspiracy ... and it's right here in New York/Philadelphia/The arse-end-of-nowhere." And what do you do? ... You get abducted ... get taken to Jupiter – and back again – then dumped ... with a tattoo on your head that says "Aliens have just had it off with me".' And yet, as 'Grant' notes, at the end of every single episode she still ends up saying into her dictaphone ' "I think something happened, but it wasn't the paranormal ..." Mulder would be better off being partnered by Angus Deayton. At least he's not so bloody cynical.' The most infuriating thing about this pastiche, of course, is that it's *exactly* what many fans have been saying since episode two.

Perhaps it is inevitable that a series like *The X-Files* should become such an obvious name to drop – TV programmes as diverse as *Brookside*, *2 Point 4 Children* and *Fantasy Football League* have referred to it. This is nothing new, of course. TV has always enjoyed nodding to its more esoteric programmes. The series has become the new subject of jokes that used to finish with the line 'It's like something out of *Doctor Who*!' But, when we hear about motorcycle and hi-fi magazines featuring Mulder and Scully on their covers, or the tenth newspaper this week to point out that the Romanian footballer Dan Petrescu looks uncannily like David Duchovny, we know we are dealing with something bigger in the public consciousness than a popular TV series. Full marks to the football magazine *90 Minutes*, by the way, who were the first to spot the uncanny resemblance Manchester United's Paul Scholes bears to Scully!

70: 'Avatar'

US Transmission: 26 April 1996
UK Transmission: 23 July 1996 (Sky One)
Writers: Howard Gordon,
from a story by David Duchovny and Howard Gordon
Director: James Charleston
Cast: Tom Mason, Jennifer Hetrick, Amanda Tapping,
Malcolm Stewart, Morris Panych, Michael David Simms,
Tasha Simms, Stacy Grant, Janie Woods-Morris

Skinner wakes beside a dead woman, and claims to have lost his memory of the night before. He won't take a polygraph test. Mulder and Scully discover the woman was a prostitute, and go to see her madam, who says that Skinner paid for her.

Skinner, meanwhile, is having visions of a mysterious old woman as he meets his (soon to be ex-) wife. He's being treated for a sleep disorder that prompts nightmares. Scully discovers a phosphorescent trace left on the dead woman's mouth. Skinner's wife is run off the road and badly injured. It turns out that the old woman Skinner is seeing saved his life during a near-death experience in Vietnam. Mulder finds the image of a man on one of the airbags in Skinner's wife's car: she was driven off the road deliberately. At a hearing, Skinner is dismissed. The madam is killed in a fall, but Mulder and Scully discover that the man whose face is on the airbag hired the prostitute. They set a trap for him, but it's obvious, and he prepares to spring it. Skinner goes to see his comatose wife, electing not to divorce her, and the old woman gives him a message. He arrives to shoot the man who injured his wife, thus clearing himself. He won't reveal the nature of the message.

Don't Be in the Teaser: Skinner gets his end away: the scariest thing we've ever seen in *The X-Files*. *She* turns into a hag, and he wakes up beside a woman with her head on back to front.

Scully Here is a Medical Doctor: She does the autopsy on Skinner's apparent victim.

Ooze: Luminescent traces on the woman's mouth and nostrils.

Scully's Rational Explanation of the Week: Skinner is suffering from REM sleep behaviour disorder.

Dialogue Triumphs: Mulder: 'At least they were having safe sex.'

Scully (on the sumptuous surroundings of the escort agency): 'Business must be booming.' Mulder: 'You mean banging.'

Skinner: 'I was no choirboy. I inhaled.'

The Conspiracy Starts at Closing Time: This is an attempt to frame Skinner, the conspiracy having failed to kill him.

The stuff on the prostitute's face is presumably the chemical that wiped Skinner's memory. They probably take the sample of it from Scully's case. It may be just their good luck that Mulder gets off on his succubus riff, or perhaps they're aware of the nature of Skinner's dreams from the treatment that he's having, and have read enough of the sort of book Mulder reads to guess he'd start thinking this. At any rate, they nearly get Mulder and Scully fired as well as Skinner.

Continuity: Skinner is trying to get a divorce, and now only has to sign the final paper. He and his wife Sharon haven't been together for eight months. Their wedding ring is inscribed 'Love forever, Sharon'. Skinner mentioned Mulder to her, saying that he respected him. Skinner drinks whiskey, and took drugs (probably marijuana) in Vietnam. His middle name is (incredibly) Sergei. The Office of Professional Conduct believe that Mulder has 'enchanted' both Skinner and Scully into believing his own wild theories. There's a mention of Mulder's aide Danny (see 'Conduit', 'The Erlenmeyer Flask' and others).

The Truth: The old woman gives Skinner messages from some outside source, or perhaps (she being one of the archetypes, the wise old woman) from his own subconscious. (It's possible that, if Mulder and Scully are registering their investigation as they go, he could have logically followed them to the trap, the only subconscious cue being the idea that they might be in danger.)

Trivia: Mulder has one of the New Zealand UFO photos (obviously a misidentification of a planet) on his wall. The scenes with Sharon in the red coat are taken from *Don't Look Now* (only, in this case, Sharon looks ridiculous in the coat). Jennifer Hetrick, who plays Sharon, also played Captain Picard's girlfriend Vash in *Star Trek: The Next Generation*. She must have a thing for bald, authoritative, telefantasy icons.

Scientific Comment: It's stated that sodium metal coats the interior of the airbag. Sodium is an extremely reactive metal.

It should never be handled. So it's difficult to believe that it would be in an airbag even after it's been activated.

The Bottom Line: PC: A clever, complicated maze of a story, that tries to be a little too clever for its own good. If Skinner would tell anybody his weird story, it would be Mulder. And how, exactly, does he get off the charges against him? He's proved there's a plot going on, but the initial evidence is still rather damning. *X-Files* scripts often purposely confuse two different phenomena, which audiences, used to the straighter through-lines of regular US television, tend to initially see as one. In this case, Skinner's hag experience is overlaid upon the attempt to frame him, and the twists and turns of the plot mean that it takes quite a bit of thought to separate them out, especially when Mulder (the lead usually tells the audience the truth) muddies the ground between them still further.

MD: Poor Old Skinner (Part Whatever) – don't you just want to hug him at the beginning? No? OK. This is a fantastic little story, and I especially liked the scene with Skinner explaining his emotional coldness to his unconscious wife. But I just can't believe you can get an impression of a face from a discharged airbag . . .

KT: 'He's behaving like a guilty man.' Love Skinner's wedding photo – with such an obvious toupee that it takes on the quality of grand kitsch! More *JFK* imagery and dialogue and 'several questions remain unanswered . . .' To be honest, I lost the plot of this one quite early on and never really recovered. Not that it's bad, necessarily, just a little over-complicated. Of course, it's still better than 95 per cent of other stuff on TV.

71: 'Quagmire'

US Transmission: 3 May 1996
UK Transmission: 30 July 1996 (Sky One)/
20 November 1996 (BBC1)
Writer: Kim Newton

Director: Kim Manners
Cast: Chris Ellis, Timothy Webber, R. Nelson Brown, Mark Acheson, Peter Hanlon, Terrance Leigh

Missing persons around Heuvelmans Lake, Georgia, which is associated with a monster, 'Big Blue', attract Mulder's attention. Dr Faraday, a biologist, denies that he killed a man who was sceptical about his work, and tells Mulder that the lake's frog population has declined. A half-eaten body is found, and, after further disappearances, the lake is 'shut down'. Scully's dog is snatched from her by something in the bushes. Mulder and Scully take a boat out onto the lake, and end up marooned on a rock, which turns out to be very close to shore. Mulder becomes convinced that the monster lives in the woods, and, hunting it, is attacked by a huge alligator, which he kills. But after the two agents leave, a real lake monster appears.

Don't Be in the Teaser: Dr Bailey, a 'frog holocaust' sceptic, gets dragged into the lake.

How Did He Do That?: Faraday asks the question for us, concerning Mulder's frog/food-chain leap.

Scully Here is a Medical Doctor: She puts a tourniquet on Faraday's leg.

Scully's Rational Explanation of the Week: Lake monsters are folk tales born of a collective fear of the unknown. It's a busy lake, people get killed, by boats and by drowning. One body's flies are undone, so he must have fallen in while relieving himself. The fish ate one of the torsos. As the sheriff says, 'I'm not at all convinced we're dealing with an aquatic menace.'

Phwoar!: Scully's sadness over her dog makes you want to hug her, but Mulder just doesn't understand. Marooned on the rock, they manage some very charged small talk, prompting Mulder to ask, 'Scully, are you coming on to me?' But very obviously they don't attempt to keep each other warm. Mulder's stutter reappears as he reveals another small piece of his soul: that he'd prefer to have a handicap than an obsession, because a handicap would give him good cause to work hard and improve. Faraday arrives with 'Hope I'm not interrupting anything', and Scully's reaction is pure comedy guilt. They're able to talk now about the nature of their dispute earlier this season (does Mulder pursue the truth without reason?). And Scully comes to understand and accept him a bit more.

Dialogue Triumphs: Stoner: 'Dude, what's wrong with you? You made me drop my toad.'

Faraday: 'If you'll excuse me, I have some amphibians to release.'

Continuity: Scully has apparently lost some weight lately (as we all know . . .). Her father taught her to respect nature ''cos it has no respect for you'. She won't put her dog in kennels (problem solved) and can pilot a small boat. As a child, Scully was interested in the mysteries of the deep. Then 'I grew up, and became a scientist.' Mulder, too, is familiar with *Moby Dick*.

The Truth: A big alligator has been eating people and frogs. But there is also (badly animated though it might be) a real sea serpent in Heuvelmans Lake.

Trivia: Tyler Labine and Nicole Parker reprise their roles of Stoner and Chick from 'War of the Coprophages', still trying to open the 'doors of perception'. This story begins on a Saturday. Big Blue is possibly a reference to IBM (after Gates was the villain in Kim Newton's last script . . .). Mention is made of the Loch Ness, Lake Champlain and Ogopogo monsters. Heuvelman's Lake is named after Van Heuvels, a Dutch cryptozoologist who was an expert on sea serpents. The Doors, Jimi Hendrix, Hole and Primus are referenced by the kids, along with the Discovery Channel and *Unsolved Mysteries*. There are visual references to *Jaws*, and an extended metaphor around *Moby Dick*, with Scully's little dog being called Queequeg (whose death Mulder, cast as Ahab, ignores in his obsessive pursuit). Interestingly (given what it was doing to its previous owner in 'Clyde Bruckman's

Final Repose'), in *Moby Dick*, Queequeg was a cannibal.

The Bottom Line: PC: This one resembles nothing more than one of those Vodaphone adverts starring Kyle Maclachlan. It's way cool, though, the cult of Darin Morgan having taken the two Kims for members. The series has started to demonstrate that what some newspaper critics have alleged (that fans watch the show believing it to reveal 'the truth') is nonsense. This episode is a case in point, as our gaze is invited to rest on such implicitly silly sights as Scully piloting a boat, and that first shot of her little dog, which has the viewers yelling, 'He's dead meat!' The sitcom direction holds everything in an ironic frame, recognising that, before the third season, our lead characters had so solidified as icons that seeing them doing ordinary things like washing dogs is hilarious, and that this trick can be played without damaging their credibility. Mulder and Scully tracking monsters with a little dog in tow is wonderful to watch, and the viewers are smart enough to dig this stuff. The only problem with the script is that once we've started to recognise and enjoy the *Moby Dick* metaphor, Scully actually tells us it to make sure we all got it. And the mountains of Georgia were nice. Just when we're thinking it's refreshing to see such closure from *The X-Files* (there was a monster, and Mulder shot it), we get that final frame, which is cheesy, but yeah, in that it encapsulates the continuing search for mystery . . . is rather sweet.

MD: A wonderful monster story that's as comfortable as a pair of old slippers. Simple subversions – the fisherman catching a corpse (not the expected monster), the man in boots being chased by a similar-footed creature, the duck in the mist – are balanced by little elements such as Mulder and Scully's discussion of cannibalism. Not for the first time, though, I can't help but think that only sickos read their kids *Moby Dick* at bedtime.

KT: 'You slew the Big White Whale, Ahab.' I like this one a lot (especially Faraday's rant about pseudo-scientists chasing fairytales). The scene on the rock is another definitive *X-Files* moment.

72: 'Wetwired'

US Transmission: 10 May 1996
UK Transmission: 6 August 1996 (Sky One)
Writer: Mat Beck
Director: Rob Bowman
Cast: Colin Cunningham, Tim Henry, Linden Banks,
Crystal Verge, Andre Danyliu, Joe Maffei, John McConnach,
Joe Do Serro, Heather McCarthy

Mulder gets a tip-off from someone he doesn't recognise concerning a man who's killed five people, thinking that they were all the same person. The killer taped cable news. Scully watches it, and finds mention of a Serbian war criminal on the nights of the killings. That night, she sees Mulder in conversation with the Smoking Man. Many other similar killings occur. Mulder pursues a TV engineer, and finds a strange golden attenuator in a cable TV box, which the *Lone Gunman* editors explain sends signals between the frames of a TV picture. Scully gets more and more paranoid, and shoots at Mulder. The FBI begin to hunt her. Mulder is told she's dead, but it's not her. Mulder goes to Mrs Scully's house, and finds Scully hiding there, afraid, ready to kill him. Her mother persuades her not to. Mulder deduces that the doctor who examined the first killer is controlling this experiment: he's met with the Smoking Man. But just as Mulder tracks him down, X arrives and kills all involved. He and Mulder have a confrontation. X explains that he tried to let Mulder get to these people first, but he let himself be sidetracked by Scully. X meets with the Smoking Man, and tells him that the security leak has been closed: his position is still safe.

Don't Be in the Teaser: A poor chap kills two people, including his partner, thinking they're a war criminal.

Scully's Rational Explanation of the Week: Amphetamine abuse and too much TV-watching.

Scully's Irrational Explanation of the Week: That Mulder has sold them out to their enemies.

Phwoar!: Mulder's utter lack of visible reaction until he knows that isn't Scully's corpse. His kick at the car. Scully, armed and dangerous, is an extraordinary sight to behold.

Dialogue Triumphs: Scully has got so used to the conspiracy stories by now that her first question to Mulder about his contact is: 'What does he want us to recover?'

Mulder: 'Yeah, but those studies are based on the assumption that Americans are just empty vessels, ready to be filled with any idea or image that's fed to them, like a bunch of Pavlov dogs.'

The Conspiracy Starts at Closing Time: X is the Smoking Man's lieutenant, and his position is still secure, because his superior doesn't know he's leaking information. In this case, X leaked news of the television experiment to Mulder via a contact (whom he was then forced to kill to cover his tracks), and then found himself ordered, because of this breach of security, to kill the men running the experiment and clean it all up. He pursued them as slowly as he could, while encouraging Mulder to get to them first, but found that he couldn't help but win this race. Since the Smoking Man knows there's an information leak at a higher level, it seems that X's days are numbered. A weapon which sends people crazy via their TV, and encourages them to, ahem, trust no one, would be a wonderful pre-invasion weapon, and this seems to be why the conspiracy are developing it. The ultimate aim – according to X – certainly transcends commerce or politics.

Continuity: Mulder is red/green colour-blind. He toys with a basketball. He doesn't believe that cow flatulence is depleting the ozone layer, or that violence on TV causes real violence, which he thinks is 'political bunkum', making him rather left-wing, if politically innocent. (He's probably so pro-TV because it's been his constant companion for so long . . . and he's not paranoid at all!) Scully's greatest paranoias are that Mulder may be working for the conspiracy, and that her home is bugged (though both Mulder and Scully are by now used to the idea that their phones are tapped). Her final collapse is set off by stumbling into a scenario very like that of Melissa's murder. Mrs Scully has photos of herself and a baby and of both the Scully sisters by her bed. Special Agent Pendrell of the Sci Crime Lab is mentioned, as is Danny (see 'Avatar').

The Truth: The conspiracy have developed a weapon that uses television signals to make viewers paranoid, fearful and violent.

Trivia: Two incredibly self-conscious girls with flowers walk down the hospital corridor, eyeing up Mulder. Whose nieces were those?

One of the tapes Scully watches is labelled *Jeopardy*.

Die Hard is on the TV as the cable man cuts the connection.

Scientific Comment: The *Lone Gunman* editors state that television is a rapid sequence of still pictures fired against the tube. At best this is a highly misleading description, at worst it's plain wrong. A TV picture is a set of lines with half of the lines repeating at 50 cycles/sec, and the other half also at 50 cycles/sec between these. The episode's description makes it sound like a very fast slide show. It's then stated that the subliminal messages are in the signal between the frames. If this was so, the messages would never be 'fired at the screen' (using their terminology) and so wouldn't be seen. To be seen, the subliminal messages would have to replace the picture itself.

The Bottom Line: PC: A non-conspiracy conspiracy episode which manages to bring a breath of fresh air to the activities of the Smoking Man by offering us another nice, solid bit of closure. We now know who X works for. And he really ought to stop leaving those cigarettes around. It's odd to find Mulder talking about pseudo-science and being the non-paranoid one, but it's great to see the series finally recognising that Mulder and Scully would, by now, be hiding in their houses with the wardrobe against the door. The TV effects are wonderful, though it's a little worrying to find that cable news (and shopping channels!) are the culprits, rather than action series (a bit too close to home?). Still, with another astonishing performance from Gillian Anderson, another routine episode gets the magical touch of season three.

MD: Season three certainly ends with a fine clutch of stories. This is really rather good (though – I may as well be the first to say it – it is very like 'Blood').

KT: 'Television does not equal violence, I don't care what anyone says.' This *is* like 'Blood', but it has a wonderful anger of its own. Mulder's rant about those who use TV to make political points had me jumping up and down shouting 'yes . . . yes'.

73: 'Talitha Cumi'

US Transmission: 17 May 1996
UK Transmission: 13 August 1996 (Sky One)
Writer: Chris Carter,
from a story by David Duchovny and Chris Carter
Director: R.W. Goodwin
Cast: Roy Thinnes, Angelo Vacco, Hrothgar Mathews,
Stephen Demopoulos, John Maclaren, Cam Cronin,
Bonnie Ray

A gunman goes crazy in a burger bar. A man called Jeremiah Smith heals the victims, then vanishes from the scene. Mrs Mulder meets with the Smoking Man, who asks her to remember something. Mrs Mulder is then hospitalised, having had a stroke, and writes Mulder a note saying 'palm'. The Smoking Man finds Smith working at a social security office, and imprisons him. X shows Mulder photos of Mrs Mulder and the Smoking Man, telling Mulder that the stroke happened after the man left. Smith, meanwhile, turns himself in to the FBI, and answers all questions blandly, essentially closing the investigation. Mulder searches his mother's beach house. 'Palm' turns out to be an anagram of 'lamp': inside a lamp is a weapon similar to the one used by the alien bounty hunter. The Smoking Man interviews Smith in his cell. Smith is a shapeshifter, one who wants to offer humans hope. He tells the Smoking Man that he's dying of lung cancer and it's implied that he cures the Smoking Man, who then frees him. Mulder and Scully find 'their' Smith, but he escapes by shapeshifting. He is the alien bounty hunter. The bounty hunter arrives at the cell to kill Smith, but he's vanished. The Smoking Man visits Mrs Mulder in hospital, and tells Mulder that Smith has information about Samantha. X, seeking the alien weapon, meets Mulder. They fight, and back away from a stand-off. Scully is visited by Smith, who starts to tell her of a plan that involves Samantha. Mulder meets with them, and asks Smith to come and heal his mother, but the alien bounty hunter arrives, intending to kill Smith.

Don't Be in the Teaser: Well, in this case, do, because everybody ends up OK despite four people being shot.

How Did He Do That?: Mulder makes a connection between the two palms – 'You think it's a leap?' – and gets it absolutely wrong, but he does work it all out in the end.

Scully Here is a Medical Doctor: She gives Mulder an update on his mum's condition.

Scully's Rational Explanation of the Week: Mrs Mulder's linguistic centres have been scrambled: correct!

That's a Mouthful: The Smoking Man: 'This becomes a responsibility. The thing I'm now called upon to put right, and put down.'

Phwoar!: Mulder sobbing at his mum's bedside just demands a warm towel and some cocoa.

Dialogue Triumphs: Smith to the Smoking Man: 'You live in fear. That's your whole life.'

Dialogue Disasters: That whole muddled and misty verbal

duel between Smith and the Smoking Man. 'You talk!' shouts the Smoking Man. Indeed. We learn nothing and are simply bored by this undramatic mess of pseudery.

The Conspiracy Starts at Closing Time: The Smoking Man and the Mulders used to hang out together at the summer house. The Smoking Man knew the Mulders' children (unless Fox's memories have been severely tampered with, this must have been before he can remember). And he knew Mrs Mulder before Mulder was born. There's a hint that the Smoking Man and Mrs Mulder may have been lovers. He certainly cares for her. You don't think –? No, of course not. Although that would explain why the Smoking Man, who uses violent solutions on everybody else, has never used them on Mulder (except, of course, in 'Anasazi' – oh well, bang goes *that* theory!). X called an ambulance for Mrs Mulder, and wants Mulder to know of her and the Smoking Man's acquaintance. He knows that something is stored in the beach house, but only after Mulder finds it does he know what. And then he immediately wants it. Perhaps X knows that, at the moment of truth, the weapon will be the proof he needs to show somebody in authority, or, more likely, he wants the only weapon that can kill a shapeshifter for personal protection or for a planned assassination.

Smith used to be one of the conspiracy, a junior member, if his lowly but useful position in social security is anything to go by, but has now decided to give the humans 'hope'. He no longer believes in the 'greater purpose'. His touch can not only heal wounds, but suck up blood and dematerialise bullets. It doesn't patch up clothes (so we're not talking about a trick with time here), but perhaps that would just be unnecessary work. This sort of matter/energy manipulation is just the sort of thing that a real shapeshifter would have to be able to accomplish, and presumably all shapeshifters could do it if they wanted to. This is the first sign that their powers can extend to other people (and, in addition, that they can possibly influence their thoughts, as Smith almost does right at the beginning). The Smoking Man knows all too well that only a blow on the back of the neck by an alien weapon can kill a shapeshifter, so he summons the alien bounty hunter to act as Smith's executioner.

A date has been set for the colonisation of Earth (we're betting it's 13 October). To achieve this colonisation, humans must, for some reason, lose their belief in everything but science (either because this will leave them vulnerable to the various perception-altering weapons of the shapeshifters, or because this is the shapeshifters' own credo, which humans will be made to conform to). The Smoking Man is a human being, but wants to be a 'commandant', ruling over his own people (the image is of concentration camps) when the process (the transformation and mutation of humanity?) begins. The elaborate plan, or project, involving Samantha, may or may not be the colonisation plan itself. Perhaps, since the fate of Samantha is knowledge common to both the shapeshifter mainstream and the rebels, the plan may be some attempt by the rebels to gain the upper hand. 'I have a long and complicated story to tell you.' Let's hope we get to hear it. Skinner used to know how to contact the Smoking Man, but, as we suspected he would after Mulder went to his house, the man's made sure that this is no longer true. It's confirmed that he doesn't know the Smoking Man's real name.

Smith transforms into Bill Mulder and Deep Throat during his conversation with the Smoking Man (which seems to alarm him unduly: perhaps he wasn't aware that a lowly acolyte like Smith would know of these two high-rankers or the Smoking Man's former relations with them both).

Continuity: After her divorce, Mrs Mulder vowed never to return to the summer house at Quonochontaug, Rhode Island. Bill Mulder was a good water-skier, but nowhere near as good as the Smoking Man. That wasn't all Bill was the lesser man at, he says.

The Truth: see The Conspiracy Starts at Closing Time above.

Trivia: 'Talitha cumi' (or 'talitha koum') is New Testament

Greek for 'little girl, get up', and are the words used by Jesus when healing a child in Mark 5:41. (Both an apt reference for Smith's activities, an explicit reference to Mulder's desire to have his mother healed, and a nod in the direction of Samantha: is she now in a position to achieve something big?)

Angelo Vacco, a production assistant, appears as one of the healed gunshot victims. In real life, William B. Davis is a top veteran water-skier (what an extraordinary mental picture that conjures up . . .) The Smith/Smoking Man confrontation is a take on a scene from Dostoyevsky's *The Brothers Karamazov*. The original has a returning Jesus arrested by church leaders, and told that he burdened mankind with too much freedom, which they took away, because people want to be led. (So it's not only crap, it's unoriginal too . . .)

There are two separate references to '11.21'. It's the time when Mulder visits his mother in hospital, and, on another day, it's when Scully finds the pictures of Smith on her computer.

The Bottom Line: PC: The solid feel of the conspiracy stories in season three continues, with Diet Conspiracy, a firm, fast-paced story that doesn't try to lump in all the usual ingredients (Krycek, the *Lone Gunman* boys, etc.) for the hell of it, but just gets on with it. Unfortunately, in the middle of all that is an empty dialogue that proves, once and for all, that Chris Carter has never quite got the idea that drama is about doing, not talking. It's actually insulting that such sound and fury signifying nothing is supposed to be lapped up by the fans as deep and meaningful. We've seen deep and meaningful, and it's in the so-called 'comedy' episodes of Darin Morgan. That apart, this is a fitting end to the best season of *The X-Files*, one that saw Scully empowered, a lot of clichés flattened, and some intelligent thought put into developing and solidifying the back-story behind the most subversive, high-quality and zeitgeist-surfing television series on the planet.

MD: A hugely enjoyable finale with some fantastic effects.

There's just one dark cloud on the horizon. I'm not into wilful obscurity, but the writers – by starting to show us just what the blazes is going on – are beginning to paint themselves into a corner with this (massive) invasion/subversion/world domination thing. Next season this aspect will either have to be dropped or undermined in some way, or *The X-Files* will be on the verge of becoming the TV equivalent of *Independence Day*. In this context, the return of Morgan and Wong from *Space: Above and Beyond* is just a coincidence, isn't it?

KT: 'He's here to kill me . . .' A bit rambling in places, though I really enjoyed Mulder's fight with X. Judgement deferred on this one, I think. Time will tell whether it's a disappointing blind alley, or another link in one of the most remarkable story arcs series television (especially American series television) has ever produced. My money's on the latter.

Fourth Season

45-minute episodes

Created by Chris Carter

Co-Producers: Paul Rabwin, Vince Gilligan, Frank Spotnitz
Consulting Producers: Ken Horton, James Wong,
Glen Morgan
Associate Producer: Lori Jo Nemhauser
Producers: Joseph Patrick Finn, Kim Manners,
Rob Bowman
Executive Producers: Chris Carter, R.J. Goodwin,
Howard Gordon

Regular Cast: David Duchovney (Fox Mulder), Gillian
Anderson (Dana Scully), Mitch Pileggi (Walter Skinner, 74,
76, 78, 81), Brendan Beiser (Pendrell, 74, 76, 81), Rebecca
Toolan (Mrs Mulder, 74), Steven Williams (X, 74), William
B. Davis (Smoking Man, 74, 80, 81), Brian Thompson (The
Pilot, 74), Laurie Holden (Marita Covarrubias, 74, 76, 81),
Bruce Harwood (Byers, 80), Tom Braidwood (Frohike, 80),
Jerry Hardin (Deep Throat, 80), Nicholas Lea (Alex Krycek,
81), John Neville (Well-Manicured Man, 81)

74: 'Herrenvolk'

US transmission: 4 October 1996
Writer: Chris Carter
Director: R.W. Goodwin
Cast: Roy Thinnes, Morris Panych, Garvin Cross,
Ken Camroux, Michael David Simms

Smith and Mulder escape, Mulder stabbing the Pilot in the
back of the neck with the alien weapon. Smith takes Mulder
to see both the great plan ... and his sister. They head for
Canada, where they find a repairman stung to death by bees.

The revived Pilot forces Scully to find out where they're going and follows them. Meanwhile, the conspiracy are aware of a security leak, and let X know that Mrs Mulder is under threat. Skinner has found five Smiths across the country, all compiling data. Scully manages to decipher that data: it's an inventory of protein tags put into humans as part of the Smallpox Eradication Programme. Her superiors find that hard to believe. Mulder and Smith find covered fields of an unknown shrub and, working on the farm, many copies of his sister at the age she was abducted. The Pilot arrives at the farm, and Mulder hides with Smith and 'Samantha' in a vast apiary. The Pilot, badly hurt, chases Smith and leaves Mulder. Mulder returns to the hospital, where Scully, advised by X, has placed a guard on his mother. But there is no threat; it's a trick by the conspiracy to test X's loyalty. He's ambushed and shot, writing 'SRSG' in blood before he dies. That means: 'Special Representative to the Secretary General' of the UN. Mulder meets Marita Covarrubias, the assistant to that person, in New York and, while rebuffing all his claims about the farm, she covertly gives him photos of Samantha. Smoking Man makes the Pilot heal Mrs Mulder, saying that Mulder, who is important to the project, must always have something to lose.

Don't be in the Teaser: Scully is surprised by the Pilot's sudden reanimation.

Scully Here is a Medical Doctor: 'You show a twenty-letter code to any scientist and they immediately think "protein amino acid sequence code"!' She does a great job with the smallpox vaccination information.

Ooze: From the back of the Pilot's neck, and on the face of the stung repairman.

Scully's Conspiracy Theory: Smallpox jabs plant a protein used as a tag, a genetic marker. This has been going on for fifty years. 'This sounds like something we might have expected from Agent Mulder,' one of the FBI men tells her.

That's a Mouthful: Smith: 'A flowering shrub, but its specific epithet can't be found on any of your taxinomic charts.'

Phwoar!: Mulder tells Scully that he needs her to know that he's OK. Scully holds Mulder by his mum's bedside. Pendrell gets all hot under the collar, and Mulder's new 'Deep Throat' seems very sympathetic. They're not going to set up romantic complications here, are they?

Dialogue Triumphs: X: 'Protect the mother.'
Marita: 'Not everything dies, Mr Mulder.'

The Conspiracy Starts at Closing Time: The human race are apparently being tagged and inventoried through fifty years of smallpox innoculations. This indicates that each individual person will have a specific use when the shapeshifters arrive. Either that, or they're just incredibly finicky about knowing who they've got left to round up. The New-York-based Special Representative to the United Nations (one of several) is certainly part of the conspiracy.

The shapeshifters may feed on the honey produced by bees feeding on the pollen of their alien shrub. This foodstuff may explain why the bees' stings are deadly. The shapeshifters' agrarian workforce consists of serial ovatypes, clones who, at least in the case of these particular drones, can't speak. Smith himself is a drone, but presumably his function dictated the need for communication. The farm worker drones and Smith are immune to the bee stings, so it's slightly odd that the Pilot (who presumably therefore isn't a drone) is not. The fact that these clones include a clone of Samantha, a human, is also odd. Either the shapeshifters have a limited store of human shapes to copy (which could be one use for their genetic register, and suggests that the rebel shapeshifters of 'Apocrypha' kept the same tactics as their former faction), or there's something very special about Samantha. Considering that Mulder is regarded as important to the plan (now, since Smoking Man tried to kill him in 'Anasazi'), could it possibly be that the Mulder children are, in some way, not entirely human, perhaps having been created with shapeshifter DNA, so Samantha looked like a pre-existing shapeshifter template? Irony of ironies, if so. It could simply be that Bill Mulder took her genetic data for the shapeshifter data files before she was abducted, and it's been routinely used to churn out clones.

Smith and the Pilot both make big leaps, as we've seen shapeshifters do in the past. All shapeshifters, it would be safe to conclude, since an assassin like the Pilot can do it, can heal wounds by touch. There is only metaphor to suggest that they are at all insect-like. The plan of the invaders is known as 'the process'. Smith regards it as a new origin of species, which can't mean that the shapeshifters are going to bond with human DNA (unless their views have radically changed), but possibly that they plan to introduce many of their own species to Earth. The humans within government who are helping the aliens one might now take actually to be shapeshifters, considering that their plan is now obviously colonisation, something that most humans wouldn't really go along with. 'Everybody dies' is either a shapeshifter slogan which Marita has heard, or her mentioning the phrase is sheer coincidence.

The Truth: The shapeshifters have been preparing foodstuffs for their species on secret farms with UN backing. Scully's conspiracy theory also appears to be true: Americans are being catalogued, tagged and inventoried by a government organisation.

Trivia: From the start of this season, Mitch Pileggi gets an 'Also Starring' credit in the opening titles. Smith's boat is called the *Silver Streak*.

The Bottom Line: KT: 'Don't unlock doors you're not prepared to go through.' Strange episode this. Huge opening five-minute chase sequence with a debt to *Terminator* larger than the national debt of a third world country. Good music (particularly the industrial/techno stuff). *The X-Files* does *Swarm* with the bee metaphor plastered all over the episode. The ending is enigmatically brilliant ('you know how important Agent Mulder is to the equation') but . . . Are we ever going to get some *proper* answers? Probably not, or the series is finished!

PC: Some cool images, including insect-like conformity in farming pastureland, and some obvious steals from *Doctor Who* (the Sontarans' neck weakness, Dalek interior music for the Pilot's chase scenes), *Quatermass II*, and *The Invaders*, which could now almost be in the same canon as this show. It's good to see Scully using science as a tool to get to the truth, the demonstration of which the show's rationalist detractors often ignore. There is, however, more of that horrid 'poetic' dialogue. I'm not as disturbed by a lack of answers as I used to be. I've come to expect that, which may be a shame.

MD: Is the fourth season the one that finally reveals that the emperor has no clothes? In 'Herrenvolk' Mulder finally gets to meet Jeremiah but, instead of getting him to tell everything he knows about the conspiracy, they set off for a trek across country. And then, just when Jeremiah is about to spill the beans, the alien bounty hunter shows up. Oh, *please!* We aren't really told anything of significance during this depressingly routine episode. Although the ending is good, and the iconography memorable, 'Herrenvolk' is fatally flawed by bringing the alien killer back to life. Given that the thrust of this and previous stories is that they *can* be killed by the pointy gadget, to deny us that logical outcome is (like the lack of explanations) just plain silly.

75: 'Home'

US Transmission: 11 October 1996
Writers: Glen Morgan, James Wong
Director: Kim Manners
Cast: Tucker Smallwood, Chis Nelson Norris,
Adrian Hughes, John Trotter, Karin Konoval,
Sebastian Spence, Judith Maxie, Kenny James

Mulder and Scully arrive in the small Pennsylvanian town,

Home, after the grizzly discovery of a deformed infant body. Obvious suspects seem to be three retarded brothers who live in the family home close to the crime scene, though the local sheriff is sceptical about their involvement. Scully is shocked by the number of genetic defects displayed by the baby's body, suggesting inbreeding. The agents visit the Peacock farm and find evidence of a recent birth. Before they can be arrested the brothers murder the sheriff. Mulder and Scully, with a vengeful deputy, return to the farm where the deputy is killed. They find the men's mother, a helpless invalid, in the house and survive an attack from the men, killing two of them. The third escapes with his mother.

Don't Be in the Teaser: A newborn child is buried alive in a muddy field. Nice family entertainment there . . .

Scully Here is a Medical Doctor: She examines the dead child and is horrified by its numerous birth defects.

Ooze: Blood and mud. Urgh!

That's a Mouthful: Mulder: 'What we are witnessing, Scully, is undiluted animal behaviour. Mankind absent in its own creation of civilisation, technology and information regressed to an almost prehistoric state, obeying only the often savage laws of nature.' And several other similarly stilted rants about anything and everything. Good grief, it doesn't even *sound* like him!

Scully's Rational Explanation of the Week: The Peacocks kidnapped and raped some helpless girl and held her until she gave birth.

Phwoar!: In one of the few good scenes in the episode, Mulder comforts Scully after she is obviously upset by the state of the baby's body. He touches her back gently and asks whether her family has any history of genetic defects. She says they haven't and he tells her to 'find yourself a man with a spotless genetic make-up and a really high tolerance for being second-guessed, and start pumping out the little Uber-Scullies'! Now who on Earth could *that* refer to?!

Dialogue Triumphs: Scully: 'If you had to do without a cellphone for two minutes you'd lapse into catatonic schizophrenia.'

Continuity: Mulder used to play 'all-day pick-up games' of baseball with his sister in the vineyard of their home, which he fondly remembers along with riding their bikes to the beach and eating baloney sandwiches.

Mulder says he dreams of leaving the city behind and making his home in a small rural community like this.

The Truth: A straightforward tale of incest, infanticide and murder.

Trivia: Johnny Mathis's 'Wonderful' accompanies the murder of Sheriff Taylor.

The Bottom Line: KT: 'They're such good boys . . .' Sick. Really horrible on every level. There's nothing redeeming in this dreadful waste of time and talent; echoes of *To Kill a Mockingbird* and *Psycho* at the beginning give way to a depressingly ugly series of set-pieces taken from *The Texas Chainsaw Massacre* and *The Hills Have Eyes*. The episode contains a pre-titles warning of the carnage to come ('Due to some graphic and mature content, parental discretion is advised'). Pity they didn't include a warning about insulting the audience's intelligence too.

Only two things save it from complete worthlessness – the previously mentioned Mulder/Scully scene, which is charming, and Mulder's discovery of a newspaper from the day Elvis died. I can't believe the writers of 'E.B.E.', 'Beyond the Sea' and 'Blood' wrote this abomination.

PC: The series has been trying to address real-world savagery of late and, I suspect because it has no traditional values to fall back on (thank goodness), often slips up in doing it. This episode treats its horrors as those of a movie, which our heroes simply walk through, rather than as those of real life. Not as gruesome as Keith indicates, 'Home' is rather the victim of an uncertainty about what it's trying to be.

76: 'Teliko'

US Transmission: 18 October 1996
Writer: Howard Gordon
Director: James Charleston
Cast: Carl Lumbly, Willie Amakye, Zakes Mokae,
Maxine Guess, Bill Mackenzie, Bob Morrisey,
Michael O'Shea, Danny Wattley

Summoned to Skinner's office, Scully is asked her medical opinion on a recently discovered body. A man, an African-American, has undergone a dramatic change, losing all his skin pigmentation. Mulder's investigations (aided by Marita Covarrubias) lead him to a toxic plant from West Africa and Samuel Aboah, a recent immigrant. Aboah appears to have no pituitary gland. A minister from Burkino Faso blames the deaths on the legendary Teliko, evil spirits who drain their victims of life and colour. Mulder, however, comes to believe that the Teliko are nothing more than members of an African tribe, who hunt down other humans to steal hormones from the pituitary gland (which in turn leads to the change in skin colour of their victims). Aboah escapes the hospital and, while pursued, uses a thorn to immobilise Mulder. Scully rescues her partner, shooting the African before he can finish Mulder off.

Don't Be in the Teaser: An African turns white and dies in an aeroplane toilet.

Scully Here is a Medical Doctor: She performs an autopsy on Owen Sanders and several medical tests on Aboah.

That's a Mouthful: Scully: 'Not everything is a labyrinth of dark conspiracy. And not everybody is plotting to deceive, inveigle and obfuscate'. This doesn't even sound like *her* (see previous episode!).

Dialogue Triumphs: Mulder: 'There's a Michael Jackson joke in here somewhere, but I can't quite find it.'

Dialogue Disasters: Mulder: 'Hey, I heard you were down

here slicing and dicing. Who's the lucky stiff?'

Continuity: Pendrell seems crushed when he hears that Scully has a date.

Trivia: The episode titles replaced 'The Truth is Out There' with 'Deceive Inveigle Obfuscate'.

The Truth: Mulder's probably right. There are members of a lost African tribe who, in order to survive, must extract the hormones that they lack from the pituitary glands of other humans. Or maybe they really are ghostly entities – Scully shoots Aboah before we can find out for sure.

The Bottom Line: KT: 'I had hoped if I closed my eyes it would go away this time.' Speed-written reworking of 'Squeeze'. Some interesting bits and pieces of African tribal culture, but it's all been done before. A further example of *The X-Files* running on the spot – come on, guys, you're capable of better than this.

PC: A potential minefield just about avoided, with some cool dialogue. They're trying to find weirder fields for the series to venture into rather than explore other branches of Fortean lore as the comic strip does.

77: 'Unruhe'

US Transmission: 27 October 1996
Writer: Vince Gilligan
Director: Rob Bowman
Cast: Pruitt Taylor Vince, Sharon Alexander, Walter Marsh,
Angela Donahue, William MacDonald, Ron Chartier,
Michael Cram, Christopher Royal, Michelle Melland,
Scott Heindl

Traverse City, Michigan. A young woman has a passport photo taken and then disappears, whilst her boyfriend is killed. The developed photo shows the woman screaming surrounded by ghostly images. Soon the woman is found, having been the victim of an amateur lobotomy. Another woman is abducted in similar circumstances. While Scully follows up a possible lead concerning a construction company, Mulder takes photos from the two crime sites to Washington for enhancement. Finding hidden clues within the photo he calls Scully, who arrests a man, Gerry Schnauz, a former mental patient. Schnauz is haunted by his sister's suicide and his attack on his father, blaming both on 'the howlers', evil spirits living within people's minds. Lobotomisation is his attempt to cure the women. He escapes and captures Scully, intending to perform the same treatment on her, but Mulder arrives in the nick of time and kills him.

Don't Be in the Teaser: Mary Louise LeFante is drugged and kidnapped. Her boyfriend, Billy, is stabbed in the head.

How Did He Do That?: One of Mulder's finer leaps sussing out the presence of 'thoughtographs' on the film in Mary's camera.

Scully Here is a Medical Doctor: She graphically describes Mary's 'ice-pick lobotomy'.

Scully's Rational Explanation of the Week: Heat-damage to the film, which is also out of date. Or the photographer was involved in the kidnap. 'All right, so what's your theory?'

Dialogue Triumphs: Mulder: 'Bad year . . . What else happened in 1980?' Gerry: 'Well, John Lennon got shot. Where you going with this?'

Continuity: Scully took German in college.

The Truth: Schnauz, traumatised by personal demons, has (seemingly) developed an elaborate scheme to 'save' the women he is attracted to from their own demons ('the howlers').

Trivia: The title means 'unrest' in German.

The Bottom Line: KT: 'Let's talk about "The Howlers".' Scary. Again, loads of obvious roots are visible, including *The*

Silence of the Lambs and *The Legend of Hell House* as well as really clear debts to two of the series' own episodes, 'Shadows' and 'Grotesque'. But for all that, this is three-quarters of the way towards a really good episode – the first sign that season four has picked up from its frankly disappointing start. The ending, however, lets it down. It's somewhat sad that, given Scully's stated empathy with Schnauz in the concluding scene (a mirror-image of Mulder's descent into hell in 'Grotesque'), she still has to be tied to a dentist's chair and slavered over before Mulder comes charging in. The empowerment of much of season three seems to have gone along with Darin Morgan. Sad.

PC: Rather wonderful, but didn't we get rid of Scully strapped to chairs last season? This is all getting off to a woefully slow start as far as coherence of theme and intent go. Looking at these seasons early has always been a mistake, but let me make it again: I still think the third season has a quality that we're so far missing here.

78: 'The Field Where I Died'

US Transmission: 3 November 1996
Writers: Glen Morgan, James Wong
Director: Rob Bowman
Cast: Kristen Cloke, Michael Massee, Anthony Harrison,
Doug Abrahams, Donna White, Michael Dobson

The FBI raid the farm owned by the religious cult The Temple of the Seven Stars in Apison, Tennessee searching for a cache of weapons. Preventing the suicide of the charismatic leader Vernon and his seven wives, Mulder and Scully interrogate one of the wives, Melissa, who appears to regress to previous lives, including one in which she and Mulder were lovers. While Scully investigates possible links in the past, Mulder undergoes regression hypnosis. As the FBI continue to search for the weapons, the cult members are released and, under Vernon's instructions, commit suicide,

Melissa among them, Mulder arriving just too late to save her.

Don't Be in the Teaser: . . . Or you'll have to suffer Mulder chanting drivel at you!

That's a Mouthful: 'At times I almost dream. I too have spent a life the sage's way and tread once more familiar paths. Perchance, I perished in an arrogant self-alliance an age ago. And in that act of prayer, went up so earnest . . .'
  Like, yeah. Very poetic lads, but what the hell does it mean?

Scully's Rational Explanation of the Week: Multiple Personality Disorder (spot on – see The Truth).

Phwoar!: Mulder and Scully's heart-to-heart over their passage through time together is amazingly touching. Their friendship even survives Scully's anger at Mulder's casual use of Melissa to (hopefully) find answers about himself.

Dialogue Triumphs: Mulder: 'Souls come back together. Different, but always together. Again and again.'

Continuity: Scully says she wouldn't have changed a day of her and Mulder's four years together (although she could have 'lived without that flukeworm thing' – see 'The Host').

The Truth: Melissa and Mulder discover under hypnosis that they seem to have lived past lives as Sarah Kavanaugh and Sullivan Biddle, two Confederates during the civil war in November 1863. Mulder's claim that souls come together again and again (Scully was the sergeant of his platoon) is interesting. But rubbish. During another regression he claims he was a Jewish woman in a Nazi concentration camp and that Scully, Samantha and Melissa were related to him. Fine. Possible. But then he goes and spoils it by claiming that Smoking Man was a Gestapo guard. Despite the fact that Smoking Man would have been alive during the years of Nazi terror. Ooops. So, we're back to Scully's theory about Multiple Personality Disorder. And Mulder is susceptible enough to Melissa's fantasies to place himself into them.

Trivia: The disasters of Waco and Jonestown are both mentioned (and there are specific plot allusions to both). There are lots of Biblical quotations thrown around, most seeming pretty accurate (despite his scepticism in 'Revelations', Mulder seems surprisingly well versed in the book of 'Revelation').

The Bottom Line: KT: Now this is better! Apart from the one walloping great continuity error above (that throws the intended reincarnation/regression concept out of the window) this is a flawless script aided by a series of astonishing performances (Duchovny and Kristen Cloke especially). A couple of subplots (the child abuse one, chiefly) get lost in the maelstrom, but this script has a cohesion and focus altogether missing from those shown previously in the season. This season's 'Beyond the Sea'. Utterly impressive.

PC: This is silly! Very well done, but operatic fan fiction tosh all the same. One of those areas of weirdness that I have no interest in, though, so that affects my judgement. Shouldn't fan fiction respect continuity?

79: 'Sanguinarium'

US Transmission: 10 November 1996
Writers: Valerie Mayhew, Vivian Mayhew
Director: Kim Manners
Cast: Richard Beymer, O-Lan Jones, Arlene Mazerolle,
Gregory Thirloway, John Juliani, Paul Raskin,
Andrew Airlie, Marie Stillin, Norman Armour, Martin Evans

Greenwood Memorial Hospital, and Mulder and Scully investigate the claims of a doctor who has recently killed a patient whilst, he says, undergoing an out-of-body experience. Mulder is convinced the doctor was possessed and finds evidence of a pentagram in the operating theatre. Suspicion falls on a nurse who attacks another doctor at his home. He fights her off and she dies, having ingested hundreds of needles.

The deaths at the hospital continue and provide links to a

series of deaths ten years ago. Mulder concludes that Dr Franklin is responsible – killing patients born on sabbats in a bizarre ritual to gain a new identity. Despite Mulder and Scully saving the life of one potential victim, Franklin completes his plan and turns up at a hospital in Los Angeles wearing a new face.

Don't Be in the Teaser: Dr Lloyd liposuctions a patient to death.

Scully Here is a Medical Doctor: She's really at home in a hospital, reminding an entire operating theatre of her credentials. ('I'm an FBI agent . . . I'm a doctor!') She says that in medical school she saw 'some weird stuff' and her rant about the immorality of cosmetic surgery against managed health care is the stuff of a thousand party political broadcasts.

Ooze: Blood. Tonnes of it!

Scully's Rational Explanation of the Week: Medical malpractice. Lack of sleep. Drug use. And lots of guff about bizarre medical conditions. All of which are much easier to swallow than witchcraft.

Dialogue Triumphs: Scully: 'There is magic going on here, Mulder, only it's being done with silicon, collagen and a well-placed scalpel.'

Scully: 'If it's that simple, why don't you put out an APB for someone riding a broom and wearing a tall black hat?'

Continuity: Mulder seems to spend the episode thinking about having a nose-job.

The Truth: Black Magic, pure and simple. Dr Franklin (formerly Dr Cox) has the ability to transport objects into people's bodies (which is a really neat party trick). He is also able through means unknown to use the deaths of people born on the four sabbats in a ceremony to cut off his own face and (seemingly) grow a new one. He can also levitate. But why?

Trivia: Mulder again shows off his biblical knowledge, in this case quoting from Ecclesiastes ('Vanity, all is vanity').

The Bottom Line: KT: 'I think this patient is finished.' Wow, this is nasty! There's a lot of good characterisation on display, the switching of suspects is clever and the bathroom sequence is suitably shocking. But, really, this is nothing more than a lot of old horror clichés thrown about without much imagination. And the lack of explanations gets very annoying by the end. In a definite throwback to 'GenderBender' we're given a series of things happening and absolutely no idea why they happen (other than the fact that the occult is at work).

MD: The first couple of minutes lead you to expect a witty and shocking discussion about cosmetic surgery and self-image; instead, 'Sanguinarium' is full of mindless gore and hopeless dead ends. There is no real interaction with other characters, no investigation, no dramatic progression. It's just a series of gross set pieces (although, for me, nothing was more stomach-churning than the pre-title sequence of the doctor scrubbing his hands). Only nice bit: Mulder's hilarious reaction to Scully's quip about the APB.

80: 'Musings of a Cigarette Smoking Man'

US Transmission: 17 November 1996
Writer: Glen Morgan
Director: James Wong
Cast: Morgan Weisser, Chris Owens, Donnelly Rhodes, Dan Zukovic, Peter Hanlon, Dean Aylesworth, Paul Jarrett, David Fredericks, Laurie Murdoch

The Smoking Man enters a building opposite the *Lone Gunman* offices and eavesdrops electronically on a conversation between Mulder, Scully, Byers and Frohike in which the latter says he knows who the Smoking Man is, and who he wants to be. The Smoking Man remembers various significant moments in his life, including assassinating John F. Kennedy and Martin Luther King, and an occasion on which he and Deep Throat encountered an alien. He could easily kill Mulder, and the rest of them, but decides not to.

That's a Mouthful: Young Smoking Man: 'You've enough plausible deniability to last the rest of your nine lives.'

Later: 'Sure, once in a while there's a peanut butter cup or an English toffee, but they're gone too fast, the taste is fleeting. So you end up with nothing but broken bits filled with hardened jelly and teeth-shattering nuts.'

Dialogue Triumphs: Mulder: 'No one would kill you, Frohike. You're just a little puppy dog.'

Young Smoking Man: 'I'd rather read the worst novel ever written than sit through the best movie ever made.'

Concerning the assassination of JFK: 'Is there a cover story?' 'Tell them it was done by men from outer space!'

The Smoking Man: 'I work very hard to keep any President from knowing I even exist.'

And: 'Once again, tonight, the course of human history will be set by two unknown men standing in the shadows.'

And the marvellously unexpected: 'Life is like a box of chocolates. A cheap, thoughtless, perfunctory gift that nobody ever asks for!'

The Conspiracy Starts at Closing Time: The Smoking Man was born ('appears') on 20 August 1940 in Baton Rouge, Louisiana (on the same day that Trotsky was assassinated) (see box). His father was a Soviet spy who was executed for passing information on America's entry into World War II to the Nazis. His mother (a smoker) died of lung cancer (which would explain his early disinterest in cigarettes ('I never touch 'em'), and his reaction in 'Talitha Cumi' to being told that this is how he too will die). He was thus orphaned while still a baby, and became a lonely child who read extensively. Then, according to Frohike, he disappeared until October 1962. At this stage he appears to have been a captain in the US military, serving alongside Bill Mulder. He denies having been involved in covert action in Central America in 1961 (but then, he would, wouldn't he?). All of this sounds very like the CIA Black Ops Department. Maybe he, Bill Mulder and Deep Throat were part of a CIA team working within the military. By 1968, the Smoking Man is in such a position that he treats J. Edgar Hoover as subservient. He respected Martin Luther King ('an extraordinary man') and supported his stance on civil rights, but suggested, and carried out, his murder because of perceived communist leanings.

The 'departmental projects' he is overseeing on Christmas Eve 1991 include the Anita Hill case, the moving of the Rodney King trial, Bosnian independence ('America couldn't care less,' he says perceptively), and the Oscar nominations. The fixing of the Superbowl (for reasons unknown, the Smoking Man doesn't want to see the Buffalo Bills win the trophy as long as he's alive), and his rigging of the 1980 Olympic Ice Hockey final (in which the USA unexpectedly beat the USSR), thanks to payments to the Russian goaltender, indicate that the Smoking Man and his cohorts may control *everything* in the world. He says he'll call Saddam Hussain back!

He intends to keep a personal eye on Fox Mulder, who has managed to get himself assigned to the X-Files. (There are further hints that Mulder is his son – why else would he constantly carry a photo of Mrs Mulder and the baby Fox?) His discussion with Deep Throat is full of astonishing pieces of information. Roswell 'was concocted to keep everyone looking the wrong way' (presumably this is a reference to the subsequent media story rather than the actual crash itself – see 'The Erlenmeyer Flask'). A live E.B.E. 'could advance Bill Mulder's project by decades', but Deep Throat quotes (UN?) Security Council Resolution 10–13 (surprise!) concerning the extermination of aliens (see 'E.B.E.'). (He lies to Deep Throat, saying that he's not killed before (see box), and it wouldn't be at all surprising if he made use of a loaded coin.) The plaster he is wearing looks like a nicotine patch, but might indicate a recent implantation or removal of an (alien?) communications device.

Continuity: Fox's first word, according to his father, was 'JFK' (as this is in October 1962, he would have been eleven months old). We get another glimpse of Scully's senior thesis on Einstein's twin paradox (University of Maryland, dated

15 May 1988) – see the pilot episode.

The Smoking Man seemingly didn't smoke until November 1963. His (Zippo?) lighter is inscribed 'Trust No One'. He writes under the pseudonym Raul Bloodworth. His stories concern a secret agent named Jack Colquitt. Two novels specifically referred to in this episode are *Take a Chance*, which was brutally rejected by publishers in 1968, and *Second Chance* (concerning alien assassination) from the early nineties, which was serialised in the (salacious) magazine *Roman a'Clef* [sic], but with a rewritten ending. He is aware of the Aeschylus poem Robert Kennedy quoted at the funeral of Dr King.

In addition to *The Lone Gunman*, Byers, Langly and Frohike seem to publish another newsletter, *The Magic Bullet*. (In fact, they appear to have appropriated their original magazine's title for themselves, the plaque on the door reading 'The Lone Gunmen'.) Frohike believes the Smoking Man is trying to kill him, much to Mulder's amusement (but he's actually quite correct). Byers states that no electronic surveillance device can cut through the (aptly named!) CSM-25 Counter-Measure Filter (he's wrong!). It is implied that Deep Throat was the conspiracy's chief propagandist, being in charge of deadly 'lies'.

The Truth: The Smoking Man was the assassin of both John Kennedy (from a sewer rather than the grassy knoll!) and Martin Luther King. Both Lee Oswald and James Earl Ray were specific 'patsies' for these crimes while working for the Smoking Man. A UFO crash site during Christmas 1991 sees Deep Throat (again) killing an alien after tossing a coin with the Smoking Man.

Trivia: The episode includes five captions at the beginning of the episode and subsequently at the start of each 'act':

  ' "For Nothing can seem foul to those that win." *Henry IV, Pt 1*, Act 5, Sc. 1'
  'Part I: "Things really did go well in Dealey Plaza." '
  'Part II: "Just down the road aways from Graceland." '
  'Part III: "The most wonderful time of the year!" '

'Part IV: "The X-Files." '

Bill Mulder and the Smoking Man discuss *The Manchurian Candidate*. There are overt visual and dialogue references to *Apocalypse Now* (the scene in which the Smoking Man denies that the Bay of Pigs operation happened), *JFK* and *Forrest Gump*. Mention is made of Stokeley Carmichael and the Black Panthers.

Lee Oswald calls the Smoking Man 'Mr Hunt', presumably a reference to Howard Hunt, the CIA agent involved in Watergate and, allegedly, the Kennedy assassination (see Anthony Summers' *The Kennedy Conspiracy* for the full story).

All of the 1992 scenes featuring Scully come from stock footage from the pilot episode.

The Bottom Line: KT: 'I can kill you whenever I please. But not today.' A remarkable piece of work; a triumphant, stylish mixture of thirty years of American conspiracy theory, and a load of clever, very funny in-jokes. Love the Counter Measures Filter and the symbolic first cigarette after Lee Oswald's arrest. One of the best bits of the episode is the sequence in which the Smoking Man buys his colleagues (probably the closest thing he has to friends) identical ties as Christmas presents. At heart he's a sad, lonely, frustrated, bitter man who only wants to be a writer and would quit his job in an instant to fulfil his dream (and then turn up in *The X-Files*'s equivalent of the Village, no doubt!). He emerges from the episode with a great deal of sympathy from the audience, perhaps because we all recognise a little of ourselves and our own aspirations in him. I think if I ever got a publisher's rejection letter that included the words 'frankly crap', I'd turn into a cold-hearted killer too! Are you listening, publishers?

MD: A pretentious shaggy dog story, full of good jokes, but utterly unbelievable. This man who's killed more people than I've had hot dinners is really just a big softie who's had one novel too many rejected? No, I don't buy that for a moment. I was cringing with embarrassment at the garbage dialogue William B. Davis was given towards the end in the scene with the tramp (if his novels are anything like that, no wonder he's always getting turned down). *The X-Files* has always featured vast tracts of non-naturalistic dialogue, but in 'Herrenvolk' and in this story, it's getting way out of hand. What's worse, the show is becoming gorged on its own importance, desperate to pull in every paranoid aspect of the post-War American mythos (JFK? That was the Smoking Man. MLK? Yeah, that was the Smoking Man, too). Oh, and the conspiracy find the time to rig major sporting events. I'm sure Keith will be telling me soon that's why Newcastle lost the Premiership last year.

HOW OLD IS THE SMOKING MAN?

Frohike's statement that the Smoking Man was born (or rather, 'appeared'!) in 1940 might just fit in with the 'chronology' established in 'The Field Where I Died', but it contradicts 'Apocrypha', which has him working with Deep Throat and Bill Mulder in 1953, at which point he would have been 13! Either the events seen in 'Apocrypha' are inaccurate (a difficult position to support, as we're shown the events as a simple flashback: no one is telling the story or framing it as (possibly fictitious) narrative, although this might explain the episode title), or the facts and 'memories' in 'Musings' are not to be trusted. It is quite possible that Frohike's information is erroneous (one would expect little else of the Smoking Man), and that the 'flashbacks' seen in this episode are the Smoking Man's egotistical and fantastical rewriting of history, no more believable than his Jack Colquitt Adventures. Thus, he has made himself a pivotal figure in the history of the twentieth century (assassinating both Kennedy and Luther King) – one who didn't smoke at an early age (in 'Apocrypha', he's already smoking) and was (implausibly) an army captain by the time he was 22. If this is true, then he might not be lying to Deep Throat when he says that he has never (actually) killed anyone before.

81: 'Tunguska'

US Transmission: 24 November 1996
Writers: Frank Spotnitz, Chris Carter
Director: Kim Manners
Cast: Fritz Weaver, Malcolm Stewart, David Bloom,
Campbell Lane, Stefan Arngrim, Brent Stait

Mulder has been sent evidence suggesting the existence of a major terrorist cell. When he and an FBI team set a trap for the revolutionaries, he captures Alex Krycek, who says that he leaked the information to Mulder. He wants revenge on the Smoking Man. His clues send Mulder and Scully to the airport where they intercept a courier bag containing a piece of rock, which turns out to be a meteor fragment. Mulder takes Krycek to Skinner's apartment, then visits his UN contact, who arranges for him to follow the trail to Russia. As Krycek speaks the language Mulder takes his former partner with him. The rock seems to contain the alien oil substance, and Scully investigates the deaths of several people who came into contact with it. She and Skinner are ordered to appear before a Congress investigation into the death of the courier, killed by Krycek in Skinner's apartment. Meanwhile, in Siberia, Krycek and Mulder find a slave labour camp, and are captured. Mulder is drugged and wakes up to find himself being sprayed with the alien oil.

Don't Be in the Teaser: A 'flash-forward' as Scully addresses the Congress investigation committee and refuses to reveal Mulder's whereabouts. The *real* teaser follows this, as a customs officer becomes the latest victim of the creeping slime.

How Did He Do That?: How did Krycek manage to hang from an eighteenth-storey balcony by a pair of handcuffs?

Scully Here is a Medical Doctor: She and Pendrell get into toxic-protection suits to investigate the apparent death of the scientist investigating the 'Martian' rock.

That's a Mouthful: The Smoking Man: 'Our necessary and plausible denial is intact.'

Phwoar!: The way that Scully, dressed in black combat gear, cocks that gun at the start sends a shiver down the spine. Or something.

Ooze: Alien oil. Again.

Dialogue Triumphs: Mulder: 'You're full of crap, Krycek. You're an invertebrate scum-sucker whose moral dipstick is about two drops short of bone dry.'

Mulder: 'I'm leaving the window rolled down. If I'm not back in a week, I'll call Agent Scully to come by and bring you a bowl of water.'

The Conspiracy Starts at Closing Time: The Well Manicured Man spends some of his time at what seems to be a horse farm in Charlottesville, Virginia. The conspiracy are well aware of the experiments going on in the Siberian gulag.

Continuity: Skinner has recently moved apartments (after the irredeemable break-up of his marriage, as seen in 'Avatar'?). The Smoking Man says he is 'a friend' of Skinner's (significantly, the feeling doesn't seem to be reciprocated). Skinner gets his own back on Krycek over the former agent's attack on him in 'Paper Clip'. ('We're not even yet, boy, but that's a start!')

Krycek was released from the silo (see 'Apocrypha') by the terrorists with whom he subsequently works. Krycek's parents were Russian Cold War refugees.

The Truth: The alien oil, previously seen in 'Piper Maru' and 'Apocrypha', puts in another appearance. It seems to inhabit the rock chunk which is initially thought to be Martian and four billion years old but which may actually have come from the site of the 1908 Siberian explosion. The fact that some of the oil is inside this rock sample hints at the alien substance's longevity.

The Bottom Line: KT: 'Whatever's in that rock, it seems to be lethal.' Dull and confusing at the start, this improves as it goes along with Mulder's casual, frequent and probably very illegal abuse of Krycek anytime he seemingly feels like it being quite amusing in places. So far it's a conspiracy story only in so much as the Smoking Man and the Well-Manicured Man turn up for a couple of largely perfunctory scenes. The best bit of the episode, by far, is the end.

MD: Topical (Martian life in Antarctic rocks) but dull. There's not much wrong with this episode – although the scene in which Mulder discovers Krycek can speak Russian is absolute pants – but there's not much enjoyment to be had, either.

82: 'Terma'

US Transmission: 1 December 1996
Writers: Frank Spotnitz, Chris Carter
Director: Rob Bowman
Cast: Stefan Arngrim, Jan Rubeš, Fritz Weaver, Brent Stait,
Malcolm Stewart, Campbell Lane, Robin Mossley,
Brenda McDonald, Pamela MacDonald, Eileen Pedde,
Jessica Shcreier

A former KGB man is sent to the USA and murders the Well-Manicured Man's physician. Mulder and Krycek escape from the camp in Russia. Scully is questioned by the Senate Select Sub-Committee on Intelligence and Terrorism, and is briefly imprisoned for contempt of Congress. Meanwhile the Russian assassin kills the scientist infected by the alien 'black cancer', and steals the Tunguska rock. Mulder returns to the hearing, and he and Scully set off after the meteorite fragment, but an explosion sends it deep into the ground, and the Russian escapes.

Don't Be in the Teaser: A 'mercy killing' in Florida goes horribly wrong.

Ooze: We glimpse a 'nest' of squirming microscopic worm-like creatures in the infected scientist, but thankfully are spared the full glory of Krycek's arm being amputated.

That's a Mouthful: Skinner breathlessly explains the plot for viewers who missed the first episode: 'You owe me some answers, Agent Scully – answers I don't have to questions I'm being asked about this missing diplomatic pouch, the pouch presumably being carried by the man who was allegedly pushed off my balcony, and whose connection with a known felon I harboured in my house against all good sense I'm going to have to explain to avoid perjuring myself before a Senate sub-committee tomorrow – which, I might remind you, is a very serious crime in itself, is it not, Agent Scully?' Phew.

Phwoar!: The scene in which Mulder and Scully are reunited is extremely charged. They indulge in a very public hug, and Mulder tells her how good it feels to put his arms around her.

The Conspiracy Starts at Closing Time: The conspiracy – here much more nationalistic (i.e. American) than in previous stories – have secured a piece of alien-infected rock from Tunguska, and are overseeing a programme to work towards an 'inoculation' against the deadly 'black cancer'. To this end, Dr Bonita Charne-Sayre, Well-Manicured Man's doctor and (it is implied) lover, and one of the six most important people in the conspiracy, is using alien 'oil' on elderly patients in Florida. The Russians' own attempts to find a 'cure' (the gulag-like camp) are much more primitive, but they certainly resent the 'American' conspiracy's actions, despatching a former KGB man to kill the infected scientist, murder Dr Charne-Sayre and her human 'guinea pigs', and dispose of the rock itself. (Apparently 'black cancer' – supplied by the Russians? – was used by Saddam Hussein in the Gulf War, leading to troops being given anti-germ warfare drugs (see 'E.B.E.').)

The Smoking Man seems to imply that the conspirators having sex (with each other, or in general?!) will endanger the whole project. Even Well-Manicured Man cannot call off the Senate's investigation.

Continuity: We discover that Krycek has been a KGB agent. By the end of the episode he is missing his left arm, amputated by Russian peasants presumably attempting to remove the tracking system located in his small pox vaccination scar.

The Truth: The Tunguska rock contained a deadly alien life-form (despite visual similarities, possibly different from the space-ship-travelling, intelligent 'oil' seen in 'Piper Maru' and 'Apocrypha'). Both the Russians and now the Americans are trying to develop 'black cancer' as a weapon, or are striving to create an immunity to it.

Trivia: The shortened version of the title sequence again puts in an appearance. 'The Truth is Out There' becomes 'E Pur si Muove'.

The Bottom Line: MD: This seemed ridiculously complex, with lots of elements (hacked-off arms, Krycek's involvement with militiamen) and hoary old adventure show set pieces thrown into the mix with little thought or precision. The Russian gulag stinks of Cold War clichés, and the sequence with Mulder almost literally getting on his soapbox towards the end had me cringing. 'Tunguska' and 'Terma' form the worst multi-part *X-Files* conspiracy story so far seen. Chris Carter's name might be on the script, but it is as if his attention has switched to *Millennium*, and, for all our occasional criticism of his stilted dialogue, the programme that brought him to prominence is suffering as a result.

'I Want to Believe':
The X-Files and Faith

by Martin Day

> 'Jesus said "Everything is possible for him who believes."
> Immediately the boy's father exclaimed "I do believe; help
> me to overcome my unbelief!" '
>
> Mark 9:23b–24

We all watch television and film through a filter unique
to our preconceptions and biases. Our world-view – based
on political inclination, gender, class and a whole host of
other attitudes, some thought through, others unconsciously
assumed – will in part indicate those programmes and movies
we enjoy or admire and those we reject. Of course, there are
other (often subjective, qualitative or generic) determinants at
work, but the simple fact of the matter is (to use a personal
illustration) that I am less likely to watch *The Omen* now that
I am a Christian than a decade or so ago when I was an
atheist. Similarly, one would not expect a right-wing viewer
to list Alan Bleasdale as his or her favourite playwright, or a
gay viewer to champion *Are You Being Served?* as a sitcom
that significantly advanced the presentation of homosexual
men.

I mention this only because, on the surface, *The X-Files* – a
programme that has in no small way contributed to a massive
resurgence of public interest in the paranormal and UFOs –
might seem an unusual programme for me to enjoy, still less
to write about. Of course, those episodes that deal with
reincarnation or the spirits of the dead impacting upon the
physical world clash with my world-view: they might be
gripping slices of drama, but I am uncomfortable with them.
It's not (I hope) that I am frightened of my own views coming
under discussion or scrutiny, but one does naturally feel more
at home watching a programme that 'endorses' one's own

view of the world than one that does not. (As ever, with *The X-Files*, this unease is doubtless the very effect the programme makers want to achieve.) But in general I find myself concluding, like the priest commenting on the BBC's *Doomwatch* in the 1970s, that the programme 'strips down the pretensions, arrogance and pride of sophisticated society and shows what Christian men should be concerned with.'

The X-Files has in many ways inherited *Doomwatch*'s 'green' agenda (just think how many *X-Files* stories are prompted by environmental destruction of some sort), but more importantly, via its lead characters, desperate to see their beliefs confirmed, and via its stories, which often probe matters of theology and metaphysics, it explores deep spiritual concerns. Although study after study has shown that most people in the West still say that they believe in some form of God, 'organised religion' has been a declining influence since World War II, and society as a whole has become rationalist, materialist and consumerist. (I am not, incidentally, saying that rationalism *per se* is a 'bad thing', or that religion is inherently irrational.) As the Smoking Man says in 'Talitha Cumi', 'They've grown tired of waiting for miracle and mystery. Science is their religion.'

The X-Files seeks to suggest to us that there are more things in heaven and earth than prevailing humanism would allow, that there are paranormal and supernatural powers and forces beyond the material world (and, indeed, beyond our planet), and that death is not necessarily the end of human life. All heady areas for discussion, especially given Chris Carter's description of himself as a lapsed Baptist.

Mulder and Scully (at least until the third season) aren't shown as religious people in the usual sense of the word. But belief, faith and even dogma courses through them. The early episodes present us with a man desperate to believe in the existence of alien life and in the supernatural and a woman enslaved (professionally) to logic and science. With Mulder – and despite his frequent denials – almost everything about his current character goes back to the abduction of his sister. Indeed, I would go as far as to suggest that this moment prompted such a vast paradigm-shift that some form of childlike trust in God was shattered and replaced in an instant with contempt or disbelief and a new 'faith' in the reality of alien life and the paranormal.

His Christian or biblical 'heritage' is clear, albeit less directly addressed than Scully's. In 'Die Hand die Verletzt' he states that 'Even the Devil can quote scripture to fit his needs', referring to Jesus's temptation in Matthew 4 and Luke 4; in 'Anasazi' he shows a familiarity with the fourth commandment (calling alien life one of God's 'side projects'). He is scathing about fundamentalist preachers and their 'literal' interpretation of the Bible in '3', but in 'Quagmire' he says (tongue-in-cheek?) 'Seek and ye shall find, Scully', a reference to Matthew 7:7/Luke 11:9. In 'Revelations' he clearly recognises the phrase 'He that has ears, let him hear', much used by Jesus in the Synoptic gospels. His (adult) view of the Bible is clear: in the same story he states that it is 'a parable, it's a metaphor for the truth, not the truth itself'. (It wouldn't be at all surprising if we were to learn that he considers the angelic visitation in Ezekiel, chapter one, to be the earliest recorded encounters with a UFO!) He certainly seems unusually sour and angry in this episode, attacking Scully's beliefs much more strongly than she usually does his. Scully asks him, 'How is it that you're able to go out on a limb whenever you see a light in the sky, but you're unwilling to accept the possibility of a miracle – even when it's right in front of you?', to which Mulder replies, 'I wait for a miracle every day, but what I've seen here has only tested my patience, not my faith.' The miracle he hopes for is the return of his sister (remember the old ritual of closing his eyes and hoping (praying?) for her return, as mentioned in 'Conduit'?). One can almost imagine Mulder saying to God, 'According to the Bible, you rose from the dead, but you can't even bring my sister back!' And thus he either has no faith in God, or holds Him directly responsible for the abduction of his sister. (In 'Talitha Cumi', the Smoking Man puts this Western paradox well, although the emotion here is fear rather than contempt: 'They don't believe in Him, but they still fear Him.')

Conventional religion, in particular, strikes Mulder as being too small and limiting. Where others might look to God for a reminder of our smallness in the cosmos, Mulder looks to extraterrestrial life. And thus in 'Anasazi' he calls the cover-up of alien life the 'biggest lie of all': it's his personal 'Holy Grail'. Although at the beginning of 'Little Green Men' Mulder is saying that he 'wanted to believe', by the end of 'End Game' his belief is restored: 'I found something I thought I'd lost: faith to keep looking.' In 'Born Again' (and referring to his own hypnosis, as seen in 'Conduit'), Mulder states that he has a fundamental 'belief' in the beneficial powers of deep hypnosis. However, certain paradoxes remain: in 'Paper Clip' Mulder seems to indicate that he believes in fate, and 'Conduit' ends with Mulder praying and in tears in church before a stained-glass window of Christ crucified (which seems to me to be a conclusive counter to David Duchovny's claim that Mulder is ('ethnically'?) Jewish).

Mulder's belief in the existence of alien life is counterbalanced by Scully's unshakeable faith in science. Never is this made clearer than in 'End Game': 'Many of the things I have seen have challenged my faith in my belief in an ordered universe, but this uncertainty has only strengthened my need to know, to understand, to apply reason to those things which seem to defy it. It was science that isolated the retrovirus that Agent Mulder was exposed to, and science that allowed us to understand its behaviour, and, ultimately, it was science that saved Agent Mulder's life.' This linking of science and 'salvation' (she calls science 'sacred' in 'The Erlenmeyer Flask') seems the ultimate in humanism, but with Scully things are not as clear-cut as that (after all, most Christian scientists – from Newton onwards – have seen the world as logical and ordered precisely because a rational God created it). Science, for her, is the ultimate arbiter against irrationality and chaos (she says in 'Jose Chung's *From Outer Space*' that she'd never even considered the paranormal until she met Mulder). In 'The Blessing Way' Melissa says of Dana, 'You are so shut off to the possibility there could be any other explanation except for your rigid, scientific view of the world.' And Scully seems to be at one with Mulder with regard to the Bible, as this exchange from 'The Calusari' clearly shows:

Scully: 'Wait a second, nothing just materialises out of thin air.'

Chuck Burk: 'You've read the Bible? You remember the story about Jesus creating the loaves and the fishes?'

Scully: 'But that was a parable.'

(In one sense she's wrong, in as much as this story is presented in the Bible as an actual event, clearly delineated from Jesus's teaching and his parables. Of course, what she is actually expressing here is her belief that the whole Bible is a work of fiction, and thus symbolic.) Unlike the Smoking Man in 'Talitha Cumi', she seems to believe that you don't have to believe in miracles to believe in God.

There are early hints that Scully has some residual religious belief (most obviously in the gold cross necklace she so often wears). In 'Beyond the Sea' she is adamant that hell will not be a cold, dark place for her father or for Mulder, and in 'Miracle Man' her familiarity with the Bible leads her to believe that 'God never lets the Devil steal the show'. In 'The List' Scully mentions catechism for the first time, hinting at her upbringing as a Catholic, which is confirmed in 'Revelations'.

'Revelations' is a key Scully story, not so much in that it reveals these hidden characteristics as the fact that it explodes her previous character and presents us with a new one. Almost from the outset, and before she's seen enough to have her faith in science questioned (remember, this is the woman who will bend over backwards to make even the most obviously supernatural event an obscure scientific phenomenon), we're treated to scenes like this:

Scully: 'I believe in the idea that God's hand can be witnessed. I believe he can create miracles, yes.'

Mulder: 'Even if science can't explain them?'

Scully: 'Maybe that's just what faith is.'

This stands in complete contradiction to everything we've learnt about Scully in the past, and is one of many reasons why I found this episode somewhat disappointing. The story does, however, throw up some interesting nuggets: Scully believes in the Armageddon, was raised a Catholic, but it's been six years since her last confession. She says she's not sure why she drifted away from the Church, but she states that she doesn't question God's word (she must mean in the general sense, given her previous attitude to the Bible). Certainly, this story (no matter how contrived the character change) is something of a watershed: by 'Apocrypha' she comments on a despairing mention of a 'sign from God' by saying 'I've seen stranger things.' Of course, she has (although for much of the first season one is left wondering whether she will perpetually be in the next room when all the weird stuff happens), but the fascinating conclusion of 'Revelations' shows how much she has come to rely on her 'detached' nature as a contrast to Mulder's willingness to believe. She begins to doubt the 'miracles' she has seen simply because Mulder didn't see them (when the positions are reversed Mulder has no problem with believing what he has seen on his own). When she says, 'It makes me afraid that God is speaking, but that no one's listening', one can imagine that she's thinking particularly of Mulder, having seen the depth of his hurt and anger (and how this – as in 'Nisei'/'731' – can seemingly stand in the way of 'the truth'). However, by 'Talitha Cumi' she's very much back on form, thinking the miraculous hearings will be explained away rationally.

A number of episodes directly grapple with ideas of faith and belief in a religious, metaphysical or theological context. Not surprisingly for a programme as doggedly pluralistic as *The X-Files*, a consistent world-view is eschewed in favour of contradiction and contrast. For example, the suggestion in 'Lazarus' that the bright light at the end of the tunnel seen when dying is 'beautiful' and 'nothing to be afraid of' clashes with '3', a story that – if what the vampires say is true – puts paid to any idea of a positive afterlife. Individual stories, too, sometimes find it difficult to tackle matters of faith in a coherent or unified manner, 'GenderBender' being very much a case in point. The occasional insightful comparison between the world of belief and the unfettered but fallen physical world gives way to a conclusion that is a mess of contradictory signifiers, effectively sweeping any real-life impact under the carpet of a weird alien faction.

By comparison, 'Miracle Man' verges on the unambiguous. Despite dealing very directly with matters of Christian faith and the existence (or otherwise) of miracles in the modern age, its targets aren't so much the religious community in general as a brand of Christianity in particular. The parody of a tent ministry with regular healing services is, however, undercut by the subtle presentation of the policeman's wife, who by the story's conclusion seems to feel that she *would* have been healed by the preacher's adopted son, had her sceptical husband allowed her to attend. Although it's difficult to know what to make of the boy's resurrection – bar that the dramatic structure required a powerful conclusion – the central concept (that a man healed, supposedly by the power of God, can have such a miserable new life) causes us to question the validity (or, rather, the 'goodness') of all that we've witnessed. Perhaps it's a tale about gullibility (a man in agony and suffering massive disfigurement is seen by many as exhibiting the abundant and overflowing new life that Jesus spoke of); it certainly contains a clever message about pride. The moment that the crowds – and Samuel himself – believe that the healings come from him, rather than from God, the boy's powers become corrupted and negative. The fact that the deaths have an earthly cause doesn't change the symbolism inherent in what we witness.

In 'Red Museum' the focus switches from Christianity to a New Age church. We're invited to see it in sinister terms as the story begins, but ultimately the group are shown to be (at worst) harmless – indeed, the story ends with a possible reconciliation between the 'cult' and the suspicious locals. Although not the focus of the story, the church believes in soul transference. In an interesting exchange, Mulder states that Abraham Lincoln, Mikhail Gorbachev and Charles Colson (but not, of course, Nixon!) are believed to have been the recipients of 'enlightened spirits'. It's difficult to know what to make of this, unless the production team are attempting a slight dig at the conversion of Nixon's notorious assistant to Christianity whilst in prison (New Age 'walk-in' rather than the intervention of the God of Christianity).

'Die Hand die Verletzt' subverts all our expectations of small-town Americana. In the opening scene, a meeting to discuss possible drama productions (*Jesus Christ Superstar* would not be 'appropriate', *Grease* contains 'the f-word') sets up the prospect of a Christian school ('Deborah, why don't you lead us in prayer?'). They're impatient to conclude, but realise that they've been 'letting it slip' – encouraging us to see the teachers as normal human beings, wrestling with faith in the modern context. Only then are we presented with the candles and the intoned 'In the name of the Lords of Darkness . . .' It's a wonderful and clever device.

The story continues to show that even the 'dark people' find belief difficult to maintain in the twentieth century (it's been 'years' since their last sacrifice: 'We haven't kept our faith'). Mulder is at great pains to stress that 'witches' – followers of Wicca – are religious, that they respect life and do not cast harmful spells, and that they don't worship Satan. 'Even the Church of Satan,' he says, with a completely straight face, 'has renounced murder and torture.' But as the story progresses it becomes clear that we're dealing with more than just white witches, and the ensuing events gain much of their impact from a well-portrayed change of attitude or world-view. Jim Ausbury was raised to see Christians as evil hypocrites, and to believe that man's basic nature is selfish rather than altruistic. Mankind is no more than a race of animals. However, after Shannon's death, he begins to perceive hypocrisy in himself and others (who seek to pin the blame on her, treating her death as a worthy sacrifice): 'And at that moment I knew that I am better than an animal, that my previous beliefs were responsible for her no longer being with us . . .' He explains that he forced his daughter to take part in rituals, but did not abuse her sexually. Mulder is dismissive of their 'watered-down' ceremonies. 'Did you really think you can call up the Devil and ask him to behave?'

'Revelations' returns again to miracles within the rational

Western world, the preacher in the pre-titles sequence explaining one possible approach to the science–faith debate (that they are at odds with each other) via a story of a girl's Christian faith being disrupted by being told that the parting of the Red Sea was a natural (rather than a supernatural) phenomenon. But the man is shown to be a cheap fake and con artist who clearly doesn't understand the complexities of the argument, but does know how to fool the gullible (that theme again).

Gates – seemingly out to do more than expose false stigmatics – refers to Joel's Old Testamental description of the sun turning to darkness and the moon to blood prior to the Lord's coming. The same passage is part of St Peter's Pentecostal sermon in Acts and is referred to in Revelation (note the singular!) after the opening of the penultimate seal. Gates believes that he was 'called upon' to kill the boy 'for the New Age to come', and that his actions are part of (or run counter to) some revised world-ending apocalypse. But nothing here matches the biblical book of Revelation, nor is presented with sufficient supernatural power (bar a few parlour tricks) to lead us to believe that we are witnessing a struggle between two spiritual protagonists. Instead, we're watching one mad man attempting to kill the son of a mad man – and, tragically, by the story's conclusion, even the boy has come to believe his father's hype. Scully says, 'Maybe I'll see you again sometime', to which Kevin replies, 'You will.'

So I suppose we're back at gullibility again, another cul-de-sac in *The X-Files*' treatment of faith and belief. After three seasons we've seen much to expand our horizons and question our assumptions. Whether we're in turn drawn to God, or to other supernatural forces, or to little green men, doubtless depends on the individual. To put it another way, Christians believe that there is a God-shaped hole at the core of our psyche that will leave us unfulfilled unless we encounter God: Mulder's slot, on the other hand, is in the shape of the flying saucer that took away his sister. The desire to believe, even in the rational twentieth century, remains undimmed. As Scully says at the end of 'Avatar', 'That's why these myths and stories have endured – people want to believe.'

Acknowledgements

We would like to thank the following for their help, time and contribution: Ian Atkins, Paul Condon, Nick Cooper, Peter Darvill-Evans, Helen Day, Jeff Harth, Rebecca Levene, Claire Longhurst, Jackie Marshall, Cressida McLaughlin, John McLaughlin, John Molyneux, Carrie O'Grady, Kate Orman, David Owen, Jim Sangster, Paul Simpson, Kathy Sullivan, Kathleen Toth, Colin Topping, Lily Topping, Andrew Walker, Peter Wickham, Simon Winstone, Janet Wood, Lucy Zinkiewicz.

We would also like to thank and acknowledge the help of contributors to uk.media.tv.sf.x-files (especially Moira McLaughlin and Lee Staniforth), David Nattriss and his UK Episode Guide to *The X-Files* (http://www.i-way.co.uk/~natts/ x-files/), Laura Witte and all the contributors to the *X- Files* In-Jokes List (http://www.nashville.com/~subterfuge/ xfiljoke.html), and the inhabitants of all the other *X-Files* newgroups.

Dedicated To

Catherine Minns (MD)
Terry and Gudi Topping (KT)

End Game

This is our last book. We'd like to think that our work together has changed the way books such as these are made: we always regarded the compilation of an episode guide as a creative act in itself, not just a dry stacking of facts. Now, new and separate projects have come along, and it seems a good idea to break up the band at a positive moment. We are all, despite everything, still friends. We hope that we passed the audition.

'We made this.'